BOOKS BY ROBERT STUART NATHAN

THE WHITE TIGER
RISING HIGHER
AMUSEMENT PARK

THE WHITE TIGER

a novel by

Robert Stuart Nathan

SIMON AND SCHUSTER
NEW YORK

Copyright © 1987 by Robert Stuart Nathan
All rights reserved
including the right of reproduction
in whole or in part in any form
Published by Simon and Schuster
A Division of Simon & Schuster, Inc.
Simon & Schuster Building
Rockefeller Center
1230 Avenue of the Americas
New York, New York 10020
SIMON AND SCHUSTER and colophon are registered trademarks of Simon & Schuster, Inc.
Designed by Susan Brooker/Levavi & Levavi
Manufactured in the United States of America
10 9 8 7 6 5 4 3 2 1
Library of Congress Cataloging in Publication Data
Nathan, Robert Stuart.
  The white tiger.

  I. Title.
PS3564.A8495W4   1987   813'.54   87-4320
ISBN 0-671-63338-4

This book is for Howard Schreiber

Many Chinese, both here and in China, gave me extraordinary help in the writing of this novel. The Chinese are among the world's great storytellers, not least when recounting their own lives.

Of those in China who were so generous with their time and companionship, there are some whom for obvious reasons I cannot thank by name. But of those who helped me unwittingly, I am particularly grateful to Shen Shoujun, who with his directness and honesty made clear that China's leaders are often as aware of their weaknesses as they are of their strengths; to Li Junhua, whose endless wit cheered me in the stifling heat of Guilin; and most of all to Zhang Yaomin, who provided me with a second set of eyes and ears. If a copy of this book should reach him, he may recognize a small part of himself, in his astounding forbearance if not his politics, in its hero.

It is important to mention, however, that no character, either from history or in the present, is based on a real person. No similarity is intended, nor should any be inferred.

I am grateful also to the filmmakers Sue Yung Li and Michael Lerner, who helped pave my way to China, and to those who read the manuscript, most especially Michael Korda and Andy McKillop, and Elaine Markson, Carol Suen Shookhoff, Linda Epstein, Eugene Epstein, Robert Rosenblum, and Geri Thoma. I owe a debt, too, to many reporters and scholars, among them Jay and Linda Mathews, Fox Butterfield, Orville Schell, Jonathan Spence, Dick Wilson, and of course the late Edgar Snow.

Finally, I offer my deepest thanks to my friend Chang Xiang-ru. If I have been faithful to the lives and spirit of the Chinese, it is Chang, by bringing his fine intelligence to bear on the manuscript, who is in significant measure responsible.

—Robert Stuart Nathan
New York, December 1986

A Note on Names, Places, and Pronunciation

To help the reader distinguish Chinese personal names, I have freely mixed English spellings from both the Wade-Giles and pinyin transliterations. Also, many given names are simplified to make them more comprehensible. In pinyin, *q* is pronounced *ch* (so that the Emperor Qin, for example, is pronounced *Chin*), the opening *x* is *sh*, *zh* is a clipped *j*, and the opening *c* reads as *ts*. Most place names are rendered in pinyin, as close as possible to how the Chinese would say them; thus what Westerners have called Canton is Guangzhou, Peking is Beijing, and so forth.

When he was fifteen or twenty
He went to snatch a Tartar's horse
   and rode it away,
And in the mountains he killed with an arrow
   a white tiger....

                      —*The Old General's Song*
                      by Wang Wei

PART ONE

"The gun shoots
the bird that sticks
its neck out."

PART
ONE

1.

FRIENDS
AND
ENEMIES

White bunting, black armbands, red roses. Death was dressed in strong colors.

At the steel-gated entrance to the walled compound on Tsungenwai four young soldiers, no more than boys, really, fresh from the provinces, stood guard under the high curved archway. They scrutinized the lengthening line of mourners, they inspected identification papers with absurd meticulousness, they checked names against their lists. They had reason to be edgy: let the wrong person into this compound and a posting to the edge of the Gobi Desert would seem a reprieve.

From around the corner, turning off the Avenue of Everlasting Peace, trotted a group of middle-school joggers in regimental blue shorts. At the sight of so many important cadres they slowed their pace, gaping wide-eyed at the white crepe stretched atop the gate, then at the phalanx of Red Flag limousines crowding the curb, rear and side windows curtained in white gauze. Also seven new Shanghai sedans, also curtained. To those who never ride in them, cars are glorious machines. One daring jogger, older than the others, stepped forward, his arm already shot half into the air. For a moment, like a schoolboy sure of his answer but at the last instant doubting it, he held himself in check. Then he summoned his courage and tapped a tall, bespectacled man on the shoulder. The boy had selected this particular cadre, perhaps, because of the fresh crease in his blue cotton pants or the crisp white-on-white weave of his shirt—signs of rank even to the unobservant eye—or maybe only because the man looked friendly.

Which high cadre, the boy asked timidly, had died?

"A great and glorious man," replied Lu Hong, who had come in neither a new Shanghai nor a Red Flag, but on a stiflingly hot Haidian District bus. "A great servant of the people."

The joggers waited for Hong to say more, but then seemed to sense either his sadness or his reticence, and pursuing his answer no further hurried on past the entrance to the compound at Number Eight. If not for the security rules, Hong would have told them that Sun Sheng, whose memorial service this was, had been more than a great man. He had been a genuine hero, and there were few enough of them even among the living.

Hong felt utterly dismal. Sun Sheng, dead. Even now, he knew, the full force of it had not yet struck him. And why, he asked himself, after waking at two in the morning, had he stupidly remained awake reading old Ba Jin stories of misery and deprivation? They had only made him feel worse.

At the sentry post next to the arch, he slipped his identification folder from his breast pocket and, as he might examine suspect papers, considered his own picture: a young, serious man with thick hair, who now had less hair and was considerably less serious. When the internal passport was issued four years ago he had not worn glasses, and now he was all too aware that his thick wire-framed lenses emphasized his impending entrance into middle age. He presented his folder to the nearest guard, a beardless peasant boy in a baggy green uniform. The boy was sweltering, but had probably been transferred to Beijing from some mud-

and-dust village and was no doubt deliriously happy to work anywhere with sidewalks. He returned the identification folder, regarding Hong with no more expression than he might offer a corpse.

Hong visited this patch of Heaven rarely. Inside, behind the high walls, seven three-story houses—nicely painted in tan, with wide windows and handsome shutters—faced the courtyard. Strips of white crepe, sagging from the shutters of Sun Sheng's house at the center of the compound, wilted in the damp afternoon heat, splotched by water dripping from the air conditioners. Hong passed a crew of white-jacketed street policemen waiting on the stoop. They gave no sign of recognizing him, just another assistant deputy director. There were how many assistant deputy directors in Public Security nowadays? Twenty? Thirty? Titles proliferated like swans. But then again, while power was better than a title, a title was better than nothing at all.

Across from the house a crowd drifted up the steps of the compound's meeting hall, once a French diplomat's mansion, where vases of marsh marigolds and white chrysanthemums on marble pedestals flanked the double doors. At the bottom of the steps was a rough wooden bin of black armbands, and as Hong reached in he felt a strong hand clamp onto his shoulder.

"Pretty flowers," came the sly, whispered voice behind him. "Real, too. Not paper."

Hong turned. From anyone else the remark would have been rude. From Liu Chan, Hong's assistant, it was both an escape from the fact of Sun Sheng's death and an expression of political disharmony. At the memorial for Chan's brother, burnt to death in a truck accident nine years ago, real flowers were deemed atavistic—an inappropriate peasant obsession wasteful of precious resources. Tell that to the peasants, Hong thought. He climbed the steps with Chan, who was short and fat from lack of exercise. Chan was a Mongol, his parents were tall, wiry peasants. By inheritance he should not have been short, and by ideology should not have been fat—no one was supposed to be fat. This condition he blamed on his Army stint in Tibet. Responding to the torture of cold, Chan explained, his body had added layers to protect itself. But the fat, like so much else about

Chan, was a species of disguise; he was hard enough underneath.

"When did you get back?" Hong asked. His assistant had
been in Tianjin, an hour and a half from Beijing by train,
searching for counterfeit bicycle nameplates.

"Last night, midnight," Chan sighed. "We were stuck on
the tracks forever. Do you think we could have a couple of
train engineers publicly criticized? Make an example of
them?" He shrugged at his joke and touched Hong's hand.
"I'm sorry about Sheng, I tried to get back on Friday, I
thought maybe I'd come over and see you, but I couldn't
get out."

Hong stopped abruptly, apparently distracted, but when
he found his voice it was casual. "Friday?" he asked. "You
got called on Friday?"

"I think so, it must have been late in the afternoon. There
was a message at the hotel."

Hong himself had not heard of Sun Sheng's death until
Saturday, and then with few details. A heart attack was all
the telephone message had said: *Friday, at his office. Taken to
hospital.* It was odd, Hong thought, that the information
should take longer to travel three kilometers than a
hundred.

"I can assure you," Chan went on, "that those Flying Pigeon nameplates aren't coming from Tianjin."

"Who was the message at the hotel from?" Hong asked.

It was Chan's turn to stop on the steps. "One of the
switchboard officers, I don't know—Li, maybe, or Zhang."
He pouted and stared from his deep sleepy eyes. "Whatever
you're thinking," Chan said, ever the lecturer, "don't."

Chan's Army tenure had turned his mind in conflicting
directions, toward accepting orders and ignoring them,
toward questioning nothing and questioning everything.
These two tendencies clashing in the same mind made the
fat Mongol a good policeman, and had endeared him to
Hong the day they met.

"I'm not thinking anything," Hong answered, and pushed
through the door.

The chilled air inside the hall gave off a metallic odor.
Ah, the wondrous Dutch air conditioners! Once installed,

they cried out to be used. Opposite the entrance were more marigolds and great sprays of roses.

Chan inhaled their aroma. "I hope that when I die somebody can afford flowers for me," he said. "If we're still allowed flowers."

Friends and enemies, hundreds of both, filled the room, a grand space with a white-beamed ceiling and high white mantelpiece and billowing white silk curtains. The blue-and-gold cloisonné lamps must have been made in the thirties, Hong thought. For these cadres only the best. In the back, between couches richly upholstered in red velvet, sat a Japanese videotape recorder and an enormous television set, the largest Hong had ever seen. Above the mantel, in a billboard-sized photograph from the fifties, the late premier Zhou Enlai lounged in a chair wearing his trademark clenched grin, a cigarette dangling from his hand as he held court with Western journalists. Hong passed under Zhou to a Qin Dynasty mahogany console table holding the eulogy book and an old photo of Sun Sheng. The photographer had captured Sheng's peculiar half-smile, which could augur anything from rage to wit. Next to the portrait was a ruby-colored urn with Sheng's ashes.

"I thought Sheng wanted to be buried," Chan said.

"He did," Hong answered, staring at the urn. The shortage of land in Beijing meant cremation even for high cadres, but Sheng had been old-fashioned; he had wanted a coffin, like his ancestors. "Of course I am only one individual," Hong could hear him say with a gravelly chortle, "and my desires are nothing next to the needs of the State. So cremate me, no? On the other hand, my body can fertilize the land. A better use for me, yes?" For certain audiences Sheng could debate the individual and the State for hours. When younger, Hong had tried to master Sheng's philosophical cast of mind, and failing that, to imitate it.

What has died here, Hong thought, is a piece of my life. What has died is a part of history that will never again exist. He leaned over the eulogy book and wrote: *Sun Sheng was a great hero of the Revolution. He offered an example to us all. He was my friend. As I live by his example, so will I miss him.*

It was going to be an awful day, an awful week. Hong laid the pen down and turned toward the front of the room, where, at the head of the crowd, he saw his mother—Cui Chun, Great Poet of the Revolution. No one ever called her simply by name; the description always followed or preceded. Next to her, his head lolling as though he were studying the bare wall, stood Hong's father. They hardly ever ventured into the city these days. His father's illness, even if unmentioned, subjected everyone to mild embarrassment. Hong supposed that today no one would mind. The clan had gathered to reminisce about when they liberated China. Heroes all—to the people, anyway, if not to each other.

Hong visited his parents less often than was proper, and approached them as always with the uncomfortable feeling of intense love colored by resentment and filial obligation. He nodded his way past the other Public Security officers and eased in next to his mother. In old age, instead of shrinking, Cui Chun had expanded. Her large round body was wrapped in a pink silk blouse, an embroidered black jacket, and a pleated white skirt. For thirty-five years she had worn only blue pants and gray loose-fitting tunics, but now that previously decadent habits were allowed, she had not hesitated to revert to the luxuries of her youth.

She glanced up at Hong with red-rimmed eyes, grazed his arm with her hand. "We've lost our best," she said in a choked voice.

Hong nodded his head in agreement. "How was the ride?"

"They sent a new Red Flag," she said and, looking toward Hong's father, "he enjoyed it. You look well. How's your wife and our beautiful grandson?"

"They're fine," Hong said, hoping she would politely not raise the subject of his divorce.

Hong's father lifted his head. "We're dead, dead," Lu Yaomin wheezed madly, tugging Hong's arm, "we're all dead now." Cui Chun put an arm around her husband, quieted him, but he leaned toward Hong and managed a crooked grin, the result either of a minor stroke or his "weakness of the nerves." Doctors would say the former explained the latter. Hong chose to believe the reverse, that Lu Yaomin's madness was cause, not effect. Considering what he had been through, it was a miracle he was still living at all, even in this condition. Hong clasped his father's hand, and again came the rasping whisper: "You're dead. We're all dead."

"Yes, now let's be quiet," Hong said soothingly.

A sudden stillness fell. A moment ago the mourners had been at half-attention, more alert to each other than the memory of the man they had come to praise. Now the eulogies were about to begin, and the cause of the lull, known collectively in Beijing as the Three Tigers, stepped to the lectern. First came the stoop-shouldered Minister of Public Security, then the Vice-Minister, and finally the Director of Investigations. About the Three Tigers, Hong could truly say he had no illusions. As Chairman Mao's earliest strongarms their reputations had been cast—they were the great reformers of traitors and running dogs. Alas, the traitors under their tutelage frequently died before being reformed. It was said that the Three Tigers had once beaten two peasant women several hours a day for an entire week to extract their confessions, and then finished by bludgeoning them to death. Maybe it was true, maybe not, but the Revolution had trained the Tigers well: they had survived, and survival, even among heroes, was the ultimate test. Now they controlled the country's municipal police investigations —those of dangerous foreign elements not assigned to the new Special Ministry for State Security, of economic crimes like embezzlement, and the antisocial crimes like burglary, rape, street theft.

The Director of Investigations stepped forward first. Years of struggle were etched in the evenly lined flesh of her angular face, the stark gunmetal gray of her short swept-back hair. The first time Hong had seen her, in the living room of his parents' house, she had seemed ancient. Now, two decades later, she looked younger. She called herself Wei Ye—the name she took during the war of Liberation, when names along with everything else could be altered to suit the moment. She had been delivering her eulogy for a minute or two before Hong sorted the rush of words from the sound of his own thoughts.

"...and now we've lost our great friend, a servant of the people, a hero of the Revolution, a man who advocated seeking truth from facts," she was saying in a rich mellow

chant. Great praise from the Three Tigers, who had com-
peted with Sheng for power as rats compete for food. Hong
glanced at his father, whose eyes dreamily examined the
ceiling, and his mother, who neither paid close attention
nor gave any sign of not listening. Somehow Cui Chun conveyed a sense of not being there at all, of having briefly
departed to a world entirely her own.

"...and his deeds on behalf of the Revolution," came Wei
Ye's voice. "If we bring nothing at birth, what do we take
away at death? The opportunity to serve the people...."

On and on Wei Ye's eulogy went. Tomorrow in *People's
Daily* she would be quoted, with the Minister and Vice-
Minister—heroes praising their late comrade, with praise
for all of them from several other heroes.

Hong squirmed, gazed down at his hands, tried to blot
out her voice. Honey in the mouth, he thought, dagger in
the belly.

Ma Sufei, Sheng's widow, embraced Hong as he came
with the others into the Suns' house. Hong draped his
arms over her shoulders and she buried her head in his
chest, holding him a long moment, her fingers clutching
hard against his spine. For an old woman she had strong
hands. "Oh, he loved you," she said finally. "He took so
much pride in you." She spoke as though Sheng had been
his father—which, in a sense, was true. Her hand went to
Hong's chin, then his cheek, his mouth, caressing as if she
were blind and taking a mental impression. Hong stared
at her, and in her soft upturned face saw not grief—her
features were too alive, moving too quickly, for grief—but
something more distressing, a restlessness, a feeling he
couldn't name.

Before he could say how much he had loved Sheng, how
much he would miss him, Hong found himself ushered
away from Ma Sufei. He followed Chan into the line moving up the steps.

"You're the son they would have wanted," Chan said in a
low voice. "You're the son they didn't have."

In the spacious second-story living room half a dozen
enormous round tables were laid with fine blue-rimmed
white china on linen tablecloths. Elsewhere in Beijing eight

or ten families would be crowded into a house this size, and without air conditioning.

"This is really something," Chan said, eyeing the china and spinning his head toward the library. "Even better than you described it. Look at all these rooms."

"Rank has its privileges."

"I know, I know, but I thought you had to be at least a deputy minister to live like this."

The rear of the house faced east and north to the compound's outer walls; reflected sunlight from the mansard roof of the guards' dormitory lit the room in amber. Hong and Chan sat by the east windows, overlooking Dongdan Park and, in the distance, the Beijing Railway Station, a Russian-style behemoth. When would the Russians come back to build again? Never, Hong hoped. Their buildings were ugly, and they drank too much. On the sidewalk below, outside the walls, two boys batted a shuttlecock over a frayed net.

"Ma Sufei seems overcome," Chan said as he poured tea for Hong. "I thought they didn't get along."

"They didn't, especially," Hong said, "but forty years is a long time." He lit a Double Nine, passed one to Chan, and watched as Ma Sufei came through the door, her two sons at either side like bodyguards. To their parents' dismay, neither son had ever commanded much respect. Sun Ch'ien, a squat little bull, worked for the Silk Trading Commission in Chongqing, a furnace of a city with air so gray from burning coal that Beijing's azure haze seemed a work of art. Sun Bairong, the younger son, was lucky. His father, neglecting Party assignment lists and going quietly through the back door, had secured Bairong a spot on the Central Committee's research staff. What anyone actually researched there was a great mystery, but attached to the position was a three-room apartment with a full kitchen and new bathroom.

Together Ch'ien and Bairong lowered their mother into an easy chair near the library. Ma Sufei touched a tissue to her cheek, took a British filtered cigarette from Ch'ien, then hugged one arm into the other and seemed physically to close herself off from anyone who might wish to offer further condolences.

It was strange, Hong thought. Hundreds had traveled to see her, to comfort her, and she avoided them.

"Your great admirers," Chan said laconically, directing Hong's eye with a flick of his pudgy wrist to the group gathered by the mantel: the Three Tigers and their assorted assistants. "In Tianjin they told me that our esteemed Minister considers you one of our most brilliant investigators."

"Our esteemed Minister, thank you very much, can't even remember my name," Hong said.

"And I also heard that our Director of Investigations has kidney problems. How long can she last?"

"Don't wish death on anybody. Besides, three years ago they said she had cancer, two years ago it was a brain tumor, and next year it will be something else. For such a sick woman, Wei Ye seems to be in astonishing good health. She'll outlast us all." As she has outlasted the others, he thought.

Opposite the Three Tigers stood two brawny figures in well-cut gray tunic suits, and it took Hong a moment to realize who they were: the Minister and Vice-Minister of Defense. Their presence took his breath away—he had never seen them in public before, only in photographs, and their appearance here was significant. The Defense Ministry, in its bid for a larger budget, had been angling for months to put more of its men in the Politburo; Public Security wanted the same seats. And yet despite the battles between the two ministries, much discussed in unofficial circles, the Defense Ministry had for some reason decided to pay its official respects.

Before he was aware of his own edginess, Hong stood and crossed to the north windows. New high-rises had erupted near Ritan Park, faced in pink granite like ordinary workers' housing but vastly superior on the inside. Out of the corner of his eye, Hong watched his mother wend her way past the Defense Ministers and the Three Tigers without so much as a greeting, and he marveled for the thousandth time that they had been comrades-in-arms. Revolution breeds curious friendships.

His mother came up next to him. "Nothing will be the same," she said, speaking more to herself than Hong. "There aren't many of us left." She smiled at her son. "I'll miss that big grin when his teeth stuck out. He always made me happy. Did you see him much lately?"

"He wasn't in the Bureau very often," Hong said, "two or three days a week at most."

"Didn't you visit him?"

"Last month," said Hong.

"And how was he?" Cui Chun asked.

"Preoccupied."

"With what?"

"He didn't say."

It had been an odd day. Hong had come to the compound, self-invited, for what turned out to be a disturbingly unsatisfying discussion of his cases. Sun Sheng had been distracted. An abduction ring in Shandong, bicycle forgers, a German lawyer apparently more concerned with troop movements on the Russian border than negotiating contracts for canvas shoes—none of them could draw his interest. Sheng, who had loved nothing more than spies, should have at least cared about the German. A man who lived fraudulently in someone else's country, according to Sheng, demanded a finer intelligence than a man who lived fraudulently in his own. And yet for the better part of an afternoon their conversation passed like a typical telephone call—connect, disconnect, connect again, the shouting of "hello, are you there" across stubborn, crackling wires.

Even more disturbing was Sheng's behavior a week later. He had been scheduled to lecture the Investigations Division on military security, and Hong had stopped by his office to pick him up. But Sheng was on his way out, and in a hurry. Not only had he forgotten the lecture, he instructed Hong to cancel it. Why? What was so important? "Matters of State," Sheng had said, brushing aside Hong's objections with uncharacteristic bluntness. That was the last time Hong had seen him.

Cui Chun glanced toward the mantel and Hong saw the Minister of Public Security catch her eye. When Cui Chun parted her lips and nodded, the Three Tigers read the gesture as an invitation and joined them by the windows. The Minister, full of himself and his overdone grief, had to be reminded that Hong worked in Public Security. With Cui Chun he sparred politely, exchanging the pleasantries of former friends who saw each other only at funerals and on reviewing stands. The Minister inquired about her house in Dongshanmiao, her husband's health, whether at her advanced age, which was also his own, she had the energy to work. But no one referred to the fact, not even obliquely, that the Three Tigers still held power, while she and Hong's father did not.

"You gave a beautiful eulogy," Cui Chun said to Director of Investigations Wei Ye. "I was moved."

Hong could hardly believe what he was hearing; he stared at his mother.

Wei Ye thanked her, and the Minister chimed in. "Sun Sheng was a great man," he said. "I remember when both of you addressed us on art, on serving the masses. Whom to serve, how to serve—they were great questions."

"And still are," Cui Chun replied professorially, as if a stupid but energetic pupil had missed an important point.

"Yes. Yes, of course—and still are," the Minister answered forcefully, immune to insult. "And still are."

Hong listened as if to pandas growling in a zoo. They were speaking a foreign language known only to themselves, full of rich and hidden animosities.

Sun Ch'ien, Sheng's older son, came across the room. "Excuse me," he said, putting an arm around Hong's mother, "we want to take some pictures. You know, the old guard."

The Three Tigers and Cui Chun dutifully moved to the library, posing with Ma Sufei and nine old men against the display of books. Hong turned toward the mantel. In a lacquered red frame was a photograph from the late 1940s taken in the Party's holy land—at the headquarters in Yanan. If you had served in Yanan, if you were there with Chairman Mao from the beginning, you had earned a permanent place in the history of Liberation. In the photograph, seeming to gaze down and contemplate their older selves, stood the young revolutionaries: forty-two men and six women wearing identical peaked caps and loose shirts, posed in four rows with Chairman Mao standing at the center and wearing his customary blank expression. Self-absorbed, maybe, or bored. Surrounding the Old Man were his loyal intellectuals—writers, painters, military strategists. Some still held power; some, like Hong's parents, had lost the reins, regained them, lost them again. And the others? Well, most of the rest were dead, and now Sun Sheng had joined them. Hong picked him out in the back row, a head of high bushy hair like Bakunin, round steel-framed glasses resting on his aristocratic nose and catching a sparkle of sun.

Cui Chun returned from the photo-taking. "Immortalized once again," she said cheerfully. It was amusing to be an immortal. She struck Hong as remarkably sedate today—no harangues on the decay of China.

Hong covered his mouth with his hand. "How could you talk about Wei Ye's eulogy like that?"

"Courtesy is pleasant, and it doesn't cost much."

"And too much courtesy is a craft." He glanced toward the Three Tigers with evident disgust.

"You always forget they're different from us," his mother said, and then paused, as though she could not quite decide which of her many stories to tell. "I know it sounds strange, but we had it easier. When I was growing up—"

"Please," Hong said, holding up a hand.

"When I was growing up we heard the executions outside of town—when my aunt was shot, my grandfather, anybody who wrote the wrong words. I used to count the rifle reports. But in the countryside, where they were, it wasn't war, it was barbarism. The soldiers cut off people's heads and mounted them on spikes and paraded them through town dripping blood. The peasants sat at their windows and watched, and by the end of the day the mud in the streets was red. That shapes you, that changes you."

It was incredible to Hong: she could justify their barbarism today because of what they had endured fifty years ago. She reached into his pocket, took his cigarettes and lighted a Double Nine, and coughed violently. Every three or four months brought a new anti-smoking campaign, while at the same time the State tobacco industry kept adding new brands.

"I had a letter from your brother," Cui Chun went on. "He's coming to visit."

"Factory business?"

"Of *course,*" she said brightly. "Factory business that in-
cludes a night at the circus and a fine banquet of duck with
his friends at the Commerce Ministry."

"He's very good at what he does," Hong said, in the awk-
ward position of defending his brother Lin. "Since he took
over, output is up thirty percent."

"I hope they published that statistic. To make it true."

"In this case, it seems to *be* true."

The others from the photo-taking session gathered
around Cui Chun. Hong excused himself and wandered
into the library. There was an unusual mood among the
mourners, but he had trouble defining it. Many were
strangers to each other and guarded in their speech—when
with strangers, leave seven parts unsaid. All the same, Hong
heard a different music, a dark undertone in the chatter
itself. Were they uneasy, and not because of death? You're
imagining things, he told himself.

For all the air conditioning the second floor grew warm
with the heat of the crowd. By the end of July they would
heave off to the beach at Beidaihe, leaving the people
behind to sweat. Hong unobtrusively slipped out, down
the carpeted stairs, and stood listening to the musicians
in the paneled sitting room—chimes and harp. Outside in
the courtyard the younger Bureau staff lounged with the
drivers against their polished limousines. They passed the
time as officers did everywhere: smoking cigarettes, bantering about the availability of meat, and thanking fate for
putting them here, not in some remote little town.

Hong hung back inside the doorway for a moment, not
wanting to intrude, then edged out along the wall of whitewashed concrete planters, studying the flowers, ocher and
pink and a bizarre shade of green that seemed dyed rather
than real. He wished he could recall their species, and wondered abstractedly if he wouldn't have made a fair botanist
after all, a career effectively ruled out when the universities
closed. Life would have been simpler—studying plants,
breeding a hardier strain of wheat.

A senior officer with an athlete's broad shoulders and a
wisp of unshaven mustache was telling an old joke about a

rural soldier visiting Beijing to see Chairman Mao. The new men from the farm towns listened raptly. "And so the soldier came again on the next day and said 'I want to see Chairman Mao,' and the guard said, 'I told you already, I told you yesterday, he's dead.' The soldier waited a while, and then left. On the third day the soldier showed up again and said, 'I want to see Chairman Mao.' This time the guard lost his temper. 'Two days ago you came and asked to see him and I told you he was dead. Yesterday you came and I told you again that he's dead. Now what's the matter with you, why do you keep coming back?' And the soldier said, 'Nothing's wrong with me. I just like to hear you say it.'"

Even Hong had to chuckle. But suddenly the officers realized that joking about death might be inappropriate, and the laughter broke. Hong felt them staring at him, the assistant deputy director maundering over flowers. They think I'm too deep in grief to be bothered. Distract me, bother me, he wanted to say. Annoy me with trivia.

The senior officer, the jokester, slid from the bumper of a Shanghai sedan—a Comrade Wang, from the Bureau's motor pool. What was his given name? Wang Li? Wang Jian? There were thousands, millions of Wangs.

"Comrade Lu Hong, you were close to Director Sun," Wang said sympathetically.

"Yes. Yes, I was," Hong replied after a pause, as if the matter required some thought.

"He was the nicest of them upstairs, always a pleasant word for us whenever he came down." Wang shook his head meaningfully. "It was so quick, the fever."

Fever? No, they had found Sheng slumped over his desk. A heart attack, the message said.

"A man at seventy," Hong said, shrugging at the mystery of life and showing not even mild interest at this mention of a quick fever. "A man at seventy," he repeated, "a candle in the wind. You were at the Bureau on Friday?"

"On duty at the dispatcher's desk. I saw them carry him out to the ambulance."

"And was he very ill?"

"Yes, he looked terrible. But the doctor said it was nothing, and the Hospital for Infectious Diseases has a good reputation. But you're right, a candle in the wind. . . ."

"So," Hong said with finality, "so. We should all go so peacefully."

Wang bobbed his head up and down in some obscure variety of commiseration. It was curious, Hong thought, that no one else had spoken of Sheng's fever. On the other hand, gossip about details would be offensive. We don't live a hundred years, Sheng had said, but we worry enough for a thousand.

Hong excused himself, crossed the courtyard, and started up the steps.

At the second-floor landing he found Chan, contentedly sipping a glass of sweet osimanthus wine.

"Sheng didn't have a heart attack in his office," Hong said.

"Yes, he did. That's what they told me on the phone."

"It was a fever, some kind of infection."

"Hong, you're being distasteful."

"All in one day," said Hong with no expression. "An infection, fever, a heart attack."

Chan, exasperated, set his glass down on a sideboard. "He had a weak heart, Hong. He was old. The man was seventy years old."

"His father lived to be ninety, and his mother almost a hundred."

"And he had a weak heart," Chan repeated slowly and quietly.

They were summoning the mourners to dinner. Hong passed the photograph on the mantel and stopped to look once more. In the second row his mother glowed, plump and smiling, his father beaming joyously beside her. It occurred to Hong that he might have been forming in his mother's belly at the very moment the photographer snapped the shutter. Was he being born into a new dream as the old one was dying? He turned, felt Chan tug his arm and say something about Sheng having gone to a better world than this one. A debatable idea but an easy way to look at death.

Hong glanced back at the picture. A fever? A heart attack? For as long as he could remember Hong had tried to expunge suspiciousness from his nature, but it grew stronger in him, as natural as bark on a tree. Sheng, the tyrannical philosopher, had always urged him on. Be suspicious, he would say. Is there a better armor?

2.

STIRRING
THE
POT

On Tuesday, in his grief, or in something deeper and more troublesome, Hong decided not to go to his office. Instead he remained home in his barren one-room apartment and for much of the morning wandered like a blind man from one wall to the other, distractedly picking up odd objects, a picture frame here, a book there. He consciously avoided thinking about the previous day, or his son or his wife—who would soon be his former wife—or the five-room apartment they had shared. What occupied his mind were the horrors of the Cultural Revolution—the blood years that a decade earlier had torn the country apart and ruined so many lives—and, more specifically, memories of the day fourteen years ago when he had left the Army.

It was a Sunday, a cool afternoon in May. He had come by plane from Nanning and taken a grimy military transport bus from the airport. Two years had passed since his previous trip to Beijing, but no one was at his parents' old single-story courtyard house off Dianmen to greet him. His brother, unable to secure discharge papers, was stranded in Taiyuan, and a note from his mother said she had gone to the hospital to visit Hong's father. Hong carried his green khaki bags to his old room at the back of the house. Things remained almost as he had left them—his Youth League posters of Marx and Zhou Enlai, the wind-up alarm clock that had belonged to his grandfather, even the giant stylized portrait of Chairman Mao hanging over his desk. Hong was tempted to tear the stupid thing down and shred it.

He looked out the window into the garden, saw the familiar knotty wooden benches. In the corner a figure seemed to be moving through the vines, and at first Hong thought it a trick of the sunlight, then realized someone was tying paper bags over the bunches of purple grapes—a way of protecting them from insects and children. Who could it be? One of the neighbors? The figure turned, bending for another bag, and Hong saw that it was Sun Sheng.

Sheng had been only a shadow in Hong's life, one of the crowd of his parents' friends from Yanan. Hong knew that Sheng held a high post in Public Security, and that he had tried to protect Hong's father from the Chairman's wrath, but beyond that Sheng was a cypher, as parents' friends often are to their children. Hong set his duffel bags down and went out through the tiny alcove kitchen to the courtyard.

"Welcome home," Sheng said. "Your mother's sorry she couldn't be here."

Hong said he understood.

"It's difficult for her tending these grapes, she hasn't had time. And it's a delicate business. Put the bags on too soon, they don't ripen. Too late, and they spoil."

Sheng went on discussing the care of grapes, never directly referring to the political turmoil that had ruined Hong's father. Finally, after inquiring about conditions in the countryside, Sheng asked what Hong planned to do now.

It was the kind of question a father would have asked. Even the tone was protective. Hong said that despite his father's disgrace maybe he would apply to one of the universities that had reopened.

"It may be too soon for that," Sun Sheng said.

Well then, Hong replied, maybe he would try for a political position where he could prove his ideological purity.

"It may be too late for that," said Sheng.

Hong smiled and mentioned an Army friend who claimed back-door connections to jobs in the Foreign Ministry. The man's family, however, had an unpleasant reputation for providing back-door favors and then, if anyone complained, shifting blame and denying responsibility.

"You should listen to your own caution," Sheng said. "There's always time to be trusting...but as with the grapes, not too soon and not too late."

Hong understood that Sheng's appearance in the garden had not been an accident. A month later an officer from the Public Security Ministry called and suggested that Hong would be an ideal addition to the Ministry's staff. With his Army experience, he could begin as a foot-patrol officer. Hong appeared for training on the appointed day, and felt himself lucky. Within two years he had risen to the level of investigator.

At the time it had seemed a noble pursuit.

If for the rest of the day following the memorial service Hong thought about anything else, it was with a kind of dedicated, practiced ignorance. Make no connections, they'll make themselves. In mid-afternoon there was a knock on his door—his building watcher, a widow named Ou whose husband had been a Bureau messenger and who, with the blessings of all concerned, still kept their large one-room apartment. She wanted to know if Hong was ill. Hong said yes, he was feeling queasy, maybe the first touch of a summer cold, and was taking a precautionary day off. Old Ou volunteered to accompany him to the clinic. "Your eyes are tired," she said, which was true, though not in the way she meant. They were tired from seeing too much.

One day's recuperation was enough, and at five-thirty the following morning, as workers strolled to the parks for their *taiji* exercises, Hong woke, drank a glass of soy milk, and bicycled to the Bureau's building on Qianmen. The unease that had interrupted his sleep two nights ago had continued. Again he had twisted the sheets around himself all night, and again the unconscionable mugginess had yanked him awake. Even before he had reached the Planetarium and crossed Xizhimenwai he was tired and bleary-eyed, a condition noticeably worsened by a mauve crown of pollution settling onto the horizon.

The twin-winged headquarters building of the Bureau of Public Security, once a part of the British legation and expanded in late-Russian monolith style of pure concrete, squatted unceremoniously over nearly an entire square block in the heart of the city, within sight of the Great Hall of the People and a few minutes' walk from Sun Sheng's house in the compound on Tsungenwai. The Bureau was one of many State offices where factory workers passing on their bikes never stopped to peer in, perfectly aware of what went on inside and perfectly content to be ignorant of details. Its bald immensity testified to someone's conviction —a Russian adviser? a city planner by way of the military? —that you could never have enough room for the security needs of the State.

"Comrade Lu Hong!" bellowed the guard at the gate. "I heard you had a cold!" He appeared positively gleeful at the idea. When Old Ou dutifully called she must have made it sound like pneumonia.

"I'm fine," Hong said, wheeling in his battered one-gear Phoenix.

"You'll feel better tomorrow," the guard said.

Only two other bikes, both Flying Pigeons and new, stood in the long wall of racks. To the left of the gate, their closed doors facing the street, were twelve garages, and Hong could see through the barred windows that nine were unoccupied. Nine cars gone? At six-thirty in the morning? So much for rules. No one could afford his own car, and all Bureau cars were supposed to be used only for official business. High cadres nevertheless rode home at night and ordered their drivers to pick them up the next morning.

The guard noticed Hong's glance toward the garages. "All the cars are in the repair shop," he said as if the fact were self-evident, although the shop, directly opposite the garages, was sparklingly empty.

Hong's office on the second floor barely had room for its two pine desks, a leather-seated swivel chair for Hong and a cloth-seated one for Chan, and two rickety steel bookcases filled with directives that no one ever read. Chairman Mao's portrait had been removed four years earlier, leaving a bright rectangle on the whitewashed wall. Marx and Lenin remained, the latter's Tartar eyes staring in constant reproach, along with a tattered military map of Beijing that still showed the old city arches, long since torn down as remnants of feudalism. Thank the Russians for that defacement. Beneath the single window, with its view of the narrow airshaft between the building's two wings, sat a radio stand with an old Shanghai wide-band receiver.

On Hong's desk files of his completed cases were neatly stacked. The abduction ring in Shandong, kidnapping girls and shipping them west as wives for desperate peasants, had been broken up. Two of its leaders had sorrowfully pleaded guilty and been sent for reeducation so that they would understand their antisocial conduct and never engage in such a heinous crime again. In this case, while they might never understand their crime, there was little chance of their repeating it. Reeducation had meant standing before a squad of soldiers and accepting several bullets in the neck.

And that was justice, Hong thought angrily as he snapped the file closed, scattering a fine layer of cigarette ash. Justice was an idea that seemed to have lost many shades of meaning.

A sudden fever, he thought, an ambulance. Old men did get sick.

As for the German lawyer who had pretended to be more interested in canvas shoes than troop movements on the Russian border, he had been paid a friendly visit by Chan and asked to leave the country. He responded to this request with impeccable charm. He checked out of the Jianguo Hotel, accepted an escort to the airport, and was gone, first class, on the next flight to Tokyo.

Hong stood, crossed to Chan's desk, and turned on the hotplate under the teakettle, both gifts from the manager of nearby Department Store Number One. The manager's brother-in-law had needed a new job assignment to move from Jinan to Beijing. One job assignment, one hotplate with kettle. Hong waited for the water to boil. It was entirely reasonable, he thought, for Chan to be called in Tianjin before word of Sun Sheng's death reached Hong at home. That was the nature of things: when you're near a phone, people can call you. When you aren't, messages take longer. And as for Sheng being cremated, perhaps the old man had changed his mind, or perhaps his sons convinced his widow that burial was indeed the anachronism everyone said it was. Don't waste land, they would say, serve the people.

Hong picked up his telephone, dialed Ma Sufei's office. She was out, and he made an appointment to visit her the following evening. Somehow he would work the conversation around to the question of her husband's cremation.

The water in the kettle bubbled, steam rose. Hong turned it off, poured the water into a porcelain pot, dropped in a scoop of black tea. If someone had wanted Sun Sheng dead, someone powerful, then an official order would have been given. Sheng would have been called to a meeting in the countryside, where he would have choked on a fishbone or fallen down a well. Or he would have been accused of one crime or another, had a quick trial, and been shot.

Hong let his curiosity off its leash. He wondered further about the telephone call Chan had received in Tianjin. Who else had been called? And how quickly?

He stepped into the hallway, walked purposefully to the eastern end of the building, and descended two flights. On the decrepit corkboard at the first landing were posted the new duty rosters, flanked by two photographs: one, taken a few weeks earlier, celebrated a recent meeting between the Purchasing Ministry and the Bureau's directorate, a flock of smiling faces gazing at shiny computerized switchboards and Japanese telegraph machines as if they were newborns in a hospital nursery; the other photograph, several years old, showed the entire Investigations Division at a banquet. Hong paused and thought about the faces in the older photograph, specifically those belonging to cadres who had since been transferred elsewhere.

Foolish speculation, he told himself as he had a thousand times before. The sudden flurry of transfers had happened two and a half years earlier. It was October, just after the Thirty-fifth Liberation Day parade. Nearly a dozen men were sent to odd outlying Bureau branches. Somehow, despite housing shortages, space was found for their families as well, and they disappeared from Beijing never to return. *Don't stir the pot*, Chan had said when Hong questioned the reasons why. *Don't stir unless you want to eat.* And Hong's wife had complained about his absences that month: *You embarrass people by working extra hours. What are you doing there anyway?* Going mad, he thought. Slipping into weakness of the nerves, like my father.

What he had been doing, with a studied aimlessness, was reading the personnel dossiers of the transferred men in a fruitless search for explanations.

He turned, and the Political Commissar of the Investigations Division bounced up the steps toward him. Zhu Gang was a wooden puppet carved on the southern model—blocky jaw, skinny dangling arms, with a round innocent face and a perpetual smile of graying teeth. Both the innocence and the smile were manufactured. Zhu was a former Air Force colonel and had the mind of a snail, and hence was superbly suited to his job of fostering ideological purity. Hong, when younger and obedient to a fault, had been offered the same post, which he had politely refused.

Zhu burst out with a boisterous good morning. "Young Hong, looking at pictures of the new equipment, I see. Excellent, isn't it? Modern progress."

"We need modern progress," Hong said accommodatingly. Was that the correct response? Before Hong's wife had asked for a divorce, he had seen more of Zhu Gang than he had liked.

"Yes, new communications equipment will make us more efficient and democratic," Zhu said with gusto. Democratic was a good word this year, applicable to farm directives, urban free markets, even to telex machines. "Let me extend my sympathies," Zhu went on, his face reshaped into the very picture of sympathy, "Sun Sheng was a great servant of the Revolution."

"Which one?" Hong asked, his tongue running far ahead of what he knew to be good sense. "The old Marxist one, or the new capitalist one?"

From boisterousness to sympathy in a flash, now from sympathy to disapproval. "They are the same," Zhu said quietly. "You missed last week's political education meeting. Perhaps you could come this week. I know you have to

spend time with your son. Your wife is overburdened. But
you do want to be a good servant of the people, and I want
to help you."

"I appreciate that," Hong said with obvious sarcasm, but
Zhu seemed not to notice.

"And how's the boy getting along in school? He's doing all
right at literature?"

"Yes, passed his exam finally," Hong said, not knowing if
it were true. The exams had been held last week while he
was in Chengdu trying to move two old officers into retirement.

Zhu Gang shook a finger at him. "So. You'll find time to
come to this week's meeting."

"I'll be there," Hong said, capitulating.

He continued down the steps. Fruitless searches, he
thought, taking up the thread again. It had been around
the same time as the flurry of inexplicable transfers that,
under Sun Sheng's direction, Hong had investigated the
case of three Burmese smuggling heroin through China to
Hong Kong. Six awful weeks at the border, enough rain to
rot your hair, and in the end Hong suspected but could
prove nothing against a Deputy Director who worked for
the Three Tigers. For a few weeks things were very bad.
The Bureau imploded: doors slammed shut and bolts were
thrown, directives flew like missiles, senior cadres suddenly
found their services in urgent demand elsewhere. Before a
report could be issued, the Deputy Director was also transferred, seats were shuffled on the fourth and fifth floors,
and Hong had suffered a report that could have cost him a
promotion—or worse, sent him to some provincial office
where even the mosquitoes were bored.

Were all the transfers related to the smuggling case? You
could run in circles, chase your tail, trek up and down the
same mountain forever and still be searching for motives.

My flaw, Hong thought, my weakness, as Sun Sheng had
gently but often reminded him: always seeking a motive before precisely understanding the crime. "Motive is a question of history," Sun Sheng said. "Know the history of a
crime, and the motive unveils itself."

Hong headed for the communications exchange. The exchange monitored all calls to and from the Bureau, as

everyone inside the building knew, and random calls within the Bureau, as everyone pretended not to know. Telephone conversations took on a quality of circumspection leading to the most peculiar fits and starts. You might be recorded and you might not, but why take chances? Compounding this was the terrible quality of the system itself. If you stopped talking for more than a few moments a Central Exchange operator, thinking the line was dead, might cut you off. The combination had trained the entire population to speak in a stuttering babble.

Hong turned into a narrow hallway with a soundproofed ceiling that had buckled. Brown blotches randomly speckled its pinholed tiles. In a matter of months the newly installed water pipes had leaked from above. Falling ceilings, leaky pipes—oh well, things could only get better. At the end of the hall he pushed through a steel-reinforced door leading to the former furnace room. A blue ribbon of cigarette smoke already clung to the cavernous ceiling. There were twelve consoles on blond countertops, and next to each of the operators' newly computerized switchboards was a button that routed calls to the recording machines in the next room. A desk faced the consoles from the far end, and behind it sat Chu Shoujun, the switchboard supervisor, who was said to play a violent game of Ping-Pong.

"Up early, Hong," said Shoujun, rising from his chair and floating across the room as only thin men can. "How's your cold?"

"Much better, Shoujun, thank you," Hong said, amused.

"It's the heat that probably gave it to you. Terrible, isn't it?"

"Worse than last summer," Hong absently agreed.

"My wife's wheezing from it, too, but then she's always sick, a weak constitution. How's your family, your wife and handsome little son?" Shoujun knew about the divorce but insisted on believing the situation must be temporary. Divorce was only for disturbed people who refused to resolve their differences in a healthy way.

"They're fine," Hong said, "very fine, thank you."

"And your mother and father?" Shoujun asked with great concern, though he knew neither of them.

"Oh, fine, happy in the country." How long could this

chatter go on? Shoujun had been here all night, and probably talked to the walls. Move, Hong told himself. Plunge. "May I see the logbook for Friday, please?"

"For what purpose, I have to ask."

No, you don't have to ask, Hong thought. Some men look like boys well into middle age, others develop a face that is said to have character. Hong was painfully aware that he fell into the former category, not yet possessing, as he might in a few years, the absolute presence that commands. What he had substituted in its place was a great conservation of energy, an interior force. This worked with those attentive enough, or afraid enough, to notice it, which did not include Shoujun. Also, Shoujun's mother had died when he was young; he had been raised by men, including a father and an uncle in the Army, which created in him a pronounced reverence for authority. "Give me your Friday logbook"—that would have done the trick with Shoujun, but Hong was of a generation so trained in manners that politeness came reflexively.

Now, how to get out of it? "I want to ensure that my men properly called in."

"Very good," said Shoujun. He floated back to his desk and returned with the cloth-bound journal. "You have to sign," he said, laying the heavy book on the counter.

"I'm not taking it anywhere," Hong said. He wanted no record of this, nothing on paper.

"You still have to sign." Shoujun turned to the rack of blank yellow chits behind him.

"Only if I leave with it," Hong said, and started running his finger down the page for Friday. The calls from just past three o'clock until shortly before six o'clock filled almost an entire sheet—more than forty entries of telephone numbers, informing cadres around the country and in Beijing offices of Sun Sheng's death. Party offices first, probably. Then, in the space of the first two hours, starting at three-fifteen, six calls to Sun Sheng's house in the compound on Tsungenwai. Hong flipped the page to Saturday and saw the number of his neighborhood committee room: the call to Old Ou, his building watcher. A promotion, he thought idly, would mean his own phone, a superfluous luxury since nobody he knew had a phone to get his call. He turned back to Friday. Moving his calloused palm down the page, finger extended, he marveled at the Bureau's unusual efficiency. A man gets sick, the wires grow hot; he dies, they catch fire.

"No, I'm sorry, please," Shoujun was saying, pushing a yellow chit on Hong, "you have to sign anyway."

"Which rule are you citing?" Hong asked without lifting his eyes from the journal. At twenty past five, two calls to the same number in Tianjin, the first one lasting a few seconds, a bad connection, and the second barely a minute—to Chan, obviously, at his hotel. Supervisor Chu Shoujun, courteously but in his most businesslike voice, marched on, announcing a streak of directives from Heaven only knew which department. And then a blessed relief: another operator entered, a slim, pretty girl in a steel-blue dress whose mother taught metallurgy at Beijing University. She slid quietly into a seat, turned her board on, and called to Shoujun for help. Hong silently thanked her, recalled that she had beseeched him for a recommendation to Foreign Languages Institute Number Two, and just as silently promised himself that she or her mother or her sisters could have any favor they wanted. On the journal again—here, what's this? A call to a Shijingshan exchange? Who from the Bureau could possibly live out there?

"...and everyone agreed"—Shoujun had returned, his voice bore in—"signing a chit for reading the logs is absolutely required."

"You're right," Hong said conclusively, having stretched this as far as he dared. "Excellent that you manage these details so well. But why make extra work? I'll just forget about the chit this time, no use adding to the paperwork."

Not bad: a politically correct explanation sweetened with praise for Shoujun.

Shoujun seemed satisfied. "Very good," he said, closing the book and heading for his desk. "Very good," he repeated, and then turned to call, "Pay attention to that cold. As with many things, you never know what it could turn into."

As with many things, Hong thought, pushing through the door. As with many things.

In the hallway he took a pad from his pocket and scribbled the Shijingshan number. He wondered where the operators' gossip found its final ear; he thought about his son's literature exams and decided he should call to find out if Bai had passed; he considered Switchboard Supervisor Chu, who lived by the rules and might some day be forced to condemn anyone who broke them.

At the top of the steps, turning his back on the photograph of the smiling faces from the Purchasing Ministry, Hong looked at the telephone number in his hand. Don't be a hero, he thought, then methodically tore the piece of paper to bits.

"You're so lucky," Chan said as Hong ambled into their office. Chan was at his desk, cup of tea in hand, legs propped on the radio stand. "Last night we caught a whole team of corrupt elements, five of them, with hundreds of bicycles."

He handed Hong the file. In a country of no private cars and, for most people, limited signs of status, bicycle forging was big business. Merely owning a bicycle was a luxurious necessity, costing the ordinary worker three or four months' salary, and if you couldn't own the best bicycle, at least you might have one with a Flying Pigeon nameplate. No one in Beijing would be stupid enough to pay for a nameplate, but in the countryside status could be had for an extra twenty yuan, never mind the quality of the bike. The whole matter was touchy, given the ideological impossibility that one brand of bicycle could be superior to another.

"You wouldn't believe the stacks of money," Chan said, "thousands of yuan. These crooks could have stocked a department store, they could have financed a factory."

"They'll be financing new prisons," Hong said unhappily. In his pocket the shreds of paper felt like rocks.

"You'll get credit," Chan said emphatically. "Be happy." His feet slid from the radio stand with a thud. "Listen, you don't look well, you must have exerted yourself too much yesterday. What was it, building bookcases? Fixing the shower?"

"Shower," Hong said. He poured himself a cup of tea.

"I'm never very good at cheering you up," Chan said. "I'm sorry."

"What brand of bikes did they have?"

"Everlasting, and utter pieces of junk, too, real garbage, with defective spokes and handlebars assembled with spit. It's worse than an economic crime, it's a...a..." Chan sputtered indignantly.

"A recidivist crime," Hong supplied. Recidivist was another popular word this year, applicable to just about anything.

"Yes, exactly," Chan said, pleased to have a label, any label. "Recidivist."

"Everlastings with what nameplate?" Hong asked.

"Universal."

"What's the latest price on an Everlasting?"

"The basic model, about a hundred and thirty yuan, maybe a little more."

"And a Universal?" Hong asked.

"A hundred and seventy."

"That's a nice profit. Where were the Everlastings made?"

"Here, probably."

"Which doesn't give us more arrests elsewhere. We're supposed to be finding conspiracies."

"You're impossible," Chan said. "This arrest last night is going to make you look great." He waved a piece of paper. "But with good news comes bad news. You're officially requested to appear at the Director's Office of Investigations tomorrow morning at eight."

Hong looked at the memo. What could the Three Tigers want from him? Perhaps Chu Shoujun felt obliged to call the fifth floor whenever anyone looked at a telephone log.

Hong pulled the door open. "I need fresh air."

Outside only the leaves could hear them, and leaves, as far as Hong knew, had not learned how to speak, though he wouldn't be the least bit surprised when they did. Chan followed him down the back steps to the courtyard and past the guards onto Qianmen Street. A two-wheeled cart passed, driven by an old woman on a bicycle. On the flatbed lay a child's body swathed in sheets. The powerful meet illness in ambulances, Hong thought, the poor on bicycles.

"Let's go around the corner," Chan said. "It's cooler in the shade."

"And a coal mine is cooler than a furnace."

They walked a block in silence and turned at Zhengyilu, crossing to the tree-lined meridian strip. Chan lit a Panda, an expensive cigarette, and passed one to Hong. "Whatever they want," Chan said, "you're not interested, you turn it down. No new assignments. Slogan of the day: the gun shoots the bird that sticks its neck out." Chan loved slogans; like Chairman Mao when he was alive, Chan issued one for every occasion. "Tell them we're on the verge of discovering a ring that's selling counterfeit Flying Pigeons."

"We already look terrible," Hong said. "We haven't found the source of the nameplates, and we're not going to."

Chan threw a finger into the air. "Precisely," he said triumphantly. "Which is why we need more time. Besides, it's probably an Army operation in Sichuan. Who else has the trucks to move bicycles? I'll bet the Army's in on this."

"That's ridiculous," Hong said. Army officers didn't steal; they requisitioned their luxuries. The Army was the best career, no matter how much money the farmers were earning in free markets. In good times and bad the Army ate well.

"Make something up," Chan countered vehemently, then spat on the street. It was an unsanitary habit and everyone did it. "I don't care what you tell them. Nobody upstairs knows a thing anyway. Tell them...let's see, the new efficiency directives could be helpful here...tell them we're working round the clock."

"Who works round the clock?" Hong asked. "They'd laugh."

Chan leaned against a tree and stubbed his cigarette out on the sole of his shoe. He possessed a rare wisdom, Hong knew, an almost magical second sight. He smelled trouble the way peasants smelled rain.

"If I turn down work," Hong continued, "they'll cite me for thinking like a reactionary. And I'm up for a promotion in the spring. I'll get a jeep with a driver."

"Don't pretend you care about promotions. Which you'll get anyway." Chan shook his head as if Hong were a dumb child, and then, for no apparent reason, his face lit up in an expansive grin. "I have an idea. Put together a book of poems, you're not a bad amateur. Maybe get your mother to add a few for you. Then get yourself transferred to a poetry center. Become a full-time poet, and you'll never think about promotions or jeeps or what they do above the third floor." He was in full flight, he was soaring. He should have been a teacher, Hong thought, and probably would have been; a month after he applied to Beijing University the whole place shut down for ten years. "Don't get involved in their intrigues," Chan went on, starting for the Bureau and waving Hong to join him, "and leave the interdepartmental cases to someone else. You know what goes on up there. While we're out chasing thieves, they requisition desks to sell on the black market. And you can't catch them. Sheng told me all about it. The paperwork disappears before the stuff shows up."

Chan, too late, seemed to realize his error, and turned to see Hong's face tighten. Mentioning Sun Sheng only took Hong back to his conversation with the drivers at the memorial service.

Chan stopped at the curb. "Look, even if you're right about Sheng," he said quietly, "even if it's a little odd that I heard before you did, or that he had a fever but nobody said anything, what's to gain by thinking about it? He was an old man, right? He had a weak heart, right? He—"

"Who said Sheng had a weak heart?"

"He had a full life, a rich life."

Hong felt in his pocket, his fingers grazing the scraps of torn paper. He took out his pad and pen, and discovered that he had no trouble remembering the Shijingshan number from the telephone log. He wrote it down: 43-3641. "Find out who this number belongs to, will you? Don't use the Communications Ministry, all right? Go through the back door."

Chan stared at the paper as though it were poisonous. "Why?"

"To satisfy my curiosity."

"Don't be so curious. You're too curious. And you think too much."

"I'm curious, it's my nature."

Chan made no move to take the number.

"Try a hypothetical case for me," Hong continued. "Suppose tomorrow I was denounced as a bad element, suppose our beloved Political Commissar decided that I displayed antisocial tendencies, and suppose I was on trial and about to be sent to . . . to wherever, for reeducation through labor. Would you demand the right to testify, to clear my name? Or would you be too frightened?"

Chan sighed, an expressive explosion of breaths that lowered his chin and raised his belly and fluidly bobbled everything in between. He reached out and gently tugged the slip of paper from between Hong's fingers. "Remind me," he said as they continued side by side across the street, "did I ever tell you what a fool you are?"

3.

STIRRING
THE
WIND

Beijing was the center of the universe, and the heart of the city proclaimed its glory. The next morning Hong took in the view from the fifth-floor windows of the powerful, a panorama of granite and stone built by the most powerful of them all, Chairman Mao himself. With the help of Russian planners, of course, those lovers of imperial style. To the west lay the Gate of Heavenly Peace and the Great Hall of the People, a temple of columns, a great festivity of columns. From the balcony underneath the orange-tiled roof Chairman Mao had saluted his people and smiled beneficently on the Forbidden City, where the Emperor had lived and which was, appropriately, several stories lower. The Emperor, after all, was dead, and Chairman Mao, as everyone knew, had once been immortal. In front of the Great Hall spread Tiananmen Square, the ideal realization of the Chairman's dictum: "Destroy the old to establish the new." What thirty years ago had been lanes of small old houses was now a stadium field of concrete with an assaulting ce-

ment obelisk in the center, the Monument to the Heroes of
the People. The view began to horrify Hong. When you
looked long enough, it was extraordinarily ugly.

"Beautiful, isn't it?" came the voice behind him.

Director of Investigations Wei Ye sat behind her vast oak
desk, ear to the telephone. She covered the receiver with
her hand and nodded. "Sit down, please, I'll be another
minute or two, it's the Ministry of Justice, please excuse
me."

Ah, that voice, her old woman's lilt, so sweet and light in
timbre, the voice of someone who had never bludgeoned
anyone to death, who had never so much as wished harm
on another human being. She wore no signs of her rank—
starched white blouse, blue skirt, the uniform of the upper-
level cadre—but her office displayed evidence of her
superb connections: green brocaded silk curtains, a Dutch
television set. Gazing down at Hong from above the Director's head, in a gilt frame that needed dusting, was a portrait of the late Premier Zhou Enlai.

Hong stepped away from the window and took a seat—
cushioned, protected by freshly laundered lace antimacas-
sars, and positioned directly across from the Director on a
vast flowered blue carpet. The chair was so much lower
than Wei Ye's that Hong felt like a witness at an inquisition.

The Director of Investigations smiled at him and shook
her head to indicate impatience with her caller. Covering
the mouthpiece, she said, "The Ministry of Justice is aware
of our good work. They are all grieving, too, over the loss
of Sun Sheng." Someone returned to the line and she
leaned back into her upholstered cushion of blue velvet.
Hong, at grade twelve, had only leather. With a promotion
he, too, could rest on springs and velvet. You never had to
wonder about the rank of fellow cadres. All you had to do
was look at their chairs.

Into the phone Wei Ye said, "Yes," then after a pause,
"There is no doubt of that," and after another pause, "It
isn't too clear."

The last phrase—*It isn't too clear*—was as common in daily
conversation as "Hello" or "Have you eaten?" or "Good-
bye." It meant a variety of things. Question: Can you tell me
why this prisoner hasn't been processed? Reply: It isn't too

clear—meaning nobody can explain why, we've lost the records. Or meaning a higher cadre has intervened and you shouldn't ask any more questions. Or meaning that the policy on this sort of crime changed this morning and we can't figure out what to do. When the Director of Investigations used the phrase, the caller, if he treasured his health as much as he treasured information, would move rapidly to another topic. Even if Wei Ye had survived by virtue of history, not ability, she still bent brilliantly with the political wind. As they said of survivors, she was bamboo.

She finished her call, replaced the receiver in its cradle. With no mention of her reason for summoning Hong, she inquired about his current investigations, listened with what appeared to be genuine interest, congratulated him on the removal of the German lawyer.

"We were only doing our job," Hong said. He would match her gift for false flattery with his for genuine modesty.

"Still, you handled it with excellent instincts," she said, and then without preamble, "I have a special case for which you are well suited. An American doctor is here on a three-month scientific exchange. His name is Ostrander, given name Peter, attached to Union Hospital and Medical College, sponsored by the Academy of Sciences. There are suspicions about his presence."

"Where do the suspicions originate?"

"It isn't too clear. This case was assigned to us directly by the Minister. You will become the American's guide, representing the Scientific and Technological Commission of the State Council. You will ingratiate yourself, penetrate his habits, and report regularly. You will pretend to be his friend, promoting relations between countries and peoples."

Implications multiplied like butterflies. Hong had been assigned to only a handful of cases involving foreigners. He preferred domestic criminals. Sustained contact with foreigners, any foreigners, opened cadres to charges of spiritual pollution. Campaigns against such pollution started and ended with unpredictable regularity, and even less predictable results. On the other hand, success with foreigners could lead to overseas travel—accompanying a trade mission, say, or a state visit. Visions bloomed: standing under the Arc de Triomphe, riding across the Golden Gate Bridge and climbing the Statue of Liberty, visiting the botanical gardens of Zagreb, boating on the Thames beneath the Tower of Big Ben, which he had heard chime on broadcasts of the BBC. On the third hand, Hong heard Chan's ringing siren: *You don't want anything to do with their intrigues.*

"This American, he's a spy?" Hong said. All foreigners were presumed to be spies, though most often they weren't.

"Possibly, and he may have accomplices. His father worked here as an archaeologist for the occupying enemies before Liberation. The file is on its way to you now."

Chan's siren blared louder. How did you stop a file in midair? "But if he's a spy," Hong asked with utmost reasonableness, "why not order him to leave?"

"If he has accomplices there may be a whole nest of traitors. That's what you have to find out." Her responses reeked of anticipation, as if from a script.

"Excuse me, but as in the case of the German lawyer, should we not consult the Ministry of National Defense or the Special Ministry for State Security?" Fighting a tank with bare hands paled next to a war between ministries.

"The Ministry of Defense supplied the scientist with a guide, but his English was insufficient to the task. And the case is not yet developed enough for the Special Ministry."

Avoiding this assignment required the delicacy of a cicada shedding its skin. A ritual self-effacement would be expected, of course, so the problem was how to make it stronger. Hong looked up at Wei Ye. Delivering her eulogy for Sun Sheng, she had towered over the crowd. Today, dwarfed by her huge desk, she was a tiny crow-faced woman. But frailty to her was as ever a stranger. Power kept her young, clung to her like dew to a rose, erased wrinkles from the pockets of her eyes and left her face pale and fair as parchment.

"My workload is heavy, as you know," Hong launched in, "and there are so many investigators better suited to this case. Yu Tianwei, for example, a fine mind, and so dextrous with languages—"

"Japanese and French, not English."

Hong cursed the time he spent watching English lessons

on television. Why hadn't he tried Japanese, or Urdu?

"You're getting this assignment because the Party trusts you," Wei Ye continued, "and you're effective with foreigners. The Minister himself recommended you. He watched you at the reception for British scholars at the Foreign Affairs Ministry."

"Yes, shouldn't this be their case?"

"In serving the Revolution, it doesn't matter who does the work. We all work together."

She was a walking compendium of lessons in serving the Revolution, a living and breathing propaganda treatise. Give the Three Tigers a problem and they found a revolutionary perspective. Even, no doubt, for allowing their underlings to smuggle heroin or sell desks on the black market.

"I'm trying to understand this case in its complexity," Hong said. "I apologize sincerely for being so obtuse. What's the reason, again, for taking it away from Defense?"

"They're short of staff, and they're clumsy. They'd lose patience and try to arrest this man, even though it would be counterrevolutionary now, a contradiction. We've struggled hard to eradicate arbitrary abuse of power. We're more democratic than that."

Ah, democratic! Hong allowed himself a smile. "What kind of information is the American looking for?" he asked.

"I haven't read the documents," Wei Ye said, which Hong doubted. "But you have a good mind. If a man says one thing, you understand three." She stood up. "One more thing," she added, escorting him to the door, "you must watch carefully for subversive elements. Don't bring this case up in your working group, only with your staff."

Who could be a subversive element? Anyone, depending on whom you asked. And what did it matter whether his entire unit knew of every case? Usually they were bored by his reports. Wei Ye, however, had three heads and six arms, and Hong saw a chance to protect himself. "This is highly irregular," Hong protested. "I can't recall any such instructions before. The working group discusses every case."

"Not national security cases, under no circumstances," said the Director.

"In that event, perhaps you would present this order to

me in writing, so that I can impress on my staff the crucial
seriousness of secrecy."

The tiger smiled—or bared her teeth. "You will have my
order in writing," she said after a pause, and then, dismiss-
ing him, "Serve the people."

Downstairs all was normal. On Hong's desk lay a file suggesting that farmers were stealing their own watermelons to
sell at free markets. In the campaign to rid Beijing of dogs,
two mutts had been found and shot. The office phones had
gone dead.

"A living example of Chairman Mao's legacy," said Chan,
angrily banging the phone plunger for a dial tone. "The
installation of new equipment inevitably destroys the old.
What did she want from us?"

"An American," Hong said.

"A trail job?" asked Chan, surprised. "Is that all she called
you for? Well, Americans are easier than Germans or Russians. They're so busy covering their tracks they leave a
whole new set. What's he supposed to be doing? Gathering
farm data? Taking pictures of tanks?"

"It's not too clear," Hong said ruefully. "And it's more
than that. You are looking at a guide from the Scientific and
Technological Commission of the State Council. I am to become an American doctor's friend, I am to penetrate his
habits, I am—"

"You are to be locked in Qin Cheng Prison Number One.
You are to be stood against a brick wall and shot." Chan
leaned his head all the way back and waved a fist at the
ceiling. He was worried. "You'll be a target bigger than a
Shanghai sedan. All she'll need to get rid of you is another
spiritual pollution campaign." He sat down, rested his head
in his hands. "All right, why is the doctor here? Who invited
him?"

"I'm getting the file. It's some sort of scientific exchange."

Chan peered at Hong as if trying to read a book halfway
across the room. "Why you?"

"My English is good. And she's afraid Defense will botch
it."

"A reasonable assumption. But that still doesn't explain
why she picked you."

Hong pulled out his files on dogs and thieves. In two

years virtually all dogs in Beijing had been killed or removed to the countryside, where they were also killed and
then eaten. The ideological reason leapt easily to the lips:
pets were decadent. Not every pet, however. Baby chicks
and parakeets were permitted. The practical reasons—and
pragmatism held substantial sway over Marxism this year—
were simpler: dogs eat too much but chickens and parakeets
eat little, and all three can be eaten themselves.

Hong turned to the thieves, mostly common street robbers preying on third-shift factory workers. A week ago,
however, the Second Secretary of the Textiles Division of
the Trade Ministry was left with a bruised chin when three
thugs tumbled him into a bush in Beihai Park and took his
wallet. Then two watermelon trucks had been hijacked on
the Third Ring Road. Thus ordinary antisocial activities became a crime wave. Hong felt sorry for bicycle forgers, pet
owners, street thieves—and himself for having to deal with
them. It was all slightly crazy anyway, since the official Party
position was clear: crime wasn't a problem in China.

Hong handed Chan the file on the watermelon thieves.
"Take care of this, see if you can find the ringleader and
keep the others out of it. I don't want a truckload of dead
peasants on my conscience." He picked up the rest of the
case reports, glanced through the labels, and put the whole
lot on Chan's desk. "Pass these around, too. Whoever you
think can handle them. Then go to the Bureau of Foreign
Experts and get the American's entry record. Ostrander,
first name Peter."

"Sounds Scandinavian," said Chan, who had studied
Swedish in his spare time.

"Find out which cadre sponsored him at the Academy of
Sciences, and get his foreign travel records, family history,
anything else that could lead to accomplices."

"Don't tell me you suspect anybody in the Academy."

"I don't suspect anybody, yet. Get logs of the American's
phone calls, put a round-the-clock watch on his room at the
foreigners' compound. I'll get over to Defense eventually
and see what they've got."

Chan was taking notes. "Send Zizang," he muttered. A
Comrade Zizang had been added to the Director's staff four
months ago. For one week he had appeared at his desk,

then never showed up again. But the duty roster still listed him as an employee, and every month someone collected his pay. Who was he? *Where* was he? Who collected his salary?

"You don't seem upset," Chan said.

"One of two things is true. Either this case can be wrapped up quickly, or it will drag on so long that Defense will fight to get it back."

"Why?"

"Very simple. If he's not a spy, we'll know soon enough. And if he is? Just read the newspapers. The Standing Committee of the Politburo has to appoint someone to replace Sheng as liaison to the Central Committee. Now either it's going to be Wei Ye, or someone at Defense, or some virtuous paper-pusher at the State Council. When I was in her office she was talking to one of those flunkies at Justice, probably writing her own memorial tablets and taking credit for getting rid of the German lawyer. Do you think Defense will let her take credit or this one, too?"

"Good luck to her," Chan said brightly. "Let her rise to the top, the better to be attacked and disposed of." He started gathering the files. "Your friend Boda is selling sculpture to foreigners again."

Boda was an unofficial artist, a sculptor who belonged to no working unit, no institute, and supported himself with unofficial sales, many to diplomats.

"Where did you hear that? He didn't mention it to me."

"He wouldn't. Why get you into trouble, too? Boda's going to end up mining coal in Datong and his wife will be tending lung diseases in Urumchi."

"Where did you find out he was selling to foreigners?"

"I happened to see it," Chan said matter-of-factly, "on a report at the Telecommunications Ministry."

"And what were you doing there?" Hong asked with a smile.

"Doing you a favor that will probably get us both shot."

Chan languidly lifted his bulky body from his seat. With the case files under his arm, he reached his free hand into his shirt pocket. He extracted a piece of paper, laid it on Hong's desk, and sailed into the hallway like a man without a care in the world.

Hong looked at the slip of paper. In Chan's blunt scrawl was written: telephone 43-3641, Crematorium, Yuquan Road, Shijingshan.

On the fourth floor the walls were painted a delicate lotus green, not white, the halls were wider and carpeted in deep ruby red, and the offices—well, they were nothing less than gargantuan. When you ascended toward Heaven, did the clouds grow fluffier? Crossing through the newer, Russian section of the building, Hong walked to the Military Affairs division in the northwest wing. In what had once served as the British Minister's reception room, a young cadre named Jin, Sun Sheng's assistant, was industriously moving files and cleaning Sheng's office for its new, as yet unnamed, occupant. Jin had been a welder but scored high on his university exams and so escaped the tedium of a pipefitting shop. Sheng had found him three months ago in the budget department of the Finance Ministry. Ostensibly Hong had come to offer condolences, and Jin, leading Hong into his partitioned cubicle next to the office, graciously offered his in return.

"They tell me the memorial service was beautiful," Jin said, "lots of flowers, the compound all fixed up." Jin was in his late twenties and had a luminous Han face, handsome with deepset eyes. As pretty as a girl, Hong thought.

"You've been there, to the compound?" Hong asked.

"No, I never had the privilege."

"You would have been welcome at the service."

The boy hesitated and nervously jingled his keychain. "My wife...she felt I shouldn't intrude, that only the highest cadres should attend."

"Really?" Hong said. "That's too bad."

"And was it as beautiful as they say?" Jin went on, not so subtly shifting the subject.

Hong, out of intuition or some half-knowledge expressed not even to himself, detected an evasiveness in Jin. Treading gently, Hong said yes, the ceremony had been lovely, a fitting tribute with a lengthy eulogy by Wei Ye. At the mention of the Director of Investigations, Jin's face showed only the tiniest change of expression, which was precisely what Hong had hoped to see—knowledge of

Sun Sheng's clashes with the Three Tigers. What else did the boy know?

"You weren't here on Friday?" Hong continued.

Jin seemed embarrassed. "I was here, but I arrived late and Director Sun wasn't at his desk, and then I went out to...to return some papers to the Party Archives. If I had come back, if the ambulance had been called sooner..."

Papers to the Party Archives? What would Sheng have been doing with anything from the Archives? "You can't blame yourself," Hong said. "Who did call for the ambulance?"

"Director Sun called himself. But they told me he'd already fainted by the time the attendants arrived. When I got back..."

"There was nothing you could have done," Hong said, and then, in a gambit out of nowhere, a chicken hatched from a thing even as well-sealed as an egg: "Old Sun was working too hard, too many hours for an old man."

A crack in the wall of Jin's diffidence seemed to open. He leaned toward Hong, raised his eyebrows, and glanced around the partition separating his cubicle from the hallway. "You had heard," Jin said.

Yes, Hong replied with gravity, he had heard.

"It was frightening," Jin said intensely. "To see him like that. For three months now, one stack of records after another, files upon files, here at night after everyone had gone home."

Which records? Hong wondered. But he merely nodded.

The boy went on: "He told me he was reading history, but I...I didn't believe him."

"Oh?" said Hong with no demonstrable interest.

"One reads history to absorb it. But this crazy jumble of papers all over the floor, on his desk, on the shelves—and all from the war of Liberation. He wasn't reading, he was searching."

"Which period was he most interested in?"

"His own," Jin said, "when they were all with the Chairman at the headquarters in Yanan. He had records of old military campaigns, political arguments, poring through everything like it was today's internal report."

"Did you happen to see the files he was reading?"

"No, he wouldn't let me help him. He'd been all over the city, requesting them himself."

Lightly, with an air of bemusement, Hong said, "I wonder what he could have been looking for."

"But it's obvious, I think."

Hong inclined his head. "Is it?"

"He wanted to find his childhood, he wanted to relive the greatest period of his life. The same thing happened to an aunt of mine in Xian, all she could talk about was the past. Do you think...?" This last step nearly proved too great for him. "Comrade Lu Hong, he was your friend."

"Yes, yes he was," Hong said.

"Do you think...I don't want to offend, but...do you suppose, might it be possible, that old age had overtaken his mind?"

"Yes," Hong allowed, "that happens." Which was nonsense, it was ridiculous, Sheng's mind could stir up the wind, he had a thousand changes and ten thousand variations.

Hong casually turned into Sheng's office, glanced at the three cartons of bundled files on the floor and stacks of books to be crated for removal. The musty large room smelled of furniture polish and tobacco, and testified to the extravagance of the British foreign service—oak-paneled walls, parquet floors, layered moldings around the windows and the fireplace. On the mantel sat a clock with three faces, a large one showing the time in China—there were no zones, the time was the same everywhere in the country— and two smaller faces labeled Moscow and Tokyo.

"Haven't they transferred his cases yet?" Hong asked, walking past the three cardboard boxes.

"Oh yes, of course, we started yesterday, those are his personal files, old Party documents."

Hong took a seat behind Sheng's desk. Idly running his fingers over the burnished top, he contrived to appear immensely attracted by the view out the window onto the Qianmen courtyard. In fact his eyes were fixed firmly on the three boxes a few feet away on the carpet. A corner of black leather—Sheng's desk calendar—peeked out between two files.

"I don't know who I'll be working for now," said Jin, emboldened by his newfound intimacy with Hong. "I haven't been here long enough to have any seniority, they might transfer me to one of the substations, but I hope not, I don't want to leave my wife and daughter, and I love Beijing, we're near the top of the waiting list for a new apartment and my wife's parents would be so happy...."

Hong let him continue, until after an eternity it became evident that he would never stop unless Hong promised to put in a word about keeping him in Beijing. Hong promised, and Jin, grateful to the point of fawning, escorted him to the top of the steps.

Hong remained there, watching Jin leave, holding to the rail. He was certain that Sun Sheng had not been searching for his revolutionary youth, as Jin had sentimentally but mistakenly deduced. Clearly the old man had been after something else, although he would have been happy to let Jin believe otherwise. No one knew better than Hong how cleverly Sheng could lead the young. But what exactly had Sheng been looking for in those ancient records of the war years? And why had he not used his assistant to fetch them?

Out of the storm of Hong's confusion poured an unexpected anger. Until now comfort had sufficed: work, eat, sleep, endure political folly masquerading as truth. And if you believed deceit the order of the day, if the death of a friend summoned you to battle, then perhaps you were a bad element, as Party dogma explained. But as Hong started down to his office he considered how he could get a look at those three boxes of files before Jin carted them away, and then, already inventing lies to make the feat possible, he shuddered at the idea of where this battle was taking him.

In the Bureau's rear courtyard Hong looked at his watch, an imported Japanese wonder acquired at the cost of a month's pay. The crystal was fogging in the humidity and the hands were losing fifteen minutes a day—possibly, Hong thought, reflecting its owner's feeling about his life. In two hours, at three o'clock, a divisional meeting would drag everyone from the fourth floor, and the second and third as well, to the downstairs auditorium. The corridor leading from the new building to the old, along with the corridor to Sheng's office, would be empty. It was, Hong realized, his only chance.

He crossed the courtyard to Chang'an Avenue and turned down Wangfujing, the city's main shopping street. Only two lanes wide, with trolleys impeding bicycle and car traffic on both sides, Wangfujing was under constant siege. Even in the middle of the day going two blocks was like trying to enter a sports stadium. Railings had been planted in the sidewalk to protect pedestrians from being shoved into the street. Opposite the walls of the Beijing Hotel a bicycle parking lot did brisk business, presided over by a smiling old woman in a wooden hut, while above her rose six stories of bamboo scaffolding that laced the facades of buildings under renovation. Between the buildings, in an alley barely wide enough for a man to pass with his bike, sidewalk vendors sold summer dresses and shirts sewn at home. It was the usual insanity: crowds upon crowds, neck to neck, grizzled Mongols in decorated blue smocks sitting on street corners, and, packing the plaza in front of the Beijing Department Store, newly married couples shopping for armchairs and couches against the time when they could move out of their parents' apartments into their own. Young people shopped incessantly—shopped, that is, but didn't buy, because if looking was cheap entertainment, buying was a contact sport. And so they looked at canvas zipper-bags, Toshiba refrigerators from Japan, photo albums. And color televisions, naturally, though eventually they'd settle for black-and-white. High cadres and rich farmers could afford color.

Hong stopped first at the clock shop at number 174, next to the Children's Department Store, and told the clerk about his watch. The clerk held it to his ear, shook it, and wrote out a stub.

"When will it be ready?" Hong asked.

"In a year or two," the clerk answered, smiling dourly. Then, "Three weeks minimum, maybe four."

Hong went out, turned toward Donghuamen Street, and a shroud of heat fell on him. If Guilin and Chongqing were furnaces, what was Beijing in this worst summer in a decade? All around him office workers bicycled home for lunch, although how they would get to the outlying counties and eat and return in two hours was beyond him. It used to be three hours in the summer, but the new economic policies had changed all that, too. On Hong's salary, a hundred and seventy yuan a month, more than twice that of the average city worker, he could afford to eat quite often in the neighborhood.

He asked himself again what Sheng could have been searching for in the Party Archives. Tell me, Sheng, what was so important that you went to get those files yourself, not even trusting your loyal assistant?

The dumpling restaurant at Dongfeng Market had existed for as long as Hong could remember, serving the same passable food. Occasionally the budget allowed for a coat of whitewash, new chairs, lately a neon sign, but like most of its customers the place had an air of exhaustion. Hong took a table in the front, where the clatter of dishes from the kitchen would mask any conversation. A waiter in a white smock promptly brought two glasses, a liter bottle of beer, and a smaller bottle of orange soda; Hong mixed the beer and soda into his glass, three to one, put his newspaper aside, and waited for his friend Peng Boda. Lunch with a friend was a rare occasion, and difficult to schedule, but Boda had left a message asking to see Hong.

"Gloom! You're drenched in gloom."

Hong looked up. The sculptor's high rich voice issued from a body that seemed perpetually frail—thin as a reed, always quivering in anxiety. He sat, pushed his untamed mop of hair from his forehead, and poured himself a glass of beer.

"I'm not gloomy," Hong said.

"This beer is weak," Boda said, sipping.

"It's a bad season for beer. The production quotas go up, so does the percentage of water."

"Is that the new capitalism?"

"I don't think so," Hong said. "That's the old socialism."

Lunch with Boda was an exorcism. With almost anyone else but Chan, such loose jesting brought frowns, or worse. The waiter arrived, remarked on the heat, and took their order. Hong offered to pay for lunch and encouraged Boda to eat, knowing that dinners at home were small.

"You *look* gloomy," Boda said. "I'm the one who should be depressed."

"Why?"

It was a political problem. A fellow sculptor, trying to elevate Boda from the ranks of dissidents, had nominated him for an appointment to the Beijing Art Research Institute. Nothing fancy, a low-level resident position, but it would mean free materials and a salary. This seemed to Hong good news.

"It is and it isn't," Boda explained. "If the appointment goes through everything's fine. But if it doesn't then anyone who backed me is in trouble. Then it'll be harder for them to give me clay and tools. A painter, that's what I should have been. Paper, chalk, watercolors—that stuff is cheaper. Anyway, what should I do?"

"Maybe the risk is worth it," Hong assured him. "Liberalism in art is taking hold, or so they tell me."

"Maybe this month it is," said Boda. "Next month, who knows?" He drained half his glass in a gulp and refilled it. "You're preoccupied," he added with authority.

"Not at all."

"I saw Chan at the market yesterday. He doesn't think liberalism in art is taking hold. He told me I shouldn't be selling to foreigners."

"I know," Hong said. "Who did you sell to?"

Boda sighed. "A nice little Czech girl. She bought a drawing, *one* drawing. And she wasn't willing to pay much." Boda swigged his beer. "Chan also told me about the memorial service. What did you think you were doing, gossiping with the drivers, raising suspicions? Drivers talk in the wrong places, too, you know. Min thinks you're stupid."

"She has company in that opinion." Boda's wife Min was a doctor who ran a clinic for factory workers in the Fengtai District. Min believed in silence as a creed, a way of life. If you said nothing, no one could overhear you.

"She thinks I'm stupid, too," Boda said. "Why don't I sculpt in approved forms? Why do I work in clay and metal when they're teaching wood in the schools? Why do I make historical references in my work? How, I ask you, can you *not* make references?" He leaned over the table, lowered his voice: "What did the drivers say about Sheng?"

"He died quickly," Hong said.

"And?"

"And Chan shouldn't be discussing it," Hong said. Now he knew why Boda had wanted to see him. To elaborate would only engage Boda in speculation, but Hong did need his help. "Where are you going to be this afternoon at around three?"

"Home, working on a new piece. Why?"

"I want you to do me a favor." Very quietly, Hong explained what he needed—a telephone call with specific questions asked in a specific order. Boda should go to the post office near his apartment, early enough to guarantee access to a phone so that he could call at exactly the right moment. Boda listened to this request, made no protest, and just as Hong finished the waiter appeared with two plates of dumplings and a platter of string beans and hot peppers. Boda served Hong and himself. Obviously starved, Boda started to eat, then looked up, ducked his head, and nodded to the table behind Hong. Two boys were signing to each other, their hands and wrists and fingers poking the air in a spirited dance of argument, or so it seemed to Hong. He had never known anyone who was deaf.

"It must be a blessing, some days," Boda said, "not to be able to hear."

Hong smiled. Boda was unrealistic, a romantic. Hearing, at least, never got you into trouble. Not being able to speak —*that* would be a blessing.

4.

THE RULE
OF THE
GOLDEN
MEAN

The prelude to a divisional gathering never varied. One by one the junior case officers drifted into Hong's office, delivered their reports to Chan, and found excuses to stay and gossip so they could move downstairs together and enter like an army, with Hong as their general. The smiling Wan twins from the Chaoyang branch sauntered in earliest, amiably distributing American cigarettes supplied by their father, who was a member of the Politburo and a Vice-President of the Federation of Trade Unions, then Qiao Zhifu, a stony giant in charge of substation administration, and Nie Deqing, a strapping former Youth League leader who mediated family disputes.

Hong bantered with all of them and never once looked at his telephone.

At two-forty he started gathering his own files. Boda would already be at the post office now, three blocks from his apartment. Hong had told him not to take any chances. That he had so readily consented to indulge Hong was more than chance enough. Waiting for the call, Hong began to regret his impetuous request at lunch. He had known Boda since both were six years old, when Boda's parents—his father had been a pianist of some renown, and his mother a concert organizer—moved into the house across the street in the old northern quadrant of Beijing. In those days, just after Liberation, everyone reveled in high purpose and great dreams, and the two families spent a good deal of time together anticipating the glorious future. Boda and Hong, halfway through their teens, heard that an Army lieutenant, a friend of Hong's father, had been denounced as a rightist; one March morning in 1967, early in the Cultural Revolution, they were leaving for middle school when soldiers arrived, dragged the lieutenant down the stairs, and carried him off to prison. Two months later Boda's parents, denounced as bourgeois influences, disappeared into the countryside to become farmers, while Boda and his sister were sent south to live with a cousin. By then Hong's brother had become a Red Guard, a good sign, and his parents, protected by the legacy of their comradeship with Chairman Mao, had been able to keep their house. They had even managed through old friends to get Hong into the Army. Not long afterward, however, Hong's father, with the noblest of motives, issued a critical report on declining rice production and suddenly it was decided that he, too, desperately needed reeducation. To the commune! Learn the spirit of the peasants! Conquer your dangerous thinking! Hong's father, his spirit not merely reeducated but thoroughly destroyed, eventually returned. So did the Army lieutenant, who in ten years had aged thirty; Hong still remembered going with his parents to see him step off the train maimed and crippled. Boda's parents had either died at the hands of Red Guards or succumbed to hunger on some remote commune, it wasn't too clear. In any event, Boda had no graves to sweep, no pilgrimage to make, as Hong did, to the home of his ancestors.

Nowadays people liked to believe such a terrible period

could never happen again, there would be no more Cultural Revolutions. Neither Hong nor Boda ever felt quite so confident.

Boda's call came at ten minutes to three, not a minute earlier, not a minute later. The case officers continued gossiping, with Chan leading the pack. Hong finished lighting a cigarette, reached languidly across his desk as if telephone calls were a trial, and with a desultory swipe at the receiver answered after the second ring.

"Hong, is that you?" came the arranged question.

"Yes, this is Lu Hong."

For the benefit of whoever might be listening, Boda proceeded to ask if he had reached Hong at an inconvenient time, and Hong replied that he was just on his way out to a divisional meeting. Well then, Boda said, he just wanted to know if Hong could bring a few bottles of beer to dinner next week. Of course, Hong answered, that would be no problem.

He hung up, and to the assembled group announced that he had just been summoned to the Foreign Affairs Ministry to discuss the matter of the German lawyer, and he had to go immediately, which set off a predictable round of insults for the imperious self-satisfied bureaucrats at Foreign Affairs. Chan took charge and led the case officers out.

Hong waited. He listened to a burst of footsteps in the corridor, picked out the voice of the cadre in charge of Disbursement. A minute later came another stampede, this one from the Border Security division at the far end of the floor. It would have been easier, Hong supposed, to tell Chan the truth. But he knew that Chan's slogan of the day —the gun shoots the bird with its neck out—might have dissuaded him.

By ten past three the corridor was silent. Hong stood and picked up his briefcase. He went into the corridor, turned toward the northeast stairway, and without looking back let the door close behind him. In the stairwell he met no one, climbed the two flights, and at the landing leaned against the wall and paused for breath. The veins in the tip of his thumb were throbbing, but he knew that a pause now would end this escapade before it began. You have all the right explanations for being here, he assured himself. You

are on your way to the Liaison secretary to obtain surveillance reports on the German lawyer. Foreign Affairs had in
fact requested them a week ago, should anyone happen to
check.

The fourth floor was quiet as a tomb. Every door was
closed and not a sound echoed behind any of them. A car
screeched into the Qianmen courtyard, doors slammed—
someone arriving late for the meeting. Better not to go at
all, Hong thought. The Minister favored punctuality over
performance.

Hong turned left, walked straight to Sun Sheng's office,
and turned the knob. The latch held firm; the door was
locked.

On Sheng's instructions, Jin had kept his keys on a peg in
the well underneath his desk so that Sheng could always
find them. Were they still there? Hong ducked into the partitioned cubicle, knelt and reached his hand under the desk,
and promptly caught his finger on the hook. A drop of
blood was a small price to pay: the keys fell into his hand.

He was halfway to his feet when he heard voices approaching.

"It's her grandfather," a woman said. "He worked for the
enemy before Liberation. They kept it a secret, but now
she's ruined. She'll never get into university now."

Two secretaries rounded the corner, one unlocked a door
and went in, the other took up a position at a desk at the far
end of the hall. She was old and wise and had been in the
Bureau for a century at least. Hong watched her feet from
under Jin's desk. With luck he had twenty minutes, thirty at
best. Get up, he ordered himself. Boldness is all you have
left.

He stood and padded around the cubicle's dividing wall
to Sheng's office. He figured he was in the secretary's line of
sight for at most ten seconds, and in any event she hadn't
even raised her head. He slipped the key in, snapped the
lock, withdrew the key, and closed the door behind him. For
one long moment he pressed his ear against the frosted
glass, but to the secretary at the end of the hall a thudding
door was no cause for alarm.

The cardboard boxes had been packed so tightly he had
to pry the calendar out. On his knees, he leafed through the

files, reports on Party meetings with margin notes in Sheng's handwriting. Hours of tedium here, Hong thought. On to the second carton, a collection of personnel directives, and the third, drafts of speeches on security procedures for Army bases and munitions factories. The mantelpiece clock rang the half hour, a single chime. In the calendar Hong started three months back, in March. Each page covered a week, and Sheng had recorded not only his appointments, but also who had initiated them. "At my request... At Minister's suggestion... By continuing formal agreement with Administrator, Hebei Military District." Hong had no idea what he might be looking for. Could there be a list of those old records Sheng had been reading? But there were only meetings attended, appointments kept, phone calls made.

Someone on the fifth floor dropped a cup or plate that seemed to go on shattering forever.

In the last week of April, jotted outside the black borders of the page, Hong saw a drawing of a butterfly followed by an arrow, and after the arrow *Tianjin*. Below it, another drawing, a dog maybe, or a rabbit, followed also by an arrow, then *Wuhan*.

Had Sheng traveled to either Tianjin or Wuhan? Not according to the calendar. The first and second weeks of May were nearly blank, the third and fourth completely so. June opened with homey notes on things to be fixed: the Dutch air conditioners, a tape recorder. And then nothing, no more appointments. Sheng was dead.

Hong heard a dull thunder, his own breathing in his ears. He squeezed the calendar back into the carton and pulled the corner up so that it stuck out at the proper angle. A spot of sweat landed on the spine. He wiped it off, picked up his briefcase and Jin's keys. At the frosted glass he listened again, then without deliberation went into the hall, turned on his heel, and locked the door.

From an open window on the floor directly above and across the shaft Hong heard raised voices: a rarity. The shouting lasted perhaps fifteen seconds, and then an eerie quiet descended over the entire building. No doors squeaked open or closed, no footsteps fell in the hallway, no phones rang, no teletype machines clacked.

Hong squeezed his briefcase under his arm as though it contained the country's most valuable secrets. Assuming his brisk official demeanor, he swung neatly around Jin's desk, found the hook for the keys without making a sound, and started down the carpeted hall toward the Liaison secretary. She looked up and gave him a stern smile.

"Is the meeting over already?"

Hong explained that Foreign Affairs required his presence on the matter of the German lawyer, and the secretary, expelling rancorous sighs for those meddling bureaucrats, started procuring the surveillance reports he needed. Then, without warning, the madness of Hong's behavior descended on him. His leg went into a spasm, his hands started shaking. When would the secretary summon a guard? Was she blind?

She turned with the files in her hand. "This heat is terrible, my hands are sticking to everything," she said. "You're looking very pale... oh, you were a good friend of Comrade Sun, it's very sad, very sad."

Hong agreed that it was and mustered as much grief as he could manage, but he was feeling a premium on fear just then, and hurried away so quickly that he left the secretary standing with a startled expression on her face.

He made it as far as the stairwell before his body lost the fight it had been waging with itself, and the sweat poured out of him. He thought about the girl who would never be admitted to university because her grandfather had once served on the wrong side of a long-past war, and he wondered how they had kept the secret for so long. The way all secrets were kept, he supposed—through vigilance. How did it unravel? As all secrets did—including some Hong had kept himself—by the inevitable unraveling hand of time.

He examined his heartbeat for a second. It had slowed. The subject of the secretaries' conversation left him and his mind returned to the drawings in Old Sheng's calendar, and to the blank pages of late May and early June. Hong realized with utter clarity why they showed no trips to Wuhan or Tianjin. In the last month of his life, Sun Sheng had stopped recording everything—all appointments and meetings—as if, perhaps, he had begun to suspect that his random jottings might be less than entirely private, even in his own office.

With an urge to be out of the building, Hong decided he would continue on with the job he had pretended to be doing in the first place. At the Foreign Ministry they would award him the gratitude of the people and praise his skills at deduction. And because they hosted foreigners, and therefore stocked the appropriate symbols of friendship between countries, maybe they would offer him a glass of fine liquor—something that, despite his normal abstemiousness, he would at this hour more than welcome.

On Foyou Street Hong's former neighbors greeted him as if he still lived there. It was early evening, and as he passed the open doors of Xidan Market old pensioners stopped to say hello and ask about his work. What about this crime wave, couldn't something be done? By him, they meant. Across the road, rowboaters filled the back lake of Beihai Park—telegraph employees on their day off, wheeling around in yellow-canopied pedi-boats and pumping their legs in defiance of the debilitating heat. Well, better to say there was a crime wave, maybe it could help you ignore the heat wave.

At the edge of the market Hong stopped at a stationery store to pick up a large abacus for his son. Bai's fingers were getting too large for the standard schoolboy version. Hong had asked the manager to get one with cowbone beads, available only in the far north, and the manager had a friend in Jilin. In the meantime, Hong had already paid with special Foreign Exchange Currency, and the manager now had a new Japanese cassette player. The cowbone beads were an extravagance—who spoils a child more than an absent father?—but the abacus would impress Bai's friends.

Hong turned off Foyou into a closed-end lane of three-story houses that before Liberation had been an enclave of rich merchants and bureaucrats. Several blocks—the ones with newly repaired roofs and window frames—were owned by Beijing Broadcasting, where Shen Kuang worked producing television movies. After she and Hong were married, she had secured an entire floor when several of her comrades were purged for capitalist-roader tendencies. A slight miscalculation in timing, Hong thought; now they would be promoted.

Guilt followed Hong into the lane. All marriages, given time, should produce harmony just as a commune produced wheat. Divorce was unnecessary. If a couple fought incessantly, if a meddling mother-in-law drove a frustrated wife to tears, the neighborhood committee counseled patience and moderation. In Hong's case, harmony had lasted for a few years, and thereafter degenerated first into occasional bickering and then into silence. For this he blamed himself, and catalogued his sins: he lacked social energies, shared household duties badly, was not the best provider of luxuries. Kuang had been right to ask him to leave, and to save face he had requested the papers on the basis of "complete alienation," the only grounds for automatic divorce. The fact that Kuang had not been fond of sex—indeed found her husband's sexual advances distasteful—never arose, and in truth did not seem relevant.

Hong stopped at the head of the lane. In the dimming afternoon light, with crickets chirping and the canopies of pear trees blowing in the small enclosed front yards, he could imagine bankers arriving home in their polished black carriages, bedraggled rickshaw boys humbly waiting for a tip—images from his mother's memories and the stories of Lao She. A few had been rich, many poor, but the times must have been exciting.

From the other end of the road, where one of the old city gates had stood, came the smell of cooking oil, bringing Hong back to the present. Everything was changing, the city's past was vanishing. Along with his own.

His son was still at school, and his wife, home early from her office and in no mood for excuses, was standing at the sink scrubbing a pan. Or was she his ex-wife? The papers had been approved by the court but no one had seen them yet. Which made him...what? An adulterer.

"You promised to take Bai to the zoo," Shen Kuang said.

"I have an appointment," Hong said apologetically, "it can't be avoided. If we go to the zoo, I'll be late."

"He doesn't want another boat ride, Hong, he wants to go

to the zoo, I told him you'd go. Please don't disappoint him. As it is, you hardly ever see him, even on Sundays. Who do you have an appointment with that's more important than your son?"

She turned and busied herself, preparing a snack to take to the zoo. "Everyone talks about you and that girl," she said without looking at him, talking to the window. "It's a terrible embarrassment. I would think you'd have the courtesy to wait until you get the divorce papers."

People gossip, Hong thought, it's a pastime. Hot nights dictated a sidewalk life: checkers, cardplaying, and gossip. Kuang unwrapped a bean cake. She was slim, with the high cheekbones of a Uygur and wide sparkling black eyes, and moved with the grace of an acrobat. Even in winter, she exercised outside every day. She was as beautiful to Hong as the day he met her, sixteen years ago at a conference on Youth and the Revolution led by her father, a director in the Ministry of Forestry who had helped inaugurate annual tree-planting days. She was excellent at her work, talented, and respected by her comrades. She was a good, thoughtful mother. It was all too terrible to think about.

"We have to go on with our lives," Hong said.

"Yes, but with decorum. She's young enough to be your daughter."

"Not quite," Hong said.

"Well, almost. It can't be doing you too much good at the Bureau."

Hong pictured Yamei, his girlfriend, standing at the edge of a swimming pool, encouraging her team on to even greater victories in the name of socialism. He admired her innocence, he believed he could absorb it like a sponge. With her he would find something he had lost, he thought.

"Is your mother writing again?" Kuang said, taking a seat across from him. She held out tomorrow's issue of *People's Daily*, which her office received a day in advance, and pointed to a short fable about a lowly Ming Dynasty official, a painter, who had accused a higher official of deceit and abuse of power. All such stories had two meanings, one literal and the other a comment on current events—pointing at the mulberry, it was called, while upbraiding the ash. But Cui Chun had been out of favor with the literary establish-

ment for years. The journals never even published her poetry.

"It's unsigned," Hong said, his eyes reaching the bottom
of the column.

"It's your mother's style, though," Shen Kuang said,
reaching out to take the paper. "Now let's see, the high official here kills the painter, then rapes and kills her daughter.
The painter is your mother, obviously. Painter, poet, no difference, not even a disguise. And you must be the daughter.
So the question is, who's going to rape and kill you? What
kind of trouble is she getting you into?"

"None," Hong said. "It isn't hers. She's in no position to
be writing allegories about power."

"You can call a stag a horse, but this sounds like her
work."

Hong glanced through the story again. The language was
rich in imagery, the sentences unusually rhythmic—obviously the product of someone with classical training. And
Hong knew that his position in Public Security was less secure since Sheng's death; Sheng, after all, had been his pa-
tron. But *People's Daily* could hardly be bothered by such
mundane matters, and if Cui Chun were writing stories for
publication, she would send Hong a copy and ask his advice. She was too smart to be making waves when the Party
was in turmoil. Water can float a boat, but it can also sink it.
"She's retired," Hong said firmly. "She only writes poetry,
and only for herself. Besides, this has all the marks of coming straight from the Central Committee. It's about some
battle at the top."

Shen Kuang shook her head. "Your mother's like you. I'll
never understand her. With her background she could be
on the Central Committee herself. She could protect you
from everyone. She could have one of those nice houses
near the university in Haidian. And you'd be on top, too,
getting rich like your brother." She clasped her hands on
her lap and stared at them. "I don't understand you either.
Sometimes you're so *correct*, which holds you back, and then
you offend people by not going to political meetings and by
being sarcastic about the new economic reforms."

"Who says I'm sarcastic?"

"You always are, you always have been, and lately..."

Her words hung in the air. She stopped, turned away, and it struck Hong then, how incredibly obvious: Shen Kuang had a lover, her dear friend Zhu Gang, Political Commissar of the Investigations Division. Hong recalled his conversation with Zhu on the landing at the Bureau: *Your wife is overburdened. And how is the boy getting along at school?* When butchers meet they talk of pigs, when scholars meet they talk of books, and a man courting your wife tells her about your poor attendance at political education sessions. Hong shivered in disgust. Zhu Gang would make a dreadful substitute father. Dogmatic and cold, a mind that was a dozen blunt knives without a sharpener.

"If I'd become a political commissar," Hong said tentatively, "if I'd accepted the job . . . would you have—"

She put a finger on his lips. "No. No, it's not that, I told you. You're naive sometimes. I was married too young, that's all."

A way of saying she had never loved him?

Their eleven-year-old son Bai pushed through the door, his schoolbag on his arm. Fate had blessed him with Kuang's cheekbones, her perfect full mouth.

"Papa," he burst out, "I passed my literature exams! And I scored highest in politics! Listen." He struck a pose, puffed his little chest. "After a century of heroic struggle," he recited from memory, the preamble to the Constitution, "the Chinese people, led by the Communist Party and our great leader and teacher Chairman Mao Tsetung, finally overthrew the reactionary rule of imperialism, feudalism . . ."

Bai went through all of it with the fervor of a true revolutionary. What a relief! Admission to a good middle school was more competitive than ever, even with family connections.

". . . and strive for the progress and emancipation of humanity." Bai grinned, proud of himself. "That's good, isn't it? I was the only one in my class to learn it all."

"I'm very impressed," Hong said. "At your age I wasn't near as good a student."

"Can we go to the zoo now?"

Hong said yes, they would go to the zoo. He presented Bai with the new abacus to yelps of delight, stood and fetched the basket of snacks. Outside, Bai led his parents down the street toward the bus stop, then stopped at the corner and looked up, concerned.

"What is it?" Hong asked.

"Papa, that story in the paper, is Grandma writing dangerous things? Is she going to get us into trouble?"

Hong glared at Kuang with an unspoken question. Did she have to worry the boy? Was she trying to turn Bai against him? Kuang averted her eyes.

"No," Hong said, "we're not going to be in any trouble. Everything's going to be fine."

At the compound on Tsungenwai the Army guard was the same beardless boy who had been on duty the day of Sun Sheng's memorial service. Hong presented his identification, said Comrade Sun's widow was expecting him, and waited for the gate to swing open. Instead, the guard picked up his telephone and dialed.

"But I'm expected, Comrade Ma Sufei knows I'm coming," Hong protested. The guard ignored him and pulled the gatehouse door closed. Why the delay? This was outrageous. Hong could see his own name on the approved visitors list hanging on a clipboard behind the guard.

After a short conversation on the phone, the guard swung the gatehouse door open. "You'll have to wait," he said.

"I don't understand, my name is on the list, as you can see. What's the problem?"

"You'll have to wait," the guard repeated, and closed the door.

Hong considered making a scene. An assistant deputy director of Public Security should be treated with more respect. Arguing with a soldier, however, would get him nowhere. Soldiers acknowledged no one else's rank. The Army lived in its own country, where it made all the laws.

Hong paced in the darkness, thinking about Sun Sheng and files from the war. Settling old scores? Whose? He looked up. In the compound across the street, home of the Army's General Staff, lights flashed on. Bright lights you could read by without squinting. Behind gauze curtains on the third floor a man and woman embraced, silhouettes of passion. Hong envied them, living as he did in a bare apartment he could not yet call home, meeting his son once or twice a week. At the zoo Bai had asked if the tigers minded their cages. Of course they don't, Hong had said, they have heat in the winter, they eat well.

Five minutes passed, his collar started to itch. But it was all for the best, he assured himself, I gave her no happiness. A car passed, its lights out. Nowhere in the country did anyone drive with lights on, even in the dead of night, but the General Staff burned electricity to make love, which could just as easily be done in the dark.

Hong lit a cigarette, took a few puffs, then tamped it out on the sole of his shoe and put it back in the pack. This was ridiculous, an insult. Undoubtedly Ma Sufei was waiting for him. After fifteen minutes that in the damp evening heat seemed like an hour, he caught sight of a small figure coming toward the gate from inside: a young girl who walked with a horse's slow loping gait. Hong remembered seeing her at the memorial service, but in the half-light had trouble placing who she was. Then he remembered her walk, and the affectionate name they had given her... Pony. She was Ma Sufei's secretary from the Economic Affairs Commission.

"Lu Hong, please forgive us," she said coolly as the gate creaked open. "I'm so sorry you had to wait. Comrade Ma has been preparing for a trip."

"Oh," Hong said. "To where?"

"Guangzhou, for three weeks of meetings on trade."

Sun Sheng dead not a week, and they were sending her to Guangzhou? Astounding.

Sun Ch'ien, Ma Sufei's eldest son, met them at the bottom of the steps. And what was he doing here? At the memorial service he had complained of pressing business at home in Chongqing.

"I've stayed to help my mother," he said evenly, leading the way upstairs.

"Are you packing up the whole house?" Hong asked. "Are they taking it away from her?"

Sun Ch'ien looked over his shoulder. "No, of course not," he snapped, and then, softening, "I arranged a few days' leave to keep her company."

The reception was worse than impolite. It was virtually hostile. Unexpected from the girl, it was a shock from Sun Ch'ien. Though never close friends as children, Hong and Ch'ien had shot marbles together on the playground, and later had shared courting trips to the movies. It was true that even as a boy Ch'ien lacked the humility of his mother and father. Barely into his teens, he had combed his hair straight back, like an adult. He seemed, on reflection, to have struggled from the womb as a miniature dictator, taking charge of the other children and staring down his long nose with an imperious air. But never had he treated Hong like this before.

The house felt empty to Hong. Without Sun Sheng living here, without his grand laughter, the whole world felt empty.

In Ma Sufei's office upstairs, clothes and papers covered the chairs, the desk, the floor. Next to the couch a footlocker, a red wardrobe trunk, and three suitcases lay filled to capacity. All this? For a three-week trip? Ma Sufei looked up from a cardboard box of files. With a tremor in her voice, she explained that a conference on special trade zones had been scheduled months ago, and her deputy felt unprepared to handle it alone.

"It has to be done," she concluded with resignation. "I'll put aside my grief."

"When are you leaving?"

"Tomorrow morning, on the first flight." She eased the lid onto the file box. "Come, have some tea," she said with sudden false cheer, "tell me about Bai, how's the boy doing?"

With Hong in tow, the old woman shuffled slowly to the sitting room at the back of the house. She was obviously distracted by preparations for the conference. Sun Ch'ien followed, and the secretary brought tea.

"You can go finish packing," Sufei said before they sat down.

"We'll rest with you," the girl said. Her delicate face showed love and respect, but her manner had the hardness of a watchdog. With Sun Ch'ien she sat on the couch under the windows. Their noiseless, staring presence unsettled Hong, and he rambled aimlessly about Bai's schoolwork, talked loudly over the air conditioner's incessant whir, filled the empty air with his voice. Ma Sufei held up her end, but neither of them was talking to the other. This was for the walls, for the frozen couple on the couch. Could Sufei not talk in front of her own son? She nervously patted her hair, let her tea go cold in its cup. Questions died in Hong's throat. Why had Ma Sufei decided that Sun Sheng should be cremated? Why, outwardly calm, did her every gesture speak so frantically?

Half an hour had passed when a driver appeared to load Sufei's baggage, which would travel to Guangzhou ahead of her.

"I'll see you when I return," she said to Hong, rising unsteadily and crossing to the stairs. Again the girl and Ch'ien followed, trailing behind Hong. "Wait," Sufei said, turning into the library, "I have a gift for you."

She went to the shelves of her husband's precious books and stopped at a row filled with the works of Confucius— dozens of editions old and new, with multiple copies of many. Sheng had joked that if they ever came to take away his books he had stocked enough spares for a long winter. Hong loved gazing at the books; they were the man himself. Ma Sufei, as if stroking a keyboard, delicately ran her fingers over the spines. And as she searched the shelf so did her constant companions, here only to help her pack. After a moment Ma Sufei plucked a book out, a fat new volume bound in shiny brown leather.

"Here," she said, pressing it into Hong's hands, "he would have wanted you to have this."

Hong felt the secretary's eyes move from the book to his hand. If she could have opened it at ten paces, she would have done so.

Before Hong could turn the book's cover back, Ma Sufei linked her arm through his and led him down the stairs. At the courtyard entrance she thanked him for visiting, bid him good-bye with a faint brush of her hand on his arm, then the door was closing and with her two escorts she turned away. In the last instant, Hong saw her through the door's window-paneled frame, glancing at him with a kind of vacant terror, the look of a condemned prisoner being led to the rifles.

Outside the gate, under a dim streetlight, the book sprung open in Hong's hands. The binding had barely been broken except at this one page, where a bookmark lay in the center. Hong peered at it. On the back, in Sun Sheng's rapid scrawl, was written, "If the name is not correct, the words will not ring true"—a simple Confucian awareness that a thing must be properly named before we can understand it. At the top of the marked page the heading, so often quoted by Sun Sheng, cried out: "The Rule of the Golden Mean," and beneath it, "If A is true, B is not wrong either."

5.

SEEKING
TRUTH
FROM
FACTS

Man and animal are alike. Hungry, they eat. Tired, they sleep. Mature, they mate. But man is different from the animal because he has a spirit, a soul, that propels him toward good or evil.

Or so Sun Sheng had said. The idea was anything but Marxist—the nature of man, according to Marx, was to engage in class struggle—but Hong turned it over in his mind as he bicycled to the Bureau on Friday morning. Did it mean that some men were born good and decent, and others were born smugglers or thieves? What it meant, Sheng never tired of explaining, was that the soul of a good man demanded that he seek out and destroy evil.

On the way to his office Hong stopped in the telex center to collect overnight reports from the Bureau's major urban branches. Telexes usually arrived by four or five in the morning, having been punched onto tape and fed automatically to Beijing when the lines were least busy. The Japanese machines were clacking when Hong walked in, a row of

them on one wall, tended by clerks behind a long counter
with wire baskets for each department. Just inside the door,
crates with new telex machines were being opened and unloaded, supervised by the Director of Operations, Ling
Lipin.

"Hero of the month," Ling said. "Congratulations on the
German. Look at this mess! New machines but no connect-
ing wires, and they sent the wrong ribbons."

"Nothing unusual in that," Hong said.

"No," Ling said dyspeptically, "nothing at all. Just once,
for the sake of variety, it would be nice if a shipment arrived
the way I ordered it. What kind of German was he?"

"A careless one," Hong said.

"No, I meant East or West."

"West," Hong said.

Ling, in his late forties, was a rising young cadre. He had
a degree in history from Nanjing University, a horrible tic
that caused his left cheek to throb, and the kind of supercil-
ious glare that in Hong's experience belonged only to the
very stupid.

Ling asked, "Who's going to take over Military Affairs
now that Sun Sheng's gone?"

"How would I know?" Hong replied, and wondered why
Ling should assume otherwise.

"Really? You have no idea? You saw the Director of Investigations yesterday. I thought maybe she was consulting
you—you being so close to Sun, after all."

Ling was angling for the job himself—a chance to move
into a policy position—but to assume Hong had any influence required unbelievable naivete. Still, Ling had good
sources, or he wouldn't have known about the meeting with
Wei Ye.

"Ling, nobody consults me on anything that important."

Ling leaned over the counter. "Listen, Hong, if there's
anything you think I might do to get my name mentioned..."

"I'll work on it," Hong said. He gathered his reports and
went out the door.

The secrecy order on the American that Wei Ye had
promised arrived not ten minutes later, borne by a young
cadre with a premature bald spot at the top of his head. He

had the high color and whimsical expression of a monk from one of those far northern monasteries where religion was still tolerated. No, Hong corrected himself, not tolerated. Last year religion was tolerated, now it was encouraged.

"Good morning, Assistant Deputy Director. Comrade Wei Ye requests that you sign this so that I can bring it back," said the Monk, holding out the paper.

"Excuse me, do I know you?" Hong asked.

"Wu Keping, assistant to the Director of Investigations. Perhaps you remember me. I was a student in your class at Fengtai." The Bureau maintained a training center near the Yongdingmen railway station. Hong had given classes there on constitutional procedure. Officers occasionally forgot—actually, they forgot quite often—that all people had rights, that you couldn't detain a prisoner more than ten days, for example, without a formal charge issued by a procurate. The course had been a success, the arrogant treatment of prisoners declined, but Hong had absolutely no recollection of the Little Monk.

"Yes, you seem familiar," Hong said, saving face for both of them. "You were a good student, weren't you?"

"I had to repeat the course twice," Wu said miserably.

Wu laid the secrecy order on Hong's desk. *Regarding the foreign guest Ostrander, Peter, American doctor on scientific exchange mission: It is agreed that all investigations relating to this case will not be discussed in Bureau working groups or outside the office of the Fourth Assistant Deputy Director for Investigations.* Wei Ye's signature, in small pinched script, appeared above a space for Hong's, and it was chopped—stamped—with her seal. Clumsy of her, Hong thought. Foolishly she had supplied her agreement, but she would not get his.

"I'll just hold on to this," he said to the Little Monk. "Thank you for bringing it."

The Monk blinked. "But...but..."

"Thank you again, and please thank the Director for me."

Poor Comrade Wu, trying to please an impossible master. He hesitated, but Hong merely smiled. No sooner had the Monk turned away than the door opened and Chan bounced in, looking pleased with himself. The Monk nodded a good morning, gave a half-bow, and left.

"Who was that?" Chan asked.

"Wu Keping, the Director's messenger."

"He should eat better, he looks hungry." Chan saw the sheet of paper on the desk, picked it up, and read to himself. "What's this?"

"I asked for it," Hong said.

"Why?"

Hong fished out his last cigarette, crumpled the pack, and tossed it toward the wastebasket. He missed. "When the Director of Investigations asks me to adjust the rules," he said, with the thought of the Monk lingering in the hall, "I feel that a little ink is better than a good memory."

Chan retrieved the crumpled pack and deposited it in the basket. "You are an idiot," he said, striking a match, "and you smoke too much."

Hong leaned to the flame, inhaled. "So do you, so do we all."

"That's true, that's true," Chan said thoughtfully, and plopped into his chair. "The Academy of Sciences file on the American will be here tomorrow."

"And the cadres who approved the scientific exchange?"

"I'll get a list," Chan said. "What will it tell you?"

"Nothing, probably."

Hong sniffled, cleared his throat, reached into his desk for a handkerchief.

"You talk about a cold long enough, you're bound to get one," Chan said.

"It's good you're not a doctor. I'm not sleeping well, that's why I have a cold."

"I *could* have been a doctor," Chan said dreamily from behind his desk. "If the universities hadn't closed. It's not fair, what happened to us. These kids today, they don't know how we suffered."

Hong had heard this a hundred times before and delivered the desired response. "Yes," he said, "they do know. They've read about it until they can't bear any more."

"Well, maybe. But it's still not fair."

"Whoever said it was?"

Chan loved to complain, Hong loved to listen. A bond of comradeship that Chairman Mao had not predicted.

Hong leaned back, swiveled, and took in the view of his

brick airshaft. He slid a piece of paper from the corner of his desk and lifted his ballpoint pen. This is an experiment, he told himself, the musing of an idle mind. Walk a path and see where it leads. Sheng had been reading files about the group at Yanan. Why? Old struggles, all finished. What, or whom, had Sheng been looking for? Hong called up in his memory, like a slide flashing on a screen, the photograph on Sun Sheng's bookcase, then another slide, the wall of pictures in his mother's study. Some of the old revolutionaries were dead, some alive, and some . . . well, too many years had passed, Hong had been too many places to remember. Who had died while he was in the Army? He scribbled names and came up with a list of the most important cadres—the ones Sheng would have known—who had been with Chairman Mao at Yanan. The list numbered thirty-nine: thirty-two men and seven women, one of whom was Hong's mother, and one of whom was Wei Ye. Hong then crossed names off, all of those he knew to be still alive, which left twenty-three unaccounted for. All right, he said finally to himself, how far will you go? Seek truth from facts, said Chairman Mao, and also his successors. The slogan of the decade. So where were the facts?

Hong stood, put the list into a green folder in his briefcase, and pulled a fresh pack of cigarettes from his center drawer.

"Where are you going?" Chan asked.

"For a walk."

"To where?"

"To seek truth from facts."

On Chang'an, women in gray robes and caps rode on trucks with cherrypicker ladders, spraying the locust trees. The women wore face masks, but the pesticide stung Hong's eyes. Trees cleaned the air, he thought, pesticide fouled it.

The Municipality Hall of Records was a long walk. If the Bureau's transport pool had been less efficient and not logged every single trip, he would have taken a car and driver. Biking seemed to demand more energy than he could summon. Was he indeed getting the cold he had invented two days earlier? He tried to remember how the Municipality Hall of Records kept track of inquiries. It had been years since he'd any reason to go there. A gate at the desk, Party and working unit identification required, and ...and what?

The heat overcame him, he thought he would collapse. No doubt about it, his throat was scratchy, by the end of the day he would be fighting a full-blown fever. He caught a 32 bus to the corner of North Xidan, transferred to a number 5 and sat opposite two grandmothers with babies balanced on their knees. Nervously he shredded his ticket, his impatient fingers working like a weaver's. The bus passed Jingshan Park, then a tower of latticed bamboo scaffolding. Another apartment building going up. A billboard read TIME IS MONEY, IT IS GLORIOUS TO GET RICH. One side of the new building would be a solid brick wall, so that its inhabitants, hotel workers probably, would have no view into the compound that housed the leaders of the State.

Hong stepped off the bus on Wenjin, across from the red-walled compound of the Beijing Library. He was suddenly in the Army again, on patrol along the Vietnamese border with just enough twilight to catch a bullet. As the bus pulled away, he came as close as he ever did to losing his nerve. If you turn around now, he thought, forget everything, bury your suspicions and let them rest as peacefully as the dead.

He went up the steep steps of the records hall and pushed through the door. The room was three stories high and wood-beamed. The same prints of Lenin and Marx that hung in Hong's office were perched here on a small platform beneath a row of clerestory windows near the ceiling. Along either side of the vast reception area ran long counters of scuffed blond wood with chairs for researchers. As for security, Hong absorbed everything at once: the guards were on the verge of sleep, the girl at the main desk wearing a loose red blouse would need a gunshot to be roused from her copy of *Popular Cinema,* and the inquiry book on the counter looked as though it hadn't been opened in an eon or two. Directly across from the front door was an unattended turnstile. Hong sauntered to the girl, opened his Bureau pass for her cursory approval, and strolled through the turnstile as if he came here every day.

A kiosk at the center of the main hall housed an information clerk, who was dozing over a copy of last night's *Evening News*. Hong strode purposefully across the tile floor and planted himself in front of the kiosk.

"Births and deaths?"

"All the way back and to your right," said the clerk without lifting his head from the newspaper.

Thirty years of deaths occupied a minuscule alcove, the most recent six years a room the size of Hong's office. Maybe people were dying more frequently these days, Hong thought. There were no indexes. Searching for specific names required going through the books year by year. Finding twenty-three names would take months. There had to be an easier way. Hong moved to the births section and heavenly flowers fell. Here there was an index to both births and deaths, its cottony oversized pages wrinkled and yellowed by time. Hong ensconced himself at a beautiful old desk, a fabulous work of ivory marquetry and carved woods that, water-stained and deeply gouged, seemed to have lived several lives of its own.

Within an hour he had found fourteen names—all men. Fourteen from his list of twenty-three were dead, and the pattern of their deaths was a testament to the very concept of coincidence. A fish bone here, Hong thought, a scale there. Would the fins and head reveal themselves shortly?

Chan was waiting for him when he returned. He unzipped Hong's briefcase and pulled out the green file folder.

"A list of bicycle thieves," Hong said, reaching to snatch it back.

Chan opened the folder, his eyes widening as he read. Hong had rewritten the list of fourteen names and clustered them by their dates of death.

"Crazy," Chan said.

"Fourteen old cadres who were all at Yanan," Hong said. "Here, look. Eleven of them died in twos and threes, days apart. Almost as if they'd learned something at the same time."

"Yes. That death is inevitable." Chan scanned the list. "All over the country. In different cities. And over a period of what... ten, fifteen years? They're not related, Hong, there's no connection, you're chasing wisps of smoke. There were dozens of high cadres at Yanan. A man dies in Guilin, it has nothing to do with a man dying a thousand miles away. And look here, the most recent was four months ago, one man in Dalian. Who's he related to?"

A man dies in Dalian four months ago, Hong thought, and a few weeks later, according to Young Jin, Sun Sheng is carting files to his office from archives all around the city.

Hong took the file from Chan. "Your friend at the Medical Examiner's office, he wanted some movie tickets?"

Chan looked up suspiciously. "So?"

"I have some passes to the French film week." Hong opened the filing cabinet next to his desk and retrieved a small envelope. "Why don't you take these over to him?"

"He'd be very appreciative," Chan said evenly, not taking the tickets.

"Yes, I think he would. While you're there see if you can get me a copy of Sheng's death certificate." He laid the envelope in Chan's hand and wrapped his fingers around it.

Chan tucked the tickets into his jacket the way he did everything else—methodically, with a minimum of movement. "Hong, I'm older than you, and I've learned a few things. One thing I've learned is that when a friend is heading for a trap, you try to snap it shut before he gets there. So let me be a friend and give these tickets to a butcher I know. I'll get you enough pork to last until winter."

Hong was touched. People looked out for their own necks most of the time. One man's calamity was another's promotion and, thanks to the Army, Chan already knew enough of calamity to last a lifetime. It was said that a few seasons in Tibet would teach anyone either the virtues of comradeship or selfishness. For Chan it had been comradeship. He had slept every night in a sherpa coat on a tarp over bare frozen earth—no tents, no cabins. Every morning he awoke in a puddle melted from the heat of his own body. But when he lifted his tarp into the vicious wind the water froze instantly, and with his comrades he had to chip the ice away or risk tearing the precious tarp. No spares existed. In fact, no spare guns or clothing or food existed. When Chan joked that his body responded to permanent winter by adding layers of fat, he failed to mention the stiffness in his legs that hobbled him still, or the ridges on his fingernails where they had cracked from the cold. All he wanted now was peace.

"I promise you," Hong said, "if the trap springs shut you won't be anywhere near it."

"The death certificate's just a form," Chan said, "a useless piece of paper."

"Just the same, I'd like to see it."

In the end Chan agreed to bestow the Bureau's kindness on his friend in the Medical Examiner's office, although he suggested that the swap reflected badly on Hong. "You get trouble," as Chan calculated it, "he gets French movies."

Perhaps this was so, Hong reflected, but often you had no choice but to ask for trouble. When the cock crows loudly enough, even a sleeping man has to rise and dance.

At the end of the day Hong pursued one more bit of trouble, which had been nagging at him like an unsewn thread. By choice, his mother and father lived in a secluded house in a compound three hours from Beijing. Cui Chun explained their self-imposed exile, none too convincingly, as an escape from the distractions of city life. Peace in which to compose, she said, though she wrote little. Her true reasons she kept to herself, and Hong had tired of trying to convince her that if for no other reason than the availability of good medical care they ought to live in Beijing. She seemed to nurse a resentment against the city itself, or against whatever memories she had left behind. In any event, she was unreachable. A farm forty-five kilometers away possessed the closest telephone, but farmers were quick to assert they had better things to do than relay messages to revolutionary heroes.

Before leaving his office Hong dialed the number of the New China News Agency. It rang for several minutes before one of the operators was sufficiently roused to answer.

"Li Junhua, please," Hong said.

"Your name and working unit," the operator asked.

Hong identified himself, with his title, and the internal connection was made. Junhua administered a section issuing Party statistics on economic growth, many of which he invented when there was no alternative. Hong had once helped him assemble dossiers on foreign journalists, and had been able to do him a few favors.

"Li, here."

"Junhua, it's Hong."

"I haven't heard from you lately," Junhua said. "Don't we have any more journalist spies?"

"Everywhere," Hong said. "I'm wondering if you can tell me who wrote a certain parable in today's paper, a short story set in the Ming Dynasty."

There was silence at the other end.

"Hello, hello," Hong said to keep the line open.

"I'm here. I saw the story, but I don't follow such things."

"Could you follow this one for me, please?"

"Hong, that's not in my... that is, I know so little about how those stories are chosen." His reluctance echoed down the line as clearly as his words.

"And the less you know," Hong said sympathetically, "the better you feel. But I have a personal interest in the matter."

"I'll see what I can do," Junhua said.

There was a pause again.

"Hello, hello?"

"Yes, Hong, hello. I'll look into it. Please don't call me. I'll get back to you in a few days."

The connection was broken, and a second later the dial tone disappeared. The switchboard shift had changed. Or had it? Hong held the receiver to his ear for a few moments of silence. There was a metallic squawk, the dial tone sounded, then silence again.

"This is the operator. Do you need a line, Comrade Lu?"

"No, thank you," Hong said, not having to wonder, as he lowered the phone, how she had known who was waiting.

6.

MISSING PEOPLE

A cartoon on the front page of *People's Daily* showed two men powdering each other's noses. The caption read "self-criticism session." A prescient comment on the current proceedings. Hong, accustomed to the boredom, read the paper in the last row of the Bureau's auditorium. At the front his fellow cadres stood to confess their misdeeds. "I mismanaged funds in my department, but the problem is solved and all is running smoothly," said someone from the Firearms Unit. Everything except the guns, Hong thought. He turned to an article about an explosion at Tianjin Airport. An accident, according to the dispatch, caused by a defective gasoline tank. That was one way of putting it. According to the Bureau's teletype, the gas tank had blown up when a soldier opened fire on two Muslims trying to hijack a plane to Hong Kong. What must life be like there? New plumbing and cars for everyone, lots of crime.

Chan entered the auditorium through the side door and

walked over to Hong. "The file's here," he whispered. "Come look at your American."

The records provided by the Tourism Administration and Academy of Sciences were remarkably full. Fuller, Hong thought, than one would expect for a minor guest of the State. There were a half-dozen photos, a history of Peter Ostrander's medical career, a description of his political activities in the United States, a short personality profile.

"He doesn't look like a spy," Chan joked, holding up a blurry headshot of the American, probably an enlarged passport picture. "Or a Swede either."

"What does a spy look like?"

"Heavier brows, higher forehead. Look at his hair, fuzzy like wire. A round-eye spy has wavy hair."

"Through your scientific analysis," Hong said, leafing through the papers, "he's absolutely disqualified. We have no problem. We'll close this case in a week."

"Did you see that Ming Dynasty story?" Chan asked, taking a cigarette from Hong's pack. "What's that all about?"

"Struggles at the top," Hong said. It was a relief that Chan made no suggestion about Cui Chun. "Probably about the next Congress."

Chan read from the political summary. "He was something called a Democratic councilman. Maybe that makes him a spy."

"But we're democratic, too," Hong said dryly. He pulled out the biographical section, struck by the opening line: *Ostrander, Peter, born 33.1.14, Tangshan, China.* That was all, one sentence, no elaboration.

"What could his parents have been doing in Tangshan?" Chan asked. "It doesn't say."

"Considering how big this file is," Hong said, "I'd call that a significant lapse. The Director of Investigations tells me the father was an archaeologist. Get the Defense Ministry's file on the guide they assigned him."

"I asked already. They seem to think it's been misplaced."

Hong looked up.

"That's right," Chan said. "Misplaced."

"Find out who misplaced it."

Chan picked up two other photos, those of a man identified in the file as *Ostrander, Theodore,* father of the guest of the State. In the first picture, black-and-white and slightly grainy, the elder Ostrander—dressed in shorts, a loose-fitting shirt with buttoned epaulets, and a wide-brimmed straw hat—was kneeling by a mound of dirt with two Chinese, one middle-aged, the other a boy, with a shovel planted in the dirt between them. The middle-aged Chinese was a sharp-faced Han with deep skeletal eyes, also wearing shorts and shirt. In the second photo, a clearer print, Ostrander was wearing a suit, standing with the same Chinese man in front of an ornately gabled and balconied Western-style building. It appeared to be one of several attached row-houses. Hong turned the photographs over. On the first a stripe of yellowed glue showed where a label had once been; on the second there was nothing. The second print seemed to be of recent vintage, and the first, its edges torn and the emulsion turning brown, much older. It seemed that someone had been compiling a file on the elder Ostrander long before the one on his son.

Chan lifted the first photograph close to his face.

"Chairman Mao swimming the Yangtze," he said, peering intently. Virtually all cadres with any sophistication knew that the famous photo of the aged Chairman, swimming across the river at Wuhan, was a fake: a head glued to the surface of the water. Not only could you rewrite history, you could take new pictures of it. Chan pointed to the background of the photo—the clouds behind the mound of dirt—then laid a straightedge down the middle of the sky. "There's a piece of cloud missing here."

Hong placed the straightedge in the middle of the second photo, bisecting the balconied building. The balconies' crenellations on either side of the ruler, in perfect focus, fit together precisely. But the background below the balconies—the doorways and stoops—appeared slightly blurry. Theodore Ostrander, in front of the building, was clearly in focus. A most unusual camera, Hong thought. At four meters away it was in focus, at three blurry, at two meters back in focus.

He slipped both photos into an envelope and stood to leave.

"What does a psychiatrist do, exactly?" Chan asked.

Hong's parents, before the Revolution, had counted among their friends several Western-trained doctors. "He probes the human spirit," Hong answered.

"So he's a political theorist," Chan said.

"No, he figures out why people are unhappy."

"Is that so hard? I know why I'm unhappy. First, because my cousin Zhang has three rooms and I have only two. Second, because everybody uses stolen pork coupons but I don't because I'm afraid I'll get caught." Chan sighed. "And third, because even if I wait forever, I'll never have my own jeep and driver."

The headlines read "More Male Teachers Love Their Jobs," "Fight Juvenile Delinquency," "Inner Mongolia: A Unique Culture." On the cover of the current issue of *Women in China* a beautiful little girl with bangs and a smile to light up the world held her child-sized violin. The magazine's pages were tacked onto a corkboard stretching the length of the room.

"It's a wonderful world," said Fen Like. "Our teachers are wonderful, our children are wonderful, our ethnic minorities are wonderful. My equipment, on the other hand, leaves something to be desired." The head of the production lab at the Publications Center, heavily muscled from working out with weights, heaved a box of graph paper onto his worktable. "But I do have something new that truly is wonderful."

Hong followed Fen across the enormous floor of the layout department, where a battalion of women at easels delicately glued together columns of articles and headlines. Fen had worked for Hong as a white-jacketed street policeman for three years until, with Hong's help, he moved to a much softer and much higher-paying job processing photographs. It had seemed wasteful that a man in love with cameras should be chasing peasants who illegally sold fish on the street. At the time Fen had already bought himself a German single-lens reflex and a Japanese light meter, and had assembled a collection of two-lens Shanghai box cameras. The Shanghai was a national

institution. Soldiers, students, even Mongolian peasants—
everybody owned a Shanghai.

Fen stood Hong at a row of typewriter keyboards attached to television screens. "This is a typesetting computer.
Magnificent. Each key is a pen stroke. Each stroke flashes a
light through a negative onto a little strip of tape, it's incredible. No more looking for thousands of characters in a tray
of lead type. We can do two thousand characters in a tenth
the time it used to take. Now that's what I call modernization. We can produce every language in the world. Even
Arabic." He ran his hand over the machine as if it were a
treasured family heirloom. "Do Arabs read much?"

"I think they do," Hong said.

A rank chemical smell drifted from a darkroom next to
the machines. The door opened and a woman came out,
carrying long strips of damp paper in clothespins. Fen
touched the computer again, protectively this time, as
though afraid it might suddenly disappear. "Built in Shanghai with our own technological genius."

"Really?" Hong said.

"And a little help from the Japanese."

At his giant worktable, covered with photos and clippings
of articles, Fen sat on a high-backed stool, swiveled, and
opened Hong's envelope. He glanced at the first photo—
Theodore Ostrander, father of the spy, with the two Chinese at the mound of dirt.

"A clumsy fake if I ever saw one," Fen said.

"We thought so."

Fen turned to the second photo—Ostrander in front of
the balconied building. Under Fen's large, handheld magnifying glass the balconies connected through an obvious
seam.

"Here, look," Fen said. He picked up a loupe, handed it
to Hong. Hong moved the curved magnifying glass back
and forth over the surface of the photograph.

The house in the picture was actually two; in the middle,
half of each house was missing.

"Catching spies, huh?" Fen said, taking the loupe back
and bending over the first photo. "You've been moving up
in the world."

"I'd rather be hunting dogs," Hong said.

"Running dogs?" Fen asked, meaning traitors.

"Mutts," Hong said.

Fen lifted his head. "Doctored, both of them. I could have done a much better job."

"Have you?"

"Pardon me."

"Have you done better jobs?"

Fen smiled. "It's immodest of me, but yes, if I say so myself, I've done better. Our Vice-Chairman, when he was a capitalist roader, could of course not appear at certain Party functions he had somehow managed to attend. A stroke of the razor, a new negative, a shot of white dust from the airbrush, and he disappeared. Now he has returned to those functions. In time, you see, we can all be wherever we want. Or at least have the memory of being there even if we weren't."

Hong pointed to the two photos. "I want to know who was there. Can you find the originals?"

"There's only one big collection of photographs in the city," Fen said, "and I hope never to be near it."

He meant, Hong knew, the Central Department of Investigation. The CDI—with authority to watch anyone, search any records—inspired far more fear than Public Security. Average Chinese had never even heard of it.

"If you can figure out where this was published," Fen went on, holding up the second photo, "you could search yourself."

"Published?"

"Look," Fen said, motioning Hong to the loupe. "The image is broken up into dots. That's how we print photographs, by laying a screen over them and shooting them for the press. This one was screened and turned into a plate, which means it appeared in a newspaper or magazine."

Hong could see the dots now, faint as they were. So the picture was copied from a newspaper, altered, and then turned into a new picture.

Someone had gone to a lot of trouble to stuff Ostrander's dossier with fake evidence. Why?

"Don't you have newspaper archives here?"

"Burned," Fen said. "During the Great Cultural Revolution. A band of patriotic Red Guards obliterating the past, as instructed."

"Can you at least tell me where these were taken?"

"I'll try," Fen said. "Somebody upstairs might be able to match the architecture."

"And this distinguished thin face?" Hong said, indicating the man next to Ostrander. "Can you put a name to it?"

"Maybe," said Fen. "It's strange that they aren't labeled."

"Label them for me," Hong said.

An assistant, a filament of a man with the face of a cat, dropped a stack of pages from the forthcoming issue of *China Reconstructs,* the internationally distributed propaganda magazine, on Fen's desk. Fen ran his professional eye over them and initialed the upper right-hand corner of each. A bead of sweat fell from his forehead, landed on his arm, and he reached over to his window air conditioner to turn it up full blast. "Everything here is cooled for our machines. Us, too." He adjusted a vent that was blowing on his gluepot. "I'm desperate to get out of this heat. Can your mother's favorite son get me a hotel room in Harbin for the end of the month? Lin has some friends up there, doesn't he?"

"He has friends everywhere," Hong said.

"So you'll ask him for me? I'll do some fancy enlargements for him. And you, too, you and your wife and..." Fen popped his eyes. "Sorry."

"It's all right," Hong said. "Divorce isn't the scandal it used to be."

Fen slid the two photos back into the envelope and escorted Hong to the door. "You went to Sun Sheng's memorial service," he said quietly. "How was it?"

"Uncomfortable," Hong said.

Fen said nothing.

"They cremated him in a day," Hong said.

Fen again said nothing, and his silences were beginning to say a lot.

"When can you get to my labels?" Hong asked.

"A week or two, I'm on deadline with all this color work right now." Fen waved his arm at the pages of *China Reconstructs* mounted near the door—separate editions with text in Chinese, English, Portuguese, French, German, and squiggles that Hong assumed were Arabic. Hong glanced at an article on Key Projects Under Construction in the Sixth Five-Year Plan—a machine-tool plant financed by the Germans, a new American jeep factory, a grain-storage depot designed by the French.

"Impressive," Hong said.

"Isn't it?" Fen said. "China reconstructs...with the Germans, the Americans, and the French. And all the hard work, initiative, and talents of our great Party."

The midday sun rose over the Western Hills. Twenty kilometers away the air was clear, a bright halo of orange, but a layer of black smoke the size of a rice paddy blanketed the sky above Fuxing Road.

The blanket, unlike so many other things, was permanent, a fact of geography. In Beijing all winds blow from the north, out of the bellows of Mongolia and across the Gobi Desert. New industry, therefore, was now built to the south and east, so that pollution drifted out to sea, not back onto the city. Earlier planners had not been so wise. After the Great Leap Forward, the smelting plants in the Shijingshan District had been consolidated as the Capital Iron and Steel Works. The old mills were just far enough below the wind for the smoke to keep spreading and spreading but never go away.

Hong and Chan rode under the layer of smoke in a Bureau car toward the Cemetery for Revolutionary Heroes at Babaoshan. Hong had planned to go alone, but Chan said conspiracy was harder to prove than recidivism, which was a beautiful expression of his loyalty. The car was an old Shanghai with sluggish air conditioning and the driver played his horn as a musical instrument, bashing it regularly at second-shift workers on bicycles. Neither Hong nor Chan complained; this particular driver could be trusted to log his afternoon as trips to the Defense Ministry and the Academy of Sciences.

"To be buried or burned," Chan said, "what's the difference? Once you're dead you can't feel it anyway."

"There's probably no difference," Hong said.

"So why are we here?"

"To see why a man who wanted to be buried was cremated instead."

"Burial is too expensive," Chan said. "Why pay for a vault or a spot in the ground when your working unit will pay for cremation?"

Hong looked out the window. "Sheng could have afforded whatever he wanted."

The car pulled up to the cemetery's gate behind a Datsun, a taxi. Beyond the spired main building, which housed the crematorium, lay a warren of vault rooms where ashes for anyone except high cadres could be kept for five years. For the powerful there was no time limit, their ashes would stay forever. Hong noticed gusts of whitish gray floating from the red brick crematorium chimneys. Life is short, he thought, it ends in smoke. He opened his window and poked his head out.

"What's taking so long?" he called to the guard.

The guard glared at him as if gravely insulted, strutted toward the car, then leaned down, hands on hips, and stared in. "Who are you to be so impatient?" he demanded truculently.

Hong held up his Bureau card and the guard's expression instantly changed. "Oh, oh," he said, swallowing hard and catching his breath, "I'm very sorry, I'm extremely sorry, Comrade, forgive my tone, please go right on through." He was too nervous, as Hong had hoped, to note Hong's name or the car's license plate.

Inside the crematorium, light wooden boxes were stacked six and seven high. The smell of death was like a detergent. It cleansed the nostrils. Beyond a wall of painted screens— vermilion dragons and white mountains and blue rivers— the ovens burned. There was a clang of steel doors, a lever thrown, the whoosh of flames, and a cannon blast of heat that raised the temperature a hundred degrees.

Several families sat waiting, each with its small urn. A little elf of a man appeared from behind the screens, he looked like a bank clerk, and summoned a woman waiting with a teenaged girl and an old couple. But when he saw Chan he scurried over with an outstretched hand.

"Chan, how good to see you," he gushed. "What brings you here? Not a death in the family, I hope."

"It's you, it's Chekhov!" Chan exclaimed.

Hong looked from one to the other. Chan introduced the crematorium manager, Comrade Song, explaining that they had served in the Army together.

"Yes, Chan was my lieutenant," Song said with enthusiasm. "A good soldier and a great servant of the people."

Song led them to a reception room, rang for tea and cakes, asked them half a dozen times if they were comfortable, then excused himself to check the ovens.

"You knew he worked here," Hong said.

"Not at all," Chan said.

"Does he worship everybody, or just you?"

It was all very simple, Chan said, as if anything could be. Comrade Song had joined the Army full of revolutionary fervor, despite the fact that as an only son he was exempt from military service. "And he was a real ink-and-brush man, a real scholar, loved all the Russian writers. He reads them in the original, that's why we called him Chekhov. Anyway, they offered him soft assignments, desk jobs in Shanghai or Beijing. And what did he do? He demanded the harshest post. He absolutely demanded they send him to Tibet. A total patriot, Hong, that's what he was, plain as moonlight, they should write an opera about him. They should teach his life story to children."

Two years into his term, Song's mother became ill, she was dying of some hideous disease. As an only son, Song asked to be relieved of his duties. "Did they let him go home? No, some idiot of a general refuses to process the papers. So I get in touch with an uncle of mine at the division's headquarters. He'd never been able to do a thing for me, but I said he had to do something, go through the back door, for this patriot. So Song gets his pass to Beijing and he thinks I should have red stars and braids all over my chest."

Comrade Song returned. "I have to watch the gauges," he apologized. "If the fires aren't hot enough, we have incomplete combustion."

Casually, as if the matter had no great import, Hong asked about the day Sun Sheng was cremated. Comrade Song remembered the afternoon, it was past the end of his shift, he should have been home already, but the night manager was late. First, there had been a telephone call from a cadre at the Bureau inquiring about the crematorium's schedule, and could cremation be arranged quickly so the memorial service could be held on Monday?

"We were very busy, very busy I told him. And it was the truth, honestly. I hope no one's in trouble here, we really do our best. We're not lax here, our workers don't loaf, we're not like some of those factories."

Hong assured him no one was in trouble. The first call came from the Bureau, he repeated, and then? Half an hour later, Comrade Song replied, a call came from Sun Sheng's widow, Ma Sufei. She was distraught, the poor woman, most upset. Yes, as well she might have been, Hong agreed. And why had she called? The body of her husband was on its way from the hospital, and she wanted to know when she should appear for the cremation. Hong wondered aloud if Comrade Song happened to recall which cadre had telephoned from the Bureau. No, things were so busy, he was waiting for the night manager, supervising the shift change.

Hong mentioned four names from the list he had assembled at the Hall of Records, four of the old cadres from Yanan who had died during the past fifteen years, all four in Beijing. Could Comrade Song determine if they were cremated here?

"High cadres?" asked Song.

Yes, Hong said, high cadres.

"We take care of many high cadres," Song said proudly on his way out. "I'll check."

"And the dates and time of day, please," Hong added.

Recordkeeper of the dead, he thought. No wonder Song looked like a bank clerk. Chan, head down, arms locked in a furious embrace around his chest, paced in front of a productivity chart—accidents on the job, number of bodies cremated.

"You're wearing out a good pair of shoes," Hong said.

Chan stopped. "It's not that I don't understand your feelings," he said, "but what can you hope to gain from this? You'll end up in one of those ovens yourself, long before your time."

"I want what any man wants," Hong said. "Peace of mind."

"You choose a strange way to find it."

Comrade Song hurried in, carrying his files. Of the four men, three had been cremated here, all three within hours of their deaths. How fortunate they were, Hong thought. In life they had never waited in lines for food, and in death they were rushed to the head of the line to be cremated.

He thanked the manager and walked into the courtyard. Planters on either side of the gate held roses and grape vines. A poster of two men and three women in workclothes said in bold letters, SAFETY FIRST. Inside, Chan huddled with the crematorium manager. They lit each other's cigarettes, bent close and whispered. When Chan came out he was wearing a dour expression.

"Your questions unsettled him. He may look naive, but he isn't. I impressed upon him these were issues of State, not to be discussed with anyone."

"Three men," Hong said ruminatively, contemplating the roses, "all cremated hours after they died."

"Means nothing," Chan said. "Unless connected to other facts."

As with all facts, Hong thought. Well, he would just have to find the connection. With a more determined step than he had known in some time he returned to the car for the ride into the city. Chan was deep in a sulk, but as the car pulled through the gate Hong waved at the guard and smiled for reasons that were a mystery even to himself.

The driver left Hong on Wangfujing and continued on with Chan to the Academy of Sciences and the Defense Ministry. Hong wanted to walk, breathe fresh air. He felt his head growing stuffy, his temperature rising.

From a vendor next to the post office he bought an orange juice in a plastic envelope, tore the corner and inserted a straw, and started walking south toward the Bureau. Someone powerful had killed Sheng, there was no doubt, but how? Actually, how was less important than why. If another old cadre should happen to die in the next few days, Hong thought, a link could be established. So what

did he do? Call all the survivors from the Party headquarters at Yanan and tell them not to catch colds? Or
should he simply sit and wait for a man to die? And what if
no one did? Know the history of a crime, Hong kept hearing in his mind. Know the history and the motive unveils
itself.

"But which history?" he muttered aloud. "The history of
what?"

He crossed Chang'an, went into the Bureau through the
back gate, and climbed the steps to his office. The sun was
still shining but dust caked on the window blocked out what
little light it provided. He pushed the radio to the edge of
its stand, slid his desk chair around from behind his desk,
and opened the Academy of Sciences file on the American,
Peter Ostrander. For some men paper was gold, written
records a sanctuary. Not for Hong. Particularly in the case
of personal dossiers, Hong thought he could learn more in
five minutes with the man in question.

Peter Ostrander had led a remarkably simple life, at least
according to his file. Resident of St. Louis, Missouri, physi-
cian on the staff of Barnes Memorial Hospital, research in
psychiatry on learning disabilities and senility. The file elaborated: *Loss of memory in old age now assumed by Western medicine to have physical causes.* Like my father's weakness of the
nerves, Hong thought. As physical causes went, six months
of near starvation would do.

The phone rang and Hong wheeled around to his desk.
It was Chan. "I'm at the Defense Ministry," he said. "The
Ostrander file seems to be lost."

"I thought it was misplaced."

"It was. Now it's permanently misplaced."

"Who misplaced it?"

"It isn't too clear."

Not for a telephone conversation, Hong thought. "And
what did you find at the Academy of Sciences? Who authorized Ostrander's visit?"

"Strictly formal," Chan said. "Ostrander is one of six
American doctors placed around the country, invited
through the Committee on Cultural Exchange."

"Who's on the Committee?"

Chan hesitated. "Well, it's just the regular people, the political group, nobody special..."

"You didn't get a list?" Hong asked with mild impatience.

"No, I, well..."

"Can you go back for it?"

"They're closed. I'll get it first thing in the morning."

Hong put the phone down and returned to the Academy
of Sciences dossier on the American. To hell with the Defense Ministry. Let the mothers-in-law—as everyone called
competing departments—fight among themselves, and on
a higher level, please, if possible. A daughter can only serve
one mother-in-law, and getting out of this case altogether
was his priority. Ostrander had entered China ten days ago
at Guangzhou, by train from Hong Kong. Hong looked at
the enlarged passport photograph again: a high forehead,
strong cheekbones setting off bright eyes opened wide in a
kind of shock—at the flashbulb, probably, reflected as white
dots in the pupils. Ostrander did indeed look Scandinavian:
contemplative, almost brooding.

Again Hong read the first line of the file—*Ostrander,
Peter, born 33.1.14, Tangshan, China*—and again marveled at
the absence of any reason for his parents having been there.
The degree of detail that followed raised two questions:
why had this part of the American's history been neglected,
and why, considering that he was neither a journalist nor a
diplomat, had anyone ever been sufficiently interested to
compile a dossier in the first place? That the Academy of
Sciences had instigated such an investigation demanded a
rationale.

Hong continued reading. In 1941, at age eight, Ostrander had returned to the United States. Four years later
his mother was remarried in Philadelphia, Pennsylvania, to
a heart surgeon and medical college professor. The file ir-
relevantly expounded on the distribution of medical care in
the West, and in a footnote explained geographical subdivi-
sions of the United States: "Pennsylvania is a province."

What had happened to Peter Ostrander's father, Hong
wondered, that had allowed his mother to marry again?
Maybe Theodore Ostrander had gone to jail as a disgraced
intellectual during the McCarthy Period, the Americans'

version of the Cultural Revolution. Or was that later? Hong was weak on American political history. He ran his finger down the page, then back up again to Theodore Ostrander's name. Following the name was a parenthetical notation: *(Cross-references: None.)*

None? Not a single file anywhere on a man who had been in China in 1933? On the subject of Peter Ostrander's father the dossier was otherwise mute.

The younger Ostrander's record showed no foreign travel until the age of seventeen, when he spent one year as an exchange student in West Germany. A reasonable posting for a spy, but teenaged spies were a rarity. Educated at Oberlin College, Ohio, student of psychology, attended University of Wisconsin Medical School, specializing in neurobiology, or the chemistry of the brain. Then there had been various postings to hospitals throughout the United States. Married, one child, a daughter, who was now a university professor of Shakespeare. Wife, deceased in automobile accident, had been a poet, and the file listed the titles of her books. A whole family of intellectuals, Hong thought. On 80.12.1, Ostrander had applied for a Chinese visa at the Chinese consular office, New York, New York, but few individual travelers were permitted entry then, and Ostrander was refused. Scheduled for American Psychiatric Association tour 84.6.15, but did not appear with group, no reason given, partial refund issued by Luxingshe, the travel ministry, and the Academy of Sciences.

Cancelled a trip? Why? Hong's eyes moved up the page. Ostrander's wife had died on 84.6.11, which the Academy of Sciences analyst seemed not to have noticed.

Hong turned to a personality profile gleaned from "a variety of sources"—mostly, Hong guessed, from the staff at the diplomatic compound where Ostrander had been given a two-room apartment, and whatever they could hear from the microphone built into the wall. Attributing information to a variety of sources made the Special Security bureaucrats feel important. Among the other five doctors on the exchange, Ostrander was friendly only with one, a specialist in stomach disorders assigned to a hospital in Shanghai. Ostrander liked Chinese vegetables for breakfast. He smoked a pipe and had brought his own tobacco, half a kilo. He went to Chinese movies once a week, and had not yet set foot in the International Club. Though a foreigner would immediately attract attention in a movie theater, what better place to meet an accomplice? Ostrander went to bed early, slept only four or five hours a night, was up early every morning writing in his journal, which he carried with him at all times. The compound's watchers must have been weeping for joy. Ostrander kept the same hours they did.

It would be interesting to see the American's journal, Hong thought. On the surface the contents might be meaningless, but he could learn as much from what it omitted as what it contained.

Especially curious, Hong thought as he stared at the file, was that in Ostrander's twenty-four years since finishing medical studies he had left the United States thirteen times, but only on short trips—vacations, often to Switzerland to ski, medical meetings in Europe or on Caribbean islands. What sort of operative, Hong wondered, traveled abroad but never assumed a foreign posting? He might have used other names, but then there ought to have been gaps in his history. Or these files might be grafting a flower from one tree onto another—someone else's history masquerading as Ostrander's. "To the paper lovers," Sun Sheng had said, "whatever appears in print has a store of value unmatched by any intelligence you might apply to it. Apply your own intelligence." And also, as a corollary: "Merely because something is written down doesn't mean it's useful, or true. Understanding the value of information lies in knowing where it comes from and why you have it."

The file had come from the Academy of Sciences at the direction of the Three Tigers. And the Tigers seemed to have maneuvered to take the case from Defense. Most crucial, therefore, was not the information in the file, which on the surface was useless, but rather the Tigers' interest in the American. Also crucial was Theodore Ostrander, Peter Ostrander's father. Surely he merited a dossier of his own—which might well exist despite any notation to the contrary.

Hong glanced at his watch, or rather at his wrist, since the watch was in the repair shop. The wall clock opposite his desk showed that he had been reading for almost an hour. He closed the file. In the morning he would have a look at

Ostrander and find him either harmless or, with luck, worthy of attention by much more powerful cadres. Against his conscious will, however, and his stated desire to unload this case expeditiously and without incident, Hong found himself spinning the myriad messages of Ostrander's file through his mind. Out of habit he looked for the windows, spaces opening onto the horizon where the real facts could be seen.

And certainly, he thought, it was the seemingly innocuous parenthetical following the elder Ostrander's name—(*Cross-references: None.*)—that represented the clearest window of all.

7.

SELLING
RAIN
AND
WIND

A caravan of Mercedes-Benz limousines unloaded a convention of bankers from Hong Kong at the Beijing Hotel. Hong watched them as he bicycled across Chang'an. Must be second-level bankers, he thought, or they would have rated suites at the State Guesthouse. Their wives wore flowing silk dresses and clutched small cases of mah-jongg tiles. In some circles the written ideograms for Hong Kong banker translated as "I don't care a shit about anyone." Who would they care about in a few years, Hong wondered, when Chinese soldiers occupied their backyards?

At the Bureau's motor pool a Shanghai sedan and driver waited for Hong. The Little Monk waited, too. Wu Keping, the Director's clerk, had taken up a vigil next to the garage, carrying his zippered plastic briefcase. An interview with Ostrander, which would be taped anyway, did not require two cadres, one of whom was a clerk. Thus the Little Monk must be more than a clerk.

"You're going to meet the American doctor," the Little

Monk said when Hong approached the garage. "I'll be with you to help in any way I can."

And to take notes, Hong thought. "I can manage without you," he said, "if you have other duties."

"No, I am available," said the Little Monk, which settled the matter.

They rode to the foreigners' compound on Jianguomen-wai, just west of the International Club and the Jianguo Hotel, a brick-for-brick copy of an American hotel with sheets of glass across the front and a tai-rock courtyard garden. Inside, brass railings sprung from the walls like weeds and a glass-enclosed nightclub kept a band playing every night of the week. Stupendously hideous, Hong thought, but Westerners loved it. Just before the Jianguomen flyover —a highway interchange gashing the middle of the city— the car turned at Dongdaiqiao, circled back around Ritan Park, and pulled up to the compound's gate. Hong held up his pass and waited while the guard logged his name. How did anyone expect to carry on illegal activities under such scrutiny? Westerners apparently thought all Chinese were backward peasants. Crafty and industrious, of course, but backward.

"Have you discovered what the American is looking for?" asked the Little Monk as they stepped from the car.

"Shhh," Hong whispered. "You never know who's listening." That would keep him quiet for a while.

At the reception desk, Hong told the clerk to announce them, then rode the elevator to the seventh floor. The Little Monk, awed, stole glances into open apartments, where attendants were vacuuming. The foreigners' high rise displayed extraordinary luxury—carpeted hallways, kitchens with four-burner gas stoves and giant refrigerators, central air conditioning that ran twenty-four hours a day, and new bathrooms tiled floor to ceiling.

Hong knocked at apartment 701. The door opened to reveal an imposing round-eyed giant, almost half a meter taller than Hong. He was slight but broad-shouldered, and made like a string doll: all legs with a short torso. His face, unlike the one in the photo, displayed a thick mustache streaked with gray, and his hair was wilder, a wig left in the rain. But for all his size, Ostrander possessed none of the taut assurance of other foreigners Hong had met. He was an ink-and-brush man—a thinker, not an activist.

Ostrander held the door open with one hand, his pipe in the other, outstretched to beckon Hong and the Little Monk inside. His loose khakis were rumpled and his white shirt, though of unquestionably superior fabric, was billowy and ill-fitting. With the frame of the door adding perspective, everything about the man was big: the round eyes, the teeth white as dinner plates, the hairy blond arms. And yet he did not have the lumbering-bear presence, the clumsy elephantine look, of many Westerners.

"Mr. Lu, I've been expecting you," Ostrander said, letting the door close as he shook Hong's hand, then Wu's. His greeting was in impeccable *putonghua*—the national standardized dialect. Very impressive, better by far than the German lawyer.

"That's very good," Hong said, switching to English for the required ritual compliment. "You speak our language well."

"My Chinese is awful," Ostrander responded with a smile as broad as his face. "And there isn't much of it."

A dubious protest, Hong thought. Ostrander had mastered both the language and the proper level of politeness, as an enemy of the State should.

Hong introduced the Little Monk. Ostrander, bustling in his modern kitchen, quickly produced a pot of tea. His eyes, Hong noticed, radiated a childlike merriness, and he stooped slightly, as though uneasy with his height. Hong glanced at the air duct over the entrance to the kitchen. Between the two screws at the top was a small hole—the microphone.

"I must apologize," Hong said, "for your previous inexperienced liaison. I understand that his English was not of the quality you needed."

"His English was fine, it was really very good," Ostrander said cheerily. "Your English is excellent, too."

More politeness, or a ruse? Had the guide assigned by Defense in fact been adequate? "In any case," Hong went on, "Mr. Wu and I would like to make your stay in Beijing as pleasant as possible. You must call on us, Dr. Ostrander, for anything you want."

"Call me Peter, please," Ostrander said, sitting and crossing his long legs. Instant informality. Americans thought the rest of the world should indulge in their barbarisms. Ostrander sucked on his pipe and the smell of burnt cherries filled the room. "I don't really need much help," he went on with buoyant friendliness. "I just go to the hospital and back again. I might need a train ticket or something like that, but really, I can get around by myself."

"Are you familiar with Beijing?"

"No, but I'm learning. I take buses, ride the subway. Do you know that whenever I get on a bus someone usually gives me a seat?"

"Is that so?" asked Hong, who would just as soon let a foreigner stand. The days of kowtowing were long over.

"Everyone is so nice," Ostrander said, and then, leaning forward, "except at the hospital, of course."

"Oh?" Hong said, feigning surprise.

Ostrander offered his big smile again. "You understand. First of all, I'm a foreigner. And they have this idea, I think, that because I'm a psychiatrist I can know things about them without their telling me."

Either he was a fool or a liar—no, it was unquestionably the latter. Could a spy be so unsophisticated? Ostrander delivered a good performance.

"The situation will change," Hong said, "when people know you better. We want to make friends between peoples and cultures."

"How long have you been with the Academy of Sciences?" Ostrander asked.

"Three years," Hong replied, and while his tongue issued a fictitious recitation of his work with foreign scientists, complete with digressions on his many foreign journeys and opinions on the relative merits of living in Paris or Moscow or East Berlin, he surveyed the room. An array of gadgets, like a display in a store, covered the top of Ostrander's dresser: two miniature tape recorders and stacks of cassettes, an electric typewriter with power converter, stacks of books, an electric shaver with battery attachment, a small shortwave radio, boxes upon boxes of ballpoint pens, several more cigarette lighters (one black metal, next to a canister of pressurized gas fuel), and four cameras with an assortment of lenses. On the corner of the desk were several brown leatherbound notebooks, one of which lay open with an uncapped pen in the center—Ostrander's journal. Hong had to restrain himself from drifting toward it for a closer look.

"So you liked Paris best," Ostrander said.

Hong mentally danced to retrace his steps. What had he just said about Paris? "Yes, the French food was very good," he answered, and continued with an inventory of the superb meals he had eaten.

Two of the cameras were Japanese (a Canon and a miniature pocket Minolta), one was a Leica, the last a Polaroid. The same kind of equipment the German had carried and also the typical trappings of a rich tourist. The Little Monk had taken a chair in the corner, and he too was casting an eye at the cameras. For many years Hong had dismissed as a fantasy the portrait of life in American movies—*The Sound of Music,* which he had seen three times, *Convoy,* the love story about trucks, or the television program "The Man from Atlantis." Then Channel 2 had shown a newsreel of Vice-Chairman Deng's visit to the United States. The fantasy was real: all those modern buildings, cars, highways. It was a contradiction in the socialist state. The Western way led to evil, and yet socialism promised the same result— more cars and tractors, higher productivity, a better standard of living for all. Of course the lower classes in the West went hungry, even starved, but peasants starved in China, too. If capitalism was evil, why did socialism promise what capitalism provided?

Meanwhile, Hong went on recounting to Ostrander his nonexistent career as a translator with the Scientific and Technological Commission, ending with his three months in Rome assigned to a team of biologists.

"You've led an interesting life," Ostrander put in.

Yes, Hong agreed, but it was so sad that his facility with Italian had deteriorated during the Cultural Revolution, when no foreign languages were spoken. The last part, at least, was true, and as for losing his Italian, it made a plausible story. In fact, despite the ban on foreign languages, thousands had studied secretly when the universities closed. Hong himself had smuggled copies of Dickens and Hemingway from his parents' house a week before their library was raided and, for the most part, burned. To Dickens he owed his utter conviction that the detestable rot of capitalism would lead to its downfall. Still, bemoaning the horrors of the Cultural Revolution would gain Ostrander's confidence. Criticism of the "blood years," now officially encouraged, enthralled foreigners, particularly Russians and Americans.

Ostrander was different. "The Chinese are too hard on themselves," he said. "You survived a terrible time, and now you're moving on. All we hear about is your new capitalism, less control over factories, people being able to buy refrigerators and television sets."

"We're making use of capitalism," Hong said, "but what we have is the responsibility system. Everyone is now more responsible to do his work, and so we're more productive."

"Call it what you like," Ostrander said pleasantly. "When you pay people based on what they produce, when you let the market set prices, we call it capitalism."

"Yes, the responsibility system is working well," Hong repeated, anxious to avoid political debate. Not everyone was getting rich. The unambitious and untalented were jealous and afraid. Stubborn old factory bosses who owed their jobs to Party membership fought attempts to reduce their power. "And your work?" Hong asked. "Maybe you could explain it to me."

Foreigners were like chefs and artists. They loved talking about their work. Ostrander, being a spy, had the correct pose. As a doctor, he explained, he had always been fascinated most by the inner workings of the mind—how people think, remember, make mental connections. It struck Hong as a questionable field of study. Marxism might be under attack as an economic theory, but it explained quite clearly how people thought.

"I'm putting you to sleep," Ostrander said.

Hong searched Ostrander's face quizzically. What did it mean, putting him to sleep? "Excuse me?"

Ostrander smiled. "I mean that I'm boring you."

"Oh, it's idiomatic," Hong said, understanding. "Yes, I see it now. No, please go on, you're not putting me to sleep."

"What I want to know is exactly how memory works.

What happens in the brain, chemically, when information is stored? We're just beginning to find out how complicated the brain is."

"In China, you know, we believe that what we eat is very important to mental functioning. Medicine is very concerned with diet."

"For us, too," Ostrander said with a smile, "although not in quite the same way. For example, for many years we knew very little about cancer. Now we think that certain foods cause cancer, and others protect the body against it."

"What foods protect the body?"

"Carrots, for one. And green leafy vegetables."

"Well, then, the price of carrots and green vegetables is going up immediately."

Ostrander laughed, even the silent Little Monk laughed. Ostrander stood, said he was due at Union Hospital, and began filling his briefcase, a beautiful object of polished leather with fine brass clasps. He picked up two boxes of ballpoint pens and held them out to Hong and the Monk. "One for each of you," he said. "A gift to show my appreciation for your courtesy."

"No, that's unnecessary," Hong said, waving them away.

"Please, I gave them to my last guide, too." He grinned mischievously and added, "It's all right, I'm not a spy."

Hong took the pens, passing a box to Wu, but the remark unsettled him. Why would Ostrander joke about being a spy?

In the elevator Ostrander babbled, flattering all things Chinese: the clean streets, the beauty of the Forbidden City, the tenacity of family feelings that protected the old from isolation. Outside he passed the waiting cars and drivers and headed straight for the bicycle rack, where he unlocked a new single-gear Phoenix, the cheapest model you could buy.

"When in Beijing," he said, strapping his briefcase to the rack over the rear wheel, "do as the Chinese do." He flung a leg over and prepared to ride off. "It's the only way to travel."

Especially, Hong thought, if you preferred not leaving a record of everywhere you went.

"You can reach me or Mr. Wu at the Academy," Hong said. "Please call on us for assistance."

Ostrander thanked him again and pedaled through the gate.

The Little Monk eased up beside Hong and asked conspiratorially, "What do you think?"

"I think he's a very clever spy," Hong said, though in fact he was not quite so sure as he sounded.

"Yes, I agree," said the Monk decisively.

Hong watched Ostrander disappear into the traffic on Chaoyangmen, and tried to take a measure of the man. A spy? Hong remembered a fairy tale he had heard as a child, the story of a princess locked in a cave who escaped to find a lush, beautiful world of palaces and temples. Hong felt as though he, too, had just crept from a cave, but instead onto a barren sunlit desert. There was plenty of light, but nothing to see.

Listening to his chest rasp, Hong climbed the steps from the Bureau's Qianmen courtyard entrance to the first floor and turned down the hall. He pushed through one of two ceiling-high swinging doors into Surveillance. Like all departments, Surveillance—or "the night people" as they were called—had staff trouble, and the trouble could be expressed simply: budget too small, duties too large. For the night people matters had gone from unbearable to absurd. A decade ago the country had hosted only a handful of foreigners each year. Now there were millions, far too many of whom had to be watched; there were telephone calls to record and transcribe, rooms to search, luggage to be stolen and then found.

Surveillance had expanded from half a dozen closet-sized rooms into the entire northern half of the first floor. All the walls had been demolished and partitions erected, breaking the space into hundreds of cubicles derisively called birds' nests by their occupants—spaces so small that even a bird might refuse to live in them. At the western corner of the floor was a somewhat larger office, with real walls and windows facing Chang'an, occupied by Comrade Ru Taisheng, who was the case liaison to the Investigations Division.

Hong knocked on the door, entered, and found Ru hunched over his desk eating noodles from a paper container.

"Breakfast," Ru said. "I was here until eleven last night, I haven't had a day off in two weeks, and my stomach doesn't know what time it is anymore." He put the container down. "So be warned," he continued with a grin. "Whatever you want, you can't have it." Ru was a little bird himself—balding severely, with his remaining hair pulled back from his forehead like the crown stripe on a heron.

"I've got an American," Hong said. "He keeps a diary."

"How nice for you," Ru said. "You must mean the doctor living in the foreigners' compound. I got the order from Chan and saw the building watchers' report yesterday. Sit down, pass some time. Can you spare a cigarette?"

Hong took out his pack, tapped the bottom.

"Thank you. If only you'd been here last night."

"Ostrander has a diary—"

"Which, as you know, he carries everywhere. You've seen the same reports I did. He even takes it when he jogs. Too bad he doesn't swim."

"Can you get in while he's asleep?"

"And what if he wakes up when we're there? He's a light sleeper. Three nights ago he got out of bed and started writing at four in the morning."

"I want to read it," Hong said.

"He has a stack of leatherbound notebooks, and he's on the first one. When he finishes it, presumably he'll leave it in the compound. Then we'll go in and photograph it for you."

"I'd rather not wait," Hong said.

"Tell me how to cut off a man's hand and not have him notice."

"You're right," Hong said, pulling the door open. "Please call me when he finishes the notebook."

Hong let Ru's door close, turned into the hall, and walked up to the second floor. His infected lungs cried out for relief. In the office Chan was waiting with a membership list and career summaries for the Academy of Sciences' Committee on Cultural Exchange, the cadres who had recommended that Ostrander be admitted as a foreign expert.

"I also brought files on the other five foreign doctors," Chan said.

Hong looked at a message on his desk; he was supposed to meet his brother Lin at the circus at eight o'clock. The tickets would be delivered to the Bureau before the end of the day. Superb seats, without question, second or third row and facing the center ring. Hong picked up the files on the American doctors, opened them one by one. Brief travel and educational histories, photographs, nothing more.

"These are virtually empty," Hong said.

"Not like Ostrander's, as you guessed."

"Check them anyway. Surveillance reports, telephone calls, the usual." A pointless order, Hong knew. The other doctors had no relation to this case. But better the appearance of thoroughness than a reprimand.

"What was Ostrander like? What did you learn from him?"

"Not much. Who's on this committee?" Hong scanned the list.

"Like I told you, the regular people. Two rehabilitated professors, one Party liaison who sleeps through meetings, and two watchdogs, one from Defense and one from Foreign Affairs."

The professors and Party liaison were functionaries. The two watchdogs actually made the decisions—who would be allowed in, which scientific facility would host them. Hong recognized neither of their names, but the Defense cadre's career caught his eye, a meager summary but interesting nonetheless for its breadth: posts in the General Political Department of the Army, the Secretariat of the Central Committee, a two-year stint at the Navy's district regional headquarters in Qingdao. A Defense cadre with that kind of experience should be running a military academy, not screening doctors for scientific exchanges.

"And the permanently misplaced file on Ostrander at Defense?" Hong asked.

Chan sat forward. "Now that's a story. You'll enjoy this. I went through channels, one desk to another. I got bumped from security to propaganda to staff operations. All they had was a record of Ostrander's entry and the assignment of a translator. It seems the file wasn't lost after all. They say it never existed."

"Yes, well, they can sell rain and wind to farmers," Hong said, and then, a foregone conclusion: "We'll never see it now."

He lit a cigarette, inhaled painfully, and coughed so hard his chair shook. It was crazy how Defense expected anyone to believe such nonsense. But of course they didn't. They fixed their story and stuck to it. You could stand on their shadow and they would swear it was raining.

"You're sweating," Chan said.

"I'm running a fever."

"Excellent!" Chan exulted. "There you go, it's simple, you're deathly ill."

"And that makes you happy?"

"Yes, now you can get this case transferred."

Chan was right. The battle between Defense and Public Security had taken on new and disturbing dimensions, and a war of the mothers-in-law was as good a justification as any for jettisoning Ostrander. Defense had a cadre on the Academy's screening committee, and Defense had also lost a file on their own translator. Defense was showing as much interest in Ostrander as Public Security, and at the same time trying to subvert the investigation.

Be done with it, Hong thought. Go to bed for a week, or two or three, force the Tigers to choose another assistant deputy director for the case. But Ostrander had stirred Hong's professional pride. Or so he told himself, not wanting to think about other, deeper reasons he might have for continuing. Whatever the reasons, he decided he would hold on to the American for just a while longer.

PART
TWO

"*Seek truth
from facts.*"

8.

THE
PAGODA
OF
BOWLS

The people loved the circus and tickets were cheap. The real price of admission, however, was connection, in which Lu Lin, Hong's older brother, excelled. A successful factory manager required no less, and so every three months Lin flew from Shanghai to Beijing to meet bureaucrats from the Commerce and Defense Ministries. Permits for raw materials, large advance orders from State stores, city and housing transfers for new university graduates—without these, and the connections needed to get them, Lin's electronics factory would cease functioning.

On Baishiqiao Road in front of Capital Gymnasium, a yellow square of stone, Hong searched the crowd for Cao Yamei, his girlfriend, who had to travel across the city in congested shift-change traffic. Hong had hoped to send a Bureau car for her, but every single one was booked—the Volkswagens, the new jeeps, the Shanghais, even the motorcycles with sidecars. Probably on their way here, Hong thought, bearing Deputy Ministers and Vice-Ministers and Directors. On the circular driveway behind the Exhibition Center new Japanese taxis and Shanghais and Red Flags jostled for parking spaces. Four cadres in Western suits and ties piled out of a Volkswagen and drew stares. The teardrop clusters of the streetlamps burst into light.

Hong pushed his glasses against his nose and peered anxiously across the street toward the bicycle racks. Maybe Yamei had been delayed, maybe her team's practice had gone on longer than usual, maybe she had been hurt in a bicycle accident. He enjoyed worrying about her, even needlessly, enjoyed having someone other than himself to worry about. That she had fallen in love with him was the great blessing of his life, the one poets wrote about. Without her he might well have given up hope of finding someone new to love—someone who would love him back, anyway. He had envisioned growing old alone, moving in with his son and becoming a doting grandfather whose mind had long since shut down. Even now he saw Yamei less often than both would have liked. She was expected to spend extra time with her swimming team, and the best she and Hong could manage was an evening a week. Applying for a marriage license was legally impossible for at least a year, when Yamei turned twenty-five.

Their relationship was complicated by other concerns, not the least of which were Hong's divorce and the difference in their ages. When they had met six months ago, in an introduction by Chan's cousin on the Sports Commission, Yamei was being courted by senior swimming coaches, by members of her team, and by cadres in her working unit at the Institute for Physical Culture. Like Yamei, most of her suitors had excellent political backgrounds and good salaries, and all were in their late twenties. But she had flirted with Hong, and he had been enchanted. Instead of shyly avoiding the subject of his work, as many women did, she had drawn him out, encouraged him, made him feel as important to the future of his country, if only for a moment, as he had once felt himself. Later, when it was clear that Hong's divorce papers would be approved by the court, she had sent him a note, and courageously they had met in Beihai Park for a boat ride. She told him her other suitors were boys, immature. But in choosing Hong, and in refusing to hide her interest in him, she had risked criticism. Even her friends were bold enough to suggest that perhaps her decision was unwise. Everyone found it hard to comprehend why she had not picked a more suitable marriage candidate —either someone younger and more handsome, or at least someone richer and not divorced.

Thousands of well-connected cadres thronged the entrance to the hall. Regional circuses across the country sent their best acts to Beijing for month-long stands only twice a year; for each booking that meant a mere four hundred thousand available seats—in a city of ten million, a trickle of rain in the desert. Hong spotted Yamei in the crowd, parking and locking her bicycle. He semaphored with both hands over his head, and she waved back. She was wearing a bright flowered blouse and pink scarf that she had probably carried to work. She liked to dress for him, she said, something Kuang must have done once—yes, surely she had tried to please him, but for all his certainty Hong couldn't quite remember.

"I'm sorry, practice went a little late," Yamei let out breathlessly as she loped gracefully up the steps, looking at her watch.

"We have time," Hong assured her. "Did you eat?"

"Lunch was late, too. I'm not hungry."

She quieted then, and he saw that her face, small and smooth as polished stone, was flushed from the ride. She gazed at him, smiled, took his hand and squeezed it. He felt the simple pleasure of being the object of her admiration and desire.

"You look handsome," she said.

Hong shrugged. "As handsome as I ever do," he mumbled.

Yamei laughed like a schoolgirl. "Is there a more handsome man in the world?" They started for the doors. "We're sure to win next month, I'm positive, the team has never been better."

"That's good," Hong said. In her first trip out of the country she would be accompanying her team to Hong Kong for a competition. They were her spoiled babies, the swimmers. She mothered and cajoled them, cheered them, watched their diets and listened to their troubles.

"You're not interested," Yamei said with a pout. "I know. All that matters to you are robbers and prostitutes and corrupt bookkeepers. But I want my team to beat the Russians and the Japanese. And I want them to go to the next Olympics. I have a new boy from Yuxian, he's thirteen and so cute. He's destined for world class in the fifty meter."

Her patriotic fervor was a steed, a galloping beast of optimism. The young were untainted by reality—or, rather, by the past. The rest of us are damaged, Hong thought, but our scars protect us. Yamei's purity made him frightened for her. She had no doubts, no armor. She experienced so little fear that tragedy, if it came, would destroy her.

"I wish your son could have come with us," Yamei said.

"He can't," Hong said tersely. If Kuang considered Yamei a scandal, what would she think of Bai meeting her?

Hong held out his tickets and retrieved the stubs. The seats were across the stadium, in the second row directly opposite the performers' entrance into the arena. Hong stopped to buy two cups of ice cream and two orange sodas, despite Yamei's protest that she shouldn't eat such junk. She ate it anyway, of course. Studying nutrition had never cut anyone's taste for sweets. At the top of the steps leading down to their seats, Lin was waiting with a batch of programs. He was a tall figure, standing almost a head above everyone else in the crowd. Hong had not seen his older brother since early spring, and they embraced.

"You look well," Hong said.

"I took a week of rest at the shore," Lin said casually, as if to imply that everyone took weeks at the shore. "You look sick, you need some relaxation. We're flying to the beach on Wednesday, we've borrowed a house at Beidaihe. Take a couple of days off and come with us. A swim, some good food." He turned to Yamei. "Don't you have Wednesday off? Can you get an extra day? You can tell your parents everything will be properly chaperoned."

"Well..."

"Of course you'll come. And how's your team? Winning for the glory of the people?"

Yamei ignored the sarcasm—or perhaps, Hong thought, didn't even notice it. "Yes, they're going to be champions," she said emphatically.

Lin led them to the seats, where his guests occupied half the row. Hong recognized one of them, a trim square-shouldered cadre in his early sixties with close-cropped graying hair. He was wearing an expensively tailored gray tunic and slacks, and other cadres nearby were sneaking glances, trying to place his face. His name was Deng Bo, and he had been something of a mentor to Lin, especially during Lin's days as a Red Guard. It was Deng, as an emissary from Chairman Mao, who had encouraged Lin and his rowdy comrades to smash up the graveyard at Chu Fu, the birthplace of Confucius. Lin professed regret at his destructive excesses, attributing his behavior during the blood years to the typical rebelliousness of youth, stupidly unleashed by the Chairman. But all Red Guards had not been quite so rebellious as Lin, who had, Hong thought, wallowed in his rampage.

Still, in a curious way, Hong admired his brother. Lin had stepped out of the rejected past with stunning assurance. He was not the same as Yamei, whose faith sprung from believing the future would be better for everyone. Lin simply believed the future would be better for him.

"And you remember Deng Bo," Lin was saying. "Deng, my brother Hong."

"The esteemed Deputy Minister of Defense," said Hong, half-bowing.

Deng Bo smiled broadly, exposing a set of teeth in such perfect condition that they had to be porcelain. A whole mouthful of caps. Dental work of that quality took more than connections and money. A quick trip to Hong Kong, for example, or Tokyo.

Deng reached out and patted Hong on the back. "Yes, of course, what a pleasure to see you again," he said in a booming voice full of unexpected gusto, and then, continuing with a hint of condescension, "the dedicated and hardworking Deputy Director of Public Security. Ferreting out enemies of the people."

"Only an *assistant* deputy director," Hong said. "A position of modest rank and no power."

Deng laughed. "Ah, but none of us have rank. We're all servants of the people."

Lu Lin's other guests joined in the laughter. They joked about rank, Hong thought, but not power, which was a sly joke in itself. Deng kept an office at the Defense Ministry, where officially he supervised policy on troop movements. But his real ties were to the Central Department of Investigation. And who could guess what the CDI did, or where its offices were hidden? Somewhere in a Party building no one had ever seen or heard of. Deng Bo spawned as many rumors as the CDI. In high circles, cadres credited him with aborting the attempted coup against Chairman Mao in 1971. To Hong the story sounded unlikely, given that Deng had ascended to the Army's General Staff only a year earlier. But whether the story was true or not, Hong thought, the cut of Deng's suit and quality of his teeth told as much as anyone needed to know.

Deng Bo moved over, making space for Hong, but before Yamei could take the next seat Lin eased her aside. "Let me have each of you next to me," he said to her, "my brother and his beautiful friend."

A thin-lipped cadre leaned forward and introduced himself as Ho Weiping. "We met at the State Council Conference on Justice," said Comrade Ho enthusiastically. Hong vaguely remembered him, some sort of Security Officer in the Health Ministry. "I was just telling your brother how much I admire your mother"—he turned to the cadre next to him—"the Great Poet of the Revolution," he explained, and then turned back to Hong. "And you write poetry, too, your brother tells me."

"Badly," Hong said.

"What about this crime wave? Is something being done?"

"We're marshaling all our forces to bring it to an end," Hong said.

The conversation dwelled for a while on unemployed hoodlums stealing beer from State factories, a rapist shot at a rally in Taicheng, a rash of burglaries by a gang in Anhui.

Lin leaned close to Hong and whispered. "What's the matter with you? You've got a look on your face as if you're not even here."

"It's nothing, I'm just tired."

"What are you working on that's so secret? When I called, Chan told me you had a major new case, but he wouldn't say what it was."

"An American," Hong whispered back.

Lin was impressed. "An American spy, huh?"

"Keep your voice down," Hong said.

"Well, it's either the best assignment or the worst. Are you going to get transferred to the Special Ministry?"

"I hope not," Hong said.

"Why? The privileges there..." Lin rolled his eyes, sighed at Hong's obtuseness. "I want you to do me a favor," he went on.

"What could I possibly do for you?"

"I want you to move into a new apartment."

Hong stared.

"I'll buy it for you," Lin continued. "One of the new two-bedroom units they're selling for five thousand yuan, in Chongwen. You're going to get married, aren't you? Have another child? You'll need the space."

"Why do you want to buy it for me?"

"They won't let me buy in Beijing. I'll lend you the money, and in a few years we can sell it for a profit and buy you something else."

The new apartments that people could own were in great demand. Anybody with money wanted one. Lin's offer, naturally, was shadowy. Did his brother know any other kind?

"Think about it," Lin said, "we'll split the profits." He hauled up his briefcase from under his seat, unzipped it, and let Hong look in. "I brought you some presents. A Rolex watch, Swiss, with a calendar. And a new cassette recorder, a Sony, one for you and one for Yamei. They play in both directions, you don't have to turn the tape over. We got a case of them from Hong Kong to copy the parts. Not that we will, it's too complicated, but they're useful for... well, you know."

Hong knew. Lin owed much of his success to an uncanny sense of where to distribute "trial goods"—new models of television sets, radios, and tape recorders his factory produced—and samples from abroad. Hong stared at the booty, especially the watch; a good watch was harder to come by than a bicycle. "You don't have to bribe me," Hong said.

"They're *gifts,*" Lin said. He took out the Rolex, set the time, and fastened it onto Hong's wrist.

"In that case, thank you," Hong said. "I need a new watch." Having a brother on the fringes of the black market brought benefits. But looking at the Rolex, Hong felt sullied, as if he'd stolen it.

The cadre named Ho was talking about Shanghai bank lotteries, awarding prizes for large deposits.

"Is it good?" asked one cadre. "All this emphasis on money?"

"Terrible," said another earnestly, fingering his Japanese camera. "Of course we must reform our system, and our peasants should be allowed to grow rich, but at the same time we have to be careful of spiritual pollution from the West. We have to learn from the West, but not be infected. Spiritual pollution, that's a real danger."

A brilliant theorist, Hong thought. He could cover a dozen sides of an argument in a single sentence.

"Yes, spiritual pollution, it's a problem for all of us," Lin chimed in. "Even Hong. He—"

Lin caught himself.

"Yes, even Hong," Deng Bo said. "Didn't I hear that you have a foreign element under surveillance? You have to be careful. An American doctor full of bad ideas."

Doctor? Hong winced as if he'd been slapped. Even if Deng had overheard Lin talking about the American, the word doctor had not been mentioned.

"Yes, an American doctor," he said to Deng. "How did you happen to know?"

"The CDI takes great interest in all foreign guests," Deng replied, smiling again.

It was the first time Hong had heard anyone acknowledge so openly a relationship with the Central Department of Investigation. And from Deng the revelation was anything but accidental. Hong felt Deng studying him, and in the Deputy Defense Minister's eyes he saw a glimmer of pure calculation.

"Maybe you can explain, then," Hong said, "how I was selected for the case."

"What would I know of the Bureau's internal policies? But you're a trustworthy member of the Party, and you can be counted on to do what's right."

The lights dimmed, trumpets blared. A drummer beat a fast tattoo, and out rolled the acrobats, somersaulting to the center of the stadium. Hong touched Lin's hand. "Did Deng know I was coming tonight?"

"He got the tickets," Lin whispered. "He asked me to invite you."

After the acrobats came four lions walking on red balls and leaping through flaming hoops—straight from Shanghai, the announcer said, for the first time in Beijing; another team of gymnasts "shuttling through the rings," leaping from the ground and soaring in swan dives through hoops stacked four high; a Kashmir goat following a girl across a tightrope; a crew of beribboned bicyclists speeding round and round on a single cycle performing "The Peacock in His Pride." Hong leaned forward and looked at Yamei, who was transfixed, her face glowing.

"And now," the deep-voiced announcer intoned, "the world-renowned contortionist and winner of the International Golden Clown Award, our great acrobat Li Liping of the Wuhan Acrobatics Troupe, performing the famous Pagoda of Bowls."

A spotlight narrowed on her. She was barely nineteen. Her hair was pulled back, tied with a marigold in a bun. In her white pants and orange blouse she stood shyly, nodding, acknowledging the audience's recognition. Stagehands wheeled a circular platform behind her. She climbed up, braced herself with one hand on a small padded grip atop a pole, and spread out like a bird, legs thrust behind into the air. With her free hand she began lifting saucers and clear glass bowls filled with different colored waters—blue, green, amber—tossing a set onto the tips of her toes, then another set and another, more onto her head, spinning them all the while, then one final stack of bowls kept in her hand. Dozens upon dozens of saucers and bowls were in motion, spinning light around her.

Deng Bo nudged Hong. In the din of the cheering and the applause, Hong heard his voice but the words were indistinct.

"What?"

In the crisscrossing shadows of the spotlights, Deng's face swam, turning his features ghoulish and skeletal. He winked, his eyes twinkled in satisfaction. He moved closer, talking directly into Hong's ear: "I said, this is a good one for you to watch, isn't it? All this balancing, with a Western spy on your hands."

Lin offered his Shanghai sedan, on loan from the Commerce Ministry, to take Hong and Yamei home. At the curb the driver hoisted their two bicycles into the trunk while Hong thanked Lin for the circus tickets and bid good night to Deng and the other cadres.

Inside the Shanghai, Yamei leaned against Hong. "Your brother's very generous," she said, holding her new cassette player.

"Very," Hong said.

"Don't you like him? A brother is a wonderful blessing, I wish I had one." She leaned closer. "If we have a child, you know, he'll have an uncle. Just think, with everybody having one child, in another few years there won't be any aunts and uncles."

The car passed the black dome of the Planetarium, then swung around the flickering lights at the edge of Zizhuyuan Park. Young couples huddled among the trees. Living with their parents, they had no other trysting places, nowhere they could go to touch each other. The city's parks were everyone's second bedroom. For Hong and Yamei, the question of intimacy was more difficult because privacy was easier. Tradition, even for Yamei, meant that a woman remained a virgin until marriage. And while Yamei had come of age at a time when knowledge of sex, if not more openly talked about, was more common, there was still the risk of pregnancy. Yamei had decided that since she would soon marry Hong, and so long as they kept their lovemaking a secret, she could break with tradition, and through a friend at the Sports Institute found a doctor who supplied her with a birth control device. Should anyone ever discover their secret, they knew the scandal would be disastrous. But they had been careful, and tonight would return to Hong's apartment and make love. Rapidly, of course. The later Yamei was out, the more she would face her parents' questions. She and Hong had learned how to please each other in the shortest time possible. In that respect, Hong thought, making love was like any activity supervised by the Party; it had to be efficient.

"You're in a bad mood," Yamei said.

"No," Hong said.

"Something's wrong. Am I dressed too brazenly? Did I make a bad impression? Did I talk too much?"

Hong sighed. She was so undemanding. All she asked for was his approval. "None of that, honestly."

She was silent for a long while. "Are you in trouble?" she whispered finally.

It was the second time in one week that an innocent had suggested he was in trouble. First his son Bai, in a child's fear of the unknown, and now Yamei, perceptive as only the unafraid can be.

"I've been assigned to a difficult case, that's all," Hong said. "I'm preoccupied."

"You're very good at your job, everybody says you are."

The car pulled up at Hong's building. The driver leapt out and rushed around to open the door for Hong. Hong smiled to himself. The poor driver had no idea how important his passengers might be, despite their bicycles, so he treated them as high cadres just in case.

Hong retrieved his bike from the trunk, told the driver to wait. Crossing the courtyard, he put his arm around Yamei. In his mind he pictured them living in a large house with many windows, and the view from the windows opened onto mist. Two sons played in the backyard. Hong thought about Sun Sheng and wondered what the old man had been searching for. He thought about those pictures in Ostrander's file. Who had decided to alter them, and why? He wondered why Deng Bo was so interested in Ostrander, and he thought about the Defense cadres at Sun Sheng's memorial service. He remembered the recital of foreign travels he had delivered to Ostrander, and then realized that the misty view he imagined for himself and Yamei was nothing he had ever seen except in pictures. It was Victoria Peak in Hong Kong, and then suddenly the Eiffel Tower, then the foggy towers of London in *Great Expectations*.

Yamei was hurrying up the steps. Locking his bike in the courtyard, Hong hurried, too, as if in her arms the momentary dream could come true.

9.

JELLYFISH

On the second floor of the psychiatric wing of Union Medical College five patients with reactive disorders, otherwise known as depressives, assembled paper pigeons.

"These patients have an illness, but not a disease," said the nurse-attendant, who led Hong down the hall. "There is nothing physically wrong with them. We are therefore trying to determine why they have an illness."

"Excuse me, what's the difference?"

"A disease is something that makes you sick. An illness is antisocial behavior."

She might have been reciting an old Party document, Hong thought. He wondered how she would diagnose his father. "Why are they making pigeons?"

"Therapy," the nurse said. "When they work with their hands, making paper toys for the children, they're less unhappy."

Hong glanced in at the depressives, lolling over their benches. They folded paper, stared off into space. Being here, Hong thought, would depress anyone.

"Are they antisocial, do they assault people, break things...?"

"Oh no, never. They're too drugged to do anything like that."

"Drugged by what?"

"Electroshock, a dose of electricity to the brain. That changes their attitude, makes them happy again. Of course the most serious cases are sent to Shanghai. Ours are special patients, assigned to us for experiments."

Union Medical College and Hospital used to be Capital Hospital, and before that, during the Cultural Revolution, Anti-Imperialist Hospital, and now the original name had been restored. The loudspeaker above Hong's head blared: "Supervisor Shen, please report to the second-floor reception desk."

"That's me," the nurse-attendant said, running down the hall. "I'll be right back."

Young students in white coats scuffed briskly by. Researchers, oblivious of strangers and students alike, rushed back and forth between a laboratory at one end of the hall and an office at the other. From the lab issued the *blip-blip-blip* of electronic equipment. The medical college's psychiatric division was a cheerfully busy place, Hong thought, the walls freshly whitewashed and decorated with posters declaring WASH ALL FRUIT BEFORE EATING, PROTECT FROM GERMS, the tiled floor clean and in good repair. And yet there was something strangely sad about it, too: all the students were very young and all the teachers old, a whole generation of teachers and students was missing. For twenty years mental wards had been filled not with the ill, but with radicals. There had been no psychiatry. Chairman Mao had abolished it as a "bogus bourgeois science."

The *blip-blip* from the lab grew louder. Hong peered through the open door. Five doctors surrounded an old woman strapped to a table. Acupuncture needles had been inserted into her skull at the top of her spine. Wires ran from the needles to a small generator, and more wires looped across a round green television screen to shaved patches on the woman's head, connected not to needles but to green suction cups. A jagged line, rising and falling mountains, wriggled across the screen.

A doctor holding a clipboard recited a list of numbers: "Twenty-five, fifty-two, nine, one hundred and six..." On and on the list went. When the doctor stopped, the old woman began reciting numbers back to him—different ones.

One of the doctors noticed Hong. He ran to the door and started to close it.

"What's going on in there?" Hong asked, putting a hand on the door.

"Research," the doctor said, blocking Hong's view and pushing the door toward him.

"What kind of research?" Hong asked.

"Research," the doctor said again, "now, please, this door should not be open."

The door closed and the doctor taped a sheet of paper over the little square window at the center. Hong rubbed his forehead. His fever had gotten worse, his head throbbed as if a small restless insect were nesting behind his eyes. He should have stayed home in bed and sent Chan, or even the Little Monk, for an interview that probably would yield nothing. It was the fear of being interrogated, he told himself, that kept him going: why are your files so thin? Why did you not pursue the American more thoroughly? And yet something was missing from this explanation. With the case of Peter Ostrander he had the disquieting sense of pursuing a quarry who would never run, who had no motive to run.

He glanced back at the closed lab door, then walked to the security desk at the far end of the hall and picked up a phone. The desk attendant looked up from a pile of charts.

"That telephone is not for public use," he said sharply.

"I'm not the public," Hong said.

"Just a minute now," the clerk protested, standing.

Hong was feeling uncommonly irritated. He unfolded his Public Security identification and shoved it at the clerk's nose. The clerk fell back into his seat without a word.

An operator answered. Hong gave his name, working unit, and the number of his office.

It rang twice before Chan answered.

"Do you have Ostrander's schedule?" Hong asked.

"Hold on," Chan said.

Hong listened to the rustling of papers and glanced down at the forms on the clerk's desk. *Candidate for Admission,* it said at the top, then *Date of Birth, Working Unit, Father, Mother, Education.* Which gave Hong an idea. Stupid, he told himself. Why didn't I think of it before?

The nurse-attendant returned. "We can continue now."

"In a minute," Hong said.

Chan came back on the line. "I have it here. He's at a seminar at Beijing University until two."

"Yes, I know. What's the subject?"

"'Brain Dysfunction and Learning Disorders,' whatever that means."

Hong looked at Nurse Shen, who was sifting through a pile of index cards and studiously pretending not to listen.

"About that fruitless search you made," Hong said.

"What are you talking about?"

"Three days ago."

"Someone's listening," Chan said.

"That's perceptive of you," Hong said.

"You mean the file on Ostrander's father."

"Yes, but what about the other half?"

"Other half?" Chan paused. "Oh, the mother."

"That's right. Isn't there a name attached?"

More rustling of papers. "Greene," Chan said, "as in the color."

"See what you can find on that."

"I'll try the Academy," Chan said.

"And elsewhere."

"Hong, the visa files were burned long ago."

"Elsewhere," Hong repeated. The earthquake in seventy-six probably destroyed everything, but it was worth a call.

"Oh, I see, Tangshan Municipality, where Ostrander was born. Very good. If any records survived the earthquake. I'll see what I can turn up."

Hong put the phone down and followed the nurse to the end of the hall, then up a short flight of stairs. He thought about the file on Dr. Yan, the director of psychiatric research, that he had read earlier in the morning. The old man had been educated abroad, in France and Austria. How on earth, Hong wondered, had he returned to his former post after his own subordinates had denounced him, crippled him, and then ordered him to clean toilets?

"Your appointment from Public Security," the nurse announced, turning through a door paneled in translucent white glass. "Deputy Director Lu Hong."

Hong let the misstatement of his title hang in the air; every increment of intimidation would help with a man predisposed to hating him. From his chair by the window Dr. Yan looked up as Hong entered, studied him for the briefest second, then rose haltingly, bracing himself on the edge of his desk. He wore half-lens reading glasses and a white coat, his only obvious sign of rank. He was slight and gnarled, bent and rounded, but not, Hong thought, by age. His silver hair was parted in the middle and swept back from his forehead, worn defiantly long in the manner of a young hooligan.

The doctor hobbled to the door and with obvious strain began pulling a chair to the desk for Hong to sit. Outwardly he revealed no anxiety at the presence of an officer from Public Security, but Hong noticed that except for the first moment, that quick assessment, Dr. Yan had avoided meeting his eyes. "You've come about Ostrander," he said.

"Yes," Hong said, and tried to help him with the chair.

"I can do it, thank you," Dr. Yan said, sliding the chair forward. "You see, with exercise and concentration, I can do nearly anything."

The doctor's office had the atmosphere of another time and place. High bookcases with carved moldings and pillars lined the walls, and an old Imperial trunk with painted panels of yellow dragons served as a tea table. Foreign medical journals lay open on the trunk. It reminded Hong of his father's university office, the one they had taken away and which Lu Yaomin had never cared to reclaim. Or rather, had never been in any condition to reclaim. Dr. Yan's well-worn books, the ivory pen holder and inkwell on the desk, the framed photographs from his student days, these were comforting, if only for the knowledge that some old men still had mementos they treasured. Dr. Yan lit a cigarette and offered one to Hong—a British cigarette, a 555. "For guests," said the doctor, limping to his desk, and in this case, Hong suspected, guests meant police. Lighting Hong's cigarette, the doctor held his own in the old-fashioned way, squeezed between thumb and forefinger.

"Tell me about the American's work here," Hong said.

"He's a very good choice, an excellent choice, for an exchange with us," Dr. Yan said, speaking to the wall over Hong's head and answering a question entirely of his own making.

"What does he do?"

Dr. Yan's answer was a long time coming. This is how they always are, Hong thought. Measuring words, the rank of their inquisitor, danger. In the grass and the trees, the saying went, everything seems a soldier. When Dr. Yan finally spoke his voice was tentative and breathy. "He...he observes. Our students treat many kinds of patients. Under a teacher's supervision, naturally. Mental problems, weakness of the nerves, depression. Ostrander has brought us many Western books on the subject. He joins our faculty meetings, he observes patients, makes suggestions."

"And that's all," Hong said.

Dr. Yan hesitated and flicked a glance toward the door. "Yes," he said, "that's all."

What had Dr. Yan seen behind the door? A shadow? Hong cupped a hand over his ear and leaned toward the wall. The hint of a smile opened on Dr. Yan's face as he clenched his cigarette between his teeth and expelled a gust of smoke.

"It's a beautiful day," Hong said. "Let's walk in the courtyard. If that's agreeable to you."

Dr. Yan struggled to his feet and retrieved a black cane from under his desk. Hong stopped him by holding up a palm, then inched quietly toward the door. He listened for anyone moving in the hall, peered at the translucent glass pane, then flung the door open. Nurse Shen, bearing a tray with a pot of tea, practically stumbled in.

Chagrined, she recovered quickly. "I was bringing you tea and cakes," she said pleasantly.

"We were just going outside," Hong said, and held the door for Dr. Yan. The old man moved methodically, at his own pace, but with a spring in his step as he used the cane like a walking stick to propel himself into the hall.

"I knew your parents in the fifties," he said when they reached the top of the steps. "Your mother is the poet."

"Yes," Hong said.

"Take my arm, please." Hong obliged, and Dr. Yan hopped down the stairs, holding his bad leg in the air. "It's surprising, your being in Public Security. Your brother runs a factory, is that right? I would have expected their sons to be artists or teachers."

"Children imitate their parents in all the important ways," Hong said as they reached the bottom of the stairwell. "And not necessarily to their advantage."

Dr. Yan nodded his amused approval. "Very good. You see, you are a teacher. Anyway, I liked your parents."

In the courtyard, under a covered walkway, they sat in a trellised arbor. A strong breeze rippled the leaves.

"Perhaps you know who that nurse watches me for," Dr. Yan said. "Many of them watch me. Is one of them working for you?"

"Not that I know of," Hong said.

Dr. Yan gave him a dubious grin. "I don't believe you, actually. I'd like to believe you, but I don't." His gaze drifted to the top of the arbor, a tangle of vines filtering shafts of sunlight. "There's no one else here to watch but me. All the other doctors, all my friends, are dead. They killed themselves."

"Tell me about Ostrander," Hong said.

"What can I tell you? He's a good doctor. It will be nice to have him here. Someone who doesn't ask about our astounding psychics in Dazhu County." He turned to Hong, raised his voice. "Psychics! Children who can read pieces of paper from behind screens! If you want research money, find yourself a few of them."

"I'm sure such research is—"

"Is stupid," Dr. Yan interrupted. "Twelve-year-old Wang," he went on in a mocking voice, "can read her mother's shopping list through her apron pockets. She gets mental messages. Let's test her, let's learn her secret." He snorted. "Eggs gone rotten. Garbage. The Vital Energy Masters, they call the children."

In his office Dr. Yan had been meek, his rage hidden in a

locked closet. Away from prying ears he was all bitterness.

"About Ostrander," Hong put in.

"What do you know about the brain?"

"Whatever I need to know to think," Hong said.

"As it happens, that's not a bad answer. When you have to know something, it's there, somewhere in your brain. What I am interested in, and what Ostrander is interested in, is how your brain finds what it needs." Dr. Yan stretched his cane out and drew figures in the dust on the walkway—two circles with a dot between them. "We remember and forget because of nerve connections. The circles are cells, the dot is a terminal that transmits electrical energy. If the terminal doesn't work, if the chemical isn't there to make it work, there are no connections."

"So all thought is chemical?" Hong asked.

"Superb!" Dr. Yan slapped the tip of his cane on the ground. "For a bureaucrat you have a better mind than you deserve. Yes, all thought is chemical, and also no, it is not. Both are true. Take the jellyfish, for example. A primitive nervous system, all cells are equal. It has no past, no future. It responds to stimuli, but it makes no choices. The ultimate freedom, you might say. Now man, on the other hand, has a highly developed brain, a masterwork of nature. Try to build a model of it, you will end up like my depressives upstairs. You will go crazy." He took a breath. "The human brain is not like the jellyfish. It takes past and future into account. Whereas the jellyfish simply responds."

Hong cleared his throat. "About Ostrander," he said again. "The Academy of Sciences approved his application for this exchange. Could there be any reason other than his scientific credentials?"

"You're responding, not thinking," said Dr. Yan. "Don't be a jellyfish, we have too many of them already. The whole country is a jellyfish." He tapped the ground with his cane. "Here, look in the dirt, these cells. Can I stimulate them with electricity? In the West they have discovered a chemical that makes the nerve cells grow, changes them or makes them work better, or even makes new connections altogether. Here, watch." He smudged one of the dust circles. "What happened? Has the cell gone bad? Or is there a shortage of the enzyme?"

Chemicals in the brain, Hong thought. Connections by enzymes. If only the connections he had to make were a matter of enzymes.

"I want to find out," the doctor went on, "if we can combine what they know in the West with what I know here. I want to see where memories are kept in the brain, how we call them forth when we need them. But my research isn't fashionable. Those who give the money see no potential results. I tell them I can cure the effects of old age, of stroke, of brain damage."

Hong wondered idly if old people would be well served by better memories. What many of them needed were better ways to forget. "Can you do what you promise?" he asked.

"Perhaps, perhaps not." He leaned toward Hong. "I will tell you a secret," he said in a harsh whisper. "Aren't you a protector of secrets? Do you have a guard at your mouth? I have been asking for three years to have a Western scientist. At first, the retarded pigs at the Academy called my work foolish. Then they declared it too secret. An astounding transformation, a triumph of shriveled minds, from foolish to secret. Suddenly, now, after three years and for no reason, they deliver to me Ostrander. A gift from heaven, a most precious gift. Ostrander, who is perfect for this work."

"If your research is so secret," Hong said, "he may have come to steal it."

"I desperately hope so," Dr. Yan replied. "If he takes records of my work back with him, maybe he'll write about it. Then the Academy might give me more help and more money. Whatever you do, try not to take him away from me."

Hong stood. "Ostrander thinks I'm his guide from the Academy. He'll expect to see me here occasionally. If you detect anything unusual about him, call me." He took out his card, laid it in Dr. Yan's hand.

Dr. Yan slipped the card into his breast pocket and levered himself to his feet. "But don't you see?" he said. "There's already something extraordinarily unusual about Ostrander."

"What's that?" Hong asked.

Dr. Yan smiled. "He's here."

• • •

The speechmaking of puppets was like a warm bath to
Hong. At the weekly departmental meetings he could listen
to them for hours. Actually, as with political education sessions, he sat in the back of the room and didn't listen at all,
simply let the lull of their voices wash over him while he
read *People's Daily* or wrote reports.

At the front of the room stood Political Commissar Zhu
Gang. His salt-and-pepper hair, freshly cut, was so short
you could see his scalp. How could Kuang fall in love with
him? To be replaced in her affections by this monkey, this
subhuman creature, it was enough to make Hong question
his own humanity. If she judged Zhu so badly, Hong
thought, what had she seen in me?

Comrade Zhu, alternating as if he had two mouths on a
single face, described the Bureau's current major cases
and then their ideological implications. It was truly a feat
of devotion, melding the latest Party line with decisions
made under an earlier line. Last year anyone who di-
verted State goods to his own use was charged under Part
1, Chapter 2, Article 15, Section 1 of the Constitution,
"Counterrevolutionary Crimes." This year the charge fell
under Section 2, "Ordinary Criminal Cases which call for
life imprisonment and the death sentence." Illegal economic activity thus became a crime against people instead
of the Revolution. Out of such fine distinctions would
arise greater democracy.

Zhu had moved down the list of assistant deputy directors
and reached Hong's cases, the ones he had turned over to
Chan for distribution to the investigators. Hong looked up.
Everyone seemed impressed by the reports on the German
lawyer and the bicycle thieves.

"And are there any other cases under Assistant Deputy
Director Lu Hong's jurisdiction?" came a raised voice from
the corner.

Hong lifted his head. The questioner was Tan Shu, a
beefy ex-Army corporal who scrutinized the political aspects
of all prosecutions. Tan was Mister Good-Good, a loyal and
hardworking Party member, but a little thickheaded.

"No," Hong said, "no other cases."

"Are you certain we've been informed of all of them?"
Tan Shu asked.

What was he getting at? Maybe he had heard about Ostrander. But why would he try to discuss a case that Wei Ye had declared secret?

"Yes, I'm certain," Hong said. "Comrade Zhu has covered all cases in my department."

Zhu announced the meeting completed, and the cadres filed out into the hall. There was talk of the Bureau erecting its own new apartment building, of recent directives on older cadres being forced to retire. Hong was halfway to his office when Tan Shu fell in step beside him.

"Assistant Deputy Director Lu Hong?"

"Yes, Comrade Tan, how are you?"

"Please, don't speak so loud. I wanted to ask you, were you in the Bureau last Friday, when the Director of Military Affairs became ill?"

"No, sadly, I wasn't."

"Then you didn't see the ambulance."

Hong felt the muscles in the back of his neck tighten. "The ambulance?" he repeated. "I'm afraid I don't understand. If I wasn't here, of course I didn't see it."

"The ambulance was summoned from Union Hospital, but it took Comrade Sun to the Hospital of Infectious Diseases."

"So?"

"Why would they take him, if he was ill, so far away? Union Hospital is only a five-minute ride. But Infectious Diseases is half an hour. I thought, perhaps...well, if no one else was investigating this, I thought you might have been assigned to an inquiry into how Comrade Sun died."

Many things went through Hong's mind, and all in an instant. First, that Comrade Tan was normally not bright enough to have thought this up himself, but also that Tan was too cautious to become anyone's informant. Second, Hong realized that for the past three days the Ostrander case had totally occupied his attention. Was it a coincidence, and nothing more, that he had been assigned to Ostrander so shortly after his visit to the communications exchange to see the logbooks? What conceivable relationship could there be, he wondered, between Sun Sheng's death and the appearance of Peter Ostrander? Hong thought of the Rule of the Golden Mean: If A is true, B is not wrong either.

For Tan Shu, he decided, a total dismissal was best. "Your imagination is running away with you," he said gently but with firmness. "You shouldn't start rumors like this. I happen to know that Comrade Sun had not been feeling well. And Union Hospital doesn't treat serious infections. There's no reason for an inquiry into Comrade Sun's death."

Tan bowed his head. "I'm sorry, I'm very sorry," he said, backing away. "You're right . . . it's destructive speculation . . . please forget I said anything . . ." And he was gone, tripping over himself in his rush to get away, back to the building's north wing.

Why not seek his help? Why lie to him out of fear? In a mood of self-accusation, Hong hurried to his office. The phone was ringing when he opened the door and he snatched it up. It was Li Junhua at the News Agency.

"Hong, I've looked a little further for you into that Ming Dynasty story."

"Did you find out the author's name?"

"No, even the editors weren't told. But it definitely came from the Central Committee."

"Someone currently active?"

"Yes, it seems so."

"And the actual subject matter?"

Junhua had no answer. An obscure power struggle, he said, of which the cadres at the News Agency were ignorant, and wished to remain so. Hanging up, Hong was relieved that his mother was in no way implicated. Her only friends on the Central Committee were due to "retire voluntarily."

It was strange, though, that whoever wrote the *People's Daily* story preferred to remain anonymous. In a struggle for power one wanted allies. To find them, you put a finger to the wind, sent a public message, and waited for the echo. If the echo came, you carried on. If it didn't, you forgot about the message and hoped everyone else did. The same thing happened at the beginning of every spiritual pollution campaign. It was a way of testing the Party's mood. But to send a message and not leave a return address, this was crazy. How could your allies know who you were?

Which meant, Hong thought, that whoever wrote the Ming Dynasty story had his allies in place before the article appeared. A reasonable deduction except for one thing. If you had allies, and the struggle was joined, there was nothing to gain by publicizing it.

Hong searched through his top drawer for ration coupons. He had been invited by Yamei's parents to dinner— probably so they could be assured that the trip to the beach in Beidaihe would be well chaperoned. He thought about what to bring them. Wine? No, they had plenty of wine. A can of rapeseed oil would be better. He had coupons to spare. He stood and straightened the map of Beijing, which was listing to the south. Chan had inked in the new subway, a circle crossing the old East-West link at both ends, and the extension of the Third Ring Road, completing a circle almost parallel to the inner two. Circles upon circles. Mirroring my mind, Hong thought. He picked up Ostrander's file, checked the date his guide from Defense had been removed from the case: it was the day following Hong's visit to the telephone logs.

Standing over his desk, Hong scribbled a chronology.

First, Sheng's death, perhaps related to nothing.

Second, a look at the telephone logs, a visit to Young Jin, and those empty days on Sheng's calendar.

Then, the assignment to Ostrander, and the *People's Daily* story about current power struggles. Or were they old struggles, Hong asked himself, that had left fourteen cadres dead?

Shift them around? Link them? It was purposeless.

The door opened and Chan sauntered in. "Your day for successful colors," he said, waving an envelope. "Greene, Elizabeth, mother of Ostrander. Who was listening at the hospital?"

"A nurse with a nose much too large for her face," Hong said, taking the envelope and peeling back the clasp. "Did you call Tangshan?"

"The birth was only recorded there. Ostrander was born in Choukoutien."

"So!" Hong said triumphantly. "Choukoutien! The site of archaeological excavations. That's what I call progress." More than progress, he thought to himself. Ostrander's parents had been in Choukoutien at the time of the Revolution. Now their son returns, apparently summoned by cadres from Defense just as an old revolutionary dies. They were at Sun Sheng's memorial, Hong thought, the ministers from Defense. He opened the envelope and scanned the record on *Ostrander (Greene), Elizabeth.*

"Choukoutien," Chan said. "Why is that progress?"

The door squeaked open, and the Little Monk, Wu Keping, stood with his hand on the knob, waiting for an invitation.

"Come in," Hong said. "Liu Chan has just discovered some interesting information on Ostrander."

"Evidence of accomplices?" the Monk asked.

"Who knows?" Hong said. "Ostrander was born in Choukoutien, where his father, we assume, was digging up fossils. Unless he was trying to reopen the limestone quarry."

"Which is unlikely," Wu suggested.

"Extremely," Hong said. "Chan, go on."

"Are you serious?"

"Yes, we can use Wu's perceptions here."

Chan stared at Hong with utter astonishment.

"Go on, continue," Hong said with a wry smile.

"As you wish," Chan said, and unspoken, *It's your neck.* "The mother entered at Shanghai in 1930, accompanied by the father. In 1933 she has a son, and in 1941 she leaves with the son from Beijing. The file says nothing about the father leaving."

"It wouldn't," Hong replied. "It's not his file. We can assume he didn't go with her. But he has no file, correct? The mother is documented, the father isn't."

"Not now, anyway," Chan said, taking the point.

"Why is there no file on the father?" asked Wu.

"A good question for which there is no answer," Hong said. "If a man has no file, then he doesn't exist. So we have a son with a nonexistent father."

"Like a lot of people," Chan said.

Hong picked up the file on Ostrander's mother. "Chan, have you been to the museum in Choukoutien?"

"Never, the road is terrible and it's a long ride—what is it? forty or fifty kilometers at least—and I'm a dullard. Museums are strictly for students and tourists."

"I was there last year," interjected the Little Monk. "With my nephew. All young children should be taken there. It's very important in understanding the glorious history of the

Chinese people. At Choukoutien scientists found fossils of the first intelligent beings in this part of the planet. And also evidence that we were perhaps the earth's first intelligent race."

"Some of us," said Chan. "Okay, so the father was digging up bones, we'll take that for granted. What could the son have to do with excavations for old bones fifty years ago?"

"They're missing," Hong said.

"What's missing?"

Hong turned to the Monk. "Assistant Investigator Wu, perhaps you can explain this to Chan, who was denied the proper opportunities for studying history."

"The fossils of our ancestors were lost," the Little Monk said. "They have been missing since the war. You must go to the museum at Choukoutien to study this matter. It's your patriotic obligation."

Hong turned to Chan. "The Americans were trying to ship the fossils out during the Japanese invasion. No one knows where they are."

"Slower, please," Chan said. "What's the barbarians' invasion got to do with anything?"

Hong turned to the Little Monk. "Assistant Investigator Wu?"

"Well, I'm a little unclear on the war. Maybe I should research the subject."

"Yes, do that," Hong said. "Start right now."

The Little Monk was pleased. "I'll have a report for you tomorrow before the reception." He was halfway out the door when he turned and handed Hong an envelope. "I almost forgot, I brought the schedule for you."

"Reception?" Chan asked.

"At the Foreign Ministry," Hong said. "I'm going with Ostrander. The food will be good."

When the door closed Chan waited, listened, then spun around to Hong. "You have to go to bed, go home instantly. Your illness is affecting you."

"I don't have an illness," Hong said. "What I have is a disease."

"Don't give me political arguments. What in Heaven's name do you think you're doing? That frog will go back to Wei Ye and croak. You moved the case forward."

"Nothing is what it seems," Hong said. "No file on the father, fossils missing for forty years, a translator from Defense who is assigned to Ostrander and then reassigned for no reason—"

"His English wasn't good enough."

"Maybe. Anyway, the more complications the better. Wei Ye will see that she's competing with Defense and she'll want somebody new on the case. Did you get Sheng's death certificate?"

"I'm working on it," Chan said. "And aside from moving the case forward, you slandered...well, I don't know who you slandered, but when you start talking about missing files, the Ministry of Defense obstructing an investigation....The axe has to fall somewhere. And it's liable to bounce back right into you."

"I didn't hear myself suggesting that Defense was obstructing an investigation," Hong said innocently.

"You're not being honest with me. You're not trying to lose this case. You're getting in deeper. Ostrander is nothing but trouble, he's here to find some...some what? Fossils?"

Hong seemed ready to dispute Chan's assessment of his motives, but instead retreated, chewed his lip thoughtfully for a moment, and put the file on Ostrander's mother back in the envelope. "You can return this," he said, standing and laying it on Chan's desk. "I'm going to buy some cooking oil."

"Tell me what this is all about," Chan said.

Hong folded two ration coupons into his pocket. "As soon as I know myself," he said.

A cadre from the State Energy Commission finds a husband at the People's Bank of China. Immediately they are confronted by a difficult housing choice. One floor in an old Chongwen District mansion supplied by the bank, small but elegant, or a West City four-room high-rise apartment supplied by the Energy Commission. Four rooms in a modern high-rise made more sense. That kind of luxury came once in a lifetime. But Yamei's mother, Ru Jie, had argued for the elegant mansion floor. Less austere, she said, and more breezes. Yamei's father, Cao Yun, had won out with the high-rise, and it was a good thing, too. The mansion had been torn down and all the inhabitants relocated to new towers overlooking the Lianmaqiao Ditch, which in the summer was a fetid swamp. In the meantime, Cao Yun had been able to buy an air conditioner for the West City flat. Yamei's parents had one bedroom, her paternal grandparents another, and Yamei the third.

Hong heard the television in the background as the door opened. "They've turned on the air conditioner just for you," Yamei whispered. "And be careful, don't make any political criticism of the maid."

Hong was sure he hadn't heard correctly. "Maid?"

"They hired her yesterday. To cook and do the shopping and clean. She used to work at a plastics factory somewhere in Chaoyang, but it closed."

Hong was astounded. It was well known and little talked about that high cadres and important intellectuals had domestic servants, but middle-level cadres like the Caos? How could they afford help?

Cao Yun and Ru Jie bustled to the door, where they accepted the gift of the cooking oil. "Exactly what we needed," Jie said, instantly heading back to her kitchen. "How thoughtful of you."

"Why are you keeping him out here?" said Cao Yun, who pulled Hong into the living room. The air conditioning was going full blast.

"What a relief from the heat," Hong said.

Yun turned the television set off. "Yes, it was a smart purchase," he said. "Except for the electric bills."

"But the rates are coming down," Yamei said enthusiastically. "We'll be able to use it more often."

They had a comfortable life and wanted the same for their daughter. However doubtful they might be about Hong's age and his divorce, he offered most of the "ten musts"—a good salary, a revolutionary background, access to special stores, no poor relatives to support, a bicycle, and some day, with luck, his own chauffeur-driven car.

Before Hong and Yamei's father had even sat down to have a glass of wine, raised voices could be heard from the kitchen. Cao Yun nodded at his daughter. "Go help your mother, please."

After Yamei had gone, Hong politely asked Yun about his

job, which led to a discussion of long days negotiating letters of credit for international trade. His wife Jie had also been unusually busy. These mild complaints, Hong understood, were an introduction to discussing the need for household help. As if punctuating the end of Cao Yun's speech, more loud voices came from the kitchen, and Yun fumbled to explain the maid.

"We have hired...that is, we are doing our part to alleviate unemployment. We've discovered a woman who is out of work and who wants to help with our housekeeping. Jie is having a little difficulty getting along with her."

"How did you find her?" Hong asked, then realized the question had been posed incorrectly. "That is, how did she realize you needed help?"

"Oh, it was most convenient. Through a notice at the bank. She had worked in a factory that closed, and many of their clerks and janitors needed employment. So the Director General posted a sign."

"Fortuitous," Hong said.

"And you understand that it's not exploitation."

"Of course not," Hong said.

"In fact, we're making the country stronger by hiring... by providing a position for her. Her husband is ill, and she would have no additional income." He was uneasy with his own excuse. "Look, we have the money, and she needs the money, so it's the right thing to do. We both work hard, and we never have time to shop. And the girl isn't very smart, this is a good job for her."

"I'm sure it is," Hong said. "You're to be commended."

Yun scowled, puffed his chest. "Hong, I wonder if you don't approve, if you don't consider it egalitarian."

"No, Yun, not at all. Please don't feel any need to justify yourself. We had a maid when I was growing up. And you and Jie work very hard."

Yun leapt up from his chair. "Wait," he said excitedly, "there's something I want to show you." He pawed through a stack of magazines on the breakfront and produced a copy of *Economic Daily*, published from Shanghai. "Please, read this."

It was an article by a municipal official entitled "Housework, the Distribution of Labor, and Perspectives on Employment." The author explained that while maids and cooks had once been considered decadent and bourgeois, current urban life required so much time for work and study that even middle-level cadres inevitably had to hire household help.

The article served an important purpose; Yun would be able to justify himself if the current atmosphere changed. "This is excellent," Hong said, setting the newspaper aside. "But I'm amazed you can afford her."

"The bank gave me a stipend," Yun confessed, almost abjectly, "thirty-two yuan a month. So we can pay her three days a week, and she can find someone else for the other three."

The argument in the kitchen turned out badly. The maid, not yet accustomed to her position, continued to resist joining the Caos for dinner. But if a servant ate alone, an employer might be branded an exploiter. In the end, Jie's and Yun's pleading failed, and so, without the maid at the table, dinner was served. Yun's parents had gone north for three weeks to visit their younger son, and two mouths fewer meant a large and splendid meal—abalone, squab and mushroom soup, pork dumplings, crabapple wine.

"Where will you stay in Beidaihe?" Yun asked, concerned for his daughter's honor.

Yamei's mother frowned. "Don't bother Hong with such questions."

"At an Army general's house," Hong said. "A friend of my brother."

"We'll have our own rooms," Yamei put in quickly.

"An Army general?" asked Jie. "The one whose son Lin knew in the sixties?"

"No, that was Wang Tai," Hong said. "He's still in prison."

There was a silence. The Caos preferred to pretend that everyone except the real troublemakers had been rehabilitated.

"But he was a radical," said Cao Yun.

"Not really," said Hong. "He made the mistake of criticizing the high command for corruption." He sipped his wine. "Let a hundred flowers bloom," he said in deep serious tones, quoting Chairman Mao, then added sardonically, "and let them die, too."

The silence grew worse, and Hong instantly regretted his attempt at levity.

"Well, let's have the watermelon," Yamei said.

Her mother lit up. Yamei had just solved every problem in the world. "Yes, watermelon, that's a good idea."

Jie glanced anxiously around the table, then stood and went into the kitchen, where again she could be heard asking the maid to join them, at least for this last course. Finally they appeared, Jie carrying the watermelon and the maid, a homely girl with heavy-lidded eyes, meekly clutching the bottom of her apron. Jie introduced her and she took a seat next to Hong.

Yun smiled at his wife. "Now isn't this better? We all eat together."

The maid served the watermelon slices on separate plates, passing them around the table.

"Much better," Jie said, accepting her plate and smiling broadly at Hong. Everyone was silent for another long moment, and the maid nervously worked at straightening the tablecloth. "Yes, this is good," Jie went on. "After all, this is the egalitarian way."

10.

THINKING MEN

To judge by the food at official receptions, everyone in Beijing ate like an emperor and every meal was a work of art. At each table in the banquet hall of the Foreign Ministry the hors d'oeuvres platter was a crane: the skin of a watermelon for the crown, carved slices of chicken for its feathers, a sliced lime-preserved egg for its eye, strips of pickled cucumber for the legs. Napkins, propped in the water glasses, were folded to resemble peonies, peacocks, swans.

Ostrander was thrilled. "This is fabulous," he said. "How do they do it?"

"They go to school," Hong said, leading Ostrander to a table near the dais. "We have more than three hundred master chefs in China. To become a master chef takes twelve years. Every year our chefs travel abroad—"

"Wait, wait," Ostrander said, laughing. "I was just asking about the napkins."

"Oh, for that there are special kitchen apprentices. To become an apprentice—"

Ostrander laughed louder.

"Am I funny?" Hong asked.

"Forgive me," Ostrander said. "Americans love facts, but I don't think anyone loves them as much as the Chinese."

At the entrance to the room Hong saw Wu Keping searching the crowd. What was he doing here?

"Excuse me," Hong said, "I'll return in a moment."

Hong started for the door and the Little Monk rushed over, holding his briefcase high.

"I've finished the research on Choukoutien," he said proudly. "Here are the papers."

"I don't think I'll be needing them right now," Hong said. "Why not leave them at the office?"

"I'll give them to the desk attendant to keep. I have to stay here."

"Why?"

"Because of my instructions ... that is, to help you."

"I don't need any help."

"But I am available."

This afternoon Hong wanted Ostrander to himself. He wanted Ostrander to have a few glasses of wine, maybe even a shot or two of maotai. Maotai was sorghum alcohol, one hundred and sixty proof and clear as purified water. Foreigners swigged it in one gulp, like their Chinese hosts, and it loosened their tongues. "Listen," Hong said to the Little Monk, "I'll be gone tomorrow and Thursday. I want you to make a survey of all foreigners in Beijing who are working at hospitals. Ostrander might have accomplices."

It was a silly task. Ostrander would be too clever to be tripped up by such contacts. But the Little Monk would be occupied for hours.

"I'll start right after the reception," he said.

"No, start now. It's a big job, and I want a report on Monday."

The Little Monk looked doubtful. He was like a cricket in a game played by old men in the park. Run in this direction, run in the other. He was at the bidding of so many masters that he could never be sure which to serve first.

"I believe I can help you best by remaining here."

The hammer was failing. Honey might work. "This study of foreign hospital workers is essential," Hong said, and then, an instant invention, "I've had a request from the Minister to recommend cadres for the new Special Security branch. You could become a candidate."

The scales in the Little Monk's tiny mind jiggled up and down. What a balancing act! "The Minister himself?" he asked. "You heard directly from the Minister?"

"Naturally," said Hong. "How else could he get my recommendations?"

"I'd better get to work on that survey of doctors," Wu said.

A lie, a complete fabrication. Hong had never so much as had an audience with the Minister, let alone been asked for an opinion on the talents of fellow cadres. It pained him— deceiving this child who would face Wei Ye's displeasure, deceiving in the pretense of duty. He crossed the room and took his seat at the table with Ostrander, four other foreign experts, and their translators from the hospitals, universities, and language institutes. There was a great deal of laughter, smiles for everyone, as the meal began.

"Why do the Chinese smile so much?" Ostrander asked.

"It's what makes us different from the Russians," Hong said. "In adversity, we smile. When we're embarrassed, we smile. When we don't understand a joke, we laugh and then we smile. The Russians, on the other hand, who have as much adversity as we do, are always sullen. Some people say it's because they drink too much, but I think it's their nature."

After repeated toasts with wine and maotai, served afresh with each course, the foreign experts grew thick-tongued and voluble. Ostrander mentioned that his late wife had been a poet, and one of the other translators mentioned that Hong's mother, too, had been a poet. Hong was furious, he could have reached across the table and slapped the idiot, who certainly must have known that Hong had been assigned to Ostrander by Public Security, not the Academy. Hong had not yet regaled Ostrander with fictitious tales of his humble peasant background, his mother and father the hardworking farmers, and it was the flap-mouthed incompetent's good luck. He would have soon been translating for

Ewenki deer hunters on some frozen patch of ground in Heilongjiang.

The gaffe drew everyone's attention—except for the foreigners, who were mildly drunk—and when Hong coughed loudly the other translators and scientists picked up the cue. They talked about Albert Einstein, the difficulties of translating technical journals, the problems of intellectuals in all countries. They talked about the meaning of names, and a young chemistry researcher gave the English translation of his—Defender of the Peace.

"And yours is Red," Ostrander said to Hong. "Hong means Red."

"Yes, I was born with the Revolution," Hong replied. "It's a good name." Given to him by his parents, he thought but didn't say, as a talisman, a form of protection.

"It's an American name, too," Ostrander said, "a nickname for people with red hair."

"Nickname?" Hong asked.

"It's something used among friends."

"Oh yes, we have them, too."

"When I was a student all my friends called me Captain."

"For being in the military?"

"No, because I was captain of the track team."

"Track?"

"Running," Ostrander said. "In races. A sports team."

"Who has red hair?" Hong asked, trying to imagine the sight.

Ostrander smiled. "Nobody. Not really red, but orangish, reddish, light brown."

"Oh, I see," Hong said, although he didn't.

"I wonder if I should call you Red," Ostrander said. "No, probably not. But you try to call me Peter."

"It would mean we were friends."

"Well, yes, I guess it would."

Following the meal everyone moved to the banquettes lining the walls of the outer reception hall. Ostrander was saying he hoped to visit Nanjing, to see a doctor from New York teaching at the university.

"I assume you'll want to visit Tangshan eventually," Hong said casually, "since you were born there."

"Tangshan? No, that's just where the birth certificate was sent. I was born in Choukoutien."

"Oh?" Hong said, with an ideal mixture of curiosity and surprise.

Ostrander explained that his father had been one of the youngest members of an international archaeological team at a site in Choukoutien. Geologists and paleontologists had worked the site since the early 1920s, and Theodore Ostrander had come to China when American research money was allotted for the building of a laboratory. He had then helped uncover one of the greatest archaeological discoveries of the century—the fossils of a crucial missing link between the ape and *Homo sapiens*.

"Is that an English word?" asked Hong.

"No, it's two words, in Latin, *homo*, meaning man, *sapiens*, from a word meaning 'to taste,'" Ostrander said. "The skeleton of the man they found was among the first primitive creatures who was sapient, who was aware, who could discriminate. They called him Peking Man. I suppose we should call him Beijing Man now."

"No, some names should stay as they are."

By the beginning of 1930, Ostrander went on, the archaeologists had assembled a skull, and the result stunned the world. Peking Man was younger than Java Man, discovered in Indonesia at the turn of the century. "Anyway, Java Man was really an ape. Peking Man had a larger brain. He walked upright. He ate meat and made tools. And he was the first man to use fire." Ostrander paused. "I'm putting you to sleep again," he said with a smile.

"I'm awake," Hong said. "I'm...what's the word you used? Sapient? I'm very sapient."

"Yes, you are," Ostrander said, and stared for an unusually long moment, as if he were seeing Hong for the first time, as if he had realized that Hong was not who he pretended to be. Ostrander's gaze was unnerving, clear and intense, but after a moment, whatever he suspected, his face relaxed and he continued. "Peking Man wasn't the only important discovery at Choukoutien. My father was involved in something different, and even more important."

"What was that?" Hong asked.

"Upper Cave Man," Ostrander said. "The first modern man of the East. Peking Man lived half a million years ago. Upper Cave Man lived twenty thousand years ago. Do you see what that means?"

"I know little about archaeology," Hong said. "It has not been one of my fields of interest."

"Nor mine," Ostrander said, and again came the studying gaze, held even longer. "What *are* your fields of interest?"

"Foreigners," Hong said, "and how they live. Languages. Friendship between peoples. Please, tell me more."

"All right," Ostrander said with a hint of knowingness, "if you're interested. Upper Cave Man meant that in one place they'd found two steps in evolution—the earliest evidence of a hunting man who wasn't an ape, and the earliest evidence of a man who could *think*. The Chinese might be descendants of the first thinking men on the planet."

The Chinese, Hong thought, were also in danger of becoming the first case of reverse evolution. The first men to think, and the first men to stop thinking.

In the end, Ostrander continued, the scientists had to conclude their work when the Japanese invasion threatened to overrun Choukoutien. "They packed up the bones to ship them out of the area before the Japanese arrived. But then the Japanese bombed Pearl Harbor, the Americans were put in prison camps, and the fossils disappeared."

"And what about your father?" Hong asked with no particular change of emphasis. "Did he have any idea what happened to the bones?"

"My father didn't make it either."

Hong waited.

"He disappeared, too."

"I'm sorry," Hong said. Now he knew why Ostrander's mother had remarried, but not why the file on Theodore Ostrander had disappeared. A man disappears, such things happened all the time, but his file should live beyond him.

"It was a long time ago," Ostrander said, "I was just a boy."

To Hong, family was sacred. Every spring he took the train to Suzhou, outside of Shanghai, to sweep the graves of his ancestors. Not to have ancestors, not to know where they were buried—it amazed him, he told Ostrander, that anyone could feel so little about his father's fate.

"It's not that I don't feel," Ostrander said. "But I accept what I can't change."

Not unlike the rest of us, Hong thought. "Tell me, how does a man disappear?" he asked, though he had known many who had, and could think of a dozen ways.

"I don't know, really." Ostrander glanced up toward the gilded molding on the high ceiling, and from the cast of his eyes, settling somewhere in the middle distance, he seemed to be looking back into the past. "My mother, she was never really comfortable here, and after the war started...well, we left ahead of him and he was supposed to follow us a month later. But he never did. They said he might have died in a Japanese prisoner-of-war camp. I guess I've gotten used to the idea that we'll never find out." He looked at Hong again. "This is my first trip back," he went on. "By the time I'd grown up...well, you know, traveling to China was a little harder."

"It was impossible," Hong said. "You don't need to be diplomatic."

Ostrander smiled and stretched his long frame, sliding down on the banquette. "Your mother is famous, even in the West," he said. "Did you ever think of becoming an artist?"

"To serve the masses with art, one needs a skill that I don't have."

"Does all art have to serve the masses?"

"The sole aim of literature is to extol the bright side of life and to expose exploiters and evil influences," Hong said. That was the correct line, not a word of which he believed. And he had the oddest feeling that Ostrander knew, that he recognized a parrot when he saw one.

Ostrander pulled out a pack of Winstons and offered one to Hong.

"Doctors shouldn't smoke," Hong said.

"I allow myself five a day, otherwise it's the pipe."

"That's good discipline." Hong held up his lighter, a Bic.

"Where did you get that?" Ostrander asked.

"We can buy them in special stores. How do you say it? They sell like hot dogs."

"Hot cakes," Ostrander said.

"Excuse me? Hot cakes?"

"That's the idiom. They sell like hot cakes. I should have given you a box of them instead of the pens."

"No, the pens are fine, thank you." He inhaled. "Hot cakes," he repeated. "They sell like hot cakes." He put the phrase into his vocabulary. "You were saying this is your first trip to China since your childhood. So you'll want to visit the place of your birth."

"Yes, I'd like to go out there in a couple of weeks."

"That shouldn't be a problem."

"How should we go?" Ostrander asked.

"We?"

"You'll come with me, I hope. It will give us another chance to talk. We can debate the purpose of art in a revolutionary society."

"Certainly you can make interesting debate at the medical college."

"I'd like to debate with you."

"Then I'd be pleased to accompany you," Hong said. "I suggest we take a car. The road's very good now."

"I'll probably need clearance for the ride. Maybe you can speed it up for me."

"I'm sure I won't have to," Hong said. "Those kinds of documents are easy to get."

Although this time, Hong suspected, obtaining them would be even easier than usual; the request would fly through the bureaucracy. Just as the bureaucracy had so suddenly and inexplicably met Dr. Yan's need for a scientist. And in both cases, Hong wanted to know why.

The Ministry limousine left Ostrander at the compound on Jianguomen and deposited Hong at the Bureau. In his office he picked up the accumulated messages for the outlying branches and took them downstairs to the telex center. It was already late afternoon, and the clerks were half-asleep. The new machines remained in the middle of the room, uninstalled.

At the counter Hong left his messages to be dispatched, then checked the news items tacked on the bulletin board, the ones that would either never reach the newspapers or, like the brief notice of the Tianjin airport explosion, would

be altered for political reasons. Reading internal news reports gave even the Bureau's lowliest workers a currency
more valuable than money; information sometimes opened
back doors better than twenty yuan. The stories were on a
single sheet of teletype paper stretching to the floor—a
lengthy dispatch on corruption at a ball-bearing plant in
Harbin, another on a French professor in Dalian who had
been asked to leave the country for unstated reasons.

Hong had almost turned away when the last item on the
page caught his eye. It was an obituary notice from Wuhan,
marked INTERNAL NEWSPAPERS ONLY. A cadre in the
Henan Military District of the Wuhan Administrative Region had died the previous night of a sudden illness. His
name was Su Zhen, age seventy-four, former Political Commissar of the Air Force and a member of the National Defense Council. Hong thought about the list of cadres from
Yanan, and the names he had scratched off. They were all
alive. Had Su Zhen been one of them? No, but then why
should he have been? Hong had never heard of him. Hong
read further in the Wuhan obituary notice, which wouldn't
appear in the papers before Thursday, until he came to one
striking phrase: *Made the Long March with Chairman Mao
(1934), military coordinator in War Against Japan and War of
Liberation.*

A military coordinator, possibly a colleague of Sheng's.
Hong thought about the drawing in Sheng's calendar . . . a
hare was it? Or a dog? And then an arrow pointing to
Wuhan. Below it, a butterfly and an arrow pointing to
Tianjin.

There had been no cadre in Wuhan on Hong's list, but
there had been a man in Tianjin. Without one in Wuhan,
Hong hadn't made the connection to Sheng's jottings. Stupid, he told himself. It should have been obvious. But he
had been looking for the dead, after all, not the living.

It was a few minutes before four. In afternoon traffic,
clotted with trucks, a trip to Tianjin by car could last well
into the night. Hard-seat space on the four-twenty train
would already be completely sold, but with luck, Hong
thought, he could get a soft-seat ticket.

He turned out into the hall, walked rapidly up the steps
to his office, and retrieved his list of the old cadres, the

revolutionary heroes who had served together in Yanan. There was, as Hong had remembered, only one in Tianjin: Yao Yilin, age seventy-one. From the second shelf of the radio stand Hong took a dusty and rarely consulted copy of the Party's Central Directory. Turning the oversized pages, Hong was struck by an awful thought: what if Yao Yilin had no entry, what if he had been purged and never reinstated, what if he were dead and the fact had somehow escaped notice of the registry of births and deaths?

But Yao Yilin, according to the Central Directory, was very much alive. The picture next to his entry showed a broad-faced cadre, lips slightly parted, with a deep crease across his forehead like the scar of a knife. As things happened, he had been purged during the Cultural Revolution, but had been rehabilitated and was now First Secretary of the Tianjin Municipal Committee. Hong found the most interesting aspect of Yao's life in his war record: *Made the Long March with Chairman Mao (1934–35), military and reconnaissance officer during War of Liberation.*

Had Yao Yilin worked with Sun Sheng?

Against his best instincts Hong picked up the telephone and dialed direct to a Tianjin operator, who made a connection to the Municipal Committee. Hong identified himself, and a secretary, in brisk official tones, informed him that Comrade Yao Yilin was not expected back before six o'clock.

Leaving the Central Directory on his desk and grabbing his briefcase, Hong threw the door open, bolted into the hallway, and nearly toppled Chan off his feet.

"Where are you going in such a hurry?"

"Errands," Hong said without stopping.

"Stop! You have a substation briefing at five!"

"You take it," Hong called, turning the corner and going down the stairs to the office of the Director of Operations.

The Operations anteroom, with its handsome reception desk and newly recovered couch, was unoccupied. Hong tapped on the frosted glass of the inner door and heard Ling Lipin bark, "Who's there? Come in."

The Operations Director was on the phone, arguing about the uninstalled telex machines. He begged, cajoled, pleaded—seemingly to no avail—and finally dropped the receiver into its cradle as though he would be happy to see it split apart.

"I need a seat on the four-twenty to Tianjin," Hong said.

"What's the rush?" Ling Lipin asked. "Did somebody steal a rug?" This was Ling's idea of wit; there were carpet factories in Tianjin.

"A national security case," Hong said. "I'm on my way to the station. Can you call over there for me, please, and have a ticket waiting?"

Ling yawned dramatically. "Another national security case, I'm impressed. I can see you're in a hurry, but... maybe you've been thinking about the Military Affairs directorship, maybe you could suggest that a man of my dedication..."

"But, Ling, I've already written a recommendation for you and sent it to the Deputy Minister."

Ling smiled, looked at his watch, and told Hong to see the clerk at soft-seat window number 6. "There's a lot of trouble on that line, though. You could be sitting between stations all night before you get back."

"So I've heard," Hong said on his way out, and if the only penalty for this madness was a few wasted hours on a train he would pay it gladly, and be grateful.

11.

AN

OLD

PEDDLER

The train miraculously arrived in Tianjin only ten minutes behind schedule. Hong hurried toward Central Square, opposite the East Railway Station. He could see trawlers dredging sludge from the Hai River, and over their clanking he heard, from the opposite bank, the quarter-hour chime of the department store's soaring British clock tower.

At the edge of Central Square he paused near two sad little evergreens on their tiny patch of parched lawn and spent a desultory minute apparently examining a Russian-style mass of granite three blocks long, the Number One Workers Cultural Palace. Two Public Security officers swinging their batons crossed in front of him; neither met his eye. There was an unmarked van parked at the river embankment, and a man and a woman sat next to it gazing into space. Nothing to worry about, except that it was precisely the sort of operation Hong would have run if he had wanted to observe a passenger leaving the station. He glanced over his shoulder, scanned the heat-weary travelers fanning out behind him, and strode across the pedestrian bridge to Heping Road, which had once been Roosevelt Road. It was the city's main thoroughfare, a busy boulevard of antique shops and bazaars that was Jiefangbeilu to the south and became Zhongshan on the way to the Great Wall in the northern suburbs. At a reasonably brisk pace, checking both sides of the street as he went, Hong walked two blocks to the offices of the Municipal Committee, which were housed in a French marble villa with bourgeois pilasters and sweeping arches and swirling medallions of plaster flowers. The city was an old port, rebuilt during the foreign concessions at the end of the century, and its colonial face had not yet been wiped clean by the march of progress. Hong planted himself on the opposite side of the street to wait for the end of the cadres' working day. Going inside was too dangerous; his presence would be noted and a whisper of it might reach the wrong ears in Beijing.

He did not have long to wait. At half past six workers came streaming out, most of them young, and he had no trouble examining the older men. After five minutes he spotted Yao Yilin, easily recognizable by the scar on his forehead, which had deepened and darkened with age, and which seemed incongruous on his placid face. He was a short, stocky man with large saucer eyes, a brush cut of bright white hair and thatched white eyebrows, and the kind of sturdy gait that comes only from self-imposed discipline.

It was then that Hong saw—felt really, more than saw— the motion of a green Army truck that had been parked thirty or so meters from the door of the Municipal Committee. The truck sported a long smudge of grease above its orange headlamps, and in some remote but active corner of his mind Hong had registered its presence when he arrived. The engine backfired and coughed, backfired again, and the truck moved forward. Hong watched the driver look east, lift an arm, then lower it. Half a block away was a light blue three-wheeled scooter cart with its black canvas top snapped tightly shut. Hong was certain it had not been there a moment ago. Had someone followed him to Tianjin, or sent word ahead that he was coming? Who had known?

Only Ling Lipin, and why would Ling bother to report the purchase of a train ticket? And if someone had indeed followed him, this was undoubtedly the most slovenly surveillance he had ever witnessed.

Yao Yilin had come down the steps with another old man and a girl. They walked west and the Army truck moved with them. Hong trailed behind the truck on the opposite side of the street, keeping nearly abreast of Yao. At the first corner the girl stopped and joined a bus queue. The two old men, in animated discussion, continued on past the old city market stalls. Once or twice Hong thought Yao had noticed him, something in the tilt of Yao's head, the seemingly careless darting of his eyes. At the fork to Chengdu Road the two men separated—Yao's friend heading toward the river and Yao turning south.

The truck had moved closer, the scooter stayed behind. Hong checked the side alleys and saw nobody—not a poor petitioner with a knapsack, not a single bicycling office worker, not even a pigeon. Everybody in the city had suddenly gone into hiding, run from a bomb, died. There were just the two vehicles, and to approach old Yao would reveal to their drivers the object of Hong's trip to Tianjin. Hong kept to his side of the street, hoping that the old man would kindly disappear into a courtyard. But Yao Yilin seemed in no particular hurry to go anywhere, and Hong followed him on a circuitous route through narrow streets and *hutongs*. It was a curious way to walk home. Dusk was falling and the old man faded in and out of the shadows like a curl of cigarette smoke in the glow of a lamp.

They were alone on a virtually deserted strip of pavement behind the People's Gymnasium when the truck picked up speed. Hong heard the acceleration, turned, and in an instant understood his mistake. They had not been following him at all. They were after old Yao, which was why the truck had been parked at the Municipal Committee and not the train station. Two-way radios: the truck had called for the scooter on Heping Road. The whine of the truck's engine rose like a scream, the heavy-treaded tires slapped the pavement. Hong made his decision: he sprinted into the street, leapt across the truck's path, and with the full weight of his body shoved old Yao into the space between two garbage bins. There was a screech of brakes, the scraping of metal on concrete, and when Hong raised his head the left side of the truck was up on the sidewalk and the bumper had missed them by no more than a centimeter, hitting the building instead.

It was over in less than a minute: the soldier behind the wheel of the truck jumped out, yelled that Hong had caused him to crash, then hopped back in and pulled away. Hong suppressed any urge to protest and scanned the end of the block. The scooter was gone.

"Thank you so much," Yao Yilin said mildly, unfazed by his near encounter with death. He disentangled himself from Hong and brushed a spot of white dust from his sleeve. "You're Lu Hong."

Hong stepped away.

"Don't look so worried," Yao said. "I'm not reporting you to anyone. I realized you were following me as soon as I stepped out the door."

"Was I so obvious?"

"There are some skills one never loses. I know when I'm being followed. You were lucky you reached the right secretary when you called this afternoon. Otherwise your name would have been logged, and I assume you would rather it wasn't."

Yao flexed his shoulders and started down Chengdu Road. Hong, dismayed by his inability to track a man without being seen and horrified at the potential consequences, took a moment before falling in step beside him.

"They tried to run you over," Hong said.

"Or it was an accident," Yao replied. "It's awful these days, so many people being struck by cars. Just last week I myself was almost crushed by a bus. And there was a terrible crash a month ago, a cement hauler skidding toward me in the rain."

Hong understood why the attempt had been so incompetently executed. Whoever had engineered it was desperate, and had been forced to make do with drivers less than expert at arranging accidents. Hong's only worry focused on their powers of perception; had either of the drivers seen him clearly enough to provide a description?

Yao took Hong's arm. "If I were to guess," he said, "I

would guess you've come to ask about the war."

"A military cadre who died yesterday in Wuhan—"

Yao raised his hand like a traffic officer and cut Hong off. "Please, I don't want to know. I know you were a protégé of Sun Sheng, that's enough. And the reason you're here is . . . you're thinking of writing a brief memoir of him, and you're talking to his old friends to fill in the details. Isn't that right?"

"You weren't at the memorial service."

"I'm not that significant, I wasn't invited."

"Had you seen Sheng recently, or talked to him?"

"We hadn't spoken in . . . oh, twenty years." Yao reached into the pocket of his blue jacket and produced a pack of cigarettes. He offered one to Hong, lit them both, and as he did so managed to sweep a circle with his eyes, covering the entire street. No wonder he had known he was being followed. "I think there's a concert down on Fukang Road. Let's go listen."

They had reached the broad plaza in front of the Gymnasium. The war years were exciting, Yao said, as if he had just been discussing them. He had lived here in Tianjin, behind enemy lines, proudly running a team of spies and, when he had time, serving as a courier. "We had a lot of help from the foreigners. The Japanese guarded the borders of the city, but they didn't dare touch the Western concessions. We even hid some of our men in the offices of a British bank."

A cluster of maples occupied a green island at the corner of Weidi Road. Yao walked straight toward them and stopped. That he had not once alluded to Sheng's death became to Hong increasingly unnerving, but he had a sense of standing before doors ready to spring open, and of Yao testing the territory, gauging whether Hong was friend or enemy.

Yao stepped out onto Fukang Road and crossed to a large auditorium. Hong could hear loud guitars and the steady beat of drums.

"Do you have your Public Security identification?"

Hong took out his Bureau card.

"Wave it at the ticket takers," Yao said. "They won't look too hard."

Hong did as Yao instructed and without incident they passed two stern-faced old women supervising the entrance to the arena. Dozens of young people stood on the ramp leading to the main hall, smoking cigarettes and drinking from bottles of lemon soda. No smoking was allowed inside.

The stage was lit by flashing footlights of red, blue, and orange. The performers called themselves the Guangzhou Orchestra—a large band, fifteen at least, dressed in tight-fitting white suits with purple ties. The guitars and violins and piano were electrified, there were two sets of drums each with its own drummer, and the main singer was croon- ing a love song imported from Taiwan, swiveling his hips and throwing his microphone into the air.

"Wonderful!" Yao exclaimed, raising his voice to be heard over the music. "Decadent and wonderful! They tour the country and keep the young people amused. Fifteen years ago they would all have been locked up!"

Yao led the way to the back of the auditorium and down into an alcove between two of the rear ramps. Once there, he poured out his story earnestly and quickly, and it oc- curred to Hong that he had probably been saving it for years, refining it, in anticipation of the day when someone would throw a switch, knock on the door, and say now: now is the time to remember. It also occurred to Hong that Yao might not be telling the truth about when he last saw Sun Sheng.

"In May of 1940," Yao began, "I was told to expect a visit from Sun Sheng. I couldn't fathom why anyone so impor- tant would risk his life crossing enemy lines. He was a very high officer in Yanan, and I knew him only by name and reputation. In fact, I didn't even know his name until much later, when I went to Yanan myself. We called him the Dragon then. The Party had an obsession with code names, it was the Russian influence—code names, isolation of agents so that no one could reveal anyone else's identity. Only officers in the direct line of command knew the names of their superiors in Yanan. Even here we took the same precautions. Some of my own men knew me only by my code name."

"You were the Butterfly," Hong said. "I saw—"

Again Yao raised his traffic-signal hand. "No, don't tell

me anything unnecessary." At the beginning of June that year, Yao went on, Sun Sheng arrived in Tianjin, disguised as a poor peddler. "He was brilliant. He came into the city wearing rags, bent over a broken-down wooden cart. You would have thought he was a hundred years old. I'd been told to meet him in front of the French Ministry, but his disguise was so good that I missed his signal on my first pass by the building. When I figured out that the old peddler was a high officer from Yanan, I could hardly believe it. But it wasn't until he came into my house and stood up that I appreciated his daring. The peddler vanished and under those rags was this giant of a man."

Yao's voice had been gathering urgency, forging ahead like an animal long leashed and then set free. Suddenly he drew up, retreated, and contemplated the end of his cigarette in the pulsating light emanating from the auditorium.

"Why had Sheng come to Tianjin?"

But Yao was not to be hurried, not now. "My wife massaged his back, he was sore and in pain. He'd been walking hunched over that cart for almost a week. We got him fresh clothes and we fed him. He was hungry, he ate like a starved demon."

"His mission must have been crucial for him to suffer like that," Hong offered.

"We didn't ask questions. The next day he told me that there was a man he had come to meet—a courier who was himself traveling from the south, first through enemy lines by way of Choukoutien, and then to Tianjin."

Hong showed not a flicker of interest in the fact that the courier was coming by way of Choukoutien, the city where Peter Ostrander's father was excavating the bones of China's ancestors.

Sun Sheng gave Yao the address of a bookseller who had a shop near the old harbor. "I was to go there every morning and look for a sign in the window, a painting of a dragon. It had to be me who went, no one else could be trusted."

"And Sheng still hadn't told you the purpose of the meeting, who the courier from the south was?"

There was no need for Sun Sheng to elaborate, Yao explained. It was common knowledge that month that when anyone spoke of the south they meant General Zhu De's Eighth Route Army in central Shaanxi province. The Hundred Regiments campaign was being organized to destroy the rail lines and cut off the Japanese garrisons. Yao assumed that the plans for the campaign were being delivered to Sun Sheng in Tianjin, although it was difficult to understand why a message couldn't be sent directly to Yanan.

Perhaps, Hong thought, because whatever information Sun Sheng wanted, he preferred not to have it reach Party headquarters. And perhaps there was a message not from the south at all, but from somewhere near Choukoutien.

Yao bicycled to the harbor every morning as ordered, until on the fourth day a painting of a dragon appeared in the window.

"That night Sheng put on his peddler's clothes again. He told me that he wouldn't be coming back, that after meeting his courier he would leave the city and return to Yanan. He asked me to accompany him, and I said we should carry guns. He said no, guns would identify us as military officers if by happenstance we were searched by the Japanese."

It was then that Sun Sheng dispassionately instructed Yao what to do if they should meet any trouble. The courier possessed a single piece of information. It would be only a few words, perhaps two or three—a name or a place, Yao thought. If Sheng were to be injured or taken prisoner, Yao was to save himself, get away at all costs, and wait. Someone from Yanan would contact him, mention the Dragon, and ask for the message. "I'll admit I was shaken," Yao said. "I had always been prepared to die, but not on a mission in my own city." He related this to Hong matter-of-factly, as if everyone weighed dying in some distant village versus his own front yard.

"And if you received the message," Hong asked, "and Sun Sheng were unable to leave with it, how would you know who was entitled to hear it?"

"Sheng said not to worry, I would recognize proper credentials when they were presented."

There was a curfew then, Yao continued, sporadically enforced but in existence nonetheless. So they set out in mid-evening, at twilight, with Sun Sheng in his peddler's clothing, pushing his cart, and Yao remaining a short distance behind. They took their time about it, crossing the city, slowly wending their way along the river, finally reaching the bridge over the tributary near Beima Road. While Yao kept a lookout, Sun Sheng circled the block once, and on his return signaled that all was clear.

Yao pretended to shop. He bought a sack of noodles, a newspaper. They were looking, Sun Sheng had said, for a man with a mustache who would be carrying a bundle of books under one arm. The twilight faded, the sky grew dark, and Yao began to worry about the curfew. He began to worry, too, about his own unease.

"There was no cause, everything was as it should have been—a few Japanese soldiers, the usual people on their usual business. There was an old woman selling fans, a beggar with a dog that wouldn't stop barking, all very ordinary. But I had a feeling of being watched. A courier knows these things, as I knew today that you had picked me up when I left my office. Don't ask me how a courier knows. He just does."

Hong didn't have to ask. In the Army he had met more than a few men who could smell a gun from a thousand meters.

The courier from the south was half an hour late, and Yao decided to stroll past Sun Sheng and recommend that they leave. It was at that moment, Yao said, that a figure appeared on the bridge. He had a bundle, but in the dark there was no telling if it was books. Yao almost started forward, but Sun Sheng waved him off. The man started across the bridge. "He stopped in the middle, leaned and looked into the water. He lit a cigarette, but his back was turned to us so I still couldn't see his face. I was sure it was him, though. He was taking too long, maybe he suspected something, maybe he saw something in the water, I don't know. But he adjusted his bundle and came toward us." It was then that shots exploded out of the darkness from all directions. Five guns at least, Yao thought, maybe more, and the courier on the bridge fell. Japanese soldiers appeared from nowhere, and Yao couldn't make out exactly where they'd been hiding.

"When I looked for Sun Sheng, he had already disappeared into the night. The Japanese surrounded the area and I was taken in for questioning. That's where I got this." Yao pointed to the deep crease in his forehead. "But they'd dragged half the city in, anybody they'd ever suspected, and eventually they let us go."

The audience inside the auditorium burst into applause, stamping their feet. The metal taps on their shoes set off a shattering din on the concrete floor.

"You must have wondered why Sun Sheng told you from the very beginning that there might be danger."

"That's war," Yao said. "There's always danger."

"But why," Hong asked with an air of infinite patience, "should Sheng expect the Japanese to trail this particular courier?"

"He didn't say, and I didn't ask him."

"And you never heard from Sheng again?"

"Not until I got to Yanan; the war was almost over."

"Did you ever talk about that night?"

"No, why should we?"

"Old memories, heroic times . . . you might have reminisced about it."

"We didn't," Yao said evenly.

"Then why are you telling me about it now?"

Yao stared off into the auditorium, as if the answer might suddenly be brought to him from someone out in the crowd. You're telling me now, Hong thought, because for forty years you've been wondering how the Japanese managed to surround you. You've been thinking about how they shot a man they had no right to know about. And maybe you're telling me because Sun Sheng himself called a few weeks ago, but died before he could get here himself to ask for your memories.

"My wife will be waiting for me," Yao said. "And you'll be wanting to get to the station for the last train." He started up the ramp.

"Who told you to expect Sun Sheng's arrival? Who passed the message?"

Yao stopped. "I never knew his name, he was just another courier."

"Maybe you could find out," Hong suggested.

"Now? Find a man's name after all this time?" Yao looked down, sighed. "I could ask my friends."

"And you'll call me if you learn anything?"

"You would agree, I think, that the telephone is not the best way for us to talk. There are ways to communicate if necessary."

"The courier from the south," Hong said. "Did you ever discover why he had stopped in Choukoutien?"

"I've told you everything that Sun Sheng told me." Yao turned and continued up the ramp.

"That truck accident," Hong said.

"It was lucky you were there to help me."

"It might happen again."

Yao smiled. "It might. But I have lots of friends to walk with me, to eat with me, even to sleep near me. And accidents, you know, happen in many places. One might even happen in Beijing, to someone like you."

When Hong returned to Beijing the streets were eerily quiet, empty but for an occasional cluster of cycling workers coming off shift, an exhausted student on Chang'an trudging home from night classes with his bag of books, lovers strolling toward the drooping willows and winding walkways of Dongdan Park. The entire city had retired to the glow of its television sets to watch the latest installment of "We Are Not the Sick Men of China," a martial-arts costume drama imported from Hong Kong. Feuding families, love, romance—popular television was like roasting a duck, a mixture of the right ingredients.

Hong fetched his bicycle at the Bureau. He had ridden west and crossed the intersection at North Xidan when he saw, in the glare of the bright sodium lamps in front of the Cultural Palace, a face he thought that he had forgotten, or maybe only had hoped to forget. She was walking toward him, taking tiny steps and carrying papers tied with twine. Hong could attach no name to her, but if the name was lost to him, he remembered too well what he had done to her. She had been his teacher in middle school, and the shame flooded over him with a force so overpowering that it slammed like a weight onto his back. His feet slipped from the pedals, he nearly toppled off his bike. It was January, twenty years ago, and so cold your breath froze on your lips. He had been in a crowd that lifted her onto a wooden stool in the schoolyard and poured buckets of water on her; he had hurled slogans at her, watched the ice form in her hair, called her a counterrevolutionary and a rightist and whatever other labels the Party had given him. Even then he had known it was wrong. He had watched her shiver and beg to be let go. And why? Why her? Because they had needed a target that week, because an order had come to purge the school of a few bad elements. She was chosen at random, a victim of chance.

Hong was tempted to stop and apologize, but what words would make any difference now? Any attempt would only serve to ease his guilt, and she probably preferred to forget even more than he did.

Pedaling home, he felt his fever rise—in the morning low, in the evening high, it had a rhythm of its own. He really should have seen a doctor, but for what? A prescription of antibiotics and herb teas and an order to stay in bed. Then he would lose the case of Ostrander. And now, after a lifetime of shedding politically difficult assignments, he had finally found one he needed, needed most urgently, as one needs food, sleep, a new love. A month ago he was telling himself he would keep his head down, wait for promotions, begin a new life. Never mind the schoolteacher he had tormented, never mind Shen Kuang, who had borne him a son, who had been a revolutionary but had grown up to prepare entertainment for the masses and to enjoy a far better life than anyone in her audience. Never mind that she now loved a subhuman ape. And what of the ambitious seeker of truth she had once respected? Well, never mind him, too. So perhaps he deluded himself, and others too, by imagining he had given up a career as a poet to serve the people as a protector, a stalwart enforcer of the laws. His mother would rather her son had been a mediocre poet than a good officer of Public Security. Why? "Eulogize the Proletariat!" said Chairman Mao to the makers of literature. "Eulogize the New Democracy and Socialism!" One might just as well sing the praises of angels, who also existed only in the imagination.

And so, what was left? If the proletariat and the new democracy and socialism were merely slogans, why should one powerless servant of the people bother himself with a single death? The death of an old man who would have died soon enough anyway. Because it was useless to be what Chairman Mao called "a hero with no place to display his prowess." And also because this unexpected new life was exhilarating, it lit up the sky, it lifted the assistant deputy director's spirits from the dark and lonely corners where they had recently taken up residence.

There was one problem. In this new life, the servant of the people could find an early death.

Hong passed the tower of Radio Beijing, its faint red and white lights a pair of huge tired eyes, blinking and accusing him of something. He turned onto Second Ring Road. A few days of sun might cure his cold, he thought, but what would cure him of Sun Sheng's death, and of Ostrander?

12.

A
LIGHT
IN
THE
DESERT

The early private flight to the beach at Beidaihe departed at six in the morning and arrived an hour and a half later. When Hong stepped from the plane the sun was already boiling, but the salt spray of the ocean cooled and perfumed the air. At the small military airfield on the coast a Trident, quite new, had also just landed—from Guangzhou, the captain said, but refused to reveal who his passengers were. For Lu Lin's guests three aging Datsun taxis, their fenders dented and tires perilously low on air, waited on the sticky tarmac, engines running and air conditioners at full speed. Servants of the people, relax from your labors and enjoy the sunshine. Sunshine is free, even if plane tickets are not. Poorer servants of the people, take the train. Five hours of dust and heat will help you appreciate the delights of the beach. The taxi drivers had a particularly sullen air, Hong noticed; they could have been waiting a day or a year, their expressions said, for all it mattered to them.

The Army general's grand house overlooked the beach from a secluded and terraced corner in the pines of Lotus Rock Park. Climbing West Hill in tandem, the three taxis passed women and children sitting on the curb mending fishing nets, then the small sanitoriums for recuperating workers, until finally they cruised through a narrow gate, barely wide enough for a single car, that had been neatly cut in a stone wall four meters high. Richer servants of the people, keep your villas and gardens hidden. Rest homes for the ill should be seen, palaces for the privileged should not. At the end of the steep driveway, bordered by luxuriant rows of pink roses and honey locusts and tiny dogwoods, all pruned to desperate perfection, the cars stopped and the visitors unloaded their bags. Comrade Deng Bo and his cadres from the CDI traveled with excess luggage. Did they need three suitcases for two days? Three purchasing managers for electronics from the Commerce Ministry were more modest—one bag apiece plus their own billiard cues in long plastic covers, like rifles. Four servants instantly appeared from the front door and scooped up the luggage.

Hong took Yamei's small bag and followed her up the driveway. Yamei wrinkled her nose, staring at the servants and then up at the yellow-balconied sun porch on the top floor. "This is very beautiful," she said softly, "but a little feudal, I think. Even decadent."

"And bourgeois," Hong said, laughing. "To get rich is glorious."

"Don't make fun of me," she replied tartly. "I know high cadres work hard and are entitled to privileges."

Of course they are, Hong thought. His own parents had been among them, though they had never lived quite this lavishly. The general's three-story house, probably built at the turn of the century, looked to have fifteen or twenty rooms. Tucked under the shallow eaves of the first floor's pitched roof was a wraparound, glassed-in veranda, which to guess from its pristine condition had been added recently at some unimaginable cost. Last night's arrivals—the Army general's chubby son with two Shanghai girlfriends, assorted deputy ministers from Defense and Commerce with their wives and children—were already dressed in light cotton beach jackets and swimsuits, taking breakfast on the porch. Through the open double doors a huge cassette recorder blasted pirate tapes of Taiwan love songs. Beyond the house, above Bohai Bay, the sky was a sheer plate of golden blue.

After breakfast the guests moved in a swarm to Middle Beach, toting large canvas umbrellas and baskets of beer and pickled vegetables and corn buns. Model workers on paid vacations stayed on East Beach, tourists on West Beach, with lifeguards supervising the boundaries. Hong felt a touch of retrospective envy. A day at the beach in his own youth was a rare luxury. The hotels and rest houses here had all been closed then. At the water's edge Yamei tossed an inflated blue-and-yellow ball with the children. So joyously, Hong thought. She would be a good mother. He watched her with a curious pleasure. She fretted about feudalism but could forget politics and enjoy herself. Hong had never known anyone else so able to be happy with whatever life brought. She lived on a raft. Wherever the wind blew her was fine.

Hong's brother, carrying two bottles of beer, strolled over, tossed a towel on the sand, and plopped down.

"This is great, isn't it?" He passed Hong a cold Yuchuan.

"Nice," Hong said.

"How about that house? Those bathtubs are something, huh?"

"Big enough for a whole family," Hong agreed.

"Yamei's having a good time," Lin said. "You're lucky to have found her."

"I think she found me."

Lin spread out his towel. "You really love her, don't you? More than you loved Kuang. You were too young when you got married."

"That's what Kuang always said."

"You never loved her the way you love Yamei."

"What's the point in comparing?" Hong asked.

"I think Yamei makes you a little bit crazy," Lin said with a smile. "The way you're looking at her all the time."

Hong supposed it was true. It was not so long ago that he had thought of Yamei only as a possible wife and companion, and he was surprised by how deeply he had become attached to her.

"Look, what about buying the apartment I mentioned?"

The beer, the discussion of bathtubs—all mere setting the stage. "I'll have to think about it."

Lin sipped his beer. "There's nothing wrong with making money, Hong. You get used to living simply, you start to think it's noble. And please, don't quote that Lao-tzu stuff at me—embrace plainness, have few desires."

"It's embrace simplicity, *manifest* plainness," Hong said, and was instantly sorry for his pedantry. "You know I'm not against money," he added quickly, "or even luxuries. This apartment business sounds a little risky, that's all."

"You want to talk about risk? How about you and this American doctor?"

"What about him?"

"I talked to Chan yesterday. I look out for your interests, younger brother, even if you don't always appreciate it."

"I appreciate whatever—"

Lin held up his hand. "Please, at least listen to my advice. Chan says the case is too complicated, you'll get caught between the ministries."

"Chan talks too much, and it's an interesting case. Your friend Deng Bo seems to think so, too."

"I don't know what that's about," Lin said. "I asked Deng, but he told me it was nothing, he just saw your name on an assignment list, that's all. Anyway, maybe you ought to try to pass the case on to somebody else. You'll end up spending too much time with a suspicious foreigner. A briar sticks as well as honey, you know."

"Don't you deal with foreigners? Don't you buy from them and trade with them?"

"Business, Hong. That's only business. I have to tell you, if you handle things right you could end up with a house like the general's. They're weeding out the cadres on top. They're cutting dead wood out of the Army and the Navy, those old bastards who can't write their own names without a secretary, all they can do is quote Chairman Mao and get jobs for their friends. The security ministries are next. My friends say you could be Deputy Minister, you'll have everything. A Mercedes, a house here or maybe a place in Guangzhou for the winter, foreign travel. Don't you want to see all those places you dream about? London, Paris, California?"

A thought swirled through Hong's brain before he knew it was there. If I saw California, would I want to come back? Chan had a cousin who had gone to California to study, and stayed. Could I be an expatriate Chinese poet in Rome? And then, as quickly as these insane ideas had arisen, Hong banished them, sent them away like criminals sentenced to reform-through-labor in Inner Mongolia.

"A Deputy Minister, Hong, doesn't bicycle home from work. A Deputy Minister goes to a few meetings, lunches on duck, writes a report now and then."

"A Mercedes instead of a bicycle would be nice," Hong said, "depending on what I had to do to get it."

Lin drained the last of his beer bottle and smoothed his towel. "Hong, I'm very fond of you. I would do anything for you. But sometimes I think you resent me for it."

"Nonsense," Hong said.

"You still think I was the favorite son."

"But you were," Hong said emphatically.

"No, only in your eyes. I was the steady one, but you had the better mind. Why do you think Papa used to read to you? Me, I was slow, I didn't like literature, economics. Anyway, let's buy this apartment together."

"We'll see," Hong said.

"You're worried about an apartment. I was in Shaoguan last month, looking for machine parts, gear wheels. A buyer from a silk factory in Wanxian wanted the same parts. Do you know what I had to promise? A thousand yuan for two accountants, girls for the assistant managers. Girls! So I'm a whoremaster now, just to keep my factory running."

"Come on, it's not that bad."

"It's worse than you think," Lin said. "It's worse than I can tell you. I'm a little sick with myself, to tell the truth." The inflated ball bounced at Lin's feet. He threw it back to the children. "Forget all that. Don't repeat what I said, I should keep my mouth shut. And you, you watch yourself with this foreigner. Get rid of him, let somebody else take the risks. Remember, I know you better than anybody. Don't get any ideas about being a hero."

• • •

The day ended early, before ten. The children were put to bed and the house was silent. Even the servants had gone to sleep. Hong lay on the hard double bed in his room on the second floor—a very nice room, with its own bathroom —and listened to the ocean roll into the bay. He thought about Ostrander's family being in Choukoutien almost fifty years ago, about a courier stopping in Choukoutien before meeting Sun Sheng. He thought about Lin's warning, and wondered what Lin would say to the idea that Sun Sheng had been murdered.

When Hong could listen to the ocean no longer, when the waves sounded as if they were shouting in pain, he soaked his feet with salts in the tub. At ten he put on a robe he had found hanging in the closet and tiptoed down the hall to Yamei's room. He knocked twice, two fast taps, and the door opened.

She looked both ways and stepped out. "Downstairs," she whispered. "It's safer."

They took the steps slowly but the wood creaked anyway. At the bottom they stood, hands linked, and listened like sentries. Not a sound except for the whoosh of the ocean and the wind rattling the front door.

And a distant clicking, Hong thought. Someone eating?

"Wait," he said. He crossed the central hall and peeked around the corner. Just like a policeman, he thought. He was frighteningly alert. In a far corner of the living room a pendulum clock was ticking.

Curls of moonlight broke through the glass porch, spreading crescent-shaped shadows across the faded rug. Hong waved Yamei past him. They sat on a bamboo-framed couch and Yamei nestled her head on his shoulder. She took his hand, held it to her cheek, kissed his palm, and for the first time since he could remember a sense of peace descended on him. He looked at her smooth face, the fine hair at the back of her neck. He remembered her once telling him how their love was all she needed, and his thinking but not saying that he wished it could be the same for him, too.

"You've been so worried," she said.

His hand touched her lips to quiet her, then slipped to

her neck, her breasts. She turned, lifted her head and covered his face and hands and mouth with kisses. She always surprised him with her immodesty, and her passion. He parted her robe, she tugged his open, they slid down on the couch together. They never spoke now until the end. Nakedness spoke more than anything they could say. But it was different this time, no rush against the clock, all the time in the world for their bodies to entwine and part, entwine again. He loved her face, her hands, the yielding of her body as she rose to meet him. This was a mystery, this tentative touching, the fluttering of her hands across his back like the faint beating of wings. But even as he entered, as she pulled him inside her and shivered and let out an involuntary sigh, the intoxication, the rapture he had hoped for, eluded him, and before the very moment of release he wondered if he was too old now, beyond love.

She lay against him for a long while, holding tight, as if knowing how much he needed her.

"Why do you love me?" she asked.

How could he answer? Why did anyone love? "Because you're good," he said.

"I love you," she said without his asking, "because no lake compares with the ocean."

Pretty poetry, pretty stories. He must have slept then, for she was waking him and he could see blue washing into the sky.

"They'll be coming down soon," she said urgently. "We have to go upstairs."

She kissed him once, then hurried into the hall. He followed, thinking about the fairy-tale princess escaping from the cave, thinking that this was no desert at all, because not only was there light, there was something to see.

Thursday, shopping day. A morning swim, an hour on the sand, and then the cadres from Defense and Commerce filled their wallets and trooped into the village. In Beijing they would have been more discreet. But here on the beachfront street, from the bookstore at number 89 to the specialty canned goods outlet at number 95, they sucked up delicacies like greedy worker bees, filled sacks with raffia basketware, sausages and dried fruit and sweet liqueurs, expensive clothbound volumes of Chekhov and Ba Jin and Wouk, hand-embroidered lace napkins and tablecloths, cloisonné cups from the large department store. They had a taste for beauty and finery, but more important, Hong thought with not a little rancor, they had the means to pay for it.

Yamei had gone to the beach again, and Hong strolled with his brother and Deng Bo to Kiessling and Bader, the old German beer garden across from the post office, where Lin could indulge his newly acquired taste for European food. There they settled around a front table flooded by light from the high front windows, and as Hong took his seat the heavily starched cloth crackled. From the kitchen came the smell of baking dough, Western biscuits and cakes. What a legacy of imperialism, Hong thought, a ghost of the 1930s. Any minute a troop of German diplomats would stomp in and order the Chinese out as trespassers. No dogs or Chinese allowed. The waiters had caught the spirit and took unseemly delight in laying down knives and forks of pure silver; the former proprietors' names were engraved on the shanks. In a matter of minutes the manager, with whom Comrade Deng had a laughing rapport, descended on the table and deposited platters piled high with wurst and baby shrimp and chunks of crab. A waiter brought liter bottles of Qingdao and popped the caps. It was good rich beer, and hard to come by; three-quarters of the production was marked for export.

"You'll do better to buy those parts in the south," Deng Bo was saying to Lin. "Keep the local Defense cadres happy and you'll have no problem getting orders from the Army."

Outside, Hong thought, people are hungry. Outside, at the other end of the bay, there are workers on oil-drilling platforms who see their families twice a year and who have a good chance at drowning when a random squall tears in from the ocean. Meanwhile, here at the beach we feast.

"And the world is a stage," Deng Bo said. "We're actors playing our roles on the stage of history."

"Shakespeare," Hong said.

"I thought it was Lenin," said Deng offhandedly. "Well, they had a lot in common."

Hong thought about the Defense cadre who had taken a

hand in approving Ostrander's trip to China. "I saw a file on a friend of yours the other day," he said casually. "A cadre on the screening committee for foreign exchanges at the Academy of Sciences."

Deng tilted his head back. He wrapped his palm around his chin and contrived to appear thoughtful. "A friend of mine?" he asked. "I can't think of anyone I know at the Academy."

"I've made a mistake then," Hong said.

From the rear yard, where foreign tourists sat at tables in the sun, a tall Westerner entered, paused and stared with a raised eyebrow as if he recognized Hong, and started for the table. Nearly bald, thin as a blade of grass, he looked to be Deng Bo's age, early sixties. He wore a slightly sneering half-smile, which managed to suggest his innate superiority to everyone in the room. An Englishman, Hong thought, or a Frenchman. They were experts in superiority.

"Ah, look who's here, it's Caffey," exclaimed Deng, rising from his seat and switching to English. "Come join us."

The foreigner sat down and Deng introduced him—Raymond Caffey, British subject, resident in Hong Kong, an import-export broker. The man's white linen suit had wrinkled, but seemed sleek nonetheless.

"Shrimp?" Deng offered, passing the plate. "What can we order for you?"

"Thank you, my good Comrade," Caffey said, "but no, one mustn't eat too much in this heat. Just as one mustn't take too much sun or too much exercise. Especially at my age. Some mineral water, however, would be excellent."

Deng signaled, called to the waiter, and a bottle of Laoshan appeared.

"Excuse me, is the name pronounced 'coffee'?" Hong asked. "Like the drink?"

"Please pronounce my name however you like," the Englishman said, pouring the Laoshan with a flourish from high above the glass. "What's in a name? Our true selves? But coffee is bitter, and I'm of a much sunnier disposition. Bittersweet sometimes, but not bitter." He spoke grandly, and to the world more than to anyone in particular. "You've just arrived today, have you?"

"Yesterday, from Beijing."

"Oh? By one of those marvelous special flights available to particularly important chaps?"

"Yes, by plane," Hong said.

"I favor the train myself. It's an awfully long trip, and hot, but then trains are a more decent means of travel, I think, and safer, too. I'm ashamed to admit that much as I do love traveling in your country, I find that I'm rather more comfortable not flying on your State airline, the treacherous CAAC." He winked at Hong. "Planes *do* crash sometimes, and in the most shocking circumstances."

"What kind of goods do you deal in?" Hong asked.

"The kind of goods the Chinese need," Caffey said. He had a scar on his nose, an erosion, like a rock pitted by water. Had he been struck in a fight? Or was it a birthmark? "Anything from around the world that will take China forward toward modernization."

There was no irony in the statement, which made it all the more ironic.

"And what kind of goods do we most need?" Hong asked.

Deng leaned forward. "He's a middleman, Hong. When two people want to do business, he brings them together."

"A middleman," Hong said. "That's very good. These days middlemen do very honorable work."

"Isn't all work honorable?" the Englishman asked. "From each according to his ability and so forth."

Deng leaned toward Hong, touched his arm. "And Lu Hong is a high cadre in Public Security. He recently caught a German spy."

Caffey gave a look of mock horror. "Oh? Execute him, did you? Sword across the neck?"

"We sent him home," Hong said evenly, stunned by Deng's indiscretion.

"And now he has a new case," Deng continued, "an American, a Dr. Ostrander."

In shock, Hong turned his head, but Deng had focused on Caffey with a wry smile. What accounted for Deng's loose tongue? First at the circus and now here, casually revealing secrets of State.

"Ostrander?" Caffey said with a laugh. "Peter Ostrander? American fellow? I daresay, what a silly idea! A spy!"

"You know him?" Hong asked.

"Yes, I met him at a reception...now let me think, where was it? At the American embassy, if I remember rightly. If he's a spy, well then I'm Marco Polo. Ostrander's a nice fellow doing medical research." He raised a hand and waved it grandly. "That's what the Chinese get for their isolation. You see spies in the bedsheets."

The Defense cadres burst in from their shopping. Deng and Lin rose to greet them and accompanied them to a table in the opposite corner. Hong stared at the Englishman's hand. On his index finger was a small gold ring, and just above it, on the knuckle, another scar, like the mark on his nose. All the folds on all of his knuckles had been abraded, Hong noticed.

Burns, maybe, from a fire? But why only on his hands and nose?

"I don't exactly understand," Hong said. "You are here in Beidaihe on vacation or business?"

"Business of a sort," Caffey said.

"What business is that?"

"You could call me a small cog in the wheel of world trade," Caffey said with exaggerated modesty.

But there was nothing modest about him. He was, for example, obviously rich in a way that Peter Ostrander was not. One was rumpled by accident, by not caring, the other by design.

"What does a small cog in the wheel of trade do?" Hong asked.

"It's rather simple, actually," Caffey said. "Suppose the Americans latch on to the idea of assembling jeeps in China. The Chinese would like to build jeeps for the Asian market. Now the quality of your labor is...well, let's say that at the moment it falls rather short of world standards. But it has the distinct advantage, especially to the overpaid Americans, of being unbelievably cheap. So we must first find an American automobile company willing to cope with your stubborn bureaucracy. We must then accomplish the impossible task of elevating the Chinese from their...well, shall we say old-fashioned work habits. The first has been done with a company called Chrysler, and as for the second, it remains to be seen whether the Chinese can build a good jeep even with the Americans running the factory."

"I see," said Hong. The Chinese obviously had a talent only for the inferior and the shoddy.

"Or the Spanish," Caffey went on regally. "The Spanish will do anything to sell you automated knitting machines, but you haven't enough hard currency to afford them, nor will you in the foreseeable future. And of course what do the Spanish want with a few million yuan? A worthless currency in the rest of the world. So a method has to be found to pay—barter. The barter of products. International trade is a merry-go-round. Money and products in, money and products out."

"Merry-go-round?" Hong asked.

"A circus ride for children," said Caffey. "Wooden horses on poles, a big platform turning."

"And where are you on the merry-go-round?"

"Standing at the entrance," Caffey said. "When the Chinese want to go on, they need someone who knows the other passengers. And the other passengers need someone who knows China."

A man astride two horses, Hong thought, can be torn apart if they separate. As a middleman, Caffey considered himself more powerful than either side. They, however, could survive without him, while without them he was nothing.

"And you know China?" Hong asked.

"Quite well," he said proudly, and then repeated with more satisfaction, "quite well indeed. I've been coming here a long time."

"How long?"

"A long time."

"Since when?"

Caffey's jaw tightened and his sharp sneer wavered.

"You're terribly inquisitive, aren't you? The result of your job, I assume."

"No, I'm interested in foreigners," Hong said.

"But you're in Public Security. You ask questions in your work, in finding criminals. It becomes a habit."

"Not at all," Hong said. "We have so few criminals. Crime is not a problem in China. In the West you have murderers and thieves and rapists, street criminals and beggars and prostitutes, you have white people fighting black people.

The average Chinese, what kind of crime could he commit? A stolen watermelon or two, that's the worst."

"Really? Tell me, then, what do you do all day?"

"Chase watermelon thieves, hunt the occasional bad element who attaches false labels to bicycles."

"Even with bicycles, so much meaning in a name," Caffey remarked. "The trouble with the Chinese is that you're so suspicious. For thousands of years you had the greatest culture on earth, you invented gunpowder and paper—and the noodle, good gracious let's not forget the noodle—and then you shut yourself away from all foreign influences. As a consequence, you look at all foreigners with clouded eyes. Either we're vulgar fools or spies. And that," he said forcefully, tapping the table with his index finger, "is why you mistakenly suspect people like the good Dr. Ostrander."

Hong was staring at Caffey's finger, at the scars. Caffey noticed and quickly lowered his hand to his lap. It was a bad moment, to be caught examining another's frailties, and Hong was saved from embarrassment when the door opened and another group of cadres pushed in laden with packages. Among them was Comrade Ho, the Health Ministry cadre who had been at the circus. A large haul for a middle-level cadre, Hong thought as he looked at the overflowing bags. Deng and Lin returned to the table, and the shoppers clustered around while Lin went to the bakery counter for a tray of ice cream.

"I really must be going, it's time for my nap," Caffey said, standing and shaking Hong's hand. "It's been a pleasure to meet you. I hope we'll meet again."

"Yes," Hong said, "it would be nice to talk about China's modernization."

Caffey said good-bye to Deng, then to Lin at the bakery counter. Deng's loose talk had been no accident. Why had he mentioned Ostrander's name?

Hong's eyes followed the Englishman as he made his way to the door. Caffey was spectral, taller than everyone else and of a color that seemed to push light away. The room seemed to grow brighter when he left. After the door closed behind him, Hong spun on Deng and shot his question like a bullet:

"Do you frequently discuss matters of State so lightly?"

Deng's face creased in ire for an infinitesimally small moment, then reverted to placid bemusement. "Caffey is an old and valued friend of China," he said dismissively, "a man to be trusted. Besides, he has no loyalty to his own country or to the Americans. If you're going to trap a foreign bad element, it's of no concern to him."

Perhaps that was so, Hong thought, but a man without loyalties to his own people was not likely to be loyal to China either. The last person in the world to trust is a man without loyalties.

13.

ARCHIVES

The plane brought them back late Thursday night, dropping them into a heat so numbingly intense it seemed like an illness. Hong descended the steps to the tarmac, walking toward a pink moon half-hidden in a flock of polluted clouds. At his glance the clouds decided to close in and the pink light retreated completely. He followed Yamei to the gate, where the arrival of a dozen passengers did nothing to rouse the Army guards asleep like dead men in their chairs, rifles slung across their knees. Inside the terminal the night porters, all women, pushed mops in a languid dance, moving dirt from one patch of tile to another.

On the short flight Hong had hardly spoken, and Yamei gently pursued the cause of his mood. Was it the cost of the trip? Lin's request to buy the apartment? Or disapproval of Hong's traveling with her, not his wife and son? To the insistent questioning Hong answered no, and no, and again no. Forgive me, I'm tired, vacations don't relax me. Particu-

larly, he thought, when a cadre from the CDI boisterously
divulged his cases to a foreigner.

At the Commerce Ministry's airport office limousines
were waiting. Hong said good-bye to Lin, who was flying to
Shanghai in the morning, and who importuned him one
last time, unsuccessfully, to buy an apartment. When Lin
finally released him, Hong rode with Yamei to her parents'
building. They left the driver in the car and walked into the
protective shadows of the poplars edging the road. Hong
touched Yamei's cheek, held her in his arms.

"I wish we had more time together," she whispered.
"Being with you is the most wonderful part of my life."
With her eyes she implored him: tell me what's wrong.

"Apologize to your parents for me," Hong said. "I make
the wrong jokes in front of them."

She squeezed his hand. "They're used to it. I think sometimes they secretly admire you for being so forthright. It's
only . . . they're afraid you'll get into trouble."

As well I might, Hong thought. And as well they might,
too, embracing every shift in the political wind as if the
wind would forever after subside. When having maids and
drawing excess housing bonuses were declared corrupt,
where would Yamei's parents be then? Hong kissed her and
waited while she crossed the yard. Inside the door she
waved good night and vanished up the half-lit stairs. When
she was gone he pulled out a cigarette and started for the
car, then had to stop and click his lighter three times before
the spark caught. It was almost out of gas. Staring at his
hand in the glow of the flame, Hong had a sudden vision of
remarkable clarity, an image stored in his brain that he had
not quite known was there. It was the look on Deng's face
when he said to the Englishman, *And now he has a new case,
an American, a Dr. Ostrander.* What would you call that look?
Self-satisfied, maybe. And the brief flicker crossing Caffey's
face? It was a sudden alertness, like a horse with its head
cocked to the electric air of an oncoming storm.

Seeing his own knuckles in the flame's blue light, Hong
thought about the scars on the Englishman's fingers, that
moment of embarrassment when Caffey had withdrawn his
hand below the table. Or, Hong wondered, had it been
more than embarrassment? Did Caffey's scars mark more

than his skin? It was a poet's notion that you could read the inside of a man from his surfaces. And an investigator's notion, too. Chan, for example, would hide the ridges on his nails, the ravages of frostbite, to spare an acquaintance the reminder of past pain. But maybe the evidence of Caffey's injury was simply evidence of injury, and nothing more. Caffey seemed the kind of man who, if he played with fire, knew the fire was hot.

Which was perhaps a great deal more, Hong thought, than he could say for himself these days.

The report on the wartime archaeological dig at Choukoutien supplied by the Little Monk had been culled straight from the history books. There were heaps of glorious praise for socialist archaeology and socialist scientists. Encountering this document on his desk Friday morning, Hong at first thought it utterly useless. There was only cursory mention of Peter Ostrander's father and no speculation as to his whereabouts after the war. For that matter, there was no speculation on the whereabouts of an even more important actor in this drama, the glorious Beijing Man himself.

From the Monk's labors, however, Hong did select one item for extended attention—a passing reference to three Chinese archaeologists who had at various times supervised the dig at Choukoutien. Perhaps one of them had worked with Peter Ostrander's father. He copied the names and appended a note: "Try these three for older man in the two photos." He called for a messenger and sent the list to Fen Like at the Publications Center.

For Wei Ye, Hong built a case summary that bolstered an illusion of efficiency. He explained, as laboriously as possible, three examples of his thorough devotion to trapping the American: the search for information on *Ostrander (Greene), Elizabeth,* the Monk's currently assigned examination of all foreigners working in hospitals, and the interview with Dr. Yan. In Hong's version the latter was crudely truncated and bore at best a resemblance to the truth. The old cynic who considered his country a giant jellyfish became, for the record, a polite scholar, a patriot of the highest order, and in the matter of Ostrander a cooperative witness. You couldn't ask for better. The interview with Dr. Yan would thus be graded "clean"—meaning that for no reason would he merit questioning by another ministry, particularly one which might try to take this case away.

Hong left the summary in a sealed envelope on a mail wagon in the hall, took the steps down to Surveillance, and walked through the warren of birds' nests to Ru's office. Ru looked up from his desk, where he was industriously composing a proposal for more staff and money.

"This deal with Nepal, what a load of trouble," Ru said when Hong entered. The border between Nepal and China had been opened a year earlier, and foreign tourists were flocking to Katmandu for the trip. "Foreigners in droves crossing to Lhasa and then coming down through Tibet. How can I keep track of all the guides?"

"Life is short," Hong said. "Don't even try." Ru was an empire builder. More staff meant more power.

"You could put in a recommendation," Ru answered. "Suppose you were to suggest that to do work for you I needed, say, six additional men. You could move a mountain for me."

"Move one for me. My request, a week ago—"

"You're still looking for Ostrander's journal and I still don't have it," Ru replied. "He hasn't left it anywhere but in his pocket. I could have him tossed off his bicycle, of course. At night, maybe. An unfortunate incident with some bad elements—a couple of terrible street thugs."

"We don't need an international incident," Hong said. "I just want to read the journal. How close is he to finishing it?"

"Given a normal life span," Ru said smoothly, "I'd guess twenty-five or thirty years." Ru chuckled. Without comedy, the salve of life, everyone would die of melancholy. "The notebook seems to have...what? A hundred and fifty leaves. He has maybe twenty to go. I'd say in a week or so he has to switch to a new blank book. So if he leaves the first one in his room, we can have it copied for you in a couple of hours."

"I'm looking forward to it," Hong said on his way through the doorway.

"About those six additional men—"

Ru was half up from his seat, his words chasing Hong like

the tail of a kite, but Hong was already heading down to the courtyard, where the Ministry cars, returned from illegal overnight use, fueled and cleaned, were in their garages. Hong stopped at the supervisor's desk. A driver from the pool motioned to a mangled Volkswagen and ambled over, clipboard in hand.

"Destination?"

"Academy of Sciences," Hong said.

Where with any luck, he thought as he climbed into the little car, he might find all three of those men who had vanished during the war, the one who had sent his wife and son home and promised to follow, and the other two who, thousands of years ago, had walked upright in the caves of Choukoutien.

The archives room of the Academy was a dark cell, windowless and consequently airless and a place of deep calm. Spidery mildew crawled across its whitewashed walls, masked by three huge posters of the Harbin winter festival —ice sculptures of pagodas, bridges, temples. Two students, waiting for books, held a hushed discussion on lasers and high-energy particle physics. Behind the counter three young clerks typed labels, watched over by an old troll name Lo, who had a veiny face and bloodshot eyes. Lo looked to be at least a hundred but had the broad shoulders and stiff neck of a soldier.

At Hong's request for the wartime files on the dig at Choukoutien, Lo threw his head back imperially. His bald pate gleamed like a polished vase.

"It will take us a month to locate them," Lo snorted. "Perhaps longer. We'll let you know."

The old man had the audacity to treat Public Security as a nuisance. With such a fool an assertion of rank was useless. "I'm in somewhat of a hurry," Hong said with as much obeisance as he could manage.

"Public Security is always in a hurry," Lo said.

"If I waited outside . . . ," Hong offered tentatively.

One of the clerks, a pale girl wearing thick lenses in heavy black frames, turned and called out: "The archaeological files are in the third aisle on the left, Senior Librarian. Two sections in, fourth shelf from the bottom."

Lo rotated toward his young assistant with bloodshot eyes full of disgust. "Perhaps," he said, then turned back to Hong. "Intellectuals are a waste of resources. Chairman Mao began as a librarian, and the intellectuals ignored him like dirt under their feet."

Librarians, at least to Old Lo's mind, were obviously not intellectuals. How did a scientist ever accomplish anything here? "Nevertheless," Hong said, "their records are sometimes needed in investigations."

The librarian talked right past him. "Chairman Mao learned wisely from the Emperor Qin. Two thousand years ago the Emperor solved all problems of the State. First he killed the intellectuals and then he burned the books. We could use some of that discipline now."

The files were on the fourth shelf from the bottom in the third aisle from the left, and Hong thought he might just as well open the gate, walk around the counter, and take them. But how soon would he need Lo's cooperation again?

"Senior Librarian Lo, we have a new feeling for intellectuals now. They're worthy members of the proletariat."

Lo shivered with a touch of rage. "They're useless, worse than useless. They sit on the pot, but they can't shit."

Chairman Mao was dead but his voice lived on. "This could be quite complicated," Hong said, "if an official request for those documents has to be filed with..." He paused, as if mulling possibilities. "With the political commissar of the Academy, I suppose. Is it still Comrade Liu? No, he's retired, hasn't he? Due to old age."

Old age and retirement were strangers to Senior Librarian Lo, whom nobody would dare retire. Or so his haughty glance would have had Hong believe. Where on earth had he come from? The not-so-bright son of an Army family, maybe? But Lo did prefer to go on working, for like a ship in a bad wind he abruptly changed course and shoved a blank reference chit across the counter.

"A formal request won't be necessary," he said. "Fill this in, please."

Hong scribbled his name, his working unit and division, and glanced up quickly enough to see the young clerks grinning into their typewriters. Two large packets, each tied with strands of frayed brown muslin, came off the shelves with great speed, and old Comrade Lo threw them onto the counter as if he were suddenly thrilled to be rid of them.

In his office at the Bureau Hong spread the files across his desk. Even as he unknotted the strands of fabric and peeled back the rough covers he was struck by the miracle of their survival. That any history at all survived was a miracle. Tear down the past, Chairman Mao had said, which too often had meant rewrite it.

The documents were in two sections—the first a series of reports on the impossibility of continuing scientific work in the turmoil of war, and the second a large slipcase of notebooks and journals collected from the various archaeological sites. The thin parchment leaves of the first section had been stitched with coarse thread into a single volume and then bound with now yellowing glue. To guess from its condition, the volume had been sitting unopened for years; although the edges of the sheets were tattered, the parchment inside had remained nearly white, and as Hong turned the pages not one of them crumbled. Many of the reports were handwritten in crisp strokes that spoke of classical training, and Hong recognized ideograms he hadn't seen since his childhood, before the language was simplified. Chan would love this, he thought, and hate it, too—a demonstration of the passionate scholarship he had been denied. There was no indication of the documents' provenance except on the covers, an imprint from a single chop in red ink that said "Archives, War Against Japan, 1937–45," with "Archaeology" filled in by hand.

Hong lit a Double Nine, coughed, and looked at his ashtray. Butts overflowed onto his desk. He spilled out the contents of an envelope labeled "Archaeological Sites, 1932–43." He sorted through the packets—Anyang, Xian, Anhui—until he found a long thin folder marker *Choukoutien*. It was wrapped in a gray silk band—an oddly loving touch, he thought. To someone these had been very important.

Inside the folder was a diary that had been kept in a student's handwriting practice book, along with occasional entries on parchment, foolscap, and sheets of graph paper—whatever had been nearby, obviously. All of the notes were written in one hand, part in English and part in

Chinese, by a secretary named Cheng Hai-lin, who had been hired in Beijing to translate for the foreigners.

The Little Monk's researchers had given Hong the background of the research at Choukoutien. The dig in the small village southwest of Beijing had begun at the turn of the century, led by a German explorer named Haberer, but had been abandoned shortly thereafter until early in the 1920s. A Swedish team then started anew, followed by dozens of scientists from all over the world—Germany, France, England, Canada. Theodore Ostrander, in Cheng Hai-lin's account, had arrived from the United States when the Rockefellers, the family who had built Beijing Union Medical College, sent money for the construction of the Choukoutien site's laboratory.

Not long after Ostrander joined the archaeological team, in 1930, the researchers began to assemble, from fragments of unearthed fossils, a human being—Beijing Man. "It is wonderful," the secretary wrote. "To think that I am a descendant of this man. Look at him, at his fine noble skull. This is my ancestor. Four hundred thousand years ago he lived here, hunting and picking berries. We are all his children."

The secretary's diary also contained long passages on her hope for a Communist victory in the civil war against the Guomindang, and an occasional allusion to friends who spied against the Japanese. "We are strong," Cheng Hai-lin wrote. "Both of us can make a difference by providing information." Both of us? Both of whom? There were several references to "we" and "us," separate from the entries on the excavation, but all of them were elliptical, circumspect.

Hong looked back to the earlier entries. In an undated note on a single sheet of paper—apparently from early 1936 to judge from the paper used for other entries that year—there was a similar odd comment unrelated to the scientists' work: "It is a difficult time. Our reports do not get through. We cannot understand why we are being ignored."

This was a total mystery. Who was being ignored? Which reports were not getting through? Not those, Hong assumed, having to do with the fossils. It was strange, of course, that Cheng Hai-lin had kept any record of her thoughts, although in those days, unlike now, she would never have expected her neighbors to break into her house and read them. Today you could scour the entire country and find hardly a diary anywhere. Thinking certain thoughts was dangerous enough, let alone writing them.

By 1939 the Choukoutien fossils had been moved to Beijing, but Cheng Hai-lin's diary revealed nothing of Theodore Ostrander's departure from China. One entry—dated "1939, March 12, Beijing"—referred to the foreign scientists' families: "Life here is too dangerous for all foreigners. Professor Ostrander and Professor Watson must begin planning to send their wives and children home. I will miss young Peter." Hong read the passage again. No reason was given for Cheng Hai-lin to miss Peter Ostrander more than the other children.

For the next two years the entries were sparse, and at the beginning of 1941 the diary broke off entirely, with nothing for several months except two brief lines dated in the second week of May: "The loneliness is terrible, but I must be strong," and, "Suffering is my fate." Again no explanations, for either her loneliness or her suffering.

Hong turned to the diary's final pages, which covered the summer and fall of 1941. "The despicable invaders may disrupt our laboratory soon," Cheng Hai-lin wrote. "We must save the scientists' work. Professor Ostrander would like to take the fossils with him to the United States, but he fears the Japanese will discover them, even destroy them. His country's diplomatic officials have refused to help, saying an agreement was made with Chiang Kai-shek's Guomindang government to keep them in the country. How can they still abide by such an agreement in a time of war?"

Eventually Cheng Hai-lin herself, aided by several of the scientists, helped pack the fossils into two redwood crates— one labeled "A" for Beijing Man, the other "B" for Upper Cave Man. "Professor Ostrander says these are the most important. They prove that modern man existed outside of Europe." Yes, Hong remembered, Peter Ostrander had told him about that, the final specimens from the site. In September 1941 the secretary wrote, "Professor Ostrander is still hopeful. General Chiang Kai-shek has told the Americans that the fossils can be taken from the country to protect them. The Marines now hold them in two footlockers, and will move them to an armed camp at Chinwangtao. But if the Marines cannot do the job, perhaps Professor Ostrander will try himself. I pray that he succeeds, for my sake. Who knows if I will survive the war?"

For my sake? What personal interest could the secretary have had in the saving of fossils?

The diary ended. Attached to the last page—unsigned and undated—was a note apparently penned by an archivist: "The Japanese went to war with the United States in December, bombing their ships at Pearl Harbor. The Marines at Chinwangtao were taken prisoner. The fossils were never seen again after this date."

Hong put the diary aside and opened the bound volume of parchment. According to an archivist's preface, the various reports, unsigned and undated, had been collected over the course of several years from Party outposts and university offices. In one of the entries, Hong thought, there might be a description of the collapse of the Choukoutien dig. The first main section was primarily concerned with the difficulties of ferrying supplies to an archaeological excavation at the Bronze Age site of Qian Jinggou on the Yangtze. The pen strokes, formed by what must have been a cheap nib, were shaky, the characters not quite so well etched, as if the writer had been old or afflicted with some disease. The entry was dated December 1939, and as Hong's eyes took in the wavering script, he felt as though he were traveling backward in time. "Scientific work cannot continue under current conditions. The past several months have seen an even greater breakdown in the United Front with the Guomindang. What kind of United Front is this? We fight each other while we try to fight the Japanese. Last month Chiang Kai-shek ordered his soldiers against us in Pingxiang and again in Hebei province. These attacks were extremely well planned. It is as though the enemy has reached into our lines of communication. Only weeks ago they destroyed the southern edge of our primary base in Yanan."

Hong stopped. An attack on Communist headquarters at Yanan? He read the passage again. What was being implied? That the Communist generals in the north had played host to a traitor, someone working for the Guomindang? How had Chiang Kai-shek's troops been able to get so close to Yanan? The rest of the passage continued with the same oblique angle of vision, suggesting but never quite stating that the Communist armies had been betrayed.

Two pages were missing from the journal, having come loose from the threads, and the next entry bore a heading that said only "Spring, 1941." The suggestions of betrayal now took on a different cast: *The capture of our soldiers and the halting of excavation work at Anhui make our suspicions more reasonable. We must begin our search.*

That was all. There was a list of Chinese scientists who had fled the war from various sites into the countryside, some to Communist-controlled cities in the north, others to the rural caves on the outskirts of Guilin in the south. No foreign scientists were mentioned.

Nothing on Choukoutien appeared until the last few pages, and these were in the form of a carbon copy of an official investigation summary, dated July 1968, on the letterhead of the Central Department of Investigation. Since the end of the war there had been several inquiries on the fate of the two redwood crates containing the fossils from the Choukoutien site. In the late 1950s, Public Security had followed a trail that began at a former American base called Camp Holcomb, which had surrendered to the Japanese after the bombing of Pearl Harbor. Attempts had been made to locate Theodore Ostrander, but to no avail. One investigator speculated that an escaped American prisoner-of-war, with help from Chinese researchers at Choukoutien, had spirited the bones to Guomindang officers. In this argument, they were said to be hidden in a museum on Taiwan. A not very reasonable scenario, Hong thought; by now they would have been on display. Another group of investigators, working just before the Cultural Revolution, suspected that the crates had been moved north by Communist officers who had deserted their troops and who had hoped to sell the fossils after escaping to Taiwan.

This last group of investigators, which included a deputy minister of National Security, now dead, had also tried to find and question Cheng Hai-lin, but she, too, had disappeared at the same time as the bones, apparently captured and killed by the Japanese.

An additional page, stapled to the back of the volume, referred the reader to personal correspondence and war reports at the Academy of Social Sciences: "See various accounts of underground organizers, local Party secretaries, etc., 1932–39, 1940–49," with docket numbers listed.

Hong lifted his eyes from the bound papers and reached across his desk for his cigarettes. He shook one out and stood the pack of Double Nines on end, staring at the two gold-colored digits. Two disappearing trunks, two disappearing people. Both the CDI and Public Security had tried to locate Ostrander and Cheng Hai-lin. Hong took from the folder a list of all troop divisions then near Beijing and wrote a note asking Chan to find addresses for any of the officers who were still alive. "And where is Cheng Hai-lin?" he added. "Did anyone ever trace her?"

He left the note and the list on Chan's desk. The idea that Peter Ostrander had come to China to retrieve the lost fossils seemed more credible than ever. All the evidence pointed in that direction. And yet, Hong wondered, why did his own feelings point in other, more complicated directions, into a dark tunnel without end?

The door to the office creaked open and the Little Monk entered.

"Assistant Deputy Director, I have preliminary results on the survey you ordered."

Survey? For a second Hong had trouble lifting his mind out of the journal. What had he asked for? "Oh, yes, foreigners working in hospitals."

The Little Monk was staring at the gray flakes of ash and cigarette butts ringing the ashtray. "Lu Hong, I think maybe you smoke too much."

"Yes, I do. Your report, please."

The Monk struck a pose and recited like a peasant brigade leader proud of his crops. There was, first of all, a team of Russian heart surgeons at Union Hospital. "All spies, but not working for the Americans," the Monk declared.

"Good deduction," Hong said.

"At several clinics we have Japanese observers. They complain about their drivers and take a lot of photographs.

They are much ruder than the Italians, but not spies."
Three German bureaucrats at the Health Ministry were re-
searching the eradication of venereal diseases. "By sleeping
with prostitutes," the Monk said with disdain. "I've informed the cadres at the Health Ministry to watch them
closely."

"Very good work," Hong said. "Prepare a full report."

"A political education session is beginning in ten minutes.
Comrade Zhu Gang suggested you would want to be there."

Hong wanted to suggest that the Little Monk push
Comrade Zhu Gang through the nearest window. He
looked at his watch, Lin's bribery that had failed. He would
have to go across the city for the underground organizers'
reports referred to on the last page of the Choukoutien volume, and now entombed at the Academy of Social Sciences.
Subtract one tedious hour for political education and with
luck he might reach the Academy by early afternoon.

"You go on without me," he said to the Little Monk. "I'll
join you."

When the Monk had left, Hong laid the journals and envelopes in the deep side well of his desk, forced the drawer
shut, and jiggled the key until the tired old lock tumbled
and slid into its latch.

14.

LINKS
IN
THE
CHAIN

Hong was not back in his office until three o'clock. At the political education lecture he had endured a coughing fit, a rise in his fever, and a bout of gastric distress. When the cramps took over he missed everything about negotiations with the Vietnamese, and in any event his mind had been occupied by Cheng Hai-lin and Theodore Ostrander. The lecture ended not in an hour, but almost two, whereupon he took a car to the Academy of Social Sciences. He had an odd sense of being followed, of cars and motorcycles moving behind him in rotation, but he attributed this to his imagination, to his illness, to the dizzying effect of the heat.

The librarians at the Academy of Social Sciences were more cordial than Comrade Lo, and effortlessly produced the war correspondence from the listed dockets. In his office, Hong locked the door and spread out the files. These, too, had been bound into volumes, but in stiff paperboard covers, and along with the personal reminiscences included newspaper clippings, randomly saved requests for supplies, reports on the progress at various excavation sites throughout the country. Hong turned the cover of the first volume, which opened with the dismal story of what had led to the war with the Japanese in 1937, and eventually to the great War of Liberation. Hong skipped through the early thirties until a new correspondent took over, apparently writing from somewhere in the south. The British, the French, and the Germans were running Shanghai. The remaining feudal warlords and their provincial governments in the west had allied with Russia. And as for Chiang Kai-shek, he had more interest in subduing his Communist opposition than in evicting the Japanese, or "the East Ocean pygmies" as the anonymous historian called them.

Throughout the journals were references to several archaeological sites—the Shang tombs at Anyang, Lake Tien in Kunming—but nothing on Choukoutien. The third section, again from the north, recounted the Marco Polo Bridge incident in 1937, which the Japanese used as an excuse to declare war against all China. By the middle of the year the Guomindang was forced to move its government further inland to Chongqing, while the Japanese drove south, slaughtering whoever stood in their way.

Where had Sun Sheng been then, Hong wondered, after the Long March? Somewhere in the Yangtze valley, perhaps, organizing for the Army, trying to break the Guomindang's grip on the people. Or had he already returned to the caves of Yanan to advise Chairman Mao?

A fourth journal began in yet another hand—this time, stunningly, given a date and an extraordinary location: *Fuxian, Shaanxi Province, November 1940*. Fuxian lay only a few miles south of Yanan, the headquarters base of Chairman Mao and his advisers.

The tone of this newest entry bore little resemblance to the others. It was the first to be less concerned with military strategy than with the politics of the Communist struggle, and also the first to hint that at Yanan optimism was a precious commodity, and increasingly in very short supply.

The Japanese retaliation for the Hundred Regiments Offensive is taking a toll. Their "Three Alls" campaign—burn all, loot all, kill all—turns the peasants to our cause, but we suffer from a blockade and shortages of food and weapons. This is causing much dissent. Our leaders say we must adhere more strongly to the "Mass Line." But although we are succeeding in the villages, there are difficulties with our intellectual comrades in Yanan.

Difficulties with intellectuals? Comrade Lo at the Academy of Sciences would be amused. Chairman Mao had relied on poets and scholars to celebrate the Revolution.

And then, as Hong leaned forward, the timing stuck him; the "difficulties" with intellectuals began after the Hundred Regiments campaign. It was only a few months earlier that Sun Sheng's courier had been cut to pieces by bullets in Tianjin.

Hong peered closer. The Fuxian correspondent wrote of those who composed stories, plays, poetry, and essays in support of the Revolution. The intellectuals were identified twice: first by the names they had been given at birth, then by the ones they had adopted. Political and intellectual figures had lived under many names; Chairman Mao's wife had used four.

Sun Sheng was mentioned, as was the youth leader Deng Bo, but as Hong scanned the entries of early 1941 his eyes were caught by a name in which he had more interest—Gan Chunqiao. She was one of the intellectuals who had walked the Long March with Chairman Mao, and who had been publishing poetry and essays under the name Cui Chun. It had been a long time, longer than Hong could remember, since anyone had called his mother by the name she was born with.

Our great poet Cui Chun appears to have lost faith in our revolution. Her story "A Soldier's Life" enforces the belief that our comrades are corrupt and selfserving in their explanations for incompetence. Her characters question the rightness of our cause. "The steel grip of the Party, the demands of the Party," Cui Chun's soldier says, "were choking him. How could he be true to himself and to the Party, too?"

Cui Chun suggests that our leaders are insufficiently

harsh on their own weaknesses. She implies in her story "In the Village" that we are no different from the capitalists. Why does Cui Chun write of a boy who is hindered in his education by incompetent Party officials? Cui Chun must be reeducated. She must learn that criticism is proper only in the right time and place.

Hong sat up. He remembered reading "A Soldier's Life" and "In the Village" when he was younger, but he had never thought of them as attacks on the Party. The entry went on to say that Chairman Mao himself had ordered Cui Chun "to root out her pessimistic tendencies. She is already infecting other comrades with her negative thoughts, particularly the intellectuals in her circle, even our military strategists...."

Who, Hong wondered, did that mean? Her friend Sun Sheng, perhaps? He had been in her circle, and had been a military strategist. Had Sun Sheng also worried about the rightness of his cause?

Hong was so deep in his thoughts that the telephone must have rung several times before he was aware of it. The caller was Fen Like at the Publications Center.

"Thanks to your list," Fen said, "I have an identification for you. The man in both photos with Theodore Ostrander is Dr. Guo Ke, an esteemed archaeologist."

"What about the building in the second photograph?"

"We matched it," Fen said. "It's in Guangzhou. It was a British trade office."

"How much space is missing from the picture?"

"Enough for two people," Fen said.

Hong thanked Fen and returned to the file. While Cui Chun's influence was waning, the Fuxian correspondent said, others were rising, among them the youth leader Deng Bo. Hong paused, too, at the name Huang Xianglin. It sound familiar. At first, living in Shanghai, she had changed her name for political organizing. She had been jailed twice, and after moving to Nanjing changed her name again to avoid being captured by the Guomindang. Finally, in the little farming town of Yanan, she entered the Party School and took a new identity, one that Hong recognized.

She became Wei Ye, a name she had kept.

Wei Ye had been a tiger then, too. As Hong read between the lines in the journal, it seemed to him that Wei Ye and several others had taken his mother's place in the affections of Chairman Mao and his lieutenants. Hong leaned over his desk and, from an entry dated in February, read more carefully about her rise in the Party hierarchy. Unlike the essayists and poets, Wei Ye was a fighter.

Our comrades are effectively locating and disposing of spies in the Japanese-controlled areas in the East. Wei Ye recently uncovered a plot to attack supply lines to the Eighteenth Group Army. A collaborator serving the Japanese was executed at Baoding. We are still searching for a peasant woman in the countryside near—

Hong turned the page. Again a section was missing, and the peasant woman was left dangling in the countryside. A handwritten note said the rest of this journal had been lost. Hong ran his fingers along the edges of the parchment. The pages had definitely not fallen out; they had been purposely removed.

Hong pushed the book aside. Never before, he thought, had he heard so clearly the reasons for his mother's fall from leadership at Yanan. He knew that she had been sent deeper into the countryside in 1942, then brought back only when Chairman Mao realized her value with foreign journalists. They loved talking with her. She and her husband were such good propaganda for the cause—their wit and enthusiasm, their devotion to growing their own vegetables and making their own clothes. But only once during Hong's childhood, at the beginning of the Cultural Revolution, had the subject of the role of intellectuals in the early days even arisen, and then in the most general way. Hong had been sitting by the portal to the living room, listening as his parents and their friends debated their history. He remembered his mother reminding the group that intellectuals were obligated to support whatever, and whomever, the Party ordered them to support. They already knew the penalty for dissent, she said. A pall fell over the room, one that even Hong could notice. The conversation stopped, and the whole group had stared at Cui Chun. "The cabinet-maker wants his clients rich," she had said then, "the coffin-maker wants them dead." She was telling them that Party policy had become a question of tactics and necessity, not ideology. Just as Hong was sorting this out, his father had seen him eavesdropping, and he was sent immediately to bed.

Hong glanced back at the ragged edges along the seam. *We are still searching for a peasant woman in the countryside near*— When had the pages been torn out? What was in them?

Hong thought about the death of a courier who had been in Choukoutien at precisely the same moment that Theodore Ostrander was plotting with American Marines to smuggle the fossils past the Japanese authorities and out of China. He thought about Deng Bo and Wei Ye, the rise of their influence, and the simultaneous disappearance of the Choukoutien secretary Cheng Hai-lin and Theodore Ostrander.

Were there connections to be drawn? Or was he trying to forge links where none existed? The Rule of the Golden Mean applied: If A is true, B is not wrong either.

Hong stood, dropped his cigarettes into his pocket. He looked at the list on Chan's desk, all the Army officers from the war, and thought about the coincidences in time. An attack on Yanan, discontent among the intellectuals, Sun Sheng's secret trip, the shooting of a courier....

So many flimsy links, Hong thought, looking at the old documents on his desk, in such a curiously strong chain.

In the courtyard he stopped at the transport pool, then thought better of leaving a trail and crossed to the bicycle racks. The Party Records Annex was only twenty streets away. He mounted his bike, pedaled through the gate, and turned west on Qianmen. The avenue was wide, with four car lanes in the middle and double bicycle lanes on either side. Hong rode past the rear plaza of Chairman Mao Memorial Hall and continued toward Xuanwumen Street. Block upon block of squat gray apartment buildings baked in the midday sun. Not a single window held an air conditioner. Well, it was common knowledge that the poor tolerated the heat better than the rich. Something in their blood, perhaps.

The Party Records Annex, an unmarked stone building down the street from the China Stamp Corporation, was a useful place for Hong's cousin Hu to work. To indulge his stamp-collecting hobby he had to stroll only a few doors west, and by now the clerks knew Hu so well that they saved proof sheets fresh from the presses. Hong parked his bike in the public lot next to the Annex, locked it, paid the two-fen fee and took a stub from the attendant. Across Xuan-wumen an old man sat on the sidewalk with a bamboo tripod of cricket cages, waiting for buyers while he talked to his caged myna bird. "It's hot, it's hot," the myna shrieked loudly. "Give me a glass of tea."

The Annex elevators were out of service. Wheezing and sweating, Hong walked the steep steps to the fifth floor.

"Zheng Hu?" he said to the clerk at the service desk.

Hu had gone to a meeting, was not expected for at least two hours. Hong thanked the clerk, trudged down the steps out onto the street, and around the corner to the Zhao Family Restaurant, an under-the-awning sidewalk affair where, as Hong expected, Old Hu sat outside nursing a cup of warm tea and a plate of noodles. The son of Hong's paternal grandfather's brother, who had died of a gangrenous leg on the Long March, Hu was an upright old man, with a permanent half-smile and a single arched eyebrow that conveyed a continual air of perplexity. His thick hair had gone gray but he had the skin of a young man, smooth from his forehead to his sharp dimpled chin.

"Not fifteen minutes away and I never see you," Hu said playfully when Hong approached his table. "Have you eaten?"

"You're never in your office," said Hong, laughing as he sat down.

"I'm much too busy conducting business of the State." Hu held up a copy of *Stamp Quarterly*. "Those old Mao stamps I bought a couple of years ago are now worth seven or eight times the issue price. I think I'll sell them." He folded the magazine and called to one of the Zhao daughters for another cup. "I heard your brother was in town. How is he?"

"Prosperous," Hong said a bit sourly.

"You look ill."

"It's the weather."

"I wrote Lin about getting me a new radio and he wrote back that it would be no problem. Just like the old days."

"And the Zhaos are doing well," Hong said, eyeing the tables crowded with young men in fashionable mirror-lensed sunglasses and workers on their way to second-shift factory jobs.

"Two years ago they were starving," Hu said. "Lucky for Zhao, he was unemployed at the perfect time. He has a real operation here—his mother cooks, his father cleans, his wife's mother keeps the books, and he has two daughters and a son-in-law serving the food. It makes me think I should retire because of my terrible health," Hu added with a conspiratorial gleam, "and then open a shoe repair shop. You could be my partner. We'll get rich."

"I didn't know your health was so terrible," Hong said with a grin.

"It might *get* terrible, you never know."

"But if you were repairing shoes you wouldn't have any time to read magazines and trade stamps."

"That's true, but I'd have more money to buy them." The cup arrived and Hu poured tea for Hong. "Anyway, you didn't come down here to humor an old man."

"I wanted to talk about what you were doing during the war."

Hu's arched eyebrow raised in increments, as if notched. "Which war?" he asked as though there had been dozens.

"Against Japan. Where were you in early 1941, for example?"

"This is a slow afternoon at the Bureau, I suppose," said Hu, taking a Double Nine from Hong's pack and lighting it. "There is so little work that at the end of the day you come down to visit and chat about history."

"Not exactly," Hong said.

Hu pinched his cigarette between thumb and forefinger and peered through the smoke as though Hong were a distant figure sighted through binoculars. Hu had been as instrumental as anyone in taking care of Hong and Lin after the Cultural Revolution, having emerged relatively unscathed himself. He might be listed as nothing more than an archivist, but he had friends on the Central Committee. He could open a thousand back doors, place people in jobs, speed up the wheels of the bureaucracy or slow them down as needed. And like everyone else, he could be suspicious even of his own young cousin.

"You were always interested in history," Hu said with great deliberation. "And botany. And poetry. You had so many interests as a child."

"About the war..."

"By the fortune of Heaven, I spent the early part of the war in Shanghai as a bartender at the Cercle Sportif and the old Hotel Park. First I served drinks to the French and the British, and then to Japanese soldiers."

"Weren't you a spy?"

"Sometimes, but nothing too important. I clipped Japanese newspapers, sent them to different addresses in Chongqing. And I had a few kids in the underground working for me, making bombs, breaking codes. Mostly I just tried to stay out of prison camps."

Family gossip had it that Hu had assembled a gang of street urchins who did his bidding—bicycling around the city depositing bombs disguised as candy tins, shooting traitors with stolen Mausers, setting fires in department stores. Anything, in short, to undermine Japanese control. A bit of sulphur, a pinch of potassium chlorate, a cheap spring-wound clock—all easily hidden in a small metal box, and who would suspect a ten-year-old of carrying a bomb? Hu had boys working in newsstands, grocery stalls, and garages listening for useful information, boys who carried messages to Chongqing, boys who printed pamphlets. Or so the stories went.

"Did you get news from the north?" Hong asked.

"Occasionally," said Hu.

"Then you might have known about the Guomindang attacks on Yanan."

Hu puffed thoughtfully on his cigarette and asked casually, "This is your own curiosity? Or an official matter?"

"Let's say a little of both."

Hu took in a view of the sky beyond the awning. "I hear things, you know. I hear you're a very respected man in Public Security, on your way up. It doesn't take much to

undo a good knot. We have riots now, hooligans attacking
our British guests at soccer matches and swimming meets,
Party officials stealing television sets and illegally importing
cars. Times will get worse, we'll need serious loyal men, and
it's hard for even the best of us to protect those who stir the
pot for their own narrow interests."

"Which narrow interests are those?" Hong asked.

"Your office is a sieve. As I said, I hear things."

Force the issue, Hong told himself. Hu will protect you as
he did once before. Someone will protect you. He wondered precisely what old Hu had heard, and from whom.
Chan, probably, trying to protect Hong from getting shot.
Hong wondered, too, whether old Hu also had doubts
about Sun Sheng's death. "The losses in 1940 and 1941,"
Hong said, "the Guomindang and Japanese killing your
spies behind the lines in Beijing and Tianjin, what did you
hear about that?"

Hu's smile widened, distorting his face, and for the first
time it occurred to Hong that the half-smile might be the
result of some damage to his jaw. Snatching a few strands of
noodles with his chopsticks, Hu glanced around at the other
tables. "I heard it was slaughter," he said mildly. "It was
chaos. Our troops in the north kept walking into ambushes.
Food trucks were blown up. Gun shipments disappeared."
Hu shook his head. "It was all very bad."

"I know that getting letters through was difficult, but did
you ever write to my parents, hear anything at all from
them, about discontent, perhaps?"

Without a pause Hu said no, not a letter or a message for
three or four years, security was important, he was too careful, too closely watched. . . .

But the words were coming in a rush and Hong was certain he was lying.

Hong invited himself up to Hu's office—"Maybe you can
show me some of the volumes from the war," he said lightly
—and laid forty fen on the table for the noodles and tea.

"On your salary?" asked Hu, his smile still fixed in place.
He stood, led Hong around the corner and up the steps.

In the Annex library were two logs from 1941 of troop
movements, attacks carried out, battles lost.

Hong remembered his conversation with Sun Sheng's assistant, and rooted in his mind for the boy's name—Jin. What had Jin said? *Papers all over the floor . . . all from the War of Liberation. He wasn't reading, he was searching. Military campaigns, old political arguments, poring through everything as if it were today's internal report. . . .* Sun Sheng had been going through boxes of files, searching for something. Had he been searching, perhaps, for patterns?

Hong looked down at the open volumes on Hu's desk. Cross-checking where people were, and when losses occurred, might be possible. Could someone have done this before, come to these dusty old books to find a traitor? Sun Sheng's face rose up before him. It's a long, dark road, isn't it, Sheng? Did they kill you on this road?

"Has anyone else checked these out lately?" Hong asked.

"They never leave here," said Hu.

"They do now." Hong slid them into his black plastic briefcase, empty but for the political education session's report on Vietnam, which he slipped inside one of the volumes.

Old Hu picked up Hong's briefcase. For a moment Hong thought he would take the books out. Instead Hu handed it back and said, "Plastic. You could have a briefcase of cloth or pigskin if you worked here."

"If I worked here, I'd die of boredom."

"We all die of something," cousin Hu said.

There was no point in going home. By the time he bicycled out to West City it would be time to turn back to Min and Boda's, where he was expected for dinner, and where he would offer uninformed appreciation of Boda's sculpture. He dug into his pocket and handed his stub to the old woman who supervised the bicycle lot, then squeezed between the rows to his beat-up Phoenix and strapped his briefcase to the rack. Office workers were pouring into the lot.

He had just wheeled onto the street when a gleaming Red Flag pulled up next to him and a head poked out the window.

"Going west? I'll give you a lift." It was Deputy Defense Minister Deng Bo. "Have you eaten?"

Hong said he was going east, but Deng insisted on offering a ride. "It's hot, come...put your bike in the trunk." Before Hong could say no, the driver leapt from behind the wheel like a scurrying rabbit, grabbed the bike, and popped it into the trunk. The rear door swung open and Hong saw someone else in the back seat—a round-faced, well-fed specimen with ripe red pockets around his eyes that gave him a primitive look. It was easy to believe he had descended from an ape. On his lap sat an impeccably groomed white Samoyed puppy.

"You haven't met the esteemed Vice-Minister of Defense Hsu Shao," Deng said as Hong climbed in. "This is Lu Hong, Assistant Deputy Director of Public Security, a man feared by criminal and revisionist elements wherever his name is known."

"Which is not many places," Hong said. "I'm pleased to meet you. That's a beautiful dog," he added, wondering what would happen if he were to have it picked up and shot. One more for the statistics.

"My wife's," the Vice-Minister said, petting the animal. "I've brought it back from the veterinarian for her." He eased over on the seat to make more room. "Your brother has quite a reputation at Defense. We can count on him to supply high-quality parts."

The limousine had turned north past the subway station on Xinhua Street.

"I thought we were going east," Hong said. "I have an appointment."

"But you'll stop with us for a moment, won't you?" Deng said.

It wasn't a request. The driver slowed halfway to Chang'an, turned into a narrow tree-shaded lane, and pulled the car to the curb. The Vice-Minister stepped out and Deng Bo gently pushed Hong toward him. They turned up the steps of a small nondescript rowhouse that might have been just another set of flats but for the obvious fact that the doorframe showed only one button. A single family living in this building? Impossible. The Vice-Minister rang the bell with great ceremony, poising his finger over the button before pressing and giving Deng Bo a wink and a glance over his shoulder. A peephole slid aside just above eye level, and a moment later the door swung open to re-

veal a slim woman in a high-necked black silk gown standing under a tiered crystal chandelier lit up like fireworks on
National Day.

The central hallway was carpeted in bright red, and bev-
eled mirrors lined both walls. Directly across from the door
was a small counter, behind which a chef was serving up
plates of cold sliced duck and steamed tomatoes and bottles
of Laoshan mineral water and Beijing-brand wine. Huge
white porcelain jars held roses and azaleas, and on either
side were small square parlor rooms, bathed in blue cigarette smoke and decorated with long scrolls of calligraphy.

From a distance Hong heard the unmistakable echoing
click of mah-jongg tiles, and then he saw, in an alcove under
the stairs, a cashier exchanging stacks of yuan notes for
round plastic chips.

"I hope you won't be arresting us," the Vice-Minister said
jovially as he checked his pet with the doorman. No, Hong
thought, but I might arrest your dog.

He peered around the corner into the north parlor,
where fast-moving games of Forty Points and Sky Nine
were quietly in progress. The feeling was of a Buddhist
temple—reverent and, if not exactly holy, a close companion. The only thing missing was incense, and the cigarette-
smoke cloud stood in just fine. This is what we fought to
stamp out, Hong thought, these are the excesses people
gave their lives to end. All the same, he liked the ambience,
the nice rich carpets and the good food and faintly lit globes
dispersing moonlight. A passing waiter offered him a plate
of duck with sauce and pancakes on the side, and despite
himself he took it. How often did he eat good duck? At the
head of the Sky Nine tables, where cards were tacked onto
green baize, a girl in a tight brocaded pink dress held a
glass-domed jar with three dice. The men at the tables laid
their chips on the cards and the girl turned the dice jar
twice. She up-ended it, revealed the dice, and another girl
swept in from the side to collect chips from the losers and
pay the winners.

"Do you gamble?" Deng said quietly to Hong.

If he said no, he would be rude and sound like a hick. If
he said yes, he would be admitting to a crime. So he said
nothing.

"Hardworking cadres need a rest, relaxation," Deng continued. "The Vice-Chairman himself is addicted to bridge. He comes here frequently. In fact, he built the place."

Hong had heard such accusations during the Cultural Revolution—that Party leaders siphoned money to build gambling dens, that secretaries carried official papers to the bridge tables for the signatures of high cadres. Scanning the tables, he recognized a few faces, members of the Central Committee he had seen on television during the trial of the Gang of Four. It was probably all true, those stories about misappropriation of State funds.

Deng was getting a stack of black chips from the cashier. There were two vacant slots at the Sky Nine tables, one at either end, and he led Hong to the nearest seat.

"Sit down, play. Here, take some chips. These are five yuan each."

Hong glanced at the Forty Points table, which was at least a game he knew. "If one is going to gamble," he said, "let it be at something requiring intelligence and skill."

"But don't we gamble in life all the time," Deng asked, running his fingernail over the edge of his chips, "and isn't luck often better than skill?" He left Hong and took the seat at the far end of the table. Hong sat and threw a five-yuan chip on the card in front of him, a nine. The dice were turned and they came up three, three, three. Remarkable. Deng had played eight, lost, and chosen eleven. Hong left his winnings on nine, added a chip, and the dice came up six, two, one. It happened again, and again. Well, nine was doing fine, how about something a little harder? He pushed the chips to fifteen—a six and nine together—and added three more chips. The dice showed six, six, three. Luck was one thing, and so was skill, and this, Hong thought, was neither. He pushed four more chips onto fifteen, left his winnings, and the dice were turned. Six, five, four. The other players were amused.

"What do you expect from the police?" said one with a chuckle, using the loudest stage whisper Hong had ever heard.

He felt the others staring, waiting to see what he would do. He pushed every chip he had onto fifteen, left the winnings, and the dice fell: five, five, five. In fifteen minutes one hundred yuan had become six hundred and fifty, more than his salary for three months. Hong stood and carried his chips to the cage.

"Your luck's very good," Deng said, coming up behind him.

"Sent from Heaven," Hong replied without turning around, and Deng laughed loudly. Hong pocketed his winnings, if they could be called that, and turned to Deng with ten crisp ten-yuan notes in payment for the initial chips. Now that I've taken his money, Hong thought, he'll be trying to collect. Deng steered him to a lounge at the rear of the house and they sat like the Emperor's advisers on down-stuffed couches.

"Western art is decadent," a young cadre was saying. "Nudity, abstractions, too much color."

"It's not only art, it's the economic ideas. Why, before you know it we'll be having workers' strikes."

"The hotel workers," said the first man. "At the foreign joint-venture hotels they get paid three times as much as at the State-owned hotels. A bad situation and we have to correct it with vigor. None of them like being servants, it's feudal, but pay them too much and you'll see, we'll have a whole class of reactionaries who want only higher wages."

Parasites, pigs, loafers. A hotel worker was on his knees cleaning floors while they sat here drinking beer. Reactionaries never died, they spawned in Party offices like crickets and cockroaches. Hong wondered how hard he would fight against them if the weapons were guns, not words.

"How is your investigation of the American going?" Deng asked.

"It's proceeding," Hong said.

"An enemy of the State, perhaps," Deng said. "But then there are enemies of the State everywhere."

"Maybe even in this room."

Deng's face tightened into a smile, and when he spoke it was with the satisfied triumphant voice of the Party lecturer. "Very good, very good. You're always on the lookout. Have you found out what Ostrander wants?"

There was something of the buffoon about Deng, a clown-ishness, but it was only the costume of a clown—and worn so carelessly as to intentionally *not* deceive. "Ostrander's purpose is obvious," Hong said broadly, as if any intelligent person would already have understood. "He's here to steal research."

"Really?"

"It's very clear," Hong said. "The hospital is doing research on psychic children. This has possible Defense implications, children who can view in their head remote military installations. Ostrander is here to steal this research."

The idea was so preposterous that Deng could only nod his amused appreciation. Hong stood, said he was late for another appointment, and made his way to the door. Deng offered the use of his car, which Hong rejected—"No, thank you very much, I'll take my bike."

The driver unloaded his Phoenix from the trunk. Hong looked at his briefcase, partly unzipped and askew in the rack. Heavy books struggling to escape. The zipper had been closed when he left Cousin Hu's office. Hong glanced back at Deng, who smiled from the stoop, then mounted the bike and started back toward Qianmen. Was it worth five hundred and fifty yuan just to know the contents of a briefcase?

At the corner he stopped and opened it; the report on Vietnam had migrated from the back of the second volume to the middle of the first.

He pedaled again toward Qianmen and had been riding east on the narrow lane for barely two blocks when in the faint light of the tulip-shaped streetlamps he saw a strip of metal glinting in front of him. He braked, tried to stop, but too late. A long pole swung out from the bushes. He ducked, but it hit him from behind, a hard crack on his shoulders, and his belly slammed into the handlebars. The bike wobbled, Hong grunted and pumped crazily to stay upright, but the tires skidded and he felt his leg buckle and twist under the frame before he crashed to the pavement.

They were on him in a minute, tearing at his pockets, holding him down. Something wooden cracked into his arm.

"Robbers!" he shouted. "Scum!"

A hand muffled his mouth, covered his eyes. He thrashed and kicked but couldn't break free. There seemed to be a dozen hands on him. A fist sank into his stomach, an arm hooked around his neck and he felt as though his head were being torn off. His eyes closed and then popped open in pain, and he saw a flash of yuan notes, a sheaf of brown paper floating over his head. Fuck, they must have known about the gambling den and waited for unsuspecting idiots.

"Hooligans," he screamed and was instantly rewarded with a booted heel in his groin, then another, and another.

When he recovered they were gone, their running footsteps echoing from the pavement. Hong lurched to his feet, rubbing his head, and could just make out the wavering forms climbing into a car. He felt his pocket for his glasses, which were miraculously intact, put them on. The car was an old 212 truck, or maybe it was new, the style hardly changed, lime green with one broken taillight.

Robbers with a truck?

Hong tried to trot toward it but his legs refused. He squinted to make out the license plate—the prefix was 31, for Beijing, but the rest of the numbers were disappearing into the night. Beijing was a dark city, at night it turned gray and brooding, hiding from itself.

Scum bastards, robbing a cadre in the middle of the city, it was a crime, an insult, an assault on the State. And since when, Hong asked himself foggily, am I such a defender of the State? He flexed his arms, and aside from a throbbing where the club had hit him, there seemed to be no damage. He gently touched and probed himself all over—a bruised palm to his knees, a finger tentatively testing the outline of his ribs. There was a scrape on his chin, a logy queasiness in his stomach, but no bones broken as far as he could tell. His left pant leg was shredded and trickles of blood ran along his calf down to his ankle.

He limped back to his bicycle. The handlebar was dented and a shard of rubber had been torn from the grip, but the wheels were untouched. The sturdy old Phoenix could take a better beating than he could. He rolled it back and forth and the tires moved as smoothly as ever.

Trucks belonged to the Army, he thought, or maybe to a production brigade with a trailer to tow. Not, however, to common hooligans. He started toward Qianmen, wheeling the bike, and it was only after he had taken a few shaky steps that he noticed something wrong with the balance. Not enough weight.

The briefcase was missing, and with it the two war volumes.

Hong thought of what Ru had said about getting Ostrander's journal: *I could have him tossed off his bicycle. At night, maybe. An unfortunate incident with a couple of terrible street thugs.* And then Hong remembered the attack on Yao Yilin in Tianjin. But in Tianjin they had been trying to kill, and this time they wanted only information.

The Vietnam report was unimportant, and so in a sense, Hong realized, were the books. Would he have found a traitor in them? Perhaps, but to know that others were curious, that was more significant. Indeed, the very absence of the war volumes was the most enlightening fact. Again he had the curious sensation, the same as at the Party Archives Annex, of tracing the footsteps of someone who had been here before him. And now others, remarkably unconcerned with hiding their own trail, were following in his.

What are they looking for, Old Sheng? Why did they kill you? What did you find?

15.

FOSTERING AMBIGUITY

Dongzhimen Street was a disaster. It was enough to weep over. Great gray-and-pink apartment houses sprouted from mud. A playing field gave way to a mound of painted cement called the Huadu Hotel, foreigners only, fenced in on Xinyuan Road by spikes shooting from the ground like prehistoric insects. The domed and columned Agricultural Exhibition Center, once a Russian architect's temple amidst greenery, sat ingloriously in clouds of dust contemplating the march of Progress. What were they doing to the face of his city? Bulldozing it into oblivion.

Hong climbed the steps to Boda and Min's apartment, weary in his body, and in his heart, too. He had not spoken to his friend since the day Boda called from the post office to help disguise Hong's absence from the divisional meeting. As Hong reached the third floor an airplane roared overhead, ascending from Capital Airport, and in the space between two steps carried him away with it. Where was it going? Anywhere, he thought, take me anywhere. He knocked, and Boda appeared at the door.

"We were worried about you, you're late," Boda said, and then, catching sight of Hong's bloody pants and the scratch on his cheek, took his arm and exclaimed, "What happened? Come in, sit down!"

"I had an accident. Some lousy Army truck driver cut me off."

Min, still wearing her doctor's smock from the clinic, bustled to the door with their baby daughter Shaojia in tow. Min worked uncountable late nights, and her oval face had a careworn beauty. She leaned down to examine Hong's leg. "The damn Army. I'm sure they didn't even stop."

"No, they didn't," Hong said.

She brought a towel and alcohol from the bathroom, dressed the scrapes with gauze, then stood and looked at Hong. She touched his forehead.

"You're running a fever."

"I've had a cold."

She scowled in disappointment. "Do you want to get summer pneumonia? Honestly, you're terrible. Come by in a few days, I'll bring something home from the clinic for you."

"You've changed your hair," Hong said, noticing that it was styled more in the shape of her face. "You look lovely."

"Oh, don't flatter me," she said, although she girlishly ducked her head.

When she was in the kitchen Boda led Hong to his worktable. "So now," he said boisterously, "after the Four Modernizations, we'll have the Five Desecrations—art, humanity, architecture, work, and housing. Then we'll have the Three Clarifications and the Seven Exterminations and who knows what else." He was obviously in a black mood. He pulled Hong around the table and whispered, "Are you ever going to tell me what that telephone call was about? It had to do with Sun Sheng's death, didn't it?"

"I'd rather not talk about it," Hong said.

Boda grimaced. "All right, all right, but be careful." He picked up one of his clay molding tools. "How was the trip to Beidaihe? How's Yamei?"

"You can't ask in front of Min, can you? She still doesn't approve."

"Min's very fond of Shen Kuang, you know, and Yamei is . . . well, she's . . ."

"Young," Hong said.

"Yes, young." Boda turned toward the table and said to the windows, "Min's pregnant."

Hong's breath caught in his throat. A peasant in the countryside might get away with a second child, but in the city . . .

"How long?"

"Seven weeks. I don't understand it. We use the pill."

"What's she going to do?"

"Abort it, obviously. If I earned more money maybe we could stand the penalties and still have enough left to feed another mouth, but as it is . . ." Boda's voice trailed off in anguish.

"I'm sorry," Hong said. In the kitchen the baby was crying.

"You're lucky. If you get married again, you can have another child. That's some price to pay, huh? Maybe we should start a new campaign—the 'One Is Enough but Get a Divorce and You Can Have Two' campaign. We could start a movement."

"You and Min are still young enough," Hong said. "Maybe the policy will change, and in a few years . . ."

They both knew that no matter what else changed, the one-child policy would probably last forever. Boda just shrugged and rested his hand on a large clay sculpture, thin shoots extending from a central column. "My latest. What do you think?"

It looked like a barren tree. Or a dancer. Or a tortured prisoner screaming.

"It's interesting," Hong said, realizing that what it looked like, actually, was whatever you wanted to see. That was the problem with unapproved art. It fostered ambiguity.

Boda touched his friend's arm. "You don't have to like it. But I'll tell you what it is. It's one woman dancing to music that only she can hear. Listen to this," he said, turning to his record player. A flute sang from the speakers and Boda wistfully closed his eyes. "Mozart's second flute quartet. Composed for royalty. They paid artists for their work, to do whatever they wanted."

Min came in from the kitchen with tea. "So maybe things were better under the Emperor?" she said with dismay. "Dinner's almost ready. Please go get Nai-nai."

Boda's mother, who lived with them, was downstairs borrowing a pot. Min closed the door behind Boda and turned to Hong.

"He's not happy," Hong said.

Things were bad, Min admitted. Boda's sister had lost her job at a refrigerator factory because of new productivity rules. "They want the dormitory space for another factory and she may have to come and live with us. Who could dream such things would happen? People losing jobs?"

Hong nodded agreement. Until just a few years ago, no one worried about a job.

"And he's not selling much work," Min went on. "Even the foreign embassy people don't come to look. We used to be able to count on fifty or sixty yuan a month. It's not the money that bothers him, really. It's the idea that nobody will ever see what he makes." On top of everything else, Min added, an old childhood friend of hers, an engineer on a scientific exchange in France, had decided not to come home, leaving his wife and two children. The news had been kept quiet.

Hong took this information with apparent calm, but he was shocked that he had heard nothing in the Bureau. He wondered about the torment of such a decision, how a man could abandon his wife and children.

"And you," Min said with sudden harshness, "what's the matter with you? You have responsibilities, you have a son."

Hong looked at her blankly.

"Boda told me about Sun Sheng," she said sternly. "And Chan told me, too. How stupid can you be! Would *your* parents, with two sons, have taken these kinds of risks?"

Maybe they had, Hong thought. Maybe they had taken precisely the same risks. He tried to explain his reasoning to Min, the cause of his suspicions, but Min had no patience.

"I know you loved him," she said sympathetically, "but he

was old." She looked down at her fists, clenched tight in frustration.

The door opened and Boda came in with his mother. Min stood and turned toward the kitchen. "What we'll do to-night," she announced, "is have a glass of wine, we'll eat and drink, and we'll forget about politics."

She seemed to think that was possible. So, if only for a night, it would be.

PART THREE

"*To truly
know a man,
you must
know his memories.*"

16.

DR. GUO KE

What a wonderful place to live, Hong thought, if you were old enough to have once owned a house here and clever enough to have held on to it. He stepped from the subway onto Andingmen Road and crossed over the Old City Moat. Apart from the occasional gaping wall split by the seventy-six earthquake, still waiting patiently for renewal like a child nobody loved, the north quadrant of the city looked as though the Emperor's scholars might be in residence. The archaeologist Dr. Guo Ke, identified by Fen Like as the man in the photograph with Theodore Ostrander, had lived here in his gray brick, one-story house before Liberation, moved out during the Japanese occupation, moved back after Liberation, out again during the Cultural Revolution, and back again after rehabilitation. According to his file, his most recent absence had lasted four years, when he was sent to a commune in Sichuan to pick vegetables. As Hong knocked on the door he gathered himself together for an ordeal. Old people had only bad memories.

The door opened and revealed a tall bearded man holding a copy of *Enlightenment Daily*. He was a true ink-and-brush figure, the very picture of an intellectual. He leaned forward and narrowed his eyes to read Hong's identification card through the bottom half of his bifocals.

"Comrade Lu Hong, from... from Public Security," Dr. Guo said, standing upright. "What an honor! It's been many years since I've had the pleasure of an official visit."

The official visits must have been less than happy, to judge from the sarcasm. The door opened wider. Hong caught sight of Empire furnishings—long maroon settees and varnished letterboxes and silk tapestries—and, at the end of a long hall, an old woman dressed in black pants and an embroidered white jacket scurrying through a curtain. I'm bringing more bad memories, Hong thought. Everybody run and hide.

"The dig at Choukoutien?" Dr. Guo said when they were settled with tea in the living room. He stroked his lush gray beard. "That was a long time ago. I'm afraid I don't remember much about it."

"How well did you know Ostrander?"

"How well do we know anyone?" Dr. Guo answered politely.

"I'm asking the questions," Hong said.

"So you are. Perhaps you should have followed proper procedure and brought a local official with you. Perhaps you should ask someone from the Public Security branch or the street committee to join us."

"This is a special investigation. Now I ask you again, how well did you know Ostrander?"

"I hardly knew him."

"A man who worked alongside you for... what? Three years? Four years? And you hardly knew him?"

"Our great leader Chairman Mao was a fourth cousin of mine," Dr. Guo replied patiently, explaining sunshine to a flower. "I never knew him very well either. In fact, when they sent me to the countryside the peasants assumed I must be particularly evil, or the Chairman would have saved me."

There was a clumping in the hall. Dr. Guo turned to the open archway and the old woman, who had until now not shown her face, made her way into the room.

Dr. Guo held up a hand. "Please, my dear, stay inside."

"Who is he?" she demanded fiercely, her face puckered in anger. "What does he want from us?"

"He's from Public Security and he wants nothing. Now, please..."

The old woman wagged a finger in Hong's face. "Go away! Leave us alone! We've been through enough!"

Dr. Guo rose, eased his arm around her, and to the accompaniment of muttered insults escorted her outside. Hong, rubbing his sore arm, went to the windows that lined the back of the room. In the shaded courtyard garden, where bunches of fat green grapes swung from the arbors, Dr. Guo was handing his wife her gardening shovel. The sun fell on her in speckles and Hong saw the true madness in her face.

When Dr. Guo returned, Hong again took up the same line of questions—Ostrander, the excavations at Choukoutien, the disappearance of the bones. Dr. Guo was immovable.

"You're everything that's wrong with our country," he said, locking a malevolent gaze on Hong's eyes. "*You're* the bones of China. You shoot a petty thief but assign the best jobs to your own family and friends. Your neighbor disappears one day and you forget his name. You forget he ever existed. And you call yourself honorable." He folded his arms and raised his head high and glared down his nose. "Go back and file your report. Tell them I'm a bad element. Tell them what you like. I won't help you."

The tirade stunned Hong; it was entirely out of proportion to an investigation concerning remote events. "The questions are simple," he said, "and your answers will harm no one."

"Someone is always hurt by your work."

"Your secretary disappeared. A woman named Cheng Hai-lin. Where do you think she went?"

"I haven't any idea at all," Dr. Guo said firmly.

"What do you think happened to the bones?"

"Maybe the Japanese discarded them. Maybe they were stolen. Maybe they were hidden and sold."

"By whom? By Ostrander, perhaps?"

Something in Dr. Guo's eyes, a brief flickering, drew Hong's attention, and this time the answer came with less force. "Ostrander was a scientist."

"That doesn't mean he wasn't a thief." Hong reached into his pocket, taking great pains to find a cigarette. Every criminal wants to speak, fill the empty air, if only to protest his innocence. Dr. Guo, however, remained silent. "Did you like Ostrander?" Hong asked.

"I already told you that I hardly knew him."

"He sent a wife and son home to the United States, and then he disappeared, too. Where did he go?"

"Maybe he tried to save our work," Dr. Guo said. "Maybe he took a boat and drowned at sea." The archaeologist rose and crossed the room to his tall bookshelves. He pulled out a thin volume. "They stole these from me once, all of them. Most of them they burned. You might recognize this one," and with his bony hands he pushed the book toward Hong: *In the Village* by Cui Chun. "By your mother, isn't it? Didn't someone tell me she had a son in Public Security? Aren't you the son of the great revolutionary poet? Are you a great revolutionary, too?"

Hong stifled a flinch. How often had his parents urged him as a child to fight for the Revolution? Merely listening to the question summoned memories of their determination to instill in him their beliefs, their passion. He ignored the book of stories extended in his direction and took out the two photos copied by Fen Like. "Do you remember when these were taken? During the war, wasn't it?"

"We were always taking pictures."

"What were you doing in Guangzhou?"

"Taking pictures, obviously." He slid the book back into its slot.

"These photographs are fakes," Hong announced. "Look at them. Someone is missing."

Dr. Guo glanced down, took the photos and held them close to his face. He looked at the first, probably taken in

Choukoutien, and after a short examination laid it aside. But when he turned to the second—the one Fen had identified as a British trade office in Guangzhou—his eyes tensed, his eyebrows lifted like tops popping off good beer, and then suddenly he went pale, as if hearing about an awful tragedy.

He had recognized the second picture, Hong thought, and he knew who was missing.

"Who was with you?" Hong asked, raising his voice.

"I . . . I can't remember. It was fifty years ago."

Hong leapt to his feet. "But you *do* remember!" he bellowed. "Who was there between you and Ostrander?"

Dr. Guo squinted at the photo a moment longer before returning it to Hong. His hands made a brushing motion on his chest, and he regained his composure. "You would like to incriminate me in your plot to get rich," he said indignantly, "turn me into an even worse bad element. No, Assistant Deputy Director, do as current policy instructs. Go and seek truh from facts . . . whichever truth you'd like to find."

"What plot are you speaking of?" Hong asked. "How could I get rich? How could I incriminate you?"

Dr. Guo let out a soft laugh, his breath escaping in short bursts. "Go," he said bitterly. "Go and serve the people."

On the sidewalk bordering Dongdan Park street peddlers sold T-shirts emblazoned with English slogans. Hong licked his vanilla ice-stick and watched Chan thumb their wares before finally choosing one. It was just as well that Chan's English was nonexistent. The shirt he had chosen, pink with purple lettering, said DEPARTMENT OF PUBLIC WORKS, BEIJING CHINA. Happy with his purchase, a gift for his teenaged nephew, Chan returned to the ice vendor's cart.

"What's that scratch on your cheek?" he asked, buying an ice-stick.

"A bike accident. I got cut off by an Army truck."

"The fucking Army, they own the streets." He started walking toward the park's eastern entrance. "Ostrander has made a friend at the hospital. A woman."

"Name?" asked Hong.

"Liang, given name Yu-shang. A troublesome element,

apparently, who was transferred from a clinic in Nankou to study hospital administration."

"And she becomes a friend of Ostrander's. How good a friend?"

"She speaks English. They eat lunch together every day."

"Too good a friend," Hong said. What kind of woman would risk such an association with a foreigner? "How did she learn English in Nankou?"

"I'm getting her file."

"What else do we have on Ostrander?"

"Other than the woman, he hasn't seen anyone suspicious, he hasn't gone anywhere suspicious, he hasn't said anything suspicious."

"He's quite a spy, isn't he?"

The heat was smothering, the air pollution the worst in history. Hong turned into the park and walked along a tree-shaded stone pathway under a white trellis. Neglecting to tell Chan that Peter Ostrander's father might well have committed one of the great crimes of the century, Hong described his confrontation with Dr. Guo and repeated the seething farewell.

"Seek truth from facts," Chan snorted with a flash of venom. "As if there were such things—either truth or facts."

"But what was he really afraid of?" Hong asked.

"You always expect me to be a thinker and interpreter on the habits of the influential. The only truly influential person I've ever known was the wife of our hero Dr. Sun Yat-sen. What a house she lived in!" Chan had once served on guard duty at Madame Sun's house, a mansion set on the Back Lake behind the Forbidden City. "Rooms upon rooms, even a little movie theater, can you imagine? Did you know she had three cars? A German one...a Benz, and a custom Red Flag, and an old black Volga big enough for a regiment."

"Yes, I know," Hong said impatiently. "Let's suppose you're Dr. Guo, and I ask you about a missing person in a photograph. You accuse me of plotting to get rich. Why?"

"Because everybody is getting rich. Dr. Guo himself is rich. He has that house, doesn't he?"

"But a plot," Hong repeated. "Why would he accuse me of trying to incriminate him?"

"Old people talk that way. They've all been accused so often by somebody of something that they think we still want to put them in jail or send them to the countryside or... or whatever they can imagine."

In the normal course of things Chan could be counted on for good sparring, the entwining of a case's complexities into a dozen different braids. But in Dr. Guo's behavior he perceived only simplicities.

Chan stopped walking to tighten the straps on his sandals, propping his foot on a bench. "Why did you go see Dr. Guo?" He lowered his foot and bent down to the other. "Why aren't you figuring out how to get rid of this case instead?"

The question no longer yielded an answer. Because I can't, Hong thought, because a man's death demands retribution, because spies do not threaten their enterprise by befriending troublesome elements, because... but he had run out of invention, somehow leaving the real reasons behind, unspoken even to himself, while he turned the case over and over in his mind.

"There are knots here to be untied," he said.

"Leave them tied the way they are."

The path led down to the park's west gate, where across the street another peddler, a tailor, was setting up shop on the sidewalk. Talk about contradictions! Capitalist activity was officially sanctioned while the latest issues of *Legal System* and *Red Flag* exhorted the proletariat to ever greater sacrifices in the name of socialism. Everyone used to say, "China has stood up," and now they said, "It is glorious to get rich." What they really meant when they said serve the people, Hong concluded in a fit of silent fury, was serve the people but do well for yourself. He spat forcefully into the gutter and wondered what was happening to him. He had never been so cynical.

At the corner of Chongwen, Chan reached into his pocket and pulled out an envelope. He held it for a moment, then asked, "Where were you on Tuesday night?"

"I told you, I was running errands."

"I suppose you needed things for the beach," Chan said.

"Yes, that's right."

"Do you usually go the whole way to Tianjin to run errands?"

Hong let out a short laugh. "You've been checking up on me."

"I'm watching your back, just in case someone decides to shoot you."

"What's in the envelope?"

"I shouldn't do this," Chan said with a sigh as he handed the envelope to Hong. "I shouldn't let you do this to yourself. But here's your death certificate."

"So you got it after all," Hong said. "Sheng's."

"And like I said," Chan added, "maybe yours too."

In the office, with Chan standing behind him, Hong opened the envelope. *Bureau of Records, Beijing Municipality, Certificate of Death, Name of Deceased, Usual Residence.* At the bottom was a statement signed by the chief administrative doctor at the Hospital for Infectious Diseases: "I certify that I attended the deceased, and I further certify that traumatic injury or poisoning did not play any part in causing death, and that death did not occur in any unusual manner and was due entirely to natural causes."

It was thoroughly regular, normal.

"What does it tell you?" Chan asked.

"Nothing, absolutely nothing at all," Hong said. "I think I have some additional movie passes..."

"No," Chan said.

"There are three other death certificates I would like to see, three men cremated by your friend Comrade Song within a few hours—"

"No," Chan said again, more firmly. "May I tell you a simple fact of my life? I am middle-aged and middle-level. I will not always be middle-aged, but middle-level is my destiny, and I've reached it. I would like to stay here and serve out my years. Someone at the Medical Examiner's office would notice a request for three more death certificates, and all the movie passes and ration coupons in the city wouldn't stop them from finding us. You've already agreed that this one tells you nothing, and three more will tell you three times nothing, which is also nothing."

"Yes, you're right," Hong said, except, he thought, that doctors, for all their tenuous, miniature power over life and death, submitted to a higher power as quickly as any common criminal with a gun to the nape of his neck. "Yes, this tells me nothing at all," he said again.

He folded the death certificate into the envelope as though it were a sacred scroll and locked it in his recalcitrant side drawer.

17.

OSTRANDER'S FRIEND

The middle-aged woman lying on the metal trolley had acupuncture needles in twos and threes across a shaved band of flesh on the mottled crown of her head. Hong watched from the hospital hallway as he had a week earlier. On one side of the trolley stood Dr. Yan, on the other Ostrander and a group of assistants armed with notebooks.

Dr. Yan began reading three-digit numbers. When fifty had been recited the woman commenced repeating them, first in reverse order, then as they had been announced. It was a remarkable feat. Dr. Yan glanced up, noticed Hong, and told Ostrander to continue the experiment. Ostrander waved cheerily to Hong, who, despite himself, waved back, his hand flapping like a clown's.

"Assistant Deputy Director Lu Hong, did you enjoy our experiment?" Dr. Yan asked, walking from the operating theater more nimbly than one would have thought possible.

"Fascinating," said Hong.

"Would you like to volunteer?" the doctor asked with an

insinuating, puckish grin. "For a short trial we wouldn't even have to shave your head."

"No, thank you," Hong said, and facing away from the door added softly, "I want to know about the woman."

"The woman on the table?" Dr. Yan replied, purposely misunderstanding the question. "She's a baker's assistant at—"

Hong sliced the air as his extended forefinger flew up to the doctor's face. "The woman Ostrander is involved with."

"But you should really try the experiment. It would be rewarding to...to watch the waves of your brain, to hear your memories." He touched Hong's hand. "To truly know a man, you must know his memories."

"How was Liang Yu-shang assigned to you?"

"Through the Health Ministry. She's studying clinic administration, maintaining records. But her behavior is so good it must be revisionist, isn't that right? So maybe you should arrest her immediately."

Hong started to walk away, and Dr. Yan followed, bouncing on his cane.

"I'm going to lose Ostrander, aren't I?" he called out.

Hong kept walking. We're both going to lose him, he thought.

"There was a Russian named Shereshevski," Ostrander was saying over tea and sweet buns in a corner of the hospital dining room. "He was a newspaper reporter, and he could remember everything that was said to him, virtually word for word. He never took notes. Repeating a list of a hundred numbers was nothing, Shereshevski could do it without trying. He didn't speak a word of French, but if you read him poetry in French, he could repeat it back to you a week later. Mathematical formulas, technical language, meaningless phrases—it didn't matter what you said, he could recall it without a mistake."

"It must have been difficult to be him," Hong said.

"Why?"

"Having all that useless information in his brain."

Ostrander laughed. "Yes, well, it was a problem, he kept finding that his memory was stuffed with things he didn't need. But he solved it. Whenever he wanted to get rid of something, he just imagined writing it on a blackboard, and then he imagined himself erasing it."

That was an even better skill, Hong almost replied, but thought better of it. "Lucky for him that it worked both ways," he said instead.

"Yes, wasn't it? Anyway, what we're trying to do is find out how to manipulate memory. Shereshevski had his own mental tricks, but if we can find where in the brain those tricks take place, where things are stored and how the brain decides when to erase them, who knows what secrets we could unlock? We'd have answers to how intelligence works, clues to senility, a whole host of diseases..."

Three women entered the room, clerks, chattering and giggling softly. Ostrander called out, "Jade, come meet my interpreter." The woman who approached was quite beautiful and, unlike the others, wore makeup: red lipstick, green eye shadow, pink rouge on her cheeks. Astonishing! Despite the fact that stores now encouraged women to buy cosmetics, Hong expected such a display only by the most daring women in Shanghai. Even Yamei, who liked new clothes and admired the women in cinema magazines, would never decorate herself so brazenly. This must be Liang Yu-shang, the woman Chan had told him about; her name translated as Jade Frost. She was in her mid-forties, Hong guessed, but had obviously been exempt from physical labor. Slim, with a smooth complexion undamaged by the sun, she looked like a billboard model advertising clothes or television sets or the "one is enough" policy. Her pale green dress fitted quite tightly—too tightly; it was the clothing of a prostitute, not a medical clerk.

"So you're making friends," Hong said, "as I predicted you would."

The woman came up to the table and Ostrander introduced her.

"Comrade Lu Hong, I'm pleased to meet you," she said in perfect English.

"Jade, please sit down," Ostrander said, pulling out a chair and pouring another cup of tea.

"Yes, please, please join us," Hong said, half rising from his chair. "Your English is excellent. Where did you study?"

Liang Yu-shang hesitated. "In California," she said, "in the United States."

"How interesting," Hong said. "When was that?"

"Before the Cultural Revolution," she said, "when my father was a professor," and then, with a broad smile belying her evident anger, turned to Ostrander and added, "a member of the 'stinking ninth' class. Intellectuals have fared better since then." She turned back to Hong. "Your English is very good, too. You must have gone to foreign languages institute to learn it so well."

"And on his travels," Ostrander put in. "He's been more places in the world than I have."

"Oh?" Liang Yu-shang said with apparently innocent curiosity. "How lucky you are! Where have you been?"

Hong sensed more than curiosity in her question. He tried to remember precisely which cities he had mentioned to Ostrander. "Rome," he said tentatively. "Moscow, Paris..."

"I've been to Paris," Liang Yu-shang said brightly, "didn't you love the sunset there, the light falling on Notre Dame?"

"Yes, it's a magnificent church," Hong said. She had wanted to see if he could identify Notre Dame as a church.

"Where did you live in Paris?" she asked.

"In the Eighth Arrondissement," Hong said evenly, meeting her gaze, "in housing for the Steel Mission near the embassy. I was working as a translator."

"That sounds like a wonderful life," she said with great enthusiasm. She picked up one of the buns and nibbled. "This is so sweet," she went on. "I wouldn't have guessed from looking at it that there were sweet beans inside. I would have thought meat." She took another bite, laughed delightedly, and shrugged. "Even with dumplings, things aren't always what they seem to be."

Hardly subtle, Hong thought, but Ostrander missed it all. Liang Yu-shang glanced at Hong charmingly but knowingly—and her smile said that she had been in this situation before, that she knew what he was.

The conversation turned to her help in translating for Ostrander, to hospital gossip, jokes about old Dr. Yan and his benevolent dictatorship, Ostrander's attempts to buy rice with the wrong ration coupons. At every moment in the banter, Hong felt himself tested by Liang Yu-shang. Yes, she certainly knew he was not a guide from the Academy of Sciences.

But what was she?

Eventually Hong excused himself, but not before hearing Ostrander invite the woman to dinner at the foreigners-only restaurant run by the French. How would Liang Yu-shang get in? Whom would she pretend to be?

At the entrance to the dining room Hong turned back and glanced at the two figures in the corner, who were blessedly oblivious to his presence. As if no one could see her, Liang Yu-shang let her hand graze Ostrander's and allowed the touch to linger a moment too long.

What a fine performer she was, Hong thought. He wondered who was writing the script.

The message on his desk from Chan said that not only had the Choukoutien site secretary Cheng Hai-lin disappeared, there was not a single shred of paper to show that she had ever existed. She had probably changed her name like everyone else, and in the middle of a war behind enemy lines no one left calling cards or forwarding addresses. As for the list of officers who had commanded Communist and Guomindang troops in the north, Chan was still working on it. The file on Liang Yu-shang would be available in the morning.

At the bottom of his note was a rapidly scrawled *Call Ru.* And after that, *Call your wife.*

He dialed for an outside line and then the number at Beijing Broadcasting. The connection, for a change, was strong and clear. No one was listening today. The extension rang in seconds.

"I'm on my way to a meeting," Shen Kuang said when she picked up. "But I wanted to tell you that I got a copy of the divorce decree."

What was he supposed to say? How pleased he was? "So they finally decided we weren't going to reconcile."

"You helped them along," she said. "You and that girl"— she never called Yamei by her name, only "that girl" or "your friend" or something equally dismissive—"have been seen in too many places."

"Well, anyway, I'm glad for your sake."

"And I need fifteen yuan for Bai," she went on.

"For what?"

"A math tutor. He's having trouble."

"Since when?"

"It's nothing serious, but I don't want him falling behind."

Hong was irrationally tempted to reply that she ought to get the fifteen yuan from Zhu Gang. Monkey, he thought. Subhuman animal. If Zhu was going to play the role of father, let him pay for the privilege. He earned twenty or thirty yuan more a month than Hong did. Or let *him* tutor Bai; he had a child's mind, after all. "Fifteen yuan is no problem," Hong answered instead. "I'll get it to you by next weekend."

"Good. Now don't be upset, but I have to go to the editing room now."

She hung up. Hong held the plunger down for a second, then dialed Ru's extension at Surveillance. Ru answered and said Ostrander had started a new diary this morning, and had left the old one in his room.

"Can you get in and photograph it today?"

"I don't have anyone available," Ru said. "We'll go in tomorrow when he leaves for the hospital."

"Today," Hong said.

"Hong, I'm running four full-time operations as it is. I just sent a team to Katmandu. Special Security took two of my best and—"

"Today," Hong repeated.

Ru sighed. "Okay, okay, tonight while he's at dinner. I'll get them developed in the morning and you'll have them before noon."

"I'd like them tonight."

Ru lost his temper. "Hong, that's ridiculous, it's out of the question. It can't be done."

"At this very moment," Hong said, "I'm writing a memo to the Director of Operations recommending that six additional officers be moved to Surveillance."

"Make it eight," Ru said.

"Didn't I say eight? I meant eight."

"And you'll send me a memo authorizing the use of sixty rolls of film."

"Sixty? That's twelve hundred shots."

"We're very short on film, too."

Ostrander's diary would take ten rolls at most. Fifty extra rolls on the black market would buy Ru two or three expensive new suits.

"I'll send the memo down today."

"The diary will be on your desk at midnight."

"Thank you," Hong said. "Serve the people."

It was a busy afternoon for the Director of Investigations. A dozen of Wei Ye's assistants lolled outside her office, waiting to deliver reports. Hong joined the others on a bench. No one talked about crime, no one complained about housing, no one mentioned politics or new directives on lightbulb rationing or riots at soccer matches. In such large groups the only safe topic was the weather. "We can discuss the heat forever," Chan liked to say, "because the Party doesn't control it."

Eyebrows raised when Hong was called ahead of the others. He shrugged dumbly as though to protest at being this week's favorite flavor, and strode through the open door. An investigator of tax fraud was on his way out.

"She's in a cross mood," he whispered without missing a step, and pulled the door closed behind him.

Wei Ye was bent over the reports Hong had submitted. Not lifting her head, she waved him forward with her cigarette, making smoke rings in the air.

"Please sit." Wei Ye looked up. "You are not exercising your best energy on this case," she said in the admonishing tone of a schoolmaster. "Are there perhaps other matters distracting your attention?"

She meant Shen Kuang, the divorce.

"No," Hong said.

"Personal matters, perhaps? Something I could help you with?" Now she was grandmotherly, a parody of tenderness.

"No, thank you, I have no distractions at all."

"Well, then. You were instructed to become Ostrander's

friend. Clearly the American is here to locate and steal the missing fossils. But he must have accomplices, and you must find out who he is working with. Spend more time with him, reveal yourself to him, and he will reveal himself to you. Think what this might lead to. Perhaps he would even try to recruit you."

"It isn't my nature to become too friendly," Hong said.

"Nature? You underestimate yourself," she said, now flattering. "In the guise of promoting friendship between peoples, you can learn a great deal."

"But surveillance of Ostrander has produced nothing. Isn't it possible that we have no case?"

"That's dangerous thinking," she said, switching from flattery to aggrieved disappointment. "Of course there is a case, as your otherwise excellent work has made so obvious. For example, you located Dr. Guo Ke and secured the files on Choukoutien. I congratulate you for that. Also for your investigations of the other doctors. And perhaps most for your astute inference that a Defense Department cadre on the Academy's screening committee was responsible for choosing Ostrander and admitting him to the country, an aspect of the case that I will look into myself."

"The Defense Ministry refuses to cooperate."

"They'll cooperate with me, I assure you. You continue with your investigation. Find Ostrander's accomplices. If not Dr. Guo, then someone at the hospital."

"He's made one friend, a woman from a rural clinic sent to study administration."

Wei Ye shot out her arm and vigorously thrust her cigarette toward Hong. "There, you see, you *are* making progress," she said excitedly, now urging him on in battle. She could be sweet or cold, she could congratulate vigorously or reprimand severely. She possessed a dozen faces and moods, all at the same time. "Interrogate this woman, search her background thoroughly. Where is she from?"

"I'm waiting for her file."

"A rural clinic, you said. Remember the case of the Burmese drug smugglers. Their accomplices were from rural communes, where they stopped to supply themselves on the journey east. This woman, if she's from the north, may even know where the fossils are. Be vigilant, grasp revolution, this is your chance to do a great service for your country."

For a moment Hong was speechless. Citing the case of the drug smugglers, in which the Three Tigers were nearly implicated, was not only a slap in his face, but a reminder of her power. As if he needed reminding.

"Yes, I'll try," he said at last.

"You lack enthusiasm. This is a bad sign. I recall now that you were hesitant to assume responsibility for this case. And Comrade Zhu tells me you have been less than diligent in attending your unit's political education sessions."

"I'll admit that I'm sometimes too busy."

She shook her head. "Comrade Lu Hong, you shame yourself. Have you no pride? You neglect your Party obligations and you neglect this case. Did you not admire Sun Sheng, our great cadre and your own inspiration? What would he have said? He would have told you that it is counterrevolutionary to refuse to pursue a case that you yourself have demonstrated is of great consequence. And with Ostrander anything could happen. Do you remember the case of the French student?"

Hong nodded. How could he forget? The Deputy Director in charge of the case had been secretly tried under some trumped-up charge and dispatched to a labor camp.

"This student traveled freely in the countryside and wrote dishonest negative reports after his departure. Ostrander is equally a threat. He speaks our language sufficiently to have allies, he could use his accomplices to find the fossils and smuggle them out of the country. Now you must intensify your efforts, and if you need additional help, just request whomever you want. Is Comrade Wu Keping useful?"

"Superb," Hong said, "a model of thoroughness." Maybe the Little Monk would get a promotion.

Wei Ye leaned forward on her arms. "You're very pale, Comrade."

"I've had a slight cold."

"Attend to it immediately," she ordered.

"Yes, I will."

She fell back in her chair. "So we understand, then? This Dr. Ostrander is engaged in crimes against the State, and you will bring in the evidence." She pushed his reports aside, waved him out, and picked up one of her new telephones to summon the next assistant deputy director.

Hong edged through the door and passed the chief investigator for foreign media, who said, "I hear she's in a cross mood."

"Yes," Hong replied, "and several others, too."

Crimes against the State, he thought as he slowly went down the steps. Traitors in the foreign embassies and their trade missions, in the foreign media, in the clubs of overseas students.

But Ostrander? In answer to this, Hong could only rely on instinct, and he began to form a picture—to first draw the dragon, as the saying went, and then to dot its eyes. Just as Sun Sheng's cremation had provided the irritation for a nervous and dangerous itch, so did the coincidences of Ostrander's presence nudge Hong toward trusting his intuition... an intuition supported by logic. Ostrander wore no masks except as everyone did, concealed no layers except as everyone concealed them. There was nothing so deep as the unspoken, but Ostrander had no secrets.

Hong held to the handrail; his palms were sweating. He thought of Sun Sheng's books, the volume of Confucius that Ma Sufei had pressed on him before her hasty departure to Guangzhou. *If the name is not correct, the words will not ring true.* He thought of the names thrown up like a desert storm from those old files, and the odd conjunctions: the anonymous correspondent's suspicions of a traitor at Yanan, the disappearance of two boxes stored in footlockers, the fragmentary ramblings of a woman named Cheng Hai-lin.

So who are you, indeed, Dr. Peter Ostrander? For what memories have you been invited here, and why do all roads, in so unlikely a fashion, lead to you?

On the steps Comrade Zhu Gang was coming toward him. You ape. You weak, sniveling, toadying...

"Ah, Comrade Lu Hong, I was going to stop in and see you about leading a session on—"

Hong brushed rudely past him as if he weren't there.

In his office he sat, propped his feet on the desk, and thought of Dr. Yan waiting for a scientist to share his research, and of a Defense cadre on the screening committee

to approve—maybe even encourage—the choice of Ostrander.

To truly know a man, you must know his memories.

A clerk knocked, opened the door, and with a cursory
greeting dropped the afternoon mail and telexes on Hong's
desk. Hong opened the envelopes first, case files from Bureau offices in the northeast, and one by one appended his
notes. He came to a thin envelope from Public Security in
Tianjin, and found an unexpected dossier concerning the
theft of wool from the Number One Carpet Factory on the
Jintang Highway. The case, Hong quickly ascertained, was
old, closed three months ago. For some reason the assistant
director in charge had issued an update—solely, said the
covering letter, to inform Beijing of the criminals' sentences
and the institution of new security procedures at the factory. For good measure, a copy had gone to the Ministry of
the Textile Industry.

Hong studied the brief file, a mere four pages. Public
Security in Beijing received such updates only on request,
and Hong had never requested this one. He stared at the
file, then picked up the envelope, reached inside. There
was a slip of paper that had not been attached to the dossier, as though it might have ended up in the envelope by
accident. On it were scribbled someone's random
notes—"Department meeting, 3 o'clock Wednesday...
review plans for assignment of street officers...." *There are
ways to communicate if necessary,* Yao Yilin had said. So Yao
had managed to trace back, through his own friends, the
courier who had prepared him for Sun Sheng's perilous
entry into Tianjin. In the corner, encircled, was a name that
at first registered only dimly with Hong... Wang Zhen.
Thousands of Wangs, millions of Wangs.

Hong opened his directory of Public Security, and no
sooner had he seen the man's title than he recalled the se-
vere face, the restrained greeting, and Sun Sheng's jovial
introduction: "Come now, Wang, don't be so cheerless. Lu
Hong is going to take over from all of us one day. Better be
friendly to him now, or you'll be begging him for favors
then." Wang Zhen had been a Deputy Director of Investigations eleven years ago, when Hong joined the Bureau.
Wang was now retired, living on his generous pension. Had

he been at Sun Sheng's memorial service? Hong couldn't
remember.

There was really no need to see Wang's biographical
sketch in the Party Directory. Hong knew precisely what he
would find, and of course, when he pulled the heavy volume up to his desk, it was there: *Military and reconnaissance,
War Against Japan and War of Liberation.*

Hong felt a pounding in his temples, a headache coming
on. If he had been superstitious it would have been an
omen, a signal to stop. Nature had her warnings: an earthquake, a storm, a pounding of blood. But there was another
aspect of nature that also occurred to him, one that he had
heard from an old farmer on a childhood visit to the countryside: when the melon was ripe, it would drop from its
stem. Some events depended on time, not will, and superstition or not, Hong thought, there could be no stopping
now.

The blocks of old houses off Lishi Road, behind Yuetan
Park, belonged to Public Security, but in fifteen years no
one had been able to secure an apartment there. All the
residents were retired, and—with a park nearby, the Xidan
Market within bicycling distance, and Yuyuan Lake close
enough to walk—none of them were going to move if they
could help it. Hong arrived as the sun was just beginning its
descent to the horizon. He parked his bike in front of a
three-story building with a street-level stoop that had recently been restored; the mason's grooves in the cement
were still fresh, and etched deep, as if done by an angry
worker. The first-floor windows were shuttered, but on the
second they had filmy curtains, and the entrance door, with
a fan-shaped window in the lintel, had actually been polished.

Hong went in, up through the dark stairwell to the second floor. Door Number Three, directly at the top, had a
small brass knocker. Hong lifted it, let it fall. From inside he
heard squeaking, a rattle, and an irregular clumping on the
floor.

"I'm coming, I'm coming, is that you, Little Ou?"

The door opened, and Wang Zhen backed his wheelchair
away at the sight of a strange visitor. Yes, Wang had been at

the memorial service. Hong remembered the wheelchair—
a wooden contraption with a cane seat and pedals at chest
level that Wang pushed with his hands. Wang's luxuriant
hair was stark white, the color of chalk.

"That's not you, Little Ou . . . who's there?"

Wang squinted, and Hong moved into the light, introducing himself and holding out his Bureau card at arm's
length. "You remember me, I was a friend of Sun Sheng's.
We met many years ago."

The old man thought for a moment. "Perhaps," he said.
"Perhaps we did." He wheeled farther back into the apartment, and waved Hong in.

"I was expecting my granddaughter," Wang Zhen said in
a slow, purposeful voice that was the very essence of con-
templation. "She comes every few days to read to me. My
eyesight is not so good."

They were sitting at the front of the apartment, overlooking the street. On a painted white table were stacks of books
and assorted magnifying glasses, on the floor a rug that had
been repaired so often the pattern was gone. Hong had
made tea, difficult for Wang since he could hardly stand. In
the kitchen they had discussed every topic imaginable—
from the heroics and brilliance of Sun Sheng to Bureau
politics to the new economic policies, but Hong had not
ventured a hint of why he was really here. Now, settled into
a chair by the window, and due on the other side of the city
in less than an hour, he could hold off no longer.

"I remember Sheng talking once about the war, how you
had worked for him behind enemy lines."

Except for an almost imperceptible change in posture,
the raising of his chin, nothing in Wang's manner implied
that this was a subject of more than passing interest. "My
eyesight was better then," he said.

"You were in Tianjin, weren't you?"

"Among many places," Wang said.

"In 1940, though, in May it would have been, you were
clearing routes for couriers around Tianjin."

Wang reached down and massaged his withered legs. "I
remember you better now," he said thoughtfully, "yes, you
were a favorite of Sun Sheng's. But he must have been more

discursive than usual when he told you about the war. I
don't think any of us have thought much about it for years."

Hong took a gamble: "Let's say, then, that I've been talking to others as well."

Wang nodded his head up and down, up and down, with
exaggerated deliberation. "Might you have a cigarette? I'm
not supposed to smoke, they say it will kill me, but I'm already near dead, so what's the difference?"

Hong leaned over and put a cigarette to Wang's lips,
clicked his lighter.

"You're a deputy director now," Wang said, exhaling.

"An assistant deputy."

"Not very high up to conduct official investigations."

"It's unofficial," Hong said.

"And you're in a different war from the last one," Wang
said, hurrying on. "You don't shoot at Japanese. You shoot
in the dark. But that suits me since I can't see anyway."

"Courier routes," Hong prompted. "May of 1940."

Wang lifted his cup of tea, set it aside, and used the
saucer for his cigarette ashes. "You're speaking of 1940. My
particular concern at the time was the transport of materials. Perhaps you're interested in that."

Hong said that his interest was in whatever Wang could
tell him.

"Well, you've never fought in a war, but you understand
that to win a war you need supplies. At the time you're concerned with, the supply situation was bad. The Japanese
had taken Xiaoshan, costing us our route to Shanghai. We
had good intelligence in Shanghai—by radio mostly, two or
three excellent men operating in the French concession—
but you can't fortify supply lines by radio, you need people
there, and by that point we didn't have access to the sea."

"What was Sun Sheng's involvement in this?" Hong
asked.

"He was in charge of moving supplies for the northern
troops. He'd been getting airplanes from the Russians, but
he needed fuel, bullets, medical supplies. It was winter, men
were hungry and sick, and we were competing with the
Guomindang for control of Shanxi. Fighting two enemies at
once..."

Wang clasped his hands together and sighed. The Communists could count on help from the British in Hong Kong, he said, but Japan controlled the coast. Supplies from Hong Kong had to be bought and then flown to the northwest.

"And how did you make those purchases, the ones in Hong Kong?" Hong asked, hearing in his head the voice of Raymond Caffey, the Englishman he had met in Beidaihe: *I've been coming here a long time,* Caffey had said.

Wang held up his cigarette and shook it. "A very good shot in the dark," he said admiringly. "We had men in Hong Kong to make transactions and pilots willing to risk Japanese artillery. The Japanese guns were better than ours, newer, but we had men willing to fly."

It was accepted that some of the pilots would be shot down. But in February, Wang explained as though it were yesterday, only half the planes survived the journey. In March, barely a third. Sun Sheng ordered the flights ended. "It was only a matter of time before Hong Kong fell to the Japanese, but stopping the flights hurt us badly."

"Around this time," Hong said, "when you were losing so many pilots, did Sun Sheng wonder—the idea might have occurred to him—that someone in Hong Kong could be responsible?"

"Our intelligence was never good enough to find out," Wang said flatly.

"And Sun Sheng?" Hong asked. "What did he think?"

"I was a courier, not a strategist, I wouldn't have been told," Wang said, closing the subject.

Hong let a moment of silence pass, but Wang refused to speculate about the loss of planes and pilots. Hong took up where he had begun: "Later that year, in May, didn't Sun Sheng make an unusual journey on one of your courier routes?"

Here Wang allowed himself a long thoughtful moment. He tapped his fingers lightly on the pedals of his wheelchair, made small sucking noises through his discolored teeth. He looked briefly out the window, studied the rug.

"Sun Sheng," Hong said. "An unusual trip on your courier routes at the end of May in 1940."

"Unusual," Wang said. "That's one way of putting it."

And how would Wang put it? Hong asked. Wang replied

that he would say the journey was unprecedented. Wang, supported by sympathetic peasants, had built a string of courier stops strung from the east, near Tianjin on the coast, to Shaanxi Province. But that anyone from Yanan should cross enemy lines was unheard of. Military strategists were too valuable to risk in actual operations. Still, in late April, a message was sent along the line for the attention of Wang himself, and Wang only, to provide a route for Sun Sheng, both to Tianjin and back again to Yanan.

Why, Hong asked, would Sun Sheng have selected Wang for this delicate operation?

"We'd worked together in Beijing before the Japanese invasion, and Sheng knew he could count on me. Of course my routes weren't perfect, it's impossible to keep an absolutely secure route. Three or four peasants shot and you had to chop out two hundred kilometers as unsafe."

"And was Sun Sheng warned that the courier routes were less than entirely secure?"

Wang drew up in his wheelchair. "Do you think we were total fools?" he replied loudly. "Naturally I warned him."

Which had no effect, Hong suggested, on Sheng's decision.

"None," said Wang.

"So he trusted you with his life," Hong said. "Did he also trust you to arrange this particular trip in such a way that no one else at Yanan knew he was making it?"

Wang's eyes narrowed, and he looked querulously at Hong. "I think you've been talking to a great many others about this trip so long ago."

"Sun Sheng requested, did he not, that no one else at Yanan discover where he was going, that he was traveling to Tianjin. In fact, he asked you to put out false information, not only to mislead the enemy, but also so that his own comrades would think he was elsewhere."

Wang looked out onto the street. "My granddaughter is on her way to the door. Maybe you should take the rear steps to the courtyard entrance. She's very patriotic, and would feel compelled to inform the neighborhood committee that she found me with a visitor."

Wang's poor eyesight, which enabled him to play the role of doddering pensioner, was apparently sufficient to see the whole way to the street. Wang began pushing his hands on the pedals of his wheelchair, turning and rolling toward the rear of the apartment.

"Send her away," Hong said. "Tell her you're not feeling well. Tell her to come back later."

"No, no, you have to go."

Hong trailed him into the kitchen. "The plans for Sheng's trip were not revealed even to his comrades at Yanan, is that right?"

Wang reached the rear door and was awkwardly twisting himself forward to open it. "Yes, you're correct," he said urgently. "The information was to be kept secret even from Yanan. Now, hurry, you must leave."

Hong stepped out and the door closed behind him. He heard the clack of Wang's wheelchair moving away.

"Is that you, Little Ou? I'm coming."

18.

DUCKWEED MEETING DUCKWEED

For five hundred years only the Emperor and members of His court entered the Forbidden City. Outside its walls His subjects might starve in crowded shanties, but ten thousand palaces inside housed the Ruler with the Mandate of Heaven. The Revolution ended all that, and now any Tibetan peasant can pass under the Meridian Gate and pose for a picture next to a Red Flag sedan facing the gilded pillars of the Hall of Supreme Harmony. Hundreds of peasants come and go, but the black car never moves; it just sits there being photographed.

On Chaoyangmen, the street running along the north wall of the Forbidden City, Hong and Yamei rode their bicycles to the Three Doors Theater. Disguised as an old Buddhist temple, with a yellow tiled roof, it lay at the end of a long driveway bordered by ancient evergreens. At the entrance to the driveway Hong and Yamei showed their Party cards, and Hong held out his special passes. A month earlier, in a fit of generosity brought on by a torrent of tears, he had provided residence papers to the sister of a beleaguered woman in the Cultural Affairs Ministry, and she had insisted on repaying him with tickets to the restricted screenings of foreign movies. Hurrying past the guards, for they were already late, Hong and Yamei continued on to the three high red doors, lodging their bikes unlocked—a theft here was impossible—in a rack to the side.

They rushed in and found their seats in the third row from the rear. Tonight's showing was of an American movie made just after the end of the Cultural Revolution. It was called *End of the World at the Moment,* a story of the Vietnamese War of Liberation. It had already begun, and like most internal screenings had been dubbed into Chinese. Helicopters sputtered across the screen, a jungle burned, a man's head upside down stared at a ceiling fan.

"Saigon," the man said. He broke a mirror with his fist and wiped blood on his face.

Yamei covered her eyes. "This is too violent."

"The human spirit is full of conflict between good and evil," the man said. The helicopters blared across the screen as the man was ordered on a river trip to find another man. Hong lost interest in the loud music, the journey up the river, and his mind drifted. He thought back to Wang Zhen's preparations for shepherding one man from Yanan to Tianjin, and wondered who in Yanan, if anyone, had discovered Sheng's purpose. He also considered, on another train of thought altogether, what sort of planning was necessary to move a woman from a remote clinic to a hospital in Beijing. How did you pick this particular woman? Many beautiful women spoke English.

At an explosion in the jungle on the screen Yamei reached for Hong's hand. Her warm touch startled him, he turned, and his chest thumped. She wanted so little from life: to travel to the next Olympics, to get married and have a son, to live in modest comfort. Was that so much? Maybe it was.

Hong looked up. American helicopters were dropping firebombs and strafing a Vietnamese village.

"Chemicals that kill people have the smell of victory," the American soldier on the screen said.

• • •

The lights came on before the final scene ended. Hong looked at his watch—almost ten o'clock. He had to admit that the filmmaking was superb, but he had already witnessed enough of death, Chinese and Vietnamese, on border patrols. What ideological point were the Americans making? That they themselves were evil?

"I don't understand," Yamei said, standing. "What was wrong with the fat man in the jungle?"

"He was just a symbol," Hong said.

"Of what?"

"Of the futility of the journey," Hong said. "Of American decadence."

"I still don't understand."

The theater emptied in minutes. In the driveway engines started up, chugged smoke, Red Flags and Shanghais rolled to the entrance. Hong and Yamei turned along the porch in front of the doors and hoisted their bicycles from the rack.

"Would you mind if I didn't ride home with you?" Hong asked.

"Of course not, it's too far," Yamei said. "Thank you for bringing me tonight."

"You didn't really enjoy it."

"But I did, the pictures were magnificent, they show me how others think. Even if it was all so sad."

Hong glanced around to see who might overhear. "Listen," he said, "I'm going to be extremely busy for the next few weeks, I might not have time to see you."

She accepted this with equanimity, simply nodding.

"And I think," he went on, "that maybe you shouldn't telephone me at the Bureau."

Her face tightened in alarm. "What's wrong?"

"It's nothing." His eyes searched the crowd again. "I hope your practice goes well. I'll see you before you leave for the competition."

"You weren't paying attention to the movie." She tugged him into the shadows cast by the porch. He bumped a tree and they were showered by pine needles. "Please tell me," she said evenly. "You're in trouble, aren't you?"

Any truth was as damaging as any lie. What he wanted to give her was impossible: an escape from him. He was silent for a moment, then kissed her. "Let's go," he whispered. "People will be noticing."

With evident reluctance she wheeled her bike out. Cars crept past them like lumbering camels, lit only by moonlight settling through the trees.

"Is that you, Comrade Lu Hong?" The voice came from behind, and Hong recognized it instantly. He turned toward the driveway and saw the gaunt Englishman leaning on the open door of a Mercedes. Again, as in Beidaihe, he wore white—expensive white linen freshly wrinkled, this time with a vest.

"Mr. Caffey," he said.

"Yes, it is you! What a delightful surprise."

A surprise, Hong thought, like duckweed on water meeting duckweed. The Englishman could have been in his car and out on Chaoyangmen by now; he had been waiting. Hong noticed the license plate—prefix 21 for Tianjin. Why? Caffey offered them a ride—"The trunk is quite large enough to hold both bicycles." Yamei politely accepted Caffey's handshake and gave a delicate smile, but said no, she preferred to ride her bike home. Hong understood that it was her fear of foreigners.

"Then perhaps Comrade Lu Hong will join me for a drink, a bit of a snack?"

"Yes, I would enjoy that," Hong said. "I'll walk down to the street and meet you there."

Caffey slid back into the seat of his car, tucking his jacket under him as he did. The door closed with hardly a sound and the rear window glided up electrically, sealing shut with a thump. The driver nosed into the line.

"Why are you going with him?" Yamei asked urgently.

"It's part of the case I'm working on."

"But is the contact authorized?"

"I can authorize it myself," Hong said. The tension welled between them and it was suddenly unbearable. "Don't call me. Don't expect me to call."

"For how long?"

"I don't know. Just understand that it's to protect both of us."

She seemed about to cry. She covered her mouth with her hand, and her breath came out in quick heaves.

Caffey's Mercedes pulled up next to them.

"Go on now," Hong said. There were tears in her eyes. Hong watched her ride out in front of the car and turn east, then look back longingly over her shoulder—for some sort of sign, perhaps. But for once, he had no sign to give.

The restaurant was called the Western Eating Room and was in an old underground bomb shelter near the Cultural Palace in Xidan. It was open late for the sons and daughters of powerful cadres. The walls were of painted concrete, but the pedestal tables were topped by squares of polished quarry stone. Caffey had chosen it, Hong suspected, because few of its patrons were likely to understand English.

"The Americans thought they would win in Vietnam," Caffey said. "How could they lose against those bloody little yellow people in pointy hats? That's the flaw in the American character. They think they're better than everyone else."

As do the British, Hong thought, and the Chinese, too. Was there a race on earth that did not feel superior to all the others? Caffey had ordered a bottle of *baijiu*—clear lightning. He roamed from topic to topic: the Vietnamese war with the Chinese, the foibles of American foreign policy. He was a man from whom chatter flowed as if from a radio. Talk was his currency.

"And the Americans here," he was saying, "all blithering on about the wonder of modern China. As if your system actually *worked*, as if your peasants weren't starving to death. I imagine our friend Ostrander talks that way. He's an idealist."

"Are they?"

"Sorry, I miss your meaning."

"Our peasants," Hong said. "Are you sure they're starving?"

"I would say so, wouldn't you? Both physically and spiritually. What does Ostrander think?"

"He hasn't said a word about them," Hong replied.

Caffey offered an English cigarette, holding up a lighter dressed in the finest green jade. "And what about his spying, has he put the touch on any State secrets yet? Taken a few snaps, possibly, of tanks and guns, that sort of thing?"

"I don't believe he's had the opportunity," Hong said, and then, on a more direct course, "I wonder if he's even a spy."

"But then why do you suppose," Caffey asked with a rising languorous drawl, "that they assigned you to watch him?"

"Maybe he'll lead us to a spy," Hong suggested airily, implying that the idea had just occurred to him. "We have a saying: he has the thread of a spider but the trail of a horse."

Caffey inhaled slowly and regarded Hong with an expression akin to admiration. "How would that happen?"

"It's only a saying. I don't know how it would happen."

"With the trail of a horse," Caffey said, "maybe he's stalking—for someone else."

"That possibility occurs to me," said Hong.

Caffey sat back and let his eyes play over the crowd. The young people pretended not to notice him, though they could hardly help gawking at his clothes, the gleam on his high black shoes. Hong, however, could see only the scars on his nose, his fingers. Step by step, Hong thought; the method Wei Ye had suggested for Ostrander was equally applicable to the Englishman. Reveal a little of yourself and his mask will fall.

"I'm quite fond of your *new* sayings," Caffey went on. "To get rich is glorious. Time is money."

"Those are good sayings, too. We mix the old and the new."

"Yes, you're learning, thank goodness. Take this business of motivating people with money. The rest of the world has known certain facts about human nature for a rather long time now. Even the Russians are getting a taste of it. Pay people more, let them earn more, and you'll build more trucks, eat more rice, have more...money."

"As long as we don't lose sight of what's truly important. Trucks and money mean nothing without spiritual happiness."

Caffey linked his fingers and, self-satisfied, rested his hands on his chest. "Comrade Lu, as a good Communist you shock me. Spiritual happiness is for artists. The only objects of value are those you can hold in your hand. Silver, gold, jade. Paintings, objects from antiquity."

Hong switched to Chinese. "*Koutour*," he said rapidly.

Caffey blinked. "Bones?"

"Not *goutour*," Hong said. "You misunderstood my accent. I meant *koutour*—suffering, hardship. They lead to wisdom, which is more valuable than jade."

"Of course, of course, I did misunderstand. I was thinking of our friend Ostrander. He was telling me the other day about his father, those missing fossils."

It was Hong's turn to be caught off guard. "You spoke with Ostrander on the phone," he said, thinking he had missed the call in the logs.

"No, at the International Club. He came for lunch."

Incompetents, Hong thought. There was no report of the meeting in the surveillance summary.

"And he spoke about his father with you?"

"Fascinating, isn't it? A man who vanishes without a trace. Prepares to leave for a train to Hong Kong and never arrives."

"For Hong Kong? On a train?"

Caffey's expression faltered. He had the disoriented look of a man suddenly and unexpectedly lost on once familiar ground. It was arriving home and finding your wife in bed with another man, it was the soldier's grasp on your arm when you were almost across the border with false papers, it was the shock of going to sleep in one country and waking in another.

How had Caffey known what Peter Ostrander had not?

Hong moved in before the mask rose again. "A train to Hong Kong. Is that what Peter Ostrander told you?"

"Uh, yes, I . . . I believe so." The mask came up. "I imagine the fossils themselves are lost forever."

"They've been lost for a long time," Hong said.

"Worth millions, I'd say, to whoever has them. If anyone does."

"Millions of what?" Hong asked.

"Yuan, dollars, pounds—whatever currency you like."

"Me? I have no use for currency. I'm a well-paid servant of the people. Only men of your importance need money."

"It was just a figure of speech, Comrade." He lit another cigarette, then passed the pack and lighter to Hong. "That's beautiful jade, isn't it? Of course the inside is German. The

Chinese are marvelous at the ancient arts, but not so adept at the modern ones. You may keep that, if you like. A gift from a friend of China."

Hong smiled. "Thank you, no, I would never be able to appreciate the craftsmanship of the inside."

Caffey slipped the lighter into his vest pocket. "You should come down to Shanghai and see my office there. I've been able to help your brother, and I'm sure I can help you."

Hong said, "I can't imagine how."

"You're more imaginative than you let on, Comrade." He put a finger to his lip. "The Chinese have a saying: if two persons are of the same mind, their sharpness can cut through metal. Might we be of the same mind?"

"Not yet," Hong said. "China is still too backward." He looked at his watch. "I'm sorry, but I must be up early."

Aboveground the air was clearer, fresher. Caffey strode to his Mercedes and held the door for Hong. But Hong waited by the trunk for his bike.

"Good night, then," Caffey said while the driver lifted it out. "I hope we'll have a chance to talk again."

"I'm sure we will," Hong said. He watched Caffey sink into the back of the car as it pulled away on Fuxingmen.

The clock on the postal-and-telegraph tower chimed the hour—midnight. Hong pedaled toward the lights of Tiananmen Square, past the tomb of Chairman Mao. The Chairman still smiled in there, embalmed with help from the Vietnamese, who were rather adept at the ancient arts themselves. On the Avenue of Everlasting Peace a road crew was hammering the pavement, installing new curbs, and behind the workers, on its plinth, the obelisk Monument to the Heroes of the People poked its red stars and carved cypresses into the sky. Granite, cement, trowels and rakes, the tools of revolution. The gold lettering on the cornice of Chairman Mao Memorial Hall sparkled across the plaza, throwing shadows on the statues of peasants, soldiers, and scientists. How appropriate, Hong could not help thinking: the people were carved in stone. It was how the architects, if the order could be given, would have them behave in life as well.

The guard at the Qianmen entrance to the Bureau jumped to attention and almost dropped his bottle as Hong rode up and rang the night bell on the gate.

"Working very late," he said.

"It's never too late for servants of the people," Hong replied. He parked his bike, waved his pass at the two guards at the door, and climbed the steps. On the first floor he leaned around the corner of the stairwell. A few lights burned—the telegraph center, the operations office. The second floor was a mausoleum. Hong turned into his office, left the overhead lights off, flicked on his desk lamp, and there in the center of his desk, as Ru had promised, were the photos of Peter Ostrander's diary, two pages to every shot. *We did our best. Ru.* Immediately Hong could see that the whole job had been hurried. The sheets were still damp from the developer, and at least a quarter of them were in soft focus.

Hong took a magnifying glass from his center drawer and bent over the pages. Ostrander was a meticulous record-keeper; every course of every meal was described, every purchase scratched in with its price, each negotiation with the bureaucracy retold in detail in his tiny but clear handwriting. Not a day had gone by without copious notations. The work of a true scholar, Hong thought. He found a passage on the cadre from Defense.

> The translator they assigned me is a surprisingly chilly guy. A hardcore believer who's memorized every slogan they've thrown at him. I can't engage him at all. This morning I caught him making notes on my conversation with the desk clerk. "Fraternizes frequently" was all I could make out. He does his job but he doesn't seem too smart—not an ounce of curiosity. Jokes go right by him, unlike Dr. Yan, who if he senses a joke and doesn't get it, wants it explained. Yan is terrific. I couldn't be luckier.

Count on Defense to supply a clumsy moron incapable of hiding his own notes, Hong thought as he lifted his magnifying glass. The following pages were filled with remarks on Ostrander's research, punctuated by innumerable references to how lucky he felt. Luck? If only you knew the reasons they brought you here. Hong stared out the window at the darkened shaft. And if only I did, he thought. He stood, slid the window up, ducked his head out. On Chang'an there was a changing of the guard—three cars next to the hotel parking lot disgorging three men, and three new ones taking their places. Not much different than a factory shift, except surveillance work was easier.

"And if only I did," Hong said aloud, and returned to his desk. Even when he had asked Ru for these pages, he had known there would be no evidence. So why had he wanted them? To be a voyeur, to know Ostrander.

Hong stopped turning the sheets when he saw his own name.

Lu Hong is different. There's a person behind those eyes. He's what I'd like to believe the Chinese are. Earnest, smart, witty—but shackled by a form of government that won't let them live. Am I projecting onto him what I want for him? I want doubt. I want him to wonder if the whole system has to change to let people live again. Maybe he does. His mother is a poet. Is that why I like him? No, I just think he's a decent man who's seen a lot of trouble. Maybe he'll tell me what kind of trouble.

Maybe I will, Hong thought. But before he did, he would get the negatives of Ostrander's diary from Ru and destroy them. Anyone else reading this would ask why Ostrander had thought Hong disloyal. He wondered if he was as decent as Ostrander imagined. Or as earnest, smart, and witty.

At the end Ostrander devoted entire pages to Liang Yushang. He wrote about marrying her and taking her back to the United States. It had been done before, he said, it could be done again. But the past did not always predict the future. Ostrander must have thought he lived in a Dickens story, where the good always found happiness in the end.

It was a few minutes before one. Hong fished for his keys, opened the side drawer, and put Ostrander's diary on top of Sun Sheng's death certificate. So let's become friends as they've ordered us to, he thought, talking to Ostrander as though he were in the room, you tell me your troubles and I'll tell you mine. We'll speak bitterness, we'll erase the past, you'll take your woman on a long journey and I'll come, too, me and Yamei and all the friends we have room for. Where's the boat? When do we leave?

He was exhausted, too exhausted to think of bicycling home, too tired even to rouse a driver and ask for a car. He saw burning jungles on the wall, exploding villages, the last images in his eyes before he leaned back in his chair and fell asleep.

19.

GETTING
RID
OF BIRDS

A haze shrouded the sun and stayed there. Even the clouds decided to park themselves in the sky, sponging up pollution and holding it for everyone to breathe.

Hong had woken at five, still curled in his chair, and gone out for breakfast. His spine ached as if a truck had rolled over him in the middle of the night. When he returned to the Bureau he collected the negatives of Ostrander's diary from Surveillance, then found a typist on the first floor, dictated two document requests, and went to the Director of Investigations' office. It was possible that asking for the Englishman's dossier at Defense would force Wei Ye to capitulate and invite the Ministry for Special Security to take responsibility. But not likely. Hong was beginning to understand that Wei Ye had her own interest in this case—for the moment invisible, he assured himself, but soon to be revealed.

"So you are afraid of spiritual pollution," she said when he told her about his not-so-coincidental encounter with

Caffey. "You feel you are unable to continue." She thought he still preferred to have the case taken from him. Hong himself was no longer sure what he wanted.

"In order to go on correctly," he said, "I must have the Foreign Ministry's file on Caffey. I want all records of his contacts, visas, and dealings with the bureaucracy."

He expected her to say no. Her relations with the Foreign Ministry were terrible.

Instead, without ceremony, she replied, "That should present no problem."

Hong unzipped his briefcase and laid the typed formal query on her desk. "It's best to move quickly," he said.

She signed at the bottom with a flourish. "Done."

This was too easy. Would his next card play so well? "I think we might ask the Defense Ministry, too." He extracted the second typed request. "I have reason to believe Caffey has had dealings with Defense."

"What reasons are those?"

To avoid implicating his brother, Hong had prepared a response. "Caffey spoke of his role as a broker, an intermediary for foreign suppliers of goods. The Defense Ministry buys goods from abroad. It's a natural conclusion."

The second card played not so well at all. Wei Ye seemed to be weighing the dangers in her mind—a fight with Defense, perhaps, versus the opportunity to export another foreigner. To prove that an old friend of China was in fact a spy, that would be a coup. Add him to the German lawyer and the Three Tigers would have two victories in two months.

Or, Hong thought, the Tigers might be clawing an entirely different victim. They might be after a certain high cadre in Defense.

Wei Ye stared at the documents, lifted her signature seal, and after another moment's hesitation chopped both of them. "My judgment of your talents turns out to be accurate," she said, jotting her signature on the second request. "As I told you, if a man says one thing, you understand three."

Chan snagged him in the hallway. "The Liang Yu-shang dossier is on your desk. And look at this."

It was a preliminary draft of a resolution for the next meeting of the National Party Congress. The NPC was endorsing several cadres from Defense for positions on the Central Committee.

"There must be something big in the works," Chan said.

Hong read the resolution again. Seats on the Central Committee were great prizes—the only route to the Politburo. The Politburo was theoretically lower in the hierarchy, but it ran the Party when the Committee was out of session.

"The Three Tigers have been campaigning for those spots for months," Hong said, wondering if the resolution was connected to Wei Ye's personal battles with Defense. "The Tigers are losing ground."

"It will be fun watching them try to regain it," Chan said dryly, and continued down the hall.

Fun? Stability was preferable to chaos.

The Little Monk was sitting on the bench outside Hong's office. His gray pants, of the cheapest imaginable fabric, were neatly pressed. An unfortunate man, Hong thought. If Wu had stayed in the countryside he'd be a rich peasant, probably have a nice trucking business with a crop on the side.

The Little Monk snapped to his feet. "I am available," he said.

"Good. I want you to go to the Jianguo Hotel. Take a car and driver. Locate an Englishman named Caffey and follow him. Before you leave, stop at Surveillance and get night relief from Comrade Ru." It should have been done sooner, Hong thought. But a week ago, for reasons that must have seemed sound but that he now had trouble retrieving, he had not wanted to alert Wei Ye to the Englishman's involvement.

"This is authorized?" the Little Monk asked, visibly nervous.

"Yes, it's authorized. Now get moving before he wakes up."

Before the Little Monk could protest, Hong yanked the door open and turned into his office. He fixed himself a pot of tea and opened the file on Liang Yu-shang.

Born 41.9.17 at Tangshan, to Liang Bairong, engineer, and Weng Ou, librarian, members of the Party.
Father worked as underground organizer for the Party
during War Against Japan, shot by Japanese troops in
February 1941. Weng Ou—

Hong paused. The Japanese were shooting a lot of spies
then; they had shot Sun Sheng's courier only eight months
earlier.

He started to read again, then stopped and looked back
at the two dates—the birth of Liang Yu-shang, and the
death of her father. Was there an error? No, it happened in
wartime; you conceived a child and hoped you lived long
enough to treasure it. Liang Bairong had not been so lucky.
His daughter Liang Yu-shang had been born eight months
after he died.

There was also the matter of her birthplace. She had
been born in Tangshan—where Peter Ostrander's birth was
recorded. Or, Hong wondered, was she, like Ostrander,
born elsewhere, and the certificate only filed in Tangshan?

The dossier went on to say that her mother remarried
early in 1943, to a scholar of literature. Taking his daughter
but not his wife, the scholar had left in 1948 to study at the
University of California in the United States. In 1956, after
finishing his studies, he had patriotically returned. Then, in
a tragedy enacted a million times, he was sent during the
Cultural Revolution to harvest vegetables near Nanjing. So
much for patriots. Alas, the Red Guards thought no more
of the need for vegetables than they did of patriotic professors, and he had been beaten to death. Ah, a "struggle session" death, so common in those days. The description of
his demise was followed by a penciled notation without a
trace of irony: "Rehabilitated in 1977 by order of the Minister of Education."

Dead for six years, then rehabilitated. Did anyone in
Heaven recognize an order from the Education Ministry?

The phone rang—Comrade Ru from Surveillance, Hong
knew before he answered it.

"A night relief follower for an Englishman?" Ru barked.
"What do you think I command down here? An army?"

"I'm requesting two additional permanent men for you," Hong said.

"It's a pleasure to work with you," Ru said.

Hong turned back to the file, where the dates again drew his attention. He thought about the turmoil at Yanan, enemy spies being rooted out by the tougher comrades, Sun Sheng's dangerous trip to Tianjin—all between 1940 and 1942.

Liang Yu-shang herself had survived somewhat better than others in her predicament. Despite her bad background, she had trained as an actress and a singer at the Nanjing Academy of Dramatic Arts. She had performed in small troupes, singing regional folk songs. For two years, from 1964 to 1966, she had been featured on tours of military outposts in the far west and on the northern border, then had returned to a troupe permanently stationed in Nanjing. Her background, as the daughter of an intellectual, unfortunately caught up with her in 1973 during the Cultural Revolution. She lost not only her position but her salary as well, and eventually moved to Nankou, near Beijing, assigned to a position as a clerk in a medical clinic. She was lucky to have found a job at all.

In fact, Hong wondered, how *had* she managed to get a job assignment in Nankou? Why would her working unit have authorized a transfer for a bad element?

Chan entered carrying a stack of telex reports from the field. "There was another riot in Jinan. Somebody actually had a gun. A tax collector took two bullets in the stomach, but he'll live."

"Sit down," Hong said. "I want to propose a theory."

"About tax collectors?"

"About Ostrander," Hong said.

Chan flopped down in the cushioned chair next to the file cabinet. "I have a peculiar hunch that I'm not going to like this."

"Let's begin with a suspected spy," Hong said, taking the floor much as he did when he gave classes on legal procedure at Fengtai. "A suspected spy assigned to me for reasons not yet clear, and who gives no evidence of being a spy. He is observing experiments previously deemed worthless and resurrected just in time for his arrival. A cadre from

Defense sits on the screening committee that admits him. We have also a high cadre in Defense, Deng Bo, who inquires about the case for no apparent reason, and who has befriended a British capitalist, who himself befriends our suspected spy and then reveals to me that he is thinking about the sacred bones of the ancestors of our people."

"Maybe," said Chan dubiously. "You led Caffey into that, you told me. You mentioned bones to him."

"And last we have Liang Yu-shang." Hong looked down at her dossier. "A very interesting case all by herself. She risks what hardly anyone else would dare—a close relationship with a foreigner."

"She's a bad element," Chan said. "What do you expect?"

"A bad element? Perhaps, but one with an inspiring past. A terrible background, a daughter of the 'stinking ninth.' And an actress, no less, a woman trained in the art of playing roles. She has had two fathers, both now dead. One shot by the Japanese—or so the file tells us. A second beaten to death."

"Come to the point," Chan said.

"This actress is able to secure a new job assignment almost immediately after losing her position as a singer. One would almost suspect her of buying her way north, but where would she get the money? Assuming very good connections, how much would it cost to buy papers for a job in Nankou, then a transfer to Beijing?"

"A heavenly sum," said Chan. "A thousand yuan at least."

"Which is what? Two years' pay for an actress?"

"Or three," Chan said.

"Who was her housing permit signed by?" Hong asked.

"You have the file," Chan said dismally.

"Yes, I do." He turned the pages. "It was signed by Comrade Ho, a Health Ministry official who I met at the circus and who happens to be a dear friend of Deputy Minister of Defense Deng Bo. And I'd like you to get the original of this, please, as soon as possible." He closed the file. "So what does that add up to?"

"Trouble," Chan said. "Although in my eyes you've left out one crucial detail in the picture."

"What's that?" asked Hong.

"You," Chan said. "Where do you fit?"

"I don't have to fit, I'm only an assistant deputy director assigned to a case," Hong said, but even he heard the hollowness in his voice.

"This all started when you were rooting around in the archives," Chan said, "with all those dead cadres from Yanan on your mind. Has it occurred to you that without the American you'd have a lot more time to pursue your suspicions? You, of all people, ought to take to heart the wisdom of your great hero. If A is true..."

Chan stopped, shook his head, nervously worked his hands.

"You're a loyal friend," Hong said.

"And you, too," Chan said. "Let me tell you, I don't have so many friends, and true friends are hard to keep. Especially if they're in a prison camp where the sun never shines, where the food is gruel, and where nobody will ever visit them again."

Union Hospital owned three low blocks of flats off Donghuamen just to the east of the Forbidden City moat. Hong had telephoned the hospital's political affairs office to report that he planned to question Liang Yu-shang and to determine her shift hours. He wanted the interrogation to take place outside the hospital, and with no one from the hospital staff present. Someone on the staff might gossip with Ostrander, but Hong was confident that Liang Yu-shang had no desire to reveal his identity as a Public Security officer. She needed Ostrander for her own reasons, of that Hong had no doubt, and she would do nothing to frighten him away.

Hong's driver pulled up in front of the third courtyard on Beizuidi Street—number 36, house number 5. On the sidewalk grandmothers tended babies and gossiped and watched him cross the courtyard. The door to number 5 was patched with a faded yellow safety poster of a smashed windshield—DRIVE CAREFULLY, AVOID ACCIDENTS—and had been nailed together from three or four different planks. Hong heard a radio inside, knocked, and when there was no answer called loudly, "Come to the door, this is an officer from Public Security."

The second hospital shift began at eight. Liang Yu-shang had to be at home.

The door opened. Half of her face was missing—or rather, not yet powdered and rouged. To Hong the makeup seemed only to obscure her beauty. In her hand she held a round pocket mirror. She glared down at him with well-contained hatred.

"Announce yourself more loudly," she said with a cold smile, "and cause me even more difficulty with my neighbors."

Hong cut past her into the tiny room. It was barely nine meters square—room for three narrow beds and dressers, a small upholstered chair, a high wardrobe, and to Hong's amazement a refrigerator. How could she afford it? Even for Hong the monthly payments were a strain. A single pane of glass let in light from the courtyard.

"Where are the others assigned to live here?" Hong asked.

"No one else has been assigned yet," she answered.

And no one will be, Hong thought.

"So you're a guide and translator," she said, smiling again. "From the Academy of Sciences. Peter has told me how friendly you are."

"You use his given name," Hong said.

"Shouldn't I? Is there a regulation against that?"

"Do you mind if I sit?"

"Of course not, please make yourself comfortable. As much as you can amidst this elegance."

Hong lowered himself into the chair. His knees were jammed together. "About your job at the hospital—"

"I'm studying for the good of my clinic. I will take back with me excellent skills so that we may have complete medical records for all of the people."

"Very well memorized," Hong said. He opened the top drawer of the dresser and poked through the blouses.

"You're supposed to have proper papers to search."

"I forgot them," Hong said, closing the top drawer and opening the next one. "Where did you buy the refrigerator?"

"Is it a crime to own a refrigerator?"

"On your salary it might be."

"I saved for it," she said.

"Tell me about how you arranged for your transfer to Beijing."

"Ask my clinic's political affairs officer. He'll tell you I'm a dedicated, educated worker."

She leaned over the dresser, propped her mirror against the wall, and continued applying her makeup. "I hope you don't mind, but I'll be late for work if I don't finish."

"You want to look good for Ostrander," Hong said. "If you continue socializing with him you'll be accused of a contradiction. You could get arrested."

"I've done nothing wrong," she said, outlining her eyes with a black pencil. "Dr. Yan will testify to my good work habits."

"You lived in the United States," Hong said.

"I've been rehabilitated."

"How did your father die?"

She paused, pretended to consider her eyes and the color on her cheeks. But for all her defiance Hong sensed a vulnerability beneath the surface. No, more than that—a terror to which she seemed as accustomed as her clothes. Fear was no enemy; it was her companion.

A bird chirped outside the window. Yu-shang looked up. "Did you know that many years ago there was a campaign to rid Beijing of birds?"

"I asked you how your father died," Hong repeated.

"The birds were unhealthy, they scavenged food, that's what the municipal government said. And so all the workers were assigned in shifts to blow whistles and beat on tin cans, to frighten the birds and keep them from alighting. For weeks the din never stopped. The birds flew and flew and flew, never coming down, until they dropped dead. And when the campaign was over, there were almost no birds left at all." She sighed deeply, as if the absence of birds was a great personal tragedy. "If one can never find solid ground, one dies."

"You can answer my questions in a cell on the other side of town," Hong said, "or you can answer them here."

She was silent.

"Your father, how did he die?"

"In a struggle session. He was a revisionist, as I told you at the hospital, a dangerous intellectual."

"No," Hong said, "I asked about your *father*, Liang Bairong."

She barely hesitated. "My father was a spy, and you probably know that, too. He was killed by the Japanese."

"And your mother?"

"She's dead, too. Of pneumonia."

"You never knew your father," Hong said.

"I learned about him from...from my mother. He was ...a hero of the Revolution."

"You're sure of that?"

"He's dead. What does it matter now?"

She was holding something back. She was not exactly lying, Hong thought, but not telling the truth either.

She had finished her makeup. "I have to be going, I'm never late."

"That must make you unusual," Hong said.

She stared at him as if he were deranged. "A Public Security officer with a sense of humor? You'll surely lose your job. They have a regulation against humor, don't they?"

"You were a singer once. Performing for the military, yes? Did you ever make friends in the Army, or in the Defense Ministry?"

"I sang," she shot back. "I wasn't a whore."

"Really?"

"Even if I were, I wouldn't sleep with you."

"Did you know a man named Deng Bo, for example?" Hong continued. "An officer in the CDI."

"I never heard of him."

"Your clinic will be happy when you return," Hong said, "now that you have new skills. You're planning to return, aren't you?"

She laughed heartily, tired of the game. "Would *you* return?" she asked through her laughter, and then, mock-serious: "I look forward to helping the sick and serving the people."

"What do you talk about with Ostrander?"

She looked down at her powders and rouges and seemed suddenly sad. "Palm trees," she replied flatly. "And places where people can look at them whenever they want. And where no one ever asks what you think about or talk about."

Her gentle tone affected him, even her voice was pretty. It was hard to conjure a world where people talked without fear of being overheard. But to live in such a world . . .

Yu-shang turned her radio off, ran a brush through her hair and then dropped it into a small canvas bag. "If you don't plan to arrest me now, I should be leaving for the bus."

The newspapers had been running articles to bolster Public Security's image with the people, and the law demanded that if Hong planned to search more thoroughly, both Liang Yu-shang and a member of her working unit or street committee should be present. But Hong wanted no interference.

"Yes, you should be going or you'll be late," he said, not getting up.

"You have a sense of humor," Liang Yu-shang said, "but not much respect for people's rights." She swung her canvas bag over her arm. "Please have the courtesy to turn the lock when you leave."

Hong searched everything in the room.

The refrigerator revealed a supply of fresh vegetables— cabbage, tomatoes, beans—and a roasted chicken. A cabinet inside the high bureau held two quarter-kilogram tins of cooking oil, far beyond a single person's ration. In the bottom drawer of the dresser he found a cardboard box of photographs: Yu-shang as a little girl, dressed in Western-style clothes, standing under a palm tree with her second father; another of her in front of an old car with a sloping roof, presumably American. There were several photos of her parents, one in particular that interested Hong. It was sepia toned, and labeled on the back, "Mama and Papa, 1940." The young man had a handsome Han face, sharp-featured with fine, full lips; that was where Yu-shang had gotten hers. The woman had the big round eyes and dark skin of the Zhuang minority. They stood in front of a small house, holding hands.

Hong put the photo in his pocket, stepped out, and shut the door behind him.

Waiting for him in the courtyard was a pale old man with a crumpled face like an old paper bag. He introduced himself as Pan Yu, the head of the neighborhood committee, a retired lathe operator. Comrade Pan invited Hong into the street's meeting room, attempted to court him with cigarettes that Hong turned down, and proudly described how he had watched Liang Yu-shang intently since she moved to Beizuidi Street.

"She keeps normal hours," the efficient Pan announced, "but every so often she does not arrive home from work until very late. Once, on Wednesday two weeks ago, she was seen getting out of a car on Donghuamen."

"What kind of car?"

"Japanese."

A taxi, with Ostrander? Or an official car belonging to ... to whom?

"Anyone else in the car?"

"It left too quickly for us to see."

"Is she friendly toward her neighbors?"

"They are very jealous of her because of her clothes and her refrigerator. Also because the other beds in her room are empty. Many of the grandmothers wonder why she pays so much attention to the children. She bestows little gifts on them—toys, sweets."

Old Pan singled out the refrigerator for particular concern. It had been brought by truck two months ago, delivered before sunrise. "The truck driver spoke with an accent from the south. I confronted him but he refused to answer my questions. Liang Yu-shang said she had hired him to bring it, but she had no receipt for its purchase. We must assume that she ... that she has ..."

"Yes?"

"Please do not take this improperly. I am not criticizing our Party."

"Go on," Hong said.

Pan took a breath. "She has friends who are high cadres, there is no other explanation." Glad to have this over with, he hurried to continue: "We think she is also not well. She mumbles to herself. She has been overheard in the morning and in the evening reciting to herself. This frightens people. She is not like us. She wears too many cosmetics and extreme clothing. We assume she suffers from weakness of the nerves."

"Yes, that's probably it," Hong said.

He thanked Pan for his hospitality, and walked toward Donghuamen. Weakness of the nerves? Highly improbable, he thought. Liang Yu-shang seemed in perfect health.

At the Bureau he found the clearance for Ostrander's trip to Choukoutien waiting on his desk. Chan was lying back in his chair, staring at the ceiling and looking glum.

"Tragedy?" Hong asked. "Are we all being transferred to the Mongolian border?"

"Worse," said Chan.

"The Liang woman has a refrigerator," Hong said. "And she's afraid of someone, but not me. She is entirely—"

"The old archaeologist is dead," Chan said. "Dr. Guo Ke."

Hong stared at him.

"Heart attack," Chan said. "This morning."

Hong felt slapped, kicked...and then numb. He had met the old archaeologist only once, and yet from that single encounter had imagined some sort of kinship. The man's death affected him deeply for no reason he could name. Such people should remain in the world as long as possible. He dreaded what he was about to hear.

"Hospital of Infectious Diseases?" he asked, hoping the answer was no.

Chan nodded solemnly. They were both thinking about Sun Sheng. Chan's lips pursed, his eyes squeezed shut as though he were in pain. "I...I can't believe it. I wanted to believe that...that you were wrong, no matter what the evidence. But now..." He slammed his fist onto the desk and shouted: "Can this still happen? Can this still go on?"

"Who signed the death certificate?" Hong asked.

"I'm getting you a copy."

"There's no point in talking to the widow, I suppose."

"She was out," Chan said.

Yes, Hong thought, of course she would be.

Dr. Guo Ke had known who was missing from the photos of Peter Ostrander's father. And they had killed Dr. Guo because of Hong's report. For almost fifty years no one had suspected that the poor old man knew anything, and it had been Hong who told them otherwise.

He slid into his chair, rested his elbows on the desk and his chin on his closed fists, and settled his gaze somewhere in the middle distance. A fierce and virulent force swept through him. He had crafted and stage-managed uncountable forms of self-deception—as did everyone who wanted to go on living, go on eating, go on working in a world turned inside out at every tick of the clock. Grasp Revolution, learn from the peasants; no, let a Hundred Flowers Bloom, a Hundred Schools of Thought Contend; no, Build Socialism, Time Is Money. Choose your movement, but choose carefully, for tomorrow it may end. He deceived himself by agreeing with anyone who proclaimed that the lives of the people had changed for the better. He deceived himself by pretending to a stronger code of honor than he actually possessed. The truth was that his first allegiance had always been to himself and to those he loved, to his friends and to his family. Given a choice between the greater good and his own, his own had always come first. We feed ourselves on little lies, he thought, so we can swallow the big ones.

He stood and waved his palm toward the door. Chan followed him out, down the back steps, and around the corner to the meridian strip of green in the center of Zhengyilu. Two old men squatting on their haunches played checkers on the ground.

"Try a new theory," Hong said when his voice was well hidden by the trees. "It's about settling old scores, a game, a competition, like a round of Forty Points. Yes, that's it, a card game, and it's been going on for a long time. Almost fifty years, I think. Everyone is gambling here, and in this game not only are the players people, so are the cards." Chan opened his mouth to speak. "No, don't interrupt. Hear me out. The cards are Ostrander, Sun Sheng, Liang Yu-shang, Dr. Guo Ke, who knows how many others...and yes, maybe me. Me, the son of a great poet who taught us that the Revolution was the center of life, that to serve the Party was to serve the people. Even when they ruined my father, my mother preached faith. But she wasn't preaching faith forty years ago, many of them weren't, maybe even

Sun Sheng wasn't, not when security at Yanan was so bad that their enemies could attack the Chairman's head-quarters without warning. What if there had been a traitor in their midst? What if for forty years the traitor worries that evidence might be uncovered—"

"What's the evidence?" Chan interrupted. "What kind of evidence is hidden for forty or fifty years?"

"I don't know," Hong said. "But people have been dying to ensure that it stays where it is."

Chan had heard enough. "I don't like these card games," he said, "and gambling is illegal. Just write your reports."

Chan was frightened. He had returned from hell at least once, but he was still frightened.

They started across the street in silence. Hong found that the fear was contagious. He, too, was afraid, but in a new and surprising way. He had always feared those around him, but now, strangely, he was afraid of something in him-self, something pushing him where he had no desire to go. He wondered if you could honestly call that fear.

Or was it perhaps ambition?

Ostrander was a balm, a painkiller. Using news of the clearance for the Choukoutien trip as an excuse, Hong had gone to the hospital to find out more about Liang Yu-shang. Or perhaps he wanted to warn Ostrander, convince him the woman was not what she seemed. But if I warn him about the woman, Hong thought, shouldn't I also warn him about me?

"There are two opposing schools of thought on human behavior," Ostrander said as Hong followed him across the hospital courtyard. "One believes that we're the result of our experiences, of the way we're raised as children. The other says that we have a fundamental nature, that we're born a certain way. Now if you extend these ideas, you get into all kinds of arguments. What do you think, Hong? Does every man have a fundamental nature?"

"Our nature is decided by the class we're born into. The nature of man is class struggle."

"And that's all?" Ostrander asked. "That's the Communist idea, but Confucius said that even if we're blank at birth, we still know right from wrong."

"That idea is outmoded," Hong said.

"So there's no human nature, we're only animals. Do you believe you can make a man do whatever you want, just by applying the right kind of pressure—punishment and reward?"

"What do you believe in?" Hong asked.

"That we're animals and that we're more than animals," Ostrander said. "What about you? Do you think punishment and reward are the only things that make us who we are?"

"I would have to give it some thought," Hong replied.

"Give it some now. I'm curious."

Ostrander, like Sun Sheng, loved debate, even on the same topics. Men were bound together, Sheng had said, by ideas as much as feelings. This gave Hong both his answer and his reason to share it.

"Behavior makes us good or evil," Hong said, "and punishment and reward are primitive. They're effective, but take no account of . . . of what you would call a soul."

Ostrander clapped his hands. "Bravo! And what about our basic nature? Are we basically good? Or evil? Or neither?"

"I think that's not the important question," Hong said.

"What is?"

"How do you discourage men from being bad, and encourage them to be good? We have a saying. When the forces of good rise one, the forces of evil rise ten."

"That's not a very hopeful saying."

"Are there so many reasons to be hopeful?"

Liang Yu-shang came toward them from the courtyard door. She gave Hong a brilliantly warm hello, and said to Ostrander, "Peter, Dr. Yan is ready for you now."

"Tell him I'll be there in a minute."

When she had left, Ostrander turned to Hong and laid a hand on his shoulder. "Hong, my friend, I want to ask you a question. What would happen if a Westerner fell in love with a Chinese and wanted to marry her, leave the country with her?"

"It's a difficult situation," Hong said, knowing that any warning would be superfluous. "The government does not usually approve."

"Maybe you could help."

It amazed Hong that they—whoever *they* were—could have been so certain of the result. To put Liang Yu-shang together with Ostrander and assume that proximity would become love, it showed great daring.

"We'll have to wait and see," Hong said. "It will be diffi-cult."

"I'm hearing that you think this is a bad idea."

"No, I've only said that it's a difficult situation."

"I love her, Hong. And I want to marry her and take her with me."

They went upstairs to the testing laboratory. Ostrander lay on the table while Dr. Yan inserted needles into his neck and head and repeated the experiment with the numbers, the one Hong had seen the old woman do; Ostrander per-formed perfectly.

"Now try to remember," Dr. Yan said, "an experience long ago. Can you recall the day you left China, for exam-ple?"

Ostrander closed his eyes. After a moment he said, "I can see the scene clearly. There's a boat in a harbor...and... peasants at the dock selling food. It's a long harbor, lots of boats. I'm feeling bad because my father has stayed behind. There's a clock tower across the street...it's a quarter to two."

On the Bund in Shanghai, Hong thought.

"The ship's there now!" Ostrander exclaimed excitedly. "A gangplank with red and blue flags, they're English flags. Jesus, there's the name of the ship! I can see it. It's the... the H.M.S. *Prince of Wales!*"

Hong stood listening. They were getting closer to Os-trander's memories. But which ones did they need?

The factory floor was a chemical swamp. Overhead con-veyor belts like giant metal snakes encircled the room. The stench was foul and the noise from the belts' grinding gears and the blast furnaces was enough to turn anyone instantly deaf. Women in pale blue caps monitored the line, men swung iron tubing from hooks, dipping it into vats of acid. They were galvanizing pipe.

Shielding his ears, Hong exited onto the loading dock. The workers stared, wondering why a well-dressed cadre would be inspecting their plant. He tramped down a flight of concrete steps, lit a cigarette to cut the taste of the chemicals in his mouth, and picked his way across the yard through mounds of scrap metal and bamboo skids piled high with new pipe.

The clinic for the families of the pipe-and-fixture complex was a whitewashed concrete bunker at the edge of the yard. Hong went around to the side, peered in the window, and saw his friend Min in her office with a patient, a ruddy girl with a long angry burn on her arm. Min dressed the wound, dispensed a prescription, ushered the patient out.

Hong tapped on the window. Min looked up, startled, and ran outside.

"What's wrong?" she said breathlessly. "Has something happened to Boda?"

"No, I came to see you about my fever," Hong said. "I'm sorry I alarmed you."

Calmed, she eyed him suspiciously. "Your fever, huh?"

"I thought you could give me something for it."

"I told you I'd bring something home for you." She grunted. "Come inside."

He followed her into the clinic and leaned against her examining table.

"What do you want?"

In his pocket Hong had Dr. Guo Ke's death certificate. It was signed, like Sun Sheng's, by the chief administrator of the Hospital of Infectious Diseases. Hong mentioned the man's name and asked if Min had ever heard of him.

"I studied chemistry under him," she said, "at Wuhan. He's number one at the Infectious Disease Hospital."

"What sort of man is he?" Hong asked.

"You can get his file. Why are you asking me?"

Hong boosted himself up onto the examining table. "How would you kill a man?" he asked.

"Hong, you know you could get me in trouble by coming here. You have experts at the Bureau, why don't you use them?"

"Tell me, how would you kill someone?"

"Is that a philosophical question?"

"No, a chemical one. How do I kill a man so no one knows I did it?"

Exasperated, she let out a breath. "Do you have someone specific in mind?"

"Just help me," Hong said.

"Extract of a plant called *Strychnos toxifera,* injected at the neuromuscular junction," Min said matter-of-factly. "Paralysis of the respiratory system."

"Would you call that a..."—he pulled the death certificate from his pocket—"a coronary incident?"

"What you want," said Min, "is potassium chloride. Injected directly into a vein. It stops the heart."

"Could you find that in the body? Would an autopsy show it?"

"No," Min said. "It would be hard to trace."

Hong was disappointed. If the chemical was hard to trace, what was the point in cremating them so shortly after their deaths?

"Not *in* the body," Min went on, "but maybe *on* the body. In someone old, you'd probably be able to find the spot of the injection." She paused and muttered something under her breath. "I assume we're talking about someone specific here," she added, "someone who was old."

Hong nodded. "Yes," he said wearily, "somebody old."

Min took a mirror, peered into his throat, told him to breathe deeply and listened through her stethoscope to his lungs, examined his eyes with a pinpoint of light. "Do you know that most people get more farsighted as they get older? Unlike you. Your eyes are the opposite. Maybe you should think about that." She opened a cabinet and found a vial of pills. "Here." She shook them out into a small white prescription envelope and handed it to Hong. "Take one of these every six hours."

He pocketed the envelope and thanked her.

"You have to go now, there are patients waiting." She held the back door open and frowned at him, but the apology was already in her eyes. "I never talked to you today," she said very softly. "You were never here."

20.

FLYING
WITHOUT WINGS

Before leaving for the Defense Ministry, Hong opened his side drawer to deposit Dr. Guo's death certificate. The key went in easily and the latch fell silently without a struggle. It struck him as odd. For seven years the lock had fought him, an inanimate and much loved enemy, and now like a criminal begging to confess it popped open without so much as a squeak—come right in, nothing dangerous here. Hong stared at it, slipped to the floor on one knee, craned his neck, and peered up into the strike-plate. No scratches. He ran his forefinger around the edge, which left a black ring of grease on his nail. Someone had opened the lock and been unable to jiggle it shut. Someone who just happened to be carrying a tin of machine oil.

Hong reached up for the death certificate of the good Dr. Guo. He thought: how did I kill you? Whom did I lead to your door? He wiped his finger on the corner of the desk, gently laid the square of paper onto the mound of documents from Choukoutien, and locked the drawer.

• • •

The Nanlishilu subway station was thick with red posters and gold banners as if for a national holiday. But the Dragon Boat Festival and Children's Day had already passed, and Army Day was still a month away. On closer inspection the fringed banners proved to be the parting shot of a safety campaign, inspired by a train accident the previous month. The subway workers had new uniforms, Hong noticed, trim tan slacks and shirts. He recalled a letter in *China Daily* from two conductors bemoaning their baggy grays. Times were changing.

He started for the street. Midway up the steps he stopped, turned, and did an up-down-up-down-I-must-be-lost dance. He patted his pockets, and frantically opened his briefcase. To a stranger he would have looked like a distraught cadre who had forgotten the most important piece of paper he would ever carry. Now you've done it, the scowl on his face said, now they'll really have your head. In the meantime, he surreptitiously examined the faces around him.

Had anyone suddenly averted his eyes? Did someone stumble, or bend over to tie a shoe, or too hurriedly unfold a newspaper?

There was no one on his heels, as far as he could tell. No sudden stops. And no one was leading the way.

If not behind or ahead, he wondered, then where?

The large book on the Englishman was waiting at the Defense Ministry's Division of Operations. This was a week for miracles. Hong opened the file on the elevator going down and saw that it began in 1939, when Caffey was twenty. The Englishman was older than he looked. When the elevator opened Hong saw the back of a familiar head, hair swept high on the top, and then the well-cut suit. Deng Bo was crossing the lobby. Hoping not to be seen in return, Hong stepped straight from the elevator and pushed into the crowd of cadres coming toward him. With luck he could hide among the stream the whole way to the door.

He made it out to the sidewalk before Deng, striding toward a new Red Flag, caught him.

"Comrade Lu Hong, we seem to be crossing paths all the time. What brings you to the Ministry?"

"Official business," Hong said, feeling ridiculous as he heard his pompous case officer's voice. He slid the Caffey book into his briefcase.

"New briefcase," Deng said.

"Yes, I lost my other one. In fact, I was robbed on the way home from our last meeting."

Deng seemed genuinely amazed. "A high cadre robbed? That's terrible. Were you hurt?"

"Only my pride," Hong said, rubbing the scrape on his face.

The chauffeur finished polishing the Red Flag's hood and opened the door. "Going back to Qianmen?" Deng asked. "I'm heading into the city."

"Considering what happened the last time, maybe it's bad luck to ride with you."

"You're of the wrong generation to be so superstitious." Deng beckoned with his hand and Hong got into the back seat. "Robbed...it's dreadful."

The car pulled from the curb. Crossing paths with Deng, Hong thought, had the same quality of coincidence as Caffey's presence at the internal film showing. But this time it was like a secret courting, a lover hiding in an alley for an accidental meeting with his beloved. Hong rested his arm on the back of the seat, glancing through the gauzy curtains covering the rear window. He saw a pale green Shanghai screech from the curb to catch up, but it turned at the first corner.

"I've just attended a reorganization meeting at the Ministry," Deng volunteered in a tone that spoke of recurrent boredom with such bureaucratic duties.

"Oh?"

"It's all I do now. One endless meeting after another. Many cadres will be retiring soon to make room for younger men, and we have to plan for the transition. I suppose it's the same at the Bureau."

"I wouldn't know," Hong said. He took in the view through the curtains again. The pale green Shanghai had circled the block and was behind them.

"You like your work there," Deng said.

"I do what's expected of me," Hong replied. Only a month ago his answer would have been a simple yes.

"Would you like to work at Defense? Or at the CDI?"

"People like you have to be concerned too much with politics," Hong said. "Me, I'd rather be arresting thieves."

"And spies," Deng said. "You did well with that German. Besides, you underestimate yourself. I sense in you the keenest appreciation of politics. And you still have the case of this American, Dr. Ostrander. How is it going? Your brother tells me you didn't like the assignment, and yet you pursue it."

"Even a trapped beast struggles," Hong said, thinking that Wei Ye had also told him he underestimated himself. "And it's not that I dislike the assignment. But it's a waste of time. The American isn't a spy."

"Is that so? Then why continue?"

"Because our Director of Investigations is thorough in following every case to its conclusion. And you know the story of the tiger and the bell."

"Your parents are intellectuals," Deng said. "Mine were poor carpet weavers."

"Fa Yen asked the assembled monks who could untie the golden bell under the tiger's neck. No one could answer. The priest T'ai Chin, when asked the same question, explained that the person who tied the bell could untie it. When the Minister and the Director for Investigations decide to untie the bell, then we'll close the case."

"The Three Tigers aren't very bright, are they?"

"They're great servants of the people," Hong said. "Why is Defense still so interested in Ostrander? Is it because your translator was removed from the case?"

"Yes, yes, it's all politics," Deng replied. "You met Caffey again, I'm told. The Englishman."

"The walls have ears," Hong said.

"No, but the guard at the Three Doors Theater has a telephone line to my office." Deng lit a cigarette, a Philip Morris, and Hong accepted the one offered. If Caffey was Deng's friend, he wondered, why would Deng need a report from a guard?

"Speaking of tigers," Deng continued, "did you hear

about the case of Han Haji? A Kazakh from Turban, an industrious fellow who came to Beijing and renounced his barbaric religious customs. Marxism would triumph over religion, he said, because it's true and scientific. This was before our leaders realized the flaws in Marxism."

"Where's Turban, exactly?" Hong asked.

"Out in the west somewhere, on the frontier. Anyway, all of this talk about the science of Marxism got him a friend in the Arts and Crafts Export Corporation, and they started an excellent business. This Kazakh would strip shrines in Tibet and sell the gold figurines and pearls to his friend, who would then sell them to foreigners. The Kazakh would have done fine, too, but he wanted too high a price for his gold figures." Deng took a long puff on his cigarette. "Of course they were both shot," he added with a smile. "Maybe today the Kazakh would be a hero. Now that getting rich is approved."

"What does that have to do with tigers?"

Deng seemed to have forgotten the reason for his story. "Oh yes, it was his friend in the Export Corporation who turned him in, hoping to save his own head. You see, it all began when the friend told him that if you don't venture into the tiger's den, then you can't get the tiger's cub. The Kazakh thought his friend was the cub."

"There's the kind of mistake a Kazakh would make," Hong said, his voice sounding a little too high. "Once he had the connection, he should have gotten rid of his friend. He probably should have found a gun and shot him."

Deng laughed heartily. "I think that's not the lesson. I know I'm not a poet like you or your mother, but what I've learned is that when two tigers fight, one of them is sure to get wounded."

There was no mistaking Deng's allusion. He considered himself a tiger, as powerful as the Minister and the Director of Investigations of Public Security. And the cub was Hong. What if Deng, supported by the forces of the Central Department of Investigation, was in fact as powerful as the cadres at the top of Public Security? Then let them fight among themselves. Come into the tigers' den, Hong thought, you'll learn nothing from me.

The car stopped in front of the Public Security Ministry.

"I hope you can make it through the gate without being robbed," Deng said.

Hong thanked him for the ride and got out. The pale green Shanghai that had been following them was nowhere in sight.

Caffey had lived a dozen lives, squeezed the histories of a dozen men into his own. He was like the Dragon King in some old peasant tale.

The bulky file on the Englishman occupied nearly a hundred pages. It showed that as a young man he had lived in Hong Kong with his parents, diplomats in the service of their King, who had conveniently secured their son a commercial post of his own. *See Appendix 3*, the file said. Appendix 3 recorded that Caffey's father had been cashiered for a smuggling offense, and been sent home to England in shame. As the sapling is bent, Hong thought, so grows the tree. Caffey, with his excellent command of Chinese, had remained in Hong Kong, arranging both trade and diplomatic agreements for the Guomindang government. His main commodities, as far as anyone could tell, had been guns and ammunition.

Most remarkable of all, he had been able to do business with the Japanese even after their occupation of the British colony during the war. Throughout the 1940s, he had traveled back and forth to Beijing several times. After Liberation, during the embargoes of the 1950s, he had been useful to the Communist government arranging shipments of medicines and, most prominently, oil.

The early 1940s, Hong thought, several trips to Beijing ...so many curious things were happening then. Had Caffey also done business with the Communists? Had he betrayed their pilots to the Japanese?

What Hong had hoped for, however, the file did not contain. There was no single key to where Caffey's connections led, which was to say that nowhere in all the lists of his visits did Deng Bo's name appear.

But this file had not been filleted. It was all of a piece, it was whole, it was as seamless as stone. Hong flipped the pages back and forth, mentally logging each visa date, trying to find cracks in the stone.

Unbidden, an astounding symmetry revealed itself. Caffey always listed organizations, ministries, and committees for his trips. In short, he named individuals only when absolutely necessary. He always negotiated with groups. The compilers would never notice the pattern, entering one fact after another, but Caffey purposefully left no footprints. To see one man, see several. Name the highest cadre, and then visit his underlings. Let an observer decide which among the many was your true host.

And so Caffey had visited the universities and research institutes, the highest Party officers and the lowest Army quartermasters. Deng Bo's name might not appear on a single record, but hadn't he been a youth leader at Yanan? And hadn't he later held posts in both the Treasury and Defense? And hadn't he praised Caffey at the Kiessling cafe in Beidaihe?

A cardboard pocket in the back of the book contained several photographs of Caffey. In one, taken near Shanghai, he stood alone, wearing khaki shorts that revealed huge knobby knees, and on his large head was perched a round-topped straw sun hat. The perfect costume, Hong thought, for a trip to a British trade office in Guangzhou.

He put the Shanghai photo in his briefcase and had an attack of conscience. What he was planning to do bothered him. He had never manufactured evidence against anyone. Not only did it run against his scruples, it was also against the law; besides, the guilty were caught easily enough. But this time, he convinced himself, was different.

So let us go back into the past, Mr. Caffey, to visit Theodore Ostrander in Guangzhou, and let us see who else we find there.

Fen Like had assembled half a dozen photographs, mounted on a bulletin board above his easel. There were the two photos Hong had originally supplied: Theodore Ostrander at Choukoutien, and again in Guangzhou. There were several blowups, in different sizes, of the British trade office, the building with the terraced balconies in the Guangzhou picture of Theodore Ostrander and Dr. Guo Ke.

"I can't find anything from Choukoutien," Fen said. "But

as you can see I've got the Guangzhou building I told you about. Built by the Portuguese in the sixteenth century."

"What were the Portuguese doing in Guangzhou?"

"Raping it," Fen said with a jolly shrug, "like everybody else."

He untacked two of the large blowups from the bulletin board and crossed to his light-table. The first, of Theodore Ostrander and Dr. Guo, and had been printed on thin, almost transparent paper. The second was one of the file shots of the British trade office building.

Fen laid the first on top of the second. "As I told you, the missing space between Ostrander and Dr. Guo is enough for two people."

Hong stared at the pillars, the tiered railings. "Do you by some chance have an old photo of Deng Bo? When he was in his early twenties? At a Party Congress, maybe, or a dedication for a dam or housing complex. Even better, an old school picture, or something taken at Yanan."

"I must have hundreds," Fen said. "The widely admired Deputy Defense Minister loves having his picture taken. Why?"

"Bring me a few," Hong said.

Fen closed one eye and pushed his lower lip out, giving Hong a look of puzzled skepticism. The look asked: what are you up to? After a moment Fen said, "This will take a few minutes."

Hong took out the photo of Caffey in Shanghai. He thought about Chairman Mao swimming the Yangtze. With Fen Like's magic airbrushes, a spot of dust here, another spot there, the Englishman and Deng Bo would fit neatly with Ostrander and Dr. Guo. Hong could imagine the scene: a breakfast of dimsum, a shopping expedition perhaps, a little sightseeing, everyone dressed for warm weather, what a pleasant day it must have been. And had there perhaps been a moment when Deng and Caffey collared Theodore Ostrander, took him aside, and made a deal for the fossils from Choukoutien?

Fen's assistant, the cat-faced thin man, came up. "Comrade Lu Hong?"

"Yes?"

"Telephone for you. I'll have it transferred."

Hong thanked him and turned back to the light-table. Theodore Ostrander's large square face seemed to mock him. Find me if you can, a voice said. The late Dr. Guo squinted into the camera, uncomfortable in the sun.

Fen's phone jangled.

"This is Lu Hong."

"Hong, it's Chan. The Monk has turned up a bad element you might want to meet."

"And you said the Monk was useless."

"I apologize. Can you meet us on Jianguomen across the street from the hotel?"

Hong said he would be there in half an hour. Fen Like returned from his library carrying a stack of prints. "The man *loves* having his picture taken." Fen laid them out— Deng Bo with a youth brigade, Deng Bo inspecting an airplane plant, Deng Bo in a commune field. In one, with Chairman Mao, he was facing the camera, hand to his forehead shielding his eyes from the sun.

"Make me a picture," Hong whispered. "Put him," pointing to Deng, "and him," pointing to Caffey, "next to Ostrander."

Fen let out a long breath through slightly parted lips. He almost whistled. "Hong, what you're asking ... I don't know, it's one thing when the order comes from above, but without something in writing ..."

"But could it be done?"

Fen tapped a finger on each of the four photographs— Caffey, Deng, the building, Dr. Guo Ke and Ostrander. "It's a tough job," he said thoughtfully, tugging at his chin, "to turn four pictures into one. Matching the backgrounds, matching the screen and the textures, getting the proportions of the bodies just right, then shooting the whole thing to make a new print that looks like an old one. If I had the German lenses I ordered ..." He moved the photos around —Caffey next to Deng, Deng next to Ostrander. "It wouldn't stand up under much scrutiny, but yes, it's possible. I'll need a week."

"I'll get you something in writing."

Fen pushed the photos into a pile. "Are you sure you know what you're doing?"

"Absolutely," Hong said.

Fen was suddenly cheerful as he tossed the pile onto his easel. "Well, what's the worst that can happen? They'll pick me up in the middle of the night and I'll be in a prison cell for twenty years. At least maybe you'll join me." He walked Hong to the door. "Besides, I've rewritten history for scoundrels. Why shouldn't I do it for you?"

The beggar Bun had no papers, no listed address, no working unit. How he survived was anybody's guess. Sometimes he was a navvy, loading trucks for a few yuan a day. Sometimes he begged by the Yongdingmen railway station. Simply remaining in Beijing was no mean accomplishment, considering that officially he did not even exist. The Party had decreed that only decadent capitalist societies produced beggars. All those ragtag children outside the station, you might call them beggars, but the Party called them "persons waiting for assignment to jobs." Bun, however, had given up waiting for a job. He was a bandit, a forager, a beggar, a dealer in this and that—in short, a skilled little hoodlum.

Hong's trip across the city had been taken, in as leisurely a manner as possible, through back streets and markets, across open plazas and parks. He thought he had seen two bicyclists split the distance in front of him and behind when he left the Publications Center. Then there was a black-helmeted motorcyclist with bug-eye goggles and a strand of white fabric floating from his empty sidecar.

The Little Monk and Chan had claimed a patch of ground opposite the Jianguo Hotel, and between them, on the sidewalk, squatted Bun the beggar. He looked to be fifteen or sixteen, but his internal papers said nineteen. He had a smooth Han face. He was well fed, surprisingly clean, and wore black-framed green sunglasses in the current fashion of youth emulating Western habits. It was the Monk, while watching Caffey's movements and interviewing the hotel's employees, who had discovered the beggar, not outside the hotel but inside, listening to music in the brass-railed discotheque. The beggar had many changes of clothes, apparently, and numerous friends on the hotel staff.

"I've even had dinner in the dining room," the impish Bun claimed.

The Little Monk corroborated the feat. "He ate right by the kitchen. He swaps cooking-oil ration coupons for favors."

"I'm checking everything else," Chan said. "He claims he's totally rehabilitated, but admits he was in Tuan He Reform Camp for receiving stolen goods and rape. If he'd been older they'd have shot him."

"Stolen goods, rape...they're pretty much the same thing," Bun chimed in. "Anyway, the rape charge wasn't true. The girl dragged me into it."

"Where do you get the oil coupons?" Hong asked.

"I work for them. If I do three nights of unloading trucks, I can get coupons instead of money."

"From whom?"

"If I told you that," the beggar said with a grin, "I wouldn't be able to get them anymore."

Chan moved to slap him on the side of his head, but the boy ducked. "The girls in the hotel say he has a productive little brick business, too. Steals from construction sites in Nankou, sells to peasants building houses."

"You're a State industry all by yourself," Hong said, and Bun smiled.

"And he's scum," Chan added. "They also say he knew a singer in Nankou, a woman who now works at a hospital."

Hong gently yanked the boy up from his haunches and leaned him against the concrete railing.

"A woman named Liang Yu-shang?" he asked softly.

At the mention of this name, the boy's attitude underwent a subtle but instantaneous evolution. Something sagged in his face, something tensed in his shoulders. Hong reached over and politely lifted the sunglasses from his nose, and it showed in the eyes, too, a quickening: this was more than the beggar had bargained for.

"I thought you were interested in the Englishman," Bun said in a rush, "in Caffey. I've seen him come and go."

"We are," Hong replied mildly, "but we're interested in Liang Yu-shang, too."

"I know her," the boy snapped out, but his voice quavered. "I know her, but that's all. I don't have anything to do with her."

Hong developed a look of kindly fatherliness to subdue

the boy's terror. No need to be afraid, we're all friends. "Now, really," he said, as tenderly and warmly as possible, "a woman comes to the city, she doesn't know anybody, maybe you helped her get some bearings. There's no crime in that."

The boy's eyes darted from Chan to Hong to the Little Monk and back again. He had expected the lash but gotten the feather. "You're right," he said finally, "maybe I helped her file for her housing permit. I think I did, I walked her around to a few places, showed her the right offices."

"And sold her a few ration coupons?" Hong inquired.

"No, honestly, I didn't sell her a thing. She didn't need them. She had plenty of her own."

"Is that so? Coupons for what?"

"For everything. For cooking oil and rice and cotton, but not from me. Honestly, she never asked me for a thing, she even had her own bicycle, I think maybe I took her to get her license, that's all, she gave me cigarettes, stacks of them."

"And did you perhaps take her to see some of her other friends in the city?"

"No, never, after a couple of days I never heard from her again."

But she must have had other friends, Hong suggested. She would have talked about them, how she was getting along, who else was helping her. On this point Bun remained firm. If Liang Yu-shang had made other friends, they were her secret.

Hong leaned a little closer. "Were you with her when she bought her refrigerator?"

Bun's eyes widened in genuine bewilderment. "She has a refrigerator?"

Chan made a loud spitting noise through his lips. "He's lying."

"No," Hong said, "I don't think so."

"He deals in foreign-exchange certificates," Chan said. "They wouldn't send him to reform camp for that."

"No," Hong agreed with an air of great sadness, "it would definitely be prison now." The idea that Bun might go to prison seemed to weigh heavily on Hong. What a tragedy it would be, said his grave expression, if they had to charge poor Bun with heinous offenses against the State. "Oh yes, prison for sure," Hong went on. "Two or three years at hard labor."

The Little Monk, unaware of what was going on, said, "Not two or three years, not these days. These days it's five or six years at least."

The beggar suddenly became a horse in harness, ready to race. He would sell them the wreaths from his ancestors' graves, buy them a whore, offer up every brick he had ever stolen. Everything now would be the truth.

"Connection," Bun said, "that's what you can say about the Englishman. Important friendships, beautiful women, he's a very valued guest of the State."

Hong and Chan had left the Little Monk at the Jianguo and moved the beggar to an interrogation room in the basement of the Bureau—bare cement, two chairs and stool, a window of wire-meshed glass so frosted with dirt that outside it could have been midnight. Two dim bulbs, unshaded, hung from cables on the ceiling. The air was fetid, an odor of sweat and flesh steaming from the walls. To leaven the atmosphere, to continue fostering the illusion of you're-among-friends, Hong had ordered a pot of tea and given a cup to the boy. He poured himself a cup, took one of the pills Min had given him, and sat, legs spread and leaning forward.

"A valued guest of the State," he repeated, lighting a cigarette. "And what makes you so convinced of Caffey's connections?"

"No one flies without wings," Bun declared. "He has a permanent room at the hotel. Cars come for him, and not taxis, but Party cars...German cars sometimes, and those new American limousines, Cadillacs, at the very least Red Flags."

"Which ministries?" Chan asked. He was leaning against the door.

"How would I know?"

"Guess," Hong said.

"Well, the drivers have a lot of friends in Army uniforms."

"Defense," said Hong.

"And some of them have prefix-21 license plates."

Registered in Tianjin, Hong thought, like Caffey's Mercedes at the Three Doors Theater. Caffey had friends in Tianjin, which meant Deng Bo and the Central Department of Investigation. Luxury automobiles were in short supply and constant demand. No ministry, other than Foreign Affairs, stationed more than a handful outside of Beijing, Shanghai, or Guangzhou. But the CDI had a virtually unlimited budget, and was rumored to maintain a large presence in Tianjin. CDI procurement officers could skirt the rules by assigning limousines to Tianjin and then have them driven back to Beijing for use by their own cadres.

"Could I have a cigarette?" the beggar asked.

Hong gave him one, struck a match and held it out. "Who visits Caffey?" he asked.

"The highest cadres," Bun said. He inhaled and sent a wave of blue smoke onto the damp walls. "Military people, business agents."

"Such as?"

"If you want their names, don't come to me. What do I know of names?"

Not much, Hong thought, and neither would anyone in the hotel except the guards. Party members never signed in. If they were dressed appropriately they flashed their identification folders and who would dare stop them?

Chan held up his hand and jerked his index finger toward the boy like a gun. "You do know their names," he said shrilly. "Because you deal with them, too. But you wouldn't want to lose a source of ration coupons, would you?"

Bun sat up straighter on his stool. "No, I don't know any of them. Why would they help me?" He tilted his head, thought a moment. "Hey, I heard that the Englishman saw somebody from Public Security. What if I tell you about a dead man? Would that be good? A dead man can't hurt anybody."

Not necessarily, Hong thought. Dead men had hurt a lot of people. He told Bun any name would do.

"Sun Sheng, do you know who he was? He died a couple

of weeks ago. Very big Party member. He came around, that's right...two or three times."

Hong was thunderstruck. Sheng? What would he have been doing with the Englishman?

Chan and Hong exchanged worried glances, holding each other's eyes. Finally, without looking at the boy, but staring at Hong, Chan asked, "How do you know it was Sun Sheng?"

"One of the chefs recognized him, said he once worked on a banquet for him. A fancy wedding."

Sun Ch'ien's wedding, a year ago last January. Sheng and Caffey...inexplicable. The Englishman had been under the jurisdiction of Defense. Sheng would never have interfered in a Defense case—unless he had been invited.

Chan was glaring, and something terrible was happening to his face—an awful hatred welling behind his brows, his cheeks, the black spheres of his eyes.

"And when did Sun come to the hotel?" he asked, still not looking at the boy.

"A year ago, maybe," Bun said. "No, it was early in the winter, that's right, just after Caffey got sick...after the doctors came."

"Sick?" Hong asked. "Sick with what?"

"How should I know? But the doctors came, a team of them. Caffey stayed in his room for a month...like a quarantine, you know. Like they'd locked him in."

"Doctors from which hospital?" asked Hong.

"How would I know?"

Caffey's file had mentioned no illness, no visits from doctors.

Chan took over again, raising his voice, practically shouting at the boy. Did you ever deal with Caffey directly? Never, Bun announced. Or perhaps introduce Liang Yu-shang to him, for a small fee. No, the beggar protested, he had already been through that, he was just escorting her around for permits.

Hong waved Chan into the hall. The steel-plated door slammed shut behind them. For a moment neither of them spoke.

"He knows more than he's telling," Chan said.

"I don't think so."

"What was Sheng doing with Caffey?"

"There's no explanation," Hong said.

"What's this business about Caffey being sick? Why wasn't he in a hospital?"

"There's no explanation for that either. I'm going over to the hotel. You take him through everything again. Then let him go."

Chan, dismayed, slapped a hand on the damp wall. "He ought to be locked up for life."

"He's somebody you can use," Hong said. "Put him on a leash, give him a couple of yuan when you want to open up a bribery ring. With what he can find out, you'll make a new case every month."

"I'll start right now," Chan said, reaching for the door.

"Control yourself," Hong said firmly. "Use your brain, not your hands."

"I'll get more with my hands," Chan said evenly, but the anger had overtaken him now. Hong realized it had nothing to do with the beggar. It was the idea that Sun Sheng, of all people, might have betrayed them, that as an actor in some traitorous scheme he had brought about his own death.

Hong refused to believe this. Sun Sheng was a hero.

"No violence," Hong declared, emphasizing both words, "not with the beggar. This isn't a struggle session, and we don't want him dead."

Chan nodded, went in, and Hong waited. There was a pleasant stillness in the building, as always when the small night crew had arrived. They were settling down to brew tea and then figure out how to make the night go faster. Hong tugged at his fingers and cracked his stiff knuckles and wondered what would lead Sun Sheng to Caffey. He wondered, too, why Caffey would be quarantined in his hotel room and not a hospital. What kind of illness would a hospital be leery of treating? Or, what illness would the Englishman prefer to keep secret?

Behind the door, the hooligan was talking. Hong lingered a moment longer, until he was satisfied that Chan would not reduce the boy's face to bruises and blood.

•   •   •

When Hong returned to his office from the hotel Chan was gone, the beggar had been sent back to the streets, and the transcripts of Caffey's calls had just been delivered. No one on the Jianguo staff had remembered anything about Caffey seeing doctors, and the hotel's infirmary showed no record of Caffey being ill. The official visitors' lists were a dead end—only an assortment of junior ministers who were undoubtedly conducting actual business. Hong looked at the transcripts of the Englishman's calls. Caffey had made a reservation with British Airways for a flight to London, three days hence, direct with no stopovers.

Three days...

Hong took out the Defense Ministry book on Caffey. Page by page, working backward, he went through the visa records. In the previous September and October Caffey had traveled between Hong Kong and Beijing four times, each time entering and exiting through Guangzhou by train, each time taking the overnight soft-seat sleeper to Beijing. The Englishman, Hong remembered, had said he would never fly CAAC. A month earlier, however, Caffey had flown direct from Hong Kong to Beijing on CAAC, stayed three days, and then gone to Guangzhou for a meeting with officials from the Department of Special Economic Zones. Many commodities had been discussed—electronics, textiles, rubber.

The August trip was the only one for which Caffey had traveled into China by plane, not train. And despite his proclaimed fear of the Chinese airline, for this particular trip he had made an exception.

As if, Hong thought, Caffey had been summoned.

As if, in fact, Caffey had been ordered by someone to put every other bit of business aside and arrive in Beijing quickly, by whatever means.

Now a specter rose in front of Hong, a link in the chain stronger than all the others. Here was a palpable presence. Here was someone playing with the cards.

On the August trip to Guangzhou, Caffey had stayed for six days at the White Swan Hotel on Shamian Island. A copy of the hotel register was attached. It had, thankfully, been printed by computer. Because of the trade fairs, the hotels in Guangzhou had been among the first to have them. For five of the six days of Caffey's stay he was charged for laundry, local telephone calls, and food from the hotel's restaurants. For one day, in the middle of the week, there were no charges at all. And yet nothing indicated that he had left Guangzhou.

Where had he gone? Where could he go by train, stay one night, and return? Or, with enough urgency pushing at his back, where could he have flown in one day?

Hong took out a map of the southern provinces and picked up a pencil. He drew a circle that took in Guangxi and Guangdong provinces and Hainan Island. He put a check mark next to every commercial airport in the area: Nanning, Guilin, Zhanjiang, and Xingning on the mainland, and Haikou on the island. If this journey was like all the others, then the listing of officials from the Special Economic Zones would be a cover for the Englishman's true purpose. Caffey would have laid his groundwork, as he always had.

Hong picked up the phone to fill in one further piece of the puzzle. It was late enough that he might catch a night clerk at the Health Ministry, one who could be bullied. He flipped through the Public Security listings, found the number of the ministry's security officer, and dialed. But the call went directly to a switchboard.

"Our equipment is not functioning," the operator said. "What number would you like?"

"Who have I reached?"

"Who is speaking?"

"What switchboard have I reached?" Hong asked.

"Who is speaking?" the operator repeated.

Hong relented and announced himself.

"Oh, Comrade Lu Hong, this is Li Weng at the Bureau switchboard. Do you remember me?"

She was the girl who had asked for the recommendation to the Foreign Languages Institute, and who had saved him by bustling into the communications exchange on the day he was checking the logs.

"Yes, of course," Hong said. "I'm trying to reach the Health Ministry. What's wrong with the equipment?"

There was a pause. "Well, uh...nothing. It's just that

your lines... from your office... we're having some trouble. Just a moment, please."

Hong pressed the receiver to his ear and listened, but a mute switch had been thrown. Ahead of me, he thought, behind me. Who was closing in?

The mute switch opened and another operator came on the line. "We're placing your call now," a man's voice said. And recording it, Hong thought. There was a short ringing. Hong contemplated hanging up, but to what end? They already had the number.

The night clerk at the Health Ministry took Hong's name, working unit, and division number, then left for several minutes to confirm the information in his own listings. In the background Hong heard the other clerks joking about a fellow cadre's ugly wife. Elsewhere in the room a heated card game was in progress. When the night clerk returned, Hong asked him to open a foreigner's treatment records. There was dead silence.

"Hello?"

"Yes, Comrade Lu Hong, I'm here. That's an unusual request. Perhaps you should wait until morning."

"This is crucial to an investigation of the highest consequence. If necessary, I will come over now and we will search the record together."

The cadres would not want their game interrupted. The clerk said he would get the records and return the call.

"I'll hold on," Hong said.

The clerk sighed. "Yes, of course." He set the phone down and Hong heard him call out, "Don't play my hand for me, you idiot. This will only take a minute."

It took less than that. Late last year the Englishman had been attended by three doctors from the Hospital for Infectious Diseases for a mild case of leprosy.

"Leprosy?"

"That's what the record indicates. Apparently he contracted it in Hong Kong."

"Are the doctors listed?"

"Only the chief administrator."

"Thank you very much for your trouble," Hong said. "Go back to your game."

Leprosy—the scars on Caffey's hands and nose. The disease had been virtually wiped out in China, and undoubtedly in Hong Kong as well. An outbreak would have made significant news. Where could Caffey be exposed to leprosy? Only in a lush climate, in the warm south, and outside the cities.

Hong pulled his map closer, looked at the marks next to each airport until his eyes reached the special trade zone on Hainan Island. Rubber was produced there, and Caffey had discussed rubber at his meetings in Guangzhou.

Hainan Island was also the site of a leprosarium.

Hong's mind turned, riffled its own internal files. But his memory groaned like the rest of his body.

Hainan Island, where else had he heard of it recently?

He dug for his key, unlocked his desk, and tore out the mountain of paper he had collected. Somewhere here...a memorandum from Chan...military officers stationed near Choukoutien during the war.

Chan had finished the compilation earlier in the week, but Hong had only glanced at the two pages of tightly spaced names. He ran his finger down the addresses until he reached one that seemed to burn holes in the paper: *Lieutenant Shun Tsung, Haikou, Hainan Island*. Lieutenant Shun had been an officer in the Hundred Regiments Offensive against the Japanese in the north.

Caffey had gone to Hainan Island—perhaps to discuss rubber, and perhaps to see Lieutenant Shun Tsung.

But why? Who was Lieutenant Shun Tsung, what role had he played fifty years ago? Why would Caffey have gone to see him?

More important, who had sent Caffey to the leprosarium? Someone had reached Caffey in Hong Kong and told him to hurry to Beijing, even if it meant flying on CAAC. Caffey had then gone on to Guangzhou, and shortly afterward had contracted leprosy.

Completing a call to Hainan would take several hours. Hong scribbled a message addressed to the director of the leprosarium, and walked it to the telex room on the first floor. He went in and found the night operator asleep. He pulled the door wide open and let it slam shut.

The operator snapped awake.

"Send this," Hong said. "Tell them I want an answer immediately."

Lieutenant Shun Tsung, it read. *Is he there? Is he alive?*

The rain broke the heat, and for the first time in days Hong felt no urge to climb into bed and sleep. He sat by his window, wearing his Japanese earphones and aiming his antenna east. Through a fine mist he could see the dome of the Planetarium, beyond it the spire of the Exhibition Center. There was a show this week, computers from around the world. Computers that would build cars, write in Chinese... and create files on everyone.

Hong tried to tune his shortwave radio, but while the rain brought relief it also fizzled the airwaves. The Voice of America came through in bursts of static, blown off the band by a Russian border station. He turned through the 14 section of the dial for the British news, but all he found was a late English-language lesson from Radio Beijing: "Turn to page two-eighteen... repeat... troop... attack... stretcher... pain." Finally, through the static, a gift: the chimes of Big Ben, and Hong could see the high tower over Westminster Square and the great church. Then a pause, followed by the rich, smooth voice that never seemed to change, that he had grown to know as a friend: "This is the BBC World Report, from London." The news was about war in the Persian Gulf, battles in France between the socialist left and the conservative right. The labels were irrelevant, here as elsewhere, but Hong was carried away by the political disputes of a country thousands of miles away. They had disputes, they argued them on the radio, they told the world.

The rain pelted down, rattling the window frames, then there was thunder and the signal died. Stripping his shirt off, Hong poured himself an unaccustomed glass of beer, and lay on the bed. Under his back the sheet stuck to him and felt like damp rubber. He thought of Yamei. He remembered the confusion in her face when he bid her good night at the theater. Was she sleeping now? Did she sleep well? He thought of Liang Yu-shang, and of how she described her love whispers with Ostrander. *Places where people can look at trees whenever they want. Places where no one ever asks what people talk about.* Hong finished his beer, left the glass on the nightstand, and turned over in the unquiet darkness. Falling into sleep, he thought about the birds kept flying by an awful din, no place to land, dying in the sky.

21.

Choukoutien

In the morning Hong made four calls. First, to Fen Like to ask if the manufactured photograph could be ready a little sooner. With his customary wit, Fen replied that if Hong would settle for the pieces glued together on a strip of cardboard, then there would be no problem, but a work of art required more time.

"Hurry, then, will you?" Hong asked urgently. "It doesn't have be a work of art." To prove a conspiracy he needed evidence; the evidence might be fake, but the conspiracy was undoubtedly real, and once Caffey had gone to England there was no telling when he would return.

"I told you a week," Fen said. "I'll do it in three days."

Hong dipped the plunger, raised it, and rang the telex operator to see whether there had been an answer from the leprosarium on Hainan Island. No, nothing, the operator said, in a tone implying that anyone who expected an overnight response was crazy. But had there been at least a confirmation? Yes, according to the local post office in Haikou the telex had arrived and been ferried to the leper colony by hand. As to how many hours might transpire before the messenger roused himself to return with a reply—well, it could be a morning, a day, a week. Special trade zone or not, Hainan was still an island, after all, where life moved slowly—

Hong interrupted, thanked the clerk, and curtly ordered a second request sent instantly. Disconnecting, he called the office of the Beijing Military Region and asked for a search of the wartime files for the service records of Lieutenant Shun Tsung.

Finally, he dialed the rear lobby desk at the Jianguo, where the Little Monk had just taken over from Surveillance's night man. The Englishman Caffey at that moment was consuming two soft-boiled eggs and gallons of tea, sitting opposite the resident negotiator for a Japanese dealer in pig hides. Where else had Caffey been in the past twenty-four hours?

"In the hotel," said the Monk. "He remained in his room all day yesterday and last night. No visitors."

"Phone calls?"

There had been two: one to British Airways to confirm his flight to London, one to his office in England.

"Transcripts?"

"They've been ordered," the Monk said.

Satisfied that nothing else could be done, Hong went down to the transport pool to pick up the car for Ostrander's trip to Choukoutien. The car was new, a cream-colored Datsun with the air conditioning quietly whirring, and the driver was new, too, a small gnome Hong had never seen before who presented himself with his credentials in hand and a bright red shirt that flapped on his little body like a flag.

A flag for patriotism, Hong thought, or for a warning.

The road to Fangshan County was clotted with trucks and peasants on wagons drawn by tired black donkeys. It was a shame, a national disgrace, that a trip of less than fifty kilometers required two hours. Outside the Datsun's sealed windows, oblivious of the strangers spewing pollutants onto their crops, farmers harvested stunted cabbages and corn. The air was so hot even the trees were wilting.

For half an hour Ostrander had sat solemnly and uttered hardly a word, his eyes casting about but fixing on nothing, as though he were in mourning. Perhaps he was, Hong thought—grieving for his dead father and his lost childhood. At the Shijingshan railway line they hit a traffic jam. The Marco Polo Bridge was completely blocked. The driver jumped out and started toward the river.

"It's very strange coming here," Ostrander said, "after all this time."

"Do you remember it?"

"No...yes...well, not really. Have you ever been to Choukoutien?"

"Never," Hong said.

"It was just a little town then."

"As it probably is now."

Ostrander sucked on his pipe. He stared at Hong frankly, as he had at the Foreign Ministry reception, seeming with his eyes to say he knew, had always known, that Hong was not what he pretended. "I wonder about you," he said softly.

"What do you wonder?"

"With your background, you might have ambitions... well, higher than taking care of me."

"Foreign visitors are very important," Hong said. "What else should I aspire to?"

Ostrander ducked his head. "I'm offending you."

"No, please, what should I have ambitions for?"

"Oh, I don't know, diplomacy? Being an ambassador?"

"I would never think of those things. Tell me, for example, how do you know what *you* want to be?"

To judge by a momentary disturbance on Ostrander's face, the question perplexed him. "This is only a theory," he said after a moment, "but I believe in it. The theory says that inside all of us there are things we want that we can't express to ourselves. They come from...from childhood. Maybe we never got quite what we wanted, so we try to get them later, without even knowing it. To understand ourselves, we have to reach inside our...our secret desires."

"But the only road to happiness," Hong said, "is to control our desires. In the West you allow everyone to express his desires and the result is chaos."

"But it's a good chaos, the chaos of being alive."

"Perhaps," Hong said, "but I don't believe I have secret desires."

"There's a story by your mother, 'In the Village,' it's about a girl working for the Party..."

"I know the story well."

"Well, it's about freedom," Ostrander said. "Don't you have a desire for that?"

"But I'm free," Hong said. "Free to work, build a better country for all the people." How often he had spoken those words, and how often had they sounded empty. "But it's better if we don't talk about politics."

Suddenly they were both nervous. Ostrander leaned his head out the window. "No one's moving."

Hong sprung his door open. At the front of the line of cars a flock of sheep were trudging across the road. Half a dozen truck drivers shooed them along with their panicked young shepherd.

"We'll be here awhile."

"That's all right," Ostrander said. "It's a nice day."

"It is?"

They looked at each other for a short moment, and then, at this unexpected and startling expression of a simple fact, both laughed. There was a recognition, a dispelling of falsehood. Hong thought: she told me to become his friend. Was this what she had in mind?

"I met a friend of yours," Hong said. "An Englishman named Caffey."

"Oh? Where?"

"He works with friends of my brother," Hong said, dodging the question.

"What does your brother do?"

"He supervises a factory in Shanghai."

"Caffey's remarkable, isn't he?" Ostrander said expansively. "At his age most people stop working. Late in his life he learns a new language, starts a new career. I admire people like that."

"Late in life?" Hong echoed.

"Well, he didn't make his first trip to China until four years ago. And now he's an international trader."

"Yes, that is to be admired," Hong said.

Caffey had lied to Ostrander, of course. He had never even seen fit to tell Ostrander that he had known his father.

Ostrander leaned closer. "I've applied to the government to marry the woman you met...Liang Yu-shang. It looks like they'll let her go home with me."

The only way they were likely to go anywhere together, Hong thought, was in chains—or caskets. "It would be nice for you," he said, "marriage is a good thing. Do you find it strange that love should come to you so quickly in a foreign place?"

"Should it seem strange? I'm older than you, Hong, I've been in love before. My wife..." Ostrander took a breath. "As we get older, we can tell when love seems too fast. This time it isn't."

"I understand that myself," Hong said. "She's very beautiful, Liang Yu-shang."

"She seems afraid of you," Ostrander said.

"Of me?" Hong exclaimed, feigning amazement.

"Yes, you frightened her, I could tell."

"People who are easily frightened usually have reason to be. For example, you said that I should not be afraid of you, that you were not a spy. This frightens me. If you are a spy, it would be very bad for me."

Ostrander, dismayed, raised his eyes and searched for meaning in the roof of the car. "Oh my God, I should have realized. You've been worrying about that ever since."

"Yes, I have."

"But everybody told me the Chinese think all foreigners are spies. It was a joke when I said it. Just a joke. I hope you believe me."

"I believe you," Hong said.

Ostrander gaped as the car moved through the market stalls at the edge of Choukoutien. On the low skyline, broken by limestone mountains, smokestacks poured pearl clouds into the sun. Bulldozers raised claw-toothed shovels from the quarries and crept on caterpillar tracks from open pits to rows of waiting trucks. Along the rail line sat giant overflowing anthills of coal.

The town itself was small, perhaps thirty square blocks of gray-shingled buildings, most no higher than two stories, laid out along narrow streets freshly paved and dotted with young balloon-shaped trees. There were no cars, no motor-cycles, no signs of life. At the far western end, lording its comfort over the valley, sat a giant sweetcake on a table: a single modern apartment house of red brick, protected by sodded lawns at the base of the mountain and faced with three columns of gleaming white balconies. The local Party officials lived well. Directly opposite, leaping up at the end of a three-lane macadam that cut straight through the town, stood an imposing limestone palace topped by a steel-girdered radio tower, the town hall.

It was gray, it was drab, it was ugly.

"I don't remember any of this," Ostrander said in a low hush. "This isn't what I imagined at all."

The museum lay on the southern crest of Dragon Bone Hill, above the railroad tracks. A bus full of schoolchildren chugged through the chain-link gate and parked next to a refreshment stand selling ice-sticks, a few brands of ciga-rettes, tattered souvenir booklets. The place had an air of meanness, of deprivation. As Hong stepped from the car a lanky horse-faced man with heavy-lidded eyes hurried down the steps from the museum. He had a scrubbed, life-less quality, like a side of beef drained of blood, and wore an expensive white shirt and brown slacks.

"You're Comrade Lu Hong?" he said in Chinese, offering his hand.

"Yes, who are you?"

His name was Wang and he was the deputy mayor of Choukoutien. "I've come to greet our honored guest."

Hong felt a prickling on his arms, in the hair on the back of his neck. A tremor rumbled through his chest. "Who told you we'd be here today?"

"I received a call from the Academy of Sciences."

The deputy mayor turned to Ostrander, introducing himself in stumbling English, and led them up the stone steps. On either side of the three doors were dying palms in

green metal pots and unkempt little flower boxes of drooping willow plants. Hong glanced up to see, behind the museum's long windows, four men in olive green uniforms.

Ostrander, followed by the deputy mayor, went inside,
examined by the children as though he were a mythical
giant, cautiously watched by the soldiers. They were officers, three-pocket men, and they bantered loudly about
their extended leave. Speak louder, Hong thought, in case
I'm deaf. Do you always wear your uniforms on vacation?

The museum's main room held an enormous glass-
enclosed scale model of the archaeological site, poster-sized
photographs of the original dig, green geological maps with
circular squiggles showing the subsoil. At one of the
mounted photos Ostrander came to a halt with his hand
over his mouth. "That's him," he whispered, his voice muffled. "There's my father. Hong, look!"

Hong complied. Theodore Ostrander stood in a deep,
wide gash in the earth, thrusting a fragment of skull up to
the camera.

"You resemble him very much," Hong said.

Ostrander was too excited to hear. Like a child at the zoo
he gawked at every display, full of questions. Deputy Mayor
Wang answered like a patient uncle. But it was not until
Ostrander had seen the diorama of the site and the rubber
models of the skull of Beijing Man that Hong began to understand the presence of Deputy Mayor Wang and his unheralded welcoming committee.

"Come, let's see the site itself," said the deputy mayor.
"There are people in the village waiting to meet you."

At the town hall a group of old people gathered around
the car. Ostrander had stood inside the cleft in the limestone mountain where the fossils were uncovered, taken
photographs of Hong and himself with his camera's timed
shutter. Now, as he stepped into the shadow cast by the
town hall tower, the old people surrounded him and chat-
tered while Deputy Mayor Wang translated. They remembered the American scientists, they said, the famous Dr.
Theodore Ostrander and his beautiful wife and son. Along
with the deputy mayor and several young cadres who appeared like beetles from the woodwork, the old people

tugged Ostrander down the street and into a graveled alley.

Deputy Mayor Wang announced proudly, "This is the place where you were born."

It was a whitewashed stone house, with square windows at eye level, set in a garden of pines blanketed with coal dust. Ostrander stared, his jaw falling, and gripped Hong's arm. "I played in this yard," he said, his voice rising in awe. "We had a nanny, an *amah,* who sometimes took care of me. She sat me right over there, there was a big old swing on ropes, and she told me fairy tales."

"An auntie?" Hong asked, apparently bemused. "Someone from the town?"

A frail, hunchbacked woman in shabby peasant clothes hobbled forward, gripping in her hopelessly gnarled fingers a walking stick carved from a tree limb. Somebody made it for her, Hong thought: those hands couldn't do anything now. And maybe never had. Her fingers were so bent and contorted they might have been caught under a tractor a hundred years ago, or snapped in a weaving machine. Her forehead and cheeks and neck were a dirtmap of creases burnt a leathery brown by a lifetime in the sun, and her feet, clad in decaying sandals, were dainty but turned inward, almost as if they had once been bound. But of course they hadn't been; it was only old age. Supported by two equally gnarled old men she stepped toward Ostrander with a quizzical expression in her eyes.

"It was me, I was the one who told you stories," she murmured. Her voice, though trembling, had an extraordinary force that all but silenced the other low voices in the crowd. Her English, though halting, was clear.

Ostrander, taken by surprise, walked slowly toward her, as if pushing through water. "Oh Jesus, it's you, you're ... I called you Auntie Helen."

Her face opened into a smile, baring a polished mouthful of gold and silver teeth. "And you are young Peter," she said with great satisfaction. "Time will always bring old friends together. Please, have tea with us."

What a surprise, Hong thought, a coincidence, that a figure from Ostrander's past should appear here, as unheralded as Deputy Mayor Wang. The old woman's face arrested Hong's gaze. She struck him as familiar, someone met long ago—a stranger passed in the night, perhaps, or a pretty street sweeper whose name you never knew but whose face had imprinted itself on your memory. But where could he have met her?

As Ostrander went inside with the old woman, Hong touched Deputy Mayor Wang's arm. "Who is she?"

"Her name is Kang Xiao-tse," the deputy mayor said irritably.

Hong took out his notebook, wrote the name. "What was her working unit?"

"She maintained accounts in the quarry office for many years."

"Why were we not informed that this was planned?"

"But I reported to the Academy," the deputy mayor shot back defiantly. "You should have received the papers. Any error is yours, not mine."

The old woman's house was clean and sparsely furnished. In the first room were two steel cots separated by a bamboo partition from an open coal stove. In the other, with a high oak wardrobe and an old polished oak bed, bookcases lined the walls—a room for intellectuals. There was a profusion of new blue-bladed fans with wire mesh covers.

Kang Xiao-tse and her husband, Shi Jun, lived with their eldest son and his wife, who poured tea while the old woman reminisced. Hong parked himself in a corner, leaned against the wardrobe, and listened as she told Ostrander of the day she watched him leave with his mother from the train station, of the time when little Peter wandered away into the countryside and got lost, brought back by a farmer atop a wagon of manure. She unveiled old paper-sheathed albums of photographs, and made a gift of one, of Ostrander as a boy sitting on his father's knee.

But the talk had an eerie sound: rehearsed, less a conversation than a drama with actors playing their parts. Hong had the same feeling as when he had first met Liang Yu-shang—a sense of a script being recited, of unseen players laying out their cards.

"And tell us," Kang Xiao-tse said, "how are your mother and father?"

"Oh, I thought you would have known," Ostrander said. "My father is dead."

The old woman translated; she and her husband exchanged nervous glances.

"It's a great sadness," she said. "We had always hoped to hear from the scientists, that your father would visit us someday. Did he have a peaceful old age?"

"My father...he never came home from China. We don't really know how he died."

The old woman nodded her head up and down. "I'm sorry. Many were lost in the war. And your mother?"

"She married again," Ostrander said, "to a very good man. She'd wanted to visit you, but she's not well enough to travel now. She did try to write you, after the war. We've often talked about you."

Kang Xiao-tse beckoned to her husband. "Please bring him the painting."

"A painting?" Ostrander asked.

"Your father left something for you."

"One of his paintings, my God..."

Another unheralded event, one that even before its revelation stirred the blood in Hong's chest. From tattered rice-paper wrapping came an old canvas nearly a meter square and tacked to a wooden frame: an oil painting of a rural scene, a large Western-style house with a brick porch, flowers on a grassy slope running down to a river. Not the work of a Chinese artist, obviously. The old woman presented it to Ostrander.

"Your father painted this while he was here," she said.

"Out in the yard," Ostrander said. "He had an easel out there."

"It was too large to travel with, so he asked us to send it to you. But the war was on, no packages were leaving the village then. And we had no address for you. So we give it to you now, with our apologies."

In the lower right corner of the canvas, Hong could see, were a signature and date scratched in black: *T. Ostrander, '40*. Ostrander seemed dazed, stupefied. He glanced at the painting, then up at the wall above the bed. A bare space showed clearly, a large rectangle unblemished by dust and whiter than the rest of the wall. At the top a single nail pierced the thin crumbling layer of plaster.

"You had it hanging there," Ostrander said, shaking his

head in amazement. "All these years..." He pulled the canvas close to his eyes, then stood and walked to the window to examine it in the light.

The old woman's husband nudged her elbow. "The letter, did you tell him?" he asked hurriedly in Chinese. "Don't forget about the letter."

Ostrander turned from the window. "A letter? From my father?"

"Yes...yes, from your father," the old woman began hesitantly. "He wrote and said that one of the scientists in Beijing would bring an address for you. But no one came."

"Do you still have the letter too?"

"No, I'm sorry, it was so long ago..."

"When did he write you? From where?"

From somewhere in the south, the old woman said. "He told us he was going to Guangzhou, and leaving the country from there."

Hong stepped toward her from the corner of the room. "When did the letter come?" he asked sharply.

The old woman's eyes fluttered, darted to Deputy Mayor Wang. Hong repeated his question.

Neither the old woman nor her husband could remember.

"Was it before Liberation?" Hong asked. "Or after?"

"We...we can't remember," she stuttered.

Ostrander moved closer. "Could he have gotten out alive? Maybe to Hong Kong..."

Deputy Mayor Wang announced that it was time for the people to return to work.

"No," Ostrander said, "let's stay. I'd like to talk with the other people who remember my parents."

"Another time, maybe," Deputy Mayor Wang said, "the people must return to their duties."

"Well, then I'd like to visit again," Ostrander said, turning to Kang Xiao-tse. "Or maybe you would like to come to Beijing?"

Flustered, the old woman glanced to the deputy mayor for a cue. He nodded, and she said, "Yes, we can do that."

Deputy Mayor Wang and his young cadres escorted Ostrander out to the waiting car, but Hong hung back, bracing his arm across the doorway and blocking Kang Xiao-tse.

"Someone ordered you to speak with Ostrander today," he said. "Who was it?"

"No...no, the neighborhood committee told us he was coming."

"Did they pay you, threaten you?"

Her lips quivered. "No payments," she said, and attempted to squeeze past him.

"The painting, where did you get it?" Hong asked, his arm not budging.

"It was entrusted to us, it was our responsibility, to send to his son."

She looked toward the street, where Ostrander waited by the open door of the car. Hong lowered his arm, dredged up a smile for the old woman, and trailed her out. With the same two old men supporting her, she hobbled her way to Ostrander on her walking stick, presented her cheek in the Western fashion for a kiss, wished him a good journey to Beijing, and thanked Heaven that they had been allowed to meet again. Ostrander, for his part, effusively said that it had been more than he could have hoped for, that it was almost unreal.

Which defined precisely how Hong felt as the car pulled away, churning up a cloud of dust.

"Could it be true?" Ostrander asked after a long silence. "A letter from him. Why wouldn't he have written us?"

"Perhaps he did," Hong said hoarsely, his throat having gone dry. "Perhaps he tried."

And also perhaps none of it was true, he thought, there had been no letter. Tomorrow it would be worth a trip to find out. He called up Kang Xiao-tse's face again, but it was one among thousands. He rolled through the indexes of his mind and found he could attach no name or place to her. And yet there her face was, on its own card, in the bin to be filed. He suspected that on his desk at the Bureau he would find a notice from the Academy, conveniently delayed by a sluggish clerk, thoroughly detailing preparations by the good cadres of Choukoutien for their foreign guest.

Ostrander picked up the canvas from the floor of the car. "My father used to sit out in the yard in front of the house," he said. "My mother told me he never really relaxed except when he was painting. I think this one is from a fairy tale, one of the stories Auntie Helen used to tell us. Or maybe it's somewhere we went." He leaned it against the door. "We actually called her Auntie Helen, you know, all the kids. The *amahs,* the aunties, they took American names for us. It's sort of awful when you think about it. Even my mother called her Helen. We could have learned her real name, but she changed it anyway."

Of course she did, Hong thought. To make the foreigners feel welcome.

Auntie Helen... Helen...

Then, like an old wooden puzzle into which the last piece has suddenly fit, it happened: a whole bagful of links clinked together and locked themselves into a chain. Not all, of course, but yes, this one was obvious.

Sun Sheng had known. Hong thought back to the bookmark in the volume of Confucius, which Ma Sufei had pressed on him before being sent to Guangzhou, and to Sheng's scrawled message: *If the name is not correct, the words will not ring true.*

The name was not correct, but Hong knew who Kang Xiao-tse really was.

He allowed himself a silent celebration. He knew where he had seen her face before: in a sepia-toned photograph that he had dropped into his pocket a week earlier. The idea lit up inside him, spun the world on its axis. He thought of Liang Yu-shang, whose birth had been recorded in Tangshan—as had Ostrander's, who was born in Choukoutien. He thought of the journal he had read, the notes from the laboratory secretary at the site where the fossils were uncovered—"It is a difficult time, our reports do not get through.... Who knows if I will survive the war?" She *had* survived, it was phenomenal. And she had persisted. But in what cause?

"A letter from the south," Ostrander said. He spun his head around, faced Hong directly. "What were you asking her at the door?"

Ostrander's recognition of Hong moved a step further, replaced by one much more insidious. From the moment Hong had leapt to question the old woman, he had known that his own mask would fall, or that Ostrander would see through it. Now, barely recovered from the shock the cadres in Choukoutien had prepared for him, Ostrander slammed into another. His frank appraising stares gave way to a burning in his eyes, a fury of accusation.

He spoke in a dead murmur: "You're not from the Academy of Sciences, are you?"

Hong sighed. "Why do you say that?" he asked, but his voice had already conceded.

"The way you went after her about the letter," Ostrander answered in the same dead tone. "And then you wouldn't let her out the door. You're . . . you're a cop."

Hong sifted the word through his mental dictionary. Cop . . . policeman, officer. He mumbled, almost to himself, "We have a saying: an honest man doesn't fear detection."

"Why a cop?" The world lit up for Ostrander, too, and he slapped his palm to his forehead. "The fossils, the skeletons, it's about my father, you think I know where they are. Oh, Jesus . . ."

Hong laid a hand on his shoulder. "You're not a spy."

"No, I already explained, that was a joke! You think that's what I'm here for." He jerked away from Hong. "You people are crazy. The man's been dead for almost fifty years, I barely knew him, how can you imagine that I . . ." He buried his head in his hands.

"They told me you were a spy," Hong said, "but it doesn't matter now."

"You think I know something that I don't!" Ostrander shouted. He was afraid. "Tell whoever you work for I don't know a thing. Do you understand? Tell them! I'm just a doctor . . ."

The driver had a taken a different route back to Beijing, and they were crossing Guanganmen by the Fayuan Temple. A bicyclist soared past, missing them by a hair and clanging his bell. Whom should I tell? Hong thought. To whom should I explain that you are only a doctor? All of them already know.

22.

INTERROGATION

A single spark was enough to set the prairies on fire. Or so it appeared to Hong shortly after the car rolled into the foreigners' compound and Chan's heavy body lumbered down the steps. Ostrander jumped out in a huff and stormed up to the door in enraged silence.

"He's had a shock," Hong said, stepping from the car.

"I can see that," Chan replied dryly, handing him a briefing report from the Academy of Sciences. "And you too, I'll bet. This came after you left."

The Academy of Sciences was pleased to inform Public Security that Ostrander would be welcomed in Choukoutien by Deputy Mayor Wang, escorted to a meeting with peasants who had served the foreigners' families, all proprieties and hospitalities to be observed to the fullest extent possible, and so forth and so on, with copies to this office, that office, and any other office showing the slightest interest.

"Any more grand theories?" Chan asked, starting to climb into the car.

"Out here," Hong said. He opened and closed his fingers like a yapping mouth and nodded toward the driver.

Chan stuck his head in and said, "Don't go anywhere yet," then slammed the door.

Hong summarized the morning's events. He did so methodically, remarking on Deputy Mayor Wang's manipulation of the scene, the rehearsed aspects of the old woman's speech, the gift of the painting. For the crowning moment —the dawning of Ostrander's awareness, his accusation and plea of innocence—Hong executed a pantomime, bowing his head into his hands. In the end he left out only his conclusion about Kang Xiao-tse's identity, though for his reticence he had no easy explanation. Was it that he had lost faith in Chan? Or was he feeling protective? The more Chan knew, the more vulnerable he, too, would become. It was neither, Hong decided. He simply wanted to wait and verify his own mad logic.

"You can get out of this right now," Chan said.

"How?"

"Report to Wei Ye that Ostrander has discovered you. Report that he knows nothing."

"If I report that he's discovered me, then I'm admitting my own failure. What would she do with me then? And to report that he doesn't know anything, I'd have to offer proof."

To this volley Chan had no reply.

"But the real point," Hong continued, "is that he was supposed to discover me. Somebody wanted him to. And they gave him the painting for a reason."

"What if I got a tire iron and cracked your skull? What if—"

"Sun Sheng is dead," Hong said, interrupting. "Dr. Guo Ke is dead. And more than a dozen others who committed the crime of knowing what we don't. Now I'd like to know what they knew."

"So you can be dead, too?" Chan asked.

"So that I can charge Deng Bo with treason. It was Deng who arranged for Ostrander to be here. And it's Deng who wants whatever Ostrander can find...the fossils, or something having to do with the fossils, something they're hiding from fifty years ago. You knew it was Deng, and so did I, when we saw a Defense cadre on the screening committee at the Academy. I haven't worked it all out yet, not completely, but Caffey is somehow Deng's accomplice. I want them exposed, I want to see them on trial, I want to see them shot."

"Maybe you'd like to pull the trigger," Chan said.

"Maybe I would."

"What would the great Sun Sheng have told you?" Chan asked rhetorically. "To seek revenge is to dig two graves."

"More than two," Hong said. "And your reference to Sheng is appropriate. In some way, I don't know how, it's all tied together—Sheng's death, Ostrander, the Englishman." He nodded toward the car. "Why did you tell the driver to wait?"

"Because of this." From his briefcase Chan lifted what appeared to be a housing order and passed it to Hong.

It was the original order from the Health Ministry for Liang Yu-shang, a virtual copy of the one that had been in her file except for two minor alterations: this one bore a chop seal from the municipal division of the Communications Ministry and included a request for a telephone. Only the highest cadres had telephones.

"You were there," Chan said. "Did you see a phone?"

Hong was stymied. He had examined every inch of that minuscule room, opened every drawer, the cabinet, the fabulous refrigerator. He looked at the housing form again. "You're sure this was processed."

"No, in fact they say it wasn't, that she never got a phone or a number."

With a start, Hong recalled the assessment of Liang Yu-shang so confidently given by Pan Yu, the neighborhood committee head. Weakness of the nerves, Old Pan had suggested. Liang Yu-shang talked to herself, all hours of the day and night.

And she was an actress.

"Get in the car," Hong said.

The grandmothers and grandfathers, towing their grandchildren, swept onto Beizuidi Street for an intimate examination of the new Datsun and its occupants. Hong and Chan moved through them brusquely and stopped at the third courtyard—number 36, house 5.

Chan looked up, waved his hand with a pointed finger. Three new poles carried electricity and telephone lines. The remains of the old ones were barely stumps in the ground, and already their replacements showed signs of vandalism.

"The wires detour around the building," Chan said. "They probably go across to Tiananmen with a stop at the Palace Museum."

"And to the north and east?" Hong asked.

"Probably to the art gallery and Dongfeng Market."

"Exactly. Lines that no one is likely to be using early in the morning or late at night."

With their eyes on the rooftops they turned into the courtyard, followed by the curious grandfathers. One telephone pole leaned against house 5. Chan wordlessly motioned to the corner of the eave where it touched the shingles.

"It's possible," Hong said, and then, after a pause, "and it's smart. It's a compromise between two risks, the chance of the phone being discovered or someone being seen with her. They picked the phone."

Inside Liang Yu-shang's room Hong drew the curtains on the single window. Awful, he thought. She had tried to cover the damp rotting smell with incense and perfume, but it was like trying to paint water. Hong took the north wall, Chan the south, running fingers along the edge of the ceiling, digging in crevices, poking at floorboards.

"Got it," Chan said.

Hong turned to see him kneeling next to the refrigerator. The floor sagged, and through the opening between the dank wood and the plaster a strand of black cord snaked in. The end had been shaved and Chan held three twisted wires in his hand—one copper, two dun colored; the three metal leads could be easily connected and disconnected.

"So where's the phone?" Chan asked, and started opening drawers.

"It's not here," Hong said. "The neighborhood committee might come in and find it." On the morning he had interrogated Liang Yu-shang, she had carried a heavy canvas bag to the hospital. He should have peeked inside then.

Chan yanked the curtains aside and they went into the courtyard, leaving the door wide open. Hong turned back, pulled the door shut. It was enough to rape her, he thought, without leaving her naked in the street.

They made a stop at the neighborhood committee room and directed Pan Yu, the old watcher, to stand outside and keep his mouth shut. Hong dialed the Bureau and asked for Comrade Ru's extension in Surveillance. The line had a nice airy sound, no one listening in, and on reaching Ru, Hong asked him to procure an incoming-call manifest for the private house line of Deng Bo.

"Hong, that's a very powerful leader of the Party you're talking about. Isn't he a liaison to the Central Committee?"

"Not yet," Hong said.

"And this relates to an official investigation?" Ru asked. "Do we have problems there?"

"No, and moreover I have a written confidentiality order on this particular case from the Director of Investigations, so you will kindly do me a favor and observe it."

"Of course, but the Communications Ministry leaks like a tar roof in winter. Speaking of which, a batch of transcripts just arrived for you. Requested by that pale shadow of yours... what's his name?"

He meant the Monk. "Wu Keping."

"Right." There was a rustling of papers. "British citizen, resident of Hong Kong, name of Caffey...oh, the one we've been covering at night. Well, I have them here. Will you be back today?"

Hong said he would and hung up. "Where's Peter...uh, where's Ostrander supposed to be now?"

Chan fished in his briefcase for the schedule. "Return from Choukoutien, then reception at American embassy. He'll tell them about you, you know. He'll run. They'll put him on the next plane...let's see now, that's tomorrow afternoon."

"I don't think so," Hong said. Love, that would keep Peter quiet, his dream of marrying Liang Yu-shang.

Outside they thanked Old Pan and explained earnestly that he was forbidden to gossip about them. He would anyway; it was his job. On Beizuidi Street the car was nowhere to be seen, and one of the grandmothers motioned them around the corner. To make room for street sweepers the car had pulled onto Andingmen. As Chan climbed in, Hong saw, on the scaffolding of a new office building rising directly overhead, a crisp blue banner with white characters: USE FOREIGN THINGS TO SERVE CHINA. Hong smiled to himself; perhaps they had been thinking of Ostrander.

Vaulting up the hospital steps Hong felt lightheaded, a dizziness that reminded him, in spite of himself, of scaling the Ailao Mountains near Jinping for a better aim at the Vietnamese enemy. A tent on his back, his body crying out for oxygen, his rifle swinging at each step, and with it all a strangely comforting fear of death. There was no rifle or tent this time, and the fear of death was anything but comforting. A good soldier expects to die, a good cadre expects to live forever.

In the third-floor laboratory a memory experiment was in progress. Hong held the door for Chan and they stepped into the anteroom. Dr. Yan and two white-coated assistants hovered over a middle-aged balding man, needles planted in his head and neck, with cables strung as before to the generator on the gray metal rack-table. The patient had a wheezing voice, it sounded like asthma, but he spoke in tones of wonder. "I'm waiting in the sun," he said, "my sister lifts me up in her arms to a branch and I...I pick an orange, a big orange. Nai-nai is here, she squeezes and hugs me and peels the orange..."

One of the assistants caught sight of Chan and touched Dr. Yan's arm. Dr. Yan looked up, met Hong's eyes. He fiddled glumly with the cap of his pen, spent an inordinately long moment reassuring the patient that the experiment was proceeding well, and with evidence of a temper grown suddenly short thrust his clipboard at the assistant, grabbed up his cane from where it hung over the edge of the generator rack, and loped into the anteroom.

"Ostrander isn't here," he said.

Hong said quietly, "We're looking for Liang Yu-shang."

Dr. Yan pursed his lips, stared at both of them, then rotated sharply on his cane. "All right," he muttered.

He led them past the nurse's station, around the outer corridor, and into a cramped room where four women, among them Liang Yu-shang, were feeding envelopes into filing cabinets. Women's work, like unraveling the cocoons of silkworms. The women raised their heads and smiled when Dr. Yan entered. Liang Yu-shang offered the broadest smile of all, and to Hong it seemed reserved for him, thrown at his eyes like a dart. He marveled that in his many years of frightening people he had never seen anyone more capable of hiding fear. Live with it long enough and it's under the skin.

She laid her handful of envelopes aside, said good-bye to the other women, and bravely marched toward Dr. Yan with her shoulders steady and her head high. Hong could not help thinking that she would have made a fine military cadre; she had the bearing. But she was too beautiful for the Army. A life in uniform would have hardened her.

She strode straight past Dr. Yan to Hong and Chan and said cheerfully, "I seem to have some important visitors."

It was then, as Hong stared at her, that the conclusion he had reached in Choukoutien was confirmed. He saw in Liang Yu-shang's face the resemblance to her mother, those big eyes carved from stone like a Buddha. She was Kang Xiao-tse's daughter. "We'd like to talk with you," he said.

"Talk?" she asked, breaking into a laugh. "*Talk?* Then let's have tea in the courtyard and we can talk till the sun goes down. We can talk of good friends and good memories, of hard work for the betterment of the people—"

Chan cut her off. "Quiet!" he said. "Show us your locker."

Her bravado undimmed, she waved happily to the other women and turned into the hall. Dr. Yan attempted to follow them to the employees' locker room. Hong stopped him.

"I think you should return to your experiment," he said as though it were a friendly suggestion.

"This woman works for me," Dr. Yan said firmly, "and if she's to be interrogated I insist on being present."

Liang Yu-shang affectionately took his free hand in hers. "No, Dr. Yan," she said, "you've done enough for me. Please, for your own sake, don't make any trouble. I'll be all right."

Dr. Yan hesitated, seemingly determined to uphold his old-fashioned principles.

"You absolutely must go," Yu-shang said softly. "I promise you, I'll be fine. There's nothing you can do."

He began walking away, then turned on his cane. "If anything happens to her," he called out, "if she disappears, I'll make a hell of a noise, you'll see."

Oh, such nobility, such courage. He had courage now, Hong thought, to make amends for when he stood by and watched his fellow doctors hauled away. It was admirable, even praiseworthy, and utterly useless.

They rode to 44 Banbuqiao, a modern prison south of the main railroad station. Its high walls discouraged any fools who might be curious enough to linger at the gates, and the grunts of exercising prisoners reminded those in the neighborhood that reform was the goal, not punishment. In winter it would be terrible, a freezing hole, but as prisons went, this one was a model—clean, not too crowded, a place for violence more against the spirit than the body.

The telephone had of course been where Hong expected to find it, folded in a towel in her canvas bag in her hospital locker. She had been toting it back and forth every day. Leaving the hospital, she had refused to comment, glancing noncommittally as if the black instrument might have belonged to someone else. But Hong had stopped caring about the phone.

At the prison he requested a large interrogation room on the third floor of L block, one he had used before. In most cases he preferred it to the dark underground cells, where a prisoner would often feel too defeated by the awesome power of the State. A criminal already conquered has nothing to give. Outside the L-block room sat two guards bearing truncheons, and inside, in front of a wall of high windows, was a single long steel table with four steel chairs. To Chan's chagrin Hong had turned down an offer of a tape recorder. He wanted none of this recorded. He sat with Chan on one side of the table, facing the far wall, with Liang Yu-shang opposite, facing the windows. In this way she was forced to stare into the light, and freedom. The late afternoon sun gave her a halo.

With her file open in front of him on the table, Hong

assured her that she had only to tell them where she obtained the phone and to whom she spoke on it, and then she would be sent back to work.

"You need papers to detain me," she said haughtily. She had started to sweat. Her face was shiny with a fine dew.

"Not for ten days we don't," Hong said, and lit a cigarette. He offered the pack to Yu-shang. "Smoke?"

"If I accepted anything from you, I'd owe you for the rest of my life."

Chan smacked the table and it rang like a chime. "You will speak respectfully to an assistant deputy director of Public Security."

"Only if you respect pigs," she said insolently.

Chan was half out of his chair, ready to maul her, when Hong blocked him. He left his lighter and the pack of Double Nines on the table.

"There's no ashtray," he said to Chan. "Please, get us an ashtray and a thermos of tea."

Chan lumbered to the door and stepped out. Hong could have done without the tea, and the floor served quite well as an ashtray. What he wanted was three minutes alone with Liang Yu-shang.

Leaning across the table, he said apologetically, "Old Chan gets a little excited, he's hard to control. Now, let's try again. Why don't we start with your mother?"

"I already told you, my mother's dead."

"Kang Xiao-tse? I saw her this morning and she seemed very much alive. Did Deng Bo threaten to kill her? Is that how he involved you in this plot?"

The actress in her sprung to life. She was brilliant: not a flicker, not a twitch. "Kang Xiao-tse? Who's she?"

"Your mother," Hong said, and then, an arrow in the dark: "She changed her name after the war to protect herself. She changed her name twice."

"My mother's name was Weng Ou, and she's dead."

"You look a great deal like her. She was obviously very pretty, even prettier than in the picture."

"You stole a photograph from my room. If Public Security has no respect for the law, how can you expect anyone else to? You're no better than the hooligans." She reached

for the Double Nines and the lighter. "I'll have that cigarette now."

Hong snagged the pack and brushed it away. If she
smoked she would take longer to answer, and time was running out. Chan would reappear any moment now. "You'll
have a cigarette the next time I offer you one. What was
your mother afraid of? Why did she change her name?"

Liang Yu-shang played deaf and stared into the sunlight.

"Did she know where the fossils were?"

Again there was no reply, but her concentration faltered.
She seemed to shiver—or was it his imagination? Hong
found that he too was sweating, beads slithering down his
back.

Finally she said, "Yes, the fossils, my mother knows where
they are."

It dawned then: this was the trail of the spider. Hong
pushed himself up from the table as if in a daze, and
stepped back. "No...," he said with amazement, looking
skyward, "no, it wasn't the fossils at all, was it? Your mother
had something else to hide, something much more valuable." He rounded on her and bent over the table, his palms
spread and his weight resting full on his arms. "It's something else...what? What was she hiding?"

Liang Yu-shang said nothing.

Hong shoved his chair away with such force that it stung
his hand. "You'll tell me," he said, "or you'll never leave
here."

The door squealed like a deranged factory siren and
Chan returned carrying a thermos, three cups, and a glass
ashtray. Peeking out of his pocket was the thonged handle
of one of the guards' truncheons.

Now the interrogation had to resume as it had begun.
Hong waited while Chan poured the tea, then sat across
from Liang Yu-shang and opened the file.

"Have a cigarette," he said.

She gave him a grin and took one.

"About this phone," he said, holding the lighter for her,
"where did you get it?"

Inhaling, she found her voice. "At the Communications
Ministry."

"Very good," Hong said. "We're making progress. And

why did you disconnect it and take it to work?"

"I was afraid someone might steal it."

"Really? Who would steal a phone? Who would be able to use it?"

"I'm from the countryside, I don't understand the ways of the city. I heard that everyone here was a thief."

"Did your friend Bun tell you that?"

"He's a boy, don't involve him."

"Such concern," Hong said derisively. "Suddenly you care for a beggar."

"I care for people more than anyone like you ever did."

"And Deng Bo? Did you care for him? How often did you speak to him? How often did you sleep with him?"

"You asked about him before. I never heard of him."

"Come now, I have right here"—he opened the file—"a list of calls from your neighborhood to Deng Bo's house. Early in the morning, very late at night. Your neighbors heard you talking to him." She had no way of knowing that the call manifest was still on Ru's desk at the Bureau.

"You can't prove anything," she said.

Chan stood up, whipped his arm at her face, and slapped her—once, a loud crack. Her head bobbled, her skin reddened then flushed white, but it was as though his hand had never touched her. Hit me, she seemed to say, I can't feel.

"When did you meet Deng Bo?" Hong asked. "When you were performing for the military? Where did he recruit you?"

"I've been in struggle sessions," she said quietly, not looking at him. "Isn't this the time for you to throw me on the floor and kick me? Or do you break my fingers first?"

Chan raised his hand.

"No," Hong said, and waved him to sit down.

"Let him beat me," she said with contempt. "You should do it, too. You, with your revolutionary parents. You, with your fine background. But you can't hurt me. You'll be here when I'm gone, but I'll be free."

"Free? Who's going to set you free? Deng Bo?"

Before Hong could stop him, Chan moved around the table and slapped her much harder. "Whore!" he shouted. "You slept with Deng Bo and you sleep with Ostrander."

She winced. "Have you ever heard of love?" she said, her

voice barely a whisper as she fought the pain.

Hong started for the door. "Leave her," he said.

"But she hasn't admitted a thing."

"She's told me everything I need to know," Hong said.

On the way out, he left the door open for her benefit. "Put her in a cell by herself," he loudly instructed the guard. "We'll send papers. In the meantime, she isn't officially here. She is not to be released to anyone."

He left Chan at the Bureau and, after the car had pulled away, told the driver to return to Choukoutien. Chan had been none too happy, suspicious that he was being excluded from the case and furious that Hong would reveal neither his destination nor why the Liang woman had been sent to her cell so quickly.

The traffic had thinned, the peasants had hauled in their horses and trucks, and Hong beat the setting sun to the Choukoutien town hall. At the Public Security office the procurate's division was just closing. Hong demanded that Kang Xiao-tse, her family, and her neighbors be brought in immediately. But it was so late, protested the procurate, who was a small-eyed little man wearing thick glasses and a standard-issue peaked cap. On whose authority, he asked, should officers be sent to arrest ordinary workers? Had they committed a crime? Call the mayor, Hong demanded. Call Deputy Mayor Wang. But unfortunately they had been driven to Fangshan for a Party meeting and would not return for several hours.

"Then you'll have to issue the order on your own authority," Hong said, bringing his hands together in a clap. And then he added, to let the procurate save face, "Or mine."

The procurate examined Hong's papers, wondering aloud what would bring a Public Security officer all the way from Beijing. "We'll do it on your authority," he said.

Two officers were sent. The procurate lent Hong his desk, ordered tea, and took a seat in the corner. Within minutes more than fifteen people had been rounded up and lodged in the vestibule outside the procurate's office.

Kang Xiao-tse, however, was not among them.

"Where's the old woman?" Hong asked the officers. They shrugged. Raising his voice, Hong turned to the neighbors: "Where is Kang Xiao-tse, the one who greeted the American today?"

A man Hong recognized as the woman's son timorously stepped forward. "My mother...she went to the market this afternoon," he began diffidently, "she was...injured by a truck." He looked down at his father, who was squatting on his haunches. The old man's eyes were bloodshot and wet from tears. "She's in the hospital."

Hong beckoned the son aside and said quietly, "How seriously is your mother hurt?"

"Her skull was fractured, she's in a coma," he said without expression. "She can't hear or speak. They think she'll die soon."

"I'm sorry." Hong paused awkwardly. Any question seemed a despicable intrusion. "Tell me, what kind of truck was it?"

"It was just...just a truck."

"An Army truck," Hong said, thinking of the three-pocket men he had seen in the museum.

"Yes, yes, it was an Army truck."

The procurate had stealthily edged in behind them, all ears. Hong bent down and offered a hand to the old man, Shi Jun, who braced himself and stood. He was quaking, and Hong could feel his speeding pulse.

"I'm sorry about your wife. Please, come with me." Terrified, the old man stared beseechingly at his son, who said nothing. "Come," Hong said, and led him outside.

The procurate hung on them the whole way to the car. Hong tapped his index finger on the window, told the driver to get out, and opened the rear door. He gestured the old man in. The procurate had started for the front door.

"I'll talk to him alone," Hong said.

"But this is my jurisdiction, I'm sure you'd like me to keep a record."

"No, it won't be necessary."

He slid in next to Shi Jun, who had obviously never been in a car in his life. Hong was counting on that, on the machine's power for intimidation, and eased the door shut.

• • •

They sat in silence for a moment. The procurate was leaning on the hood, talking with the driver. The neighbors and relatives kept their distance, staring from the town hall steps.

"My wife is going to be fine," the old man whispered hopefully, "that's what the doctors said."

"Yes, well..." The procurate was lighting the driver's cigarette, and no doubt gleaning the results of his careful listening. "I must ask you some questions. Your wife gave the American a painting today. Who ordered her to do that?"

The old man took a long time answering, wringing his frail liver-spotted hands. "No one," he said finally. "She had kept it so long—"

"It's time to tell the truth," Hong said soothingly.

"But they said we shouldn't, they said no one must know..."

"That's all right. When did they come?"

"It was five months ago, harvest time for winter wheat."

Five months...shortly before Ostrander's exchange was approved. "And they brought the painting with them?"

"No, she had always kept it, ever since the foreigners left. The two cadres came, they knew about the painting, they asked her if she had saved it."

Two cadres—from the CDI, Hong guessed. From Deng Bo.

"What did they look like?"

"They were...cadres. They came in a car. Important men."

To the powerless, the powerful all looked alike.

"Young? Old?"

"Your age...not young, not old."

"Why did Kang Xiao-tse save the painting?"

"The American gave it to her. She said it would help her punish those responsible. It would lead the good men to the evidence against the bad."

"What evidence?" Hong asked solicitously. "Who had to be punished?"

Shi Jun's voice caught in his throat. "She wouldn't tell me. I begged her, I told her she was crazy. She kept writing letters, mailing them all over the country. She said the war would never be finished for her, that the bad men had to be punished."

"Who did she write letters to?"

"To...to the Party...to...I don't know. Always sending letters. Sometimes there would be an answer, then nothing, no more replies. She would write them back, she would swear she had found an ally, and then nothing."

"Did she save those replies?"

"She burned them, she was afraid."

"Where were they from?"

"Many places...Guilin, Chongqing, Nanning, everywhere in the country."

Old men dying around the country, Hong thought, in twos and threes, and then one man in Dalian five months ago...just as Sun Sheng started his search of the Party Archives.

"And Dalian?" Hong asked. "Did she recently send a letter to Dalian?"

"I can't say, she didn't always tell me."

The inside of the car was like a steam oven. Hong opened the window a crack and touched his sleeve to his forehead. "When she wrote these letters, did she say anything about the painting?"

"She never showed me what she wrote, but I knew. She was telling them she had evidence."

Evidence of a theft? Hong wondered. Of a plan to steal the valuable fossils unearthed from the hills of Choukoutien?

Or evidence of a greater crime?

"And Theodore Ostrander?" Hong went on. "Did she write him too? Did he write her from Hong Kong, so that she would send the painting to his son?"

"There was no letter from the American," the old man said. "The cadres told her to lie. They wanted the son to believe his father might be alive."

Was he? Was Theodore Ostrander alive?

"But she worked for Ostrander," Hong continued. "Is that right?"

"We all worked for the foreigners."

The old man had broken his promises to the two cadres

sent by Deng Bo. Would he also break his promises to his wife? This was the last maze, Hong thought. This was the glimmer in the darkness he had been waiting for.

"How many years have you been married?" he asked.

The old man paused; the question made no sense to him. "Nineteen years," he said.

"But I thought you all worked for the foreigners. That was more than forty years ago. So you weren't married to Kang Xiao-tse then?"

The old man's eyes fell and he gazed at the floor.

"You won't find answers down there," Hong said. "What was your wife's name?"

The old man was trembling and wringing his hands again. Hong repeated the question, louder.

"Kang Xiao-tse," the old man replied, "her name is Kang Xiao-tse."

"I asked you what her name *was*. Before it was Kang Xiao-tse, before Liberation."

"I don't know," came the muffled reply.

"She was a Party member, she had other husbands, other names—didn't she? Before you met her?"

"Please..."

"There's no reason to be afraid," Hong said. He leaned over the seat and found, in the metal cooler on the floor, a bottle of Laoshan. The ice in the cooler had melted. Hong wiped his hand on the seat, opened the bottle, and handed it to the old man.

The old man accepted the water gratefully and sipped.

"Her name before Liberation," Hong said.

"It was W-w-weng Ou," the old man stuttered.

The name in Liang Yu-shang's dossier—her mother, Weng Ou, the librarian.

"And before it was Weng Ou," Hong said gently, "when she worked for Ostrander, what was her name then?"

The old man was weeping. "I was never to tell anyone, not even our children, no one is to know..."

"It was Cheng Hai-lin," Hong said.

"Yes, yes," the old man said into his hand. "Cheng Hai-lin."

Like the Englishman Caffey, Kang Xiao-tse had also lived many lives. As Cheng Hai-lin, she had been the secretary at

Choukoutien, when she worked for Theodore Ostrander and played with his young son and kept a diary of the foreigners' work. *I will miss young Peter.* But the foreigners preferred names they could pronounce.

Hai-lin . . . Helen. Cheng Hai-lin became Auntie Helen.

Then, when for some reason it was no longer safe to be Cheng Hai-lin, she had become Weng Ou, the librarian whose husband was shot, a man who had been an underground organizer for the Party. Before the war had ended, she had taken a third name, Kang Xiao-tse.

Hong understood the reasons she might have become Kang Xiao-tse: to avoid discovery by the Japanese, who had shot her husband. *We are still searching for a peasant woman in the countryside near—*

Or was it the Japanese? Had Liang Yu-shang's father been killed by someone else?

Whoever shot her husband, Weng Ou had not wanted to be found. That much was clear. But there was still no reason to have changed her name the first time. Who would have wanted to persecute a secretary named Cheng Hai-lin?

"Why did she become Weng Ou?" Hong asked.

"To protect herself. She believed they would find her and kill her. The bad people would find her."

Old Shi was an innocent, he had not the faintest idea who the bad people were, or who would have been looking for Cheng Hai-lin.

"That's all," Hong said, "thank you, I'm sorry to have bothered you at a time like this."

"Are you going to shoot me now?"

No one was going to shoot him, Hong said. He was free to leave.

"Please, I believe in the Party," the old man said desperately. "Please find justice for her. Please bring the bad people to justice. They ran her down like an animal under their truck. Give her justice."

Hong promised that he would, that the bad people would be punished. "There is always justice," he said.

It was past ten when Hong reached the Bureau's Qianmen gate, his mind a weary jumble of half-formed speculations. In the darkness he left the car and made for his bicycle, but the guard at the gate waved him over and said he was wanted by his assistant. Hong looked up and saw the light in the narrow airshaft reflecting from his office. Chan was still here. Hong took the stairs to the second floor.

With his desk lamp still burning, Chan was asleep, his head on his folded arms. Hong touched his shoulder and he jumped awake.

"You're back," he said in a groggy rasp.

"What's wrong? Why aren't you home in bed?"

"There's been a shooting. The Little Monk."

Hong looked down, stole a breath from the still air. When would it end? Hong had grown fond of the Little Monk— so dedicated, so anxious to help, and in the end, to Hong's surprise, more useful than anyone had a right to expect.

The Monk had been following Caffey, Chan explained. The Englishman had left the hotel at seven o'clock, just before Ru's night relief man appeared. According to the last entry in Wu Keping's notes, found with his body, the Englishman had gone to the International Club for a drink. He sat alone, talked only to the bartender, and at seven-thirty went outside and started walking. The Monk's body had been found by a foot patrolman in one of the unfinished underground civil defense tunnels, built during the previous decade as escape routes to the outlying suburbs. The tunnel was full of contraband and stolen goods—videotapes and cassettes from Taiwan, cartons of imported and domestic cigarettes, television sets from Hong Kong.

"The street officers are already satisfied that it was a murder among thieves," Chan concluded. "One smuggler killing another."

Hong pushed a noisy burst of air through his lips. "As if the poor little fellow was smart enough to be a smuggler."

"And now do I hear the grand theory?" Chan said quietly.

"Is it still theoretical?" Hong asked. "You didn't like my card games, my theories. You didn't like believing they had killed Sun Sheng, or the old archaeologist, or fourteen men dying of a disease that traveled across provinces but miraculously only struck every few years."

Chan stared at him for a moment. "I suppose," he said finally, "that you've diagnosed the disease."

"Not quite, but almost," Hong replied, and there was a

fervor in his voice. "Almost," he repeated. "What those men died of was an illness called knowledge, the knowledge of a crime, and they died looking for the evidence."

"Of what, exactly?" Chan asked.

"Of a traitor, perhaps. A thief and a murderer."

"And did Sheng find what he was looking for?"

"He must have been close enough," Hong said. "But the real evidence belongs to a woman with a painting, an old woman who has been asking for help for more than forty years."

Chan fixed his eyes on the single glowing bulb in his desk lamp. "The woman in Choukoutien," he said. "And what was her evidence?"

"Alas, before I could ask her she started her journey to Heaven. She got her skull crushed in an accident with an Army truck."

"Some accident," Chan said. "How did she know where to turn for help, this woman, how did she find Sun Sheng?"

"I'm not completely clear about that," Hong said. "She sent letters to the ones whose names she knew during the war. She'll meet them in Heaven, probably, and explain the evidence she sent them seeking. But there is one thing of which I am certain. The cure for their illness is here, and his name is Ostrander."

Chan nodded his head up and down. "One of the players in your card game," he said. "I hope for your sake he holds a winning hand."

"What he holds," Hong said, "is the location of the evidence. That's what we've been looking for, and what the middleman Mr. Caffey is looking for too. That's why Sheng went to see the Englishman. Sheng was putting the pieces together, and Caffey is one of them. But that was Sheng's mistake, and that's why he was killed."

"When you find the evidence, *if* you find it, maybe you'll tell me who committed the crime."

Hong smiled and let out a low laugh. "But I told you this morning," he insisted, and now the urgency in his words lifted his voice to a high pitch. "Who invited Ostrander? Who placed a translator with Ostrander and tried to run the case before it came to us? Who is a close friend of the Englishman? Who placed an actress in the hospital near Ostrander so that he might accidentally reveal what's in his memory? This actress, whose father was shot, whose mother nursed her own hopes for revenge for forty years. I imagine the actress might do anything if someone promised her freedom. She might help a traitor find the only evidence against him. There's one common strand in this fabric, one person who could protect himself all these years: a powerful high cadre from Defense whose real influence is at the Central Department of Investigation."

Chan pulled himself up from his chair, turned the switch on his desk lamp. "Let's go see the Monk," he said.

They rode to the entrance of the civil defense tunnel, on Zhushikou directly north of the Temple of Heaven Park. Chan had asked that the Little Monk's body not be moved until Hong arrived, and two junior officers from the municipal Public Security division were waiting to escort them down. The stairway was another city planner's nightmare, turning at right angles every fifteen steps. In an emergency anyone who had tried to use them would have been crushed.

The officers led the way with their yellow torchlights, casting ghoulish shapes on the walls. At its widest point the underground tunnel was large enough for a truck to pass, but a truck with no destination. A few hundred meters from the base of the steps the tunnel ended at a mound of dirt, blocked by crates and cartons set on strips of wood to protect them from the dampness.

In the middle of the cement floor lay Wu Keping on his back, one arm to his side, the other stretched out, his palm curled, as though in bed and reaching for a woman's hand. Hong knelt next to him. Ah, Little Monk, what have I done to you? I sent you away to keep you busy. The Monk looked extraordinarily happy, Hong thought, as if in a blissful dream, and as usual he was quite tidy except for the bullet hole and pool of blood in the center of his chest.

One of the junior municipal officers stood nearby, clipboard in hand. "Assistant Deputy Director Lu Hong?"

Hong looked up.

"Would you like to read the report?"

Hong stood. "Yes, tell me what you have," he said tiredly.

"Well, the shot was obviously fired at close range. There are powder burns on the fabric around the wound. Looks like a nine-millimeter pistol, but we won't know until they pull the bullet out." He handed over his clipboard.

According to his report the officer had been on foot patrol when, at about eight o'clock, he heard a shot through an air grating. He searched for the source of the sound, but it had been more than an hour before he reached his depot on the phone and the desk supervisor could turn up the location of the tunnel entrance. The officer had come down and found the Little Monk's body laid out as it was now, except for the notebook, which had been discovered two meters away, beyond the outstretched arm. Nothing in his pockets appeared to have been touched; there were fourteen yuan in his wallet.

How odd, Hong thought, that they would have left the Little Monk here to be found with the smuggled goods. Why not move him? Caffey, and whomever he had been meeting, had been in a hurry.

"A pistol," Hong said. "The only nine-millimeter pistols are Public Security issue."

"Or Army guard," the officer corrected him. "The Shanghai Black. And I'm sure you know that a lot of hooligans have been able to get them, smuggled from the factories."

"You've seen bullet holes before?" Hong asked.

"Yes, I have."

"Where was that?"

"In . . . in Changsha. In riots."

"You were a Red Guard?"

"No, I wasn't, honestly, but there was lots of shooting."

Hong had heard and seen enough. He motioned for the other officer to lead him up the tortured angles of the stairs.

It was midnight, but the streets had come alive with third-shift workers bicycling home. In the sky the summer moon was waning, and the tourist lights of the Temple of Heaven glowed from four blocks away. Chan lit two cigarettes and held one out for Hong.

"Thanks. Tell them they can take the body away."

"I already did. And if you're blaming yourself, don't. Half an hour later and it would have been one of Ru's men."

A green police van chugged toward them, sputtering black exhaust from its tailpipe.

"Has the Director of Investigations been told?"

"We sent a message but it may not get there. She's at a banquet in the Great Hall. They're starting the Lu Xun celebrations." It was the fiftieth anniversary of the writer's death, and there would be banquet upon banquet for weeks.

"She should be informed," Hong said.

"Do you want to interrupt her meal? I don't."

"Someone has turned the dead cat toward her," Hong said. "Someone as powerful as she is."

"Stop suggesting that," Chan said. "Slogan of the day: he who sets to work on a different strand destroys the whole fabric. The Monk got involved with smugglers, that's what the report says, and that's how you should leave it."

One more victim, Hong thought, of an old score that remained to be settled. They started for the car.

"I've been thinking," Chan said. "It's been a long time since I've been on the street, but maybe I'll clean my gun and start carrying it again."

The same idea had occurred to Hong.

PART FOUR

"*In the midst
of death,
look for life.*"

23.

SLOGANS
OF
THE
REVOLUTION

A siren woke Hong before his alarm. He was surprised to find himself alive because he had dreamed he was facing a firing squad. The ambulance erupted outside his window just as the guns were about to explode.

In the telex room two clerks, an old grizzled cadre and his nephew, lounged behind their desks. The nephew, cigarette dangling from his lips, leafed through *China Youth*. The uncle looked to be asleep. The other three clerks were late and the Japanese telex machines were dead. Not a clack. Not even a red power light. And there was still no answer from the leprosarium on Hainan Island.

"What's the trouble here?" Hong asked.

"New wiring," the nephew said, desultorily raising his eyes from his magazine. "We've been down since yesterday afternoon. They say we'll be back on line in a couple of hours." He shrugged. "But they said that yesterday, too."

Hong looked down and saw a photo of his former wife in the lead story of the magazine, which hailed a television film called "Safety First." A steel factory supervisor under quota pressure lets a priming furnace blow up, injuring his best friend. Shen Kuang was the producer. No more instructional epics for her; her most recent had been "Maintain Your Tractor for Long Service." She was quoted lavishly praising her film's director, who was only twenty-seven: "Hard work and great discipline have brought this model worker to a peak at so early an age." Hard work to be sure, and good connections, too. The model worker happened to be the son of a famous director from Shanghai Studios.

Hong picked up the telephone and asked the operator to put through a call to Public Security in Haikou on Hainan Island.

"It will take two hours at least," the operator said. "The undersea cables are booked."

Hong walked to the second floor, feeling as shaken as he had in months. An Army truck crushing Kang Xiao-tse, the shooting of the Monk. Events were spinning out of control. He considered calling Yamei, having an argument with her on the phone for the benefit of the listeners, anything to save her.

On his desk was a message from the regional Army administrator; there were no records in the Army's files for Lieutenant Shun Tsung. But there had been once, Hong thought. Somebody had removed them.

He pushed the message aside, and underneath were the transcripts of Caffey's calls. The night before, in the rush to the tunnel, he had neglected to read them. The Little Monk's name appeared at the top as the cadre who had placed the request with Surveillance. A last official duty, Hong thought, in the service of failure.

The transcripts, in both English and Chinese, showed that Caffey had changed his plane reservation. He had switched from British Airways to CAAC, and was leaving for England a day early—today, at one. Run from the scene of the crime, Hong thought, and keep running. There was also a conversation with an unnamed associate, whom the transcriber described simply as *England*.

England: "Trading desk."

Caffey: "Hello, is that you, Will? Are you there?"

England: "Yes, Raymond, how are you? How's the weather?"

Caffey: "Steamy as the rain forest. And yours?"

England: "Pouring buckets. How are our negotiations going?"

Caffey: "Excellent, Will, excellent indeed. I expect that the product will be available to us within the week. Barring complications, that is. And our friend Lord Wimsey? If I remember rightly, you were going to cut the deal with him."

England: "Yes, Lord Wimsey and his friends are prepared to pay all sums accruing. *(Laughter)* Including freight."

Caffey: *(Laughter)* "Superb, Will. That's good news. And you've made the transfer?"

England: "As instructed, to your account."

Caffey: "Let's sing a hymn then. I'll be seeing you soon."

Hong put through a call to Fen Like. It rang five times, six, seven. By the tenth ring the central exchange would cut in and demand that he relinquish the line. On the ninth ring Fen answered.

"I'm wondering about my picture," Hong said.

"I promised it today, and you'll have it today," Fen said. "Can you come by around two?"

"I need it this morning," Hong said. "In an hour."

Fen chuckled. "It just so happens that you're in luck. It's in the dryer now. But the next time you need a favor—"

Hong had already hung up.

The photo was a remarkably good job—Ostrander and Dr. Guo Ke, Deng Bo and Caffey, standing in the Guangzhou sun and looking for all the world like a group of proud boys after a soccer game. The effect was grainy, to be sure, but the missing balcony had reappeared, and even the shadows on the faces matched. "The airbrush is a great invention," Fen said. He put the picture under a loupe and crowed over his work. Not a single line was visible where the four different pictures met. "Now I'd like to put myself in Harbin for a week. Are you going to arrange that for me?"

Hong raced to the Jianguo Hotel with the two officers who had accompanied him to the Publications Center. On the front driveway Caffey's luggage was already being loaded into a Red Flag. Hong stepped from his car just as the Englishman swept out onto the pavement.

Hands on hips, a posture that announced his ownership of all creation, Caffey shouted an ebullient greeting. "Comrade Lu Hong, have you come to say good-bye?"

"No, I've come to arrest you," Hong said. The two officers padded in behind him.

Caffey pulled a look of mock-terror. "My goodness, no, what on earth have I done?"

"I arrest you under the authority of Part II, Chapter 2, Section 7, Article 91 of the Law of Criminal Procedure. The charges are attempting to smuggle archaeological treasures and the murder of an investigator from Public Security."

"That's rather a substantial charge," Caffey said, glancing at the trunk of the Red Flag as the luggage was dropped in. "Are you sure you have the right man?"

"Without a doubt," Hong said. "You are at the heart of a conspiracy. Perhaps you would find this interesting." He slipped the Guangzhou photograph from his briefcase and held it up.

For the briefest fraction of a second Caffey's composure crumbled, his face molted, and from behind his eyes an enraged animal peered out at the picture. He was a chameleon, changing shape and form. Then, in the next second, his features reassembled themselves into the placid jocular human being he had been a moment ago.

"Servant of the people," he said with tones of pity, "let me quote to you Chapter 5, Article 31 of the Law of Criminal Procedure. 'Any party that forges, withholds, or destroys evidence shall be investigated in accordance with the law.' This photograph is a forgery, and I can easily prove it so. If you arrest me with false evidence you will end up in prison yourself." He looked over at the two officers. "Are you sure you want to arrest me now?"

Hong said nothing and Caffey opened the door of the Red Flag.

"Well? I'm leaving. I have many friends who will come to my aid and demonstrate that your evidence is a forgery. Is it worth the risk?"

The picture had at first convinced Caffey, he had shuddered, but then he had known it was a fake. Hong saw himself inside a prison cell, with Deng Bo outside.

Caffey confidently folded himself into the back seat of the Red Flag. The decision made itself: arresting him was too great a risk.

The car started, the driver began pulling away.

Caffey leaned out the window. "Comrade Lu Hong," he called, "the Chinese have a saying. 'In a great degree alike, in a small degree unlike.'"

He rolled up the window and was gone.

The CAAC flight would not take off for two hours, but a call to the airport would hold it forever. The Director of Investigations had the power to keep the plane on the runway, have it searched, detain a passenger.

Wei Ye was talking on two telephones at once, first one receiver to her ear, then the other, and waved Hong to the low chair across from her desk. The portrait of Premier Zhou Enlai above her desk had been dusted since Hong's last visit, the curtains cleaned.

"Yes, a smuggler," she said into one phone. "He was found in the civil defense tunnels with stolen goods. Yes, I take complete responsibility, I should have been more vigilant. We will thoroughly root out any accomplices. It's possible that he was connected to the drug smugglers we found in our midst two years ago. We thought we had imprisoned them all, but apparently we didn't succeed."

She was trying to connect Wu Keping's death to the case of the three Burmese drug smugglers, the case that had ended in the transfer of her subordinates to the outlying Bureau offices. Those cadres had reeked of guilt. But the Little Monk, a drug smuggler? To believe that this shadow of a man, this pale dutiful cadre, had organized a smuggling ring was to believe that donkeys could fly and trucks could weep.

"Yes, this time we will succeed, I give you my complete assurances, you can be certain of it." Wei Ye hung up one phone and continued on the other. "The banquet was excellent," she said. "The delegates to the Central Committee from the Writers' Association were pleased."

This one was a vote-gathering call, Hong realized, for the liaison position on the Central Committee.

She finished the conversation and looked up. "This shooting is causing problems," she said distractedly. She might have been talking about a broken teapot. "The Minister himself was informed before the Lu Xun banquet last night, and he's been clamoring for an arrest."

"The murderer is leaving the country right now," Hong said. "The Englishman, Caffey. At the time of the shooting Comrade Wu was following him under my instructions. On your authority we can order the plane delayed and arrest Caffey."

"Lu Hong, you surprise me. You were assigned to investigate the American, Ostrander. I allowed you to extend the case to include the Englishman, Caffey, when you conjectured that he might be an accomplice. Now you assert that the Englishman has killed a Public Security cadre who was obviously committing economic crimes. That's an enormous speculation."

Hong gripped the arms of his chair. He had expected her at least to hold the plane.

"Caffey *is* an accomplice," he said, "but not of the American." He took a breath. This was farther than he had planned to go. "Caffey is working with a cadre in Defense."

Wei Ye rose upright. "A cadre in Defense?" she said, shocked. "What are you proposing?"

"That Deputy Defense Minister Deng Bo and the Englishman have engineered a conspiracy, and that Wu Keping was shot when he discovered it."

Wei Ye stood. "That is almost a traitorous accusation," she said gravely. "Would you suggest that I arrest Deng Bo as well? Unless you have proof, I suggest you refrain from this line of reasoning."

"I have evidence, based on the Englishman's travels, that he might have illegally visited—"

Wei Ye held up her hand. "Wait! *Might* have visited, you said. That's not evidence."

"So you won't order the plane delayed," Hong said.

She walked around the desk and sat down next to him. "Did I not once explain to you that such actions are un-democratic? We cannot make arrests without proof. Provide me with proof and I will order the arrest of anyone conspiring with Ostrander. Until then, we must assume that Comrade Wu was corrupted by bad elements. He engaged in unlawful acts and was killed in an argument among bandits. That is the only explanation."

"There's no case against the American," Hong said.

"But there *will* be a case," she said enthusiastically. "There most assuredly will be. You have already shown that. Stay close to Ostrander, uncover the evidence of a conspiracy, present it to me, and then we can move forward with whatever arrests you recommend."

There was a short knock at the door. Her secretary entered. "The Minister asks for your presence immediately," he said, "concerning the cadre who was shot."

"There, you see," Wei Ye said wearily, standing and walking out with Hong, "this is what happens when order breaks down. Nothing but problems."

Posters of the great writer Lu Xun hung in the windows of bookstores, restaurants, even the post office. Overnight, an instant national consensus. Hong walked to a cafeteria pinched in between the arts-and-crafts stores on Dongdan. He had no appetite for lunch, but waiting for a call from Hainan made him feel useless. He ordered a liter of Beijing beer and proceeded in short order to swig five glasses. Shop clerks around him stared.

The beer made him sweat and feel even more useless. Caffey was gone, the Little Monk was dead. Whatever Deng Bo had expected to learn from Ostrander would be impossible without Liang Yu-shang's help, and when Ostrander discovered that his beloved was in jail he would leave without her. Soon he would tell his embassy that he preferred to go home instead of finishing his scientific exchange.

Hong thought about the old woman in Choukoutien and wondered if she had died yet. The idea of her obsession interested him. How did you sustain faith? What did it cost? This is where your mind goes, he thought, with a liter of beer in your blood. He looked down and there was a cigarette ash in the foam. He wondered if anyone would ever find the evidence she had been searching for or the crime it proved, and he thought about the transcript of Caffey's call to England: *I expect that the product will be available to us within a week. Barring complications....*

Barring complications, like being forced to shoot Wu Keping. The poor Little Monk, dying with his notebook in his hand...

Hong stood up in such a hurry that he tipped over the beer bottle and it smashed to the floor. He threw three fen down to cover the deposit, called an apology to the waiter, and started back to Qianmen at a fast drunken trot.

He had not yet filed the officer's report on the shooting of the Monk, and he was hoping that Chan had been too tired.

It was still in its folder on Chan's desk, and Hong read it again. The officer on patrol had heard the shot at eight o'clock, but the body had not been discovered until more than an hour later.

But Wei Ye had said the Minister was informed of the Little Monk's death before the banquet in the Great Hall. And Chan had said that although a message was sent to Wei Ye, it would probably not reach her, that the banquet had already begun. Could it have begun later than nine?

Hong tore open the Little Monk's notebook and found Caffey's schedule in the front. Caffey, too, had been invited to the banquet, which had started at eight-thirty.

In a great degree alike, Caffey had said of the photograph, in a small degree unlike. Of course: the missing person in the photograph was not Deng Bo. Hong had put the wrong person with Caffey, he had picked the wrong conspirator. It had not been Deng Bo who traveled south and posed in the shadow of a British trade mission with Theodore Ostrander and the old archaeologist Dr. Guo Ke. Hong understood now why the Little Monk's body had been left with the smuggled goods, and why the gun had been fired at such close range. The Little Monk's murderers had been in a hurry because they had a banquet to attend, they'd had no time to move the body, and a bullet in the chest from his powerful master was the last thing the Monk had expected.

• • •

There was no heat in the Western Hills, no clouds, no weather at all. The Yiheyuan Road was nearly empty—a lone 333 bus to Xiangshan, an overloaded peasant balancing bricks on his back, a creeping oil truck. Past the Summer Palace the farms were far apart, and the pavement gave way to dirt surrounded by acres of wheat. From the road, looking back, Hong caught a glimpse of the giant marble steamboat on the spit off Kunming Lake, where the Empress Dowager had thrown grand parties on the upper deck. To build it she had blithely spent the entire budget of the Chinese Navy.

Handsome tall maples swayed in the twilight—old trees, real trees, planted not in an anti-pollution campaign but by nature herself. The car, a Shanghai assembled from a junk heap of spare parts, sped along the irrigation canal past new apartments for the Army. The road turned narrow, first stretches of gravel, then dirt, gravel again, then paved highway.

The hundred and forty kilometers to Dongshanmiao took just under three hours. Beyond the western edge of the town a dirt lane cut through fields of grapes that looked as though they needed water. The lane ran crookedly, a jog left, a jog right, into the mountains, and barely accommodated the car. At the base of the first hill, overlooking a field of ill-tended arbors, was a plain two-story wooden house.

The car pulled to a stop. Hong got out and asked the driver to wait.

The house was somehow different; his mother had fixed it up since spring. In the front, lit by a ruby glow from the setting sun, wire mesh fences circled rows of tomatoes and squash. Clucking chickens danced inside a sloping coop that wound around the porch to a pond at the rear. New green shingles covered the roof. On the ridge above were two other houses, smaller, where old friends, two retired Army officers and their wives, lived and raised ducks. It was all very pleasant, and it was also exile.

Starting toward the yard, Hong noticed that two men had appeared next to one of the houses on the ridge. Both seemed to be peering down at him through binoculars.

His mother came out onto the porch bearing a plate of
bean cakes and a porcelain mug of tea. She wore her old
clothes, baggy blues. Blue coat, blue pants, blue canvas slip-
pers. "A good son visits his mother on Sunday afternoons,
not at night," she said. "I heard the car. You'd better take
the driver something to eat so he'll keep quiet. Or doesn't
anyone worry these days about using the people's cars for
personal transportation?"

The people, always the people. But she was the expert on
survival, and Hong did as he was told. When he returned
she was waiting in the living room. Fat stuffed couches
upholstered in brown cotton faced each other across a bamboo table. Under a sheet of polished glass were pictures of
Hong and Lin—at school, at their weddings, with their
wives and children. Citations from the Party, old photos and
posters from Yanan, and announcements of her books decorated the wall next to the windows.

"Why don't you go upstairs and see him?" She poured
herself a cup of tea.

"There's been a shooting, I wanted to ask you about it."

She stopped pouring for a second, then continued. "Your
father would like to see his son."

The stairs climbed up over the rear of the house. In the
bedroom at the top his father lay in bed, swaddled in sheets
and gazing vaguely at the ceiling. His face was ruddy from
the sun and puffy from the drugs. Whatever they were giving him, it made him look incongruously healthy. Hong
stood in the doorway for as long as he could bear the sight,
then turned to leave.

"Aren't you coming in?" came the croaking whisper.

Hong went back and sat next to the bed. His father
leaned toward him.

"Did I tell you that the Chairman visited us?" He meant
Chairman Mao, he thought the Chairman was still alive.
"Last month, or maybe the month before, he brought us
potted flowers and lichees from the south, very fresh and
ripe. We're getting new assignments soon."

"That's good," Hong said.

Lu Yaomin drifted away, stared at the ceiling again. A
moment later he rolled his eyes back to Hong. "Haven't
they killed you yet?"

"No, I'm still here."

"And your brother Hong, have they killed him?"

"I'm Hong."

Another drift, another return. Minor strokes, the doctors said. Blood vessels bursting in his brain. "Where's your family? What family are you from?"

"You're my family, I'm your son."

"That's right, you're my son. Go visit your mother."

Hong took the stairs slowly. Each trip here felt as though it would be the last. In the living room his mother sat with a notebook propped on her lap, writing by the light of a single dim lamp shaded in pink.

"He's getting worse," Hong said, sitting across from her.

"Yes," she said matter-of-factly, laying the notebook aside, "yes, he is."

"There was a shooting," Hong said. "An investigator assigned to me by Wei Ye. I think she killed him herself."

"So they're shooting each other now, are they? It's only a matter of time before everybody has guns. Either they'll raise food prices again and the whole city will rebel, or we'll have ourselves a little coup and the Army will take over."

"They tried that already," Hong said, bracing himself for a tirade on the downfall of China.

"And they'll try again," Cui Chun said. "It's going to hell, the whole country. Sexual profligacy, which means venereal disease. For thirty-five years we fought to wipe it out, and watch, we'll have a plague. Greed, crime, black markets, it's decay, that's what it is."

"Did you write an article for *People's Daily*? A Ming Dynasty parable?"

She pretended not to hear, or maybe her rage blotted his voice. "Your brother sent me a Flying Pigeon, a radio, a steam heater, more clothes than I can wear. For a factory manager he serves the people very well, doesn't he?"

"What do you want him to be?" Hong asked.

"Not corrupt."

"And me, what do you hope for me?"

She took a deep breath. "That you stay alive," she said.

From the group portrait on the wall, Sun Sheng looked down at them. Hong said, "Wei Ye shot a cadre."

There was a long pause as dusk settled. The room grew

dark except for the aurora of pink light. Cui Chun folded her arms on her chest, unfolded them. "Wei Ye," she said finally, and with sadness. Her voice was so low that Hong involuntarily leaned closer to hear. "So loyal. So vicious and greedy. Chasing power." There was another long pause. "That investigation of yours...was she really smuggling heroin?"

"It seems possible," Hong said. "It might have been her."

Cui Chun shook her head with melancholy. "Nothing changes, does it? Fifty years ago it was the same. When we were..."

"Young," Hong supplied.

His mother smiled. "No, not young, we were never young. We were too busy fighting."

"But in 1941 you stopped writing stories of the resistance. You started criticizing the Party. You lost favor with Chairman Mao."

"Ah, you've been reading history," she exclaimed with false delight. "Do they let you do that now? We have to tear down the past, the Old Man said, to build the future." In a flash of temper she grabbed her notebook and threw it on the floor. "'The burgeoning trees are full with leaves, the birds cry in the hills...' That's the empty nonsense I write now."

"Are you writing for *People's Daily,* too?"

She ignored him again, sipped her tea. "Wei Ye was one of Old Mao's favorites, you know. He always liked young girls. The older he got, the younger the girls." She laughed oddly, a mixture of bitterness and world-weariness.

"What happened in 1941?"

She said nothing.

"What happened?" Hong asked again. "Why were you writing critical stories? What changed?"

"We were fighting for a great cause," his mother replied, "for the future of our country. But even a strong spirit can weaken. It wasn't always easy to keep believing."

"And what exactly happened to make you stop believing?"

Cui Chun dug between the cushions of the couch, found her cigarettes and lit one. Hong thought she would never answer. There was something in the tightening of her face, a kind of pain—almost a plea, he imagined, that he stop, carry this no further. Did she realize where he was heading?

At last she said, in a soft murmur, "There were things... things we couldn't explain."

"Like Sun Sheng losing a courier in Tianjin," Hong said. "In June of 1940."

She was startled, and she looked up. "How did you know that?"

"Never mind how I know. What else couldn't you explain?"

"Many things, many things...," she said tiredly.

"What things?" Hong pressed her.

She drew on her cigarette, picked up her cup, drank, set it back down. "Many things," she said again.

"Specifically?" Hong said, raising his voice.

For a time she simply stared at him. Leave me in peace, her expression seemed to say.

"Specifically," Hong repeated.

"Planes," she said finally. "Planes with supplies being shot down. Attacks on our guerrilla forces. Every day our intelligence sources made mistakes, one after the other."

"What kinds of mistakes?"

"Our men behind the lines, underground organizers, some of them were caught, some even thought their own operations had been betrayed..."

"But all of those things had happened earlier," Hong pressed on. "In 1941 you stopped writing your glowing stories. What happened in 1941? Was there one specific thing, perhaps?"

His mother clenched her hands, crimping her cigarette. Her fists fell to the cushions, and ashes scattered everywhere.

"*One* case," she said. "*One* case in particular."

She cleared her throat, expelled a breath. Hong waited.

"There was a man shot," she continued, "an underground organizer. The security people said he was a collaborator, a spy for the Japanese. Sun Sheng thought...others of us thought...the man had always provided good information..."

Again Hong's mind went back to the journal he had read:... *a plot to attack the Eighteenth Group Army...a collabo-*

rator serving the Japanese was executed near Baoding...we are still searching for a peasant woman in the countryside near— Cheng Hai-lin's husband, Liang Yu-shang's father...an underground organizer named Liang Bairong. Cheng Hai-lin was the woman they had been searching for; that was why she had changed her name. But according to Yu-shang's dossier, her father was shot by the Japanese. Someone had tampered with it.

"A shooting near Baoding," Hong said. "An underground organizer shot on Wei Ye's orders. Is that right?"

Cui Chun turned her head away. "You've been reading more than history," she said.

"But the man wasn't a Japanese collaborator," Hong said.

"You must realize they were terrible times," his mother said, pleading again. "We couldn't *afford* dissent, and Wei Ye was a valiant revolutionary..."

"And brutal, as you told me yourself. This supposed spy, the one Wei Ye ordered shot, what did you think was the real reason?"

"We had no proof!" she said angrily. "Only suspicions! Wei Ye was the most loyal comrade. When others weakened, when others had doubts, she remained firm. Even to suspect her..."

"But someone had proof," Hong said, "isn't that right? Someone tried to tell you that the man was innocent."

"Not then, not at the time," she said defensively.

"And since then?"

"Only suspicions," she repeated.

"Not a word from anyone? Nothing?"

"All right, maybe there were letters, but it was years later, a crazy old woman who refused to tell us who she was. Crazy letters about diaries...why should we have listened?"

"But you knew anyway," Hong said, aghast. "That's why you were disillusioned! You knew Wei Ye was smuggling the fossils from Choukoutien, trying to sell them. Still, what's smuggling? Just a matter of money. That was the kind of corruption you could tolerate. But what about betraying you to the Guomindang? And to the Japanese, too. That's why Yanan was attacked, that's why your planes were shot down. That explains all those battles you lost. She was a traitor. And when one man found out, she had him shot."

Cui Chun cringed, lowered her head, collapsed into her-self. Hong reached out and shook her violently by the shoulders. "Is that it? Am I right?"

"We couldn't be sure...we never imagined, we never really thought it was possible..."

But her defeated expression told Hong that he was right.

"Revolutionaries!" He spat the word out. "All these years you've known about her. You couldn't even warn me."

With a surprising outburst of anger his mother threw her pack of cigarettes aside and shouted: "I *never* knew! There was *no* evidence! And it wouldn't have mattered, don't you see? It was too late. She could have ruined you whenever she wanted."

"That's not the reason," Hong said, the awareness flood-ing through him. "It's because you would have had to admit to yourself that you knew. And me, you would have had to admit it to me, and you couldn't. But you started to worry when Sun Sheng died, didn't you?"

"I had suspicions..."

"Really? Why?"

"No reasons, only..."

"Only that he was in fine health," Hong said bitterly. "Only that so many others had died." He bore in on her. "And you knew *I* would wonder, too. So you wrote that story about the painter and the daughter, to warn Wei Ye, to tell her not to involve me, to tell her to stop. You were threatening to expose her."

"No, that's not true," she shot back. "I was worried about you, about your position in the Bureau, that's all."

Hong stood, went to the window. In the distant shadows of the fields, under the faint shell of the summer moon, he could see his driver, leaning on the car. He turned to his mother. "Why?" he asked, his voice breaking and dying to a whisper. "Why couldn't you admit the truth to yourself?"

His mother's eyes clouded, focused in the middle dis-tance, as if she were looking back, finding her way into the past. "I can still remember the first time we met," she began, "it was in 1934, at a Party meeting in Shanghai. She was a shy girl, small and pretty, and not very smart, we thought. But oh, how she would work, she would carry messages and recruit members. So pale and small, but it didn't matter, she was a white tiger ... she was absolutely fearless. We could have been arrested, all of us, the Guomindang was everywhere. Everywhere we went, whenever we met, we were in danger ..."

She sipped her tea, and offered the pot to Hong.

"No, go on," he said.

"I wanted to forget all this."

"But you can't," Hong said. "Go on. When did things change?"

"It's very hard to recall now. Before we got to Yanan, maybe, or else it was later. She was ... well, I suppose she was jealous of us, she felt we were better, or believed that we thought we were better. We were the scholars, we could contemplate revolution, but she would carry out the ugly tasks, things the rest of us didn't have the stomach for. But remember: no matter what, *she was one of us.* Do you understand? She had been with us from the beginning."

They had been friends, they had shared hardship, they had huddled in caves and marched the Long March. They had fought and sent others to fight. And whatever their friend had become, however the shy girl had betrayed them, they could never have accused her. If you suspect that your comrade, with whom you forged a revolution, is a traitor, how do you admit the truth? Had she not been a tiger?

Hong wondered if Wei Ye, the poorly educated peasant girl, had perhaps sensed their contempt, chafed under it and felt it as their betrayal of her. No one would ever be able to fathom her motives or the magnitude of her treason, but maybe that explained it. Still, was it explanation enough? They had not promised love, and she had promised loyalty. She sold their secrets, broke every faith. She traded with their enemy, killed their soldiers, and killed again to protect herself. And when they had won, when the country was theirs, she joined in the victory.

All of them had known, and hidden the knowledge from themselves, turning blind to the horror of Wei Ye's deceit, hoping that the sun would rise and set and rise again, and with a new day they could bask in their illusions of comradeship. And so they had been unable to admit that their staunchest comrade, once their friend, was a traitor.

But to understand was not to forgive. Hong was desolate, he felt himself betrayed. The fury rose in him, the fury that had been building ever since that day he had written his absurd little list of the dead cadres from Yanan, and he lashed out. "Revolution isn't a dinner party, you told me. You tolerated her because you'd given too much to the Revolution. You couldn't bear the thought that one of your own, one of the heroes, didn't believe as strongly as you did. And you liked being heroes, didn't you?"

His mother lifted herself to her feet.

"Heroes!" Hong shouted. "Serve the people! Serve the Revolution! Did you believe any of it? Or did you stop believing a long time ago?"

"Don't judge," she said. "We won a revolution, we won the hearts of the people."

"And what do we do now?"

"I was lucky to live out my life," she said softly. "Do whatever you have to do, but don't die for a cause."

She turned out the lamp and started to walk away.

"Not even for Sun Sheng?" he called fiercely after her. "Not even to see Wei Ye in front of a firing squad?"

He watched his mother cross the room and make her way up the stairs. The door at the top clicked open, then shut, and there was silence. But though the house was quiet, their pain, their losses, reverberated in the air.

Hong walked outside. The night was cool, the sliver of moon chasing the clouds. On the stoop he looked up at the glow coming from the second floor. You must once have believed in something, he thought. Did you fight for nothing?

Exhausted as he was, he sat at his desk with a tin of oil, a handful of cotton-tipped swabs, a rag, and a thin steel tube. The Bureau was quiet, and from across the city he heard the postal-and-telegraph clock chime: five o'clock in the morning, a nice time of day to clean a gun. Disassembling the gun was harder than he had expected. It was an old Lanzhou .38 revolver, better machined and more dependable than the nine-millimeter Shanghai Black, but encrusted with dust from years of sitting unused.

He thought about his mother, and wondered how she lived with her memories.

He swabbed the cylinder as if it were made of fine ivory, drew the rag-covered steel pin through the barrel, and oiled the breech with great respect. When he doubted himself, hatred drove him on. Let Wei Ye plan an infectious disease, he thought, a heart attack. He would shoot the doctors before he died.

There was a light tap at the door. A janitor?

"Yes, who's there?"

"Comrade Lu Hong? I have the telex you've been waiting for."

Hong wrapped the barrel and the chamber into the rag, covered them with the Bureau phone directory, then stood up and unlocked the door. The bleary-eyed night clerk held out the telex and a receipt for Hong's signature. Hong took the message first: *Shun Tsung, age 73, resident Special Clinic (Leprosarium). Director, Special Hospital Clinic 5, Evergreen Commune, Haikou, Hainan.* He signed the receipt, and when the clerk was gone riffled through Chan's top drawer for a CAAC schedule.

There was a flight to Guangzhou at 7:20, a layover of an hour, and a connection to Haikou at 12:30. From the stack at the bottom of the radio cabinet Hong got a transportation order and listed the flights. He decided he would have to do without Wei Ye's chop seal and forged her signature. The planes would be full, of course. All planes were full. And they might not even take off. A cancellation required the flimsiest excuse: the runways were crowded, the weather looked bad, the pilot had a head cold.

Hong slid the parts of his gun into two envelopes, along with the telex and a blank transportation order that he would need for his return. From his side drawer, no longer so recalcitrant now that the latch had been greased, he took a few selected reports on Ostrander and Caffey. Anyone who happened to examine the files might not notice what was missing, and retrieving them from his own apartment would be a far sight easier than returning to the Bureau. Stuffing the whole batch into his briefcase, he went downstairs to the duty officer at the Qianmen entrance, where he left a form saying he was leaving for Tianjin by train, a problem with theft at the textile factory, and would return the following afternoon.

The sun was coming up outside the duty officer's door. Across the courtyard next to the garage a truck driver was unloading posters of Lu Xun. Even here? Hong hurried past the truck to his bicycle. He had to stop at his apartment, and he wanted to be at the airport early enough to bump someone from a seat. *Don't die for a cause,* his mother had said. Pedaling away, he thought that he might not be willing to die for a cause, but living for one, that was another question altogether.

24.

LIEUTENANT SHUN TSUNG'S CONFESSION

The Guangzhou flight took off on time, minus a disgruntled purchasing agent from Beijing General Petrochemical. The plane was a cramped Ilyushin 62 with defective air-conditioning vents that belched white condensation smoke and terrified everyone. A tour group of Italians shouted at the stewardesses. The Chinese passengers studiously read their newspapers and pretended nothing was wrong. They were well-dressed, well-fed cadres of the new business class—falcons swooping. Up front were Hakkas from the south babbling in their thick-tongued dialect, and in the row across from Hong two black-robed Catholic priests from Shanghai who wisely said not a word to each other or anyone else. The stewardesses distributed CAAC souvenir keychains and paper fans decorated with mountain scenes. Hong thought about how badly his body craved sleep; to stay awake he counted the dead—Sun Sheng, Kang Xiao-tse, the Monk. In the next seat an acne-scarred cadre with nicotine-stained teeth worked over charts and columns of figures. He looked up at Hong and introduced himself.

"Are you in production?" he asked.

"No," Hong said. "You?"

"Freeze-dried foodstuffs," he said, bored. "For export. We're opening a new factory in Shenzhen." He nodded to the Catholic priests, who wore crosses on neck chains and held Bibles on their laps. "They have the best job," he added.

And why was that? Hong wanted to know.

"They study all day, they don't have to meet quotas, and no matter what the Party says their real boss is in Rome. What's your unit?"

"Public Security, Beijing."

"Honestly?"

"Yes, honestly. I don't meet quotas either."

"I shouldn't ask this," the production cadre said, leaning closer and whispering, "but is the pay good?"

"With the urban bonuses, it's okay. Yours?"

"If we have a successful year, with the new incentives I'll do pretty well. The power of incentives, you know, it makes you work harder. I have to travel a lot, so I don't see my wife much."

"Oh, that's too bad."

"No, that's good." He shrugged and smiled. "She doesn't like me, I don't like her."

"There you have it," Hong said, "another lesson in the power of incentives."

At Guangzhou, in the airport lounge, he drank tea and heavily sugared orange juice. Drenched with sweat in humidity thick as grease, he found himself staring at the Army guards stationed near the boarding gates, the local Public Security officers randomly touring the halls. This trip was a waste, reckless. Did he honestly believe he could indict a Director of Public Security for murder? For two murders, three, a dozen?

He glanced at his watch, picked up his small suitcase, and walked to the boarding area. A snub-nosed Ilyushin 14 taxied outside. Short routes used ancient Russian planes and British Tridents, long ones American Boeings. On the tar-

mac behind the Ilyushin propjet sat a dozen green Shenyang F-9s, textbook copies of Russian MIGs, powered by
Rolls-Royce engines.

Russian planes, American planes, British planes. China
reconstructs, Hong thought. Maybe soon she could recon-
struct an airplane all by herself.

Squabbling broke out at the boarding desk. A junior minister from the Sixth Ministry of Machine Building, finding
himself transferred to a flight the following day, loudly demanded the flight director, the airport manager. The gate
agent, who had bumped the junior minister to make room
for Hong, checked through the manifest, caught Hong's
eye, and apologized profusely to the minister, it was a terrible mistake but the flight had been overbooked. The minister stalked off into the terminal and Hong prayed he would
go home. If he pursued the matter, and anyone checked
with Beijing for confirmation of Comrade Lu Hong's travel
orders, soldiers with rifles would greet Hong at Haikou
Airport. For a moment he wished he had not left his disassembled revolver in his apartment, then realized that in
the event of trouble he would have had no choice but to
hand it over without a struggle.

The two Catholic priests from Shanghai were sitting
across from him, studying their Bibles. More production
cadres swarmed past, engaged in the arcana of purchasing,
supply shortages, international trade. Hong could decipher
only an occasional phrase; the dialect was impenetrable. A
small, stone-faced Hakka plopped down, ostentatiously
stowing his expensive leather bags under the chair. In his
hand was a boarding pass for Shanghai.

"Barbarians," he muttered in fractured *putonghua*. "They
ought to be locked up."

Hong caught his meaning—the priests—and ignored
him. The priests kept their heads in their Bibles.

"Valuable airplane seats," the Hakka muttered more
loudly, turning to Hong, "it's a crime to let them fly. They
should ride the train. They should be forced to walk."

"Why?"

"They're decadent, they hinder the progress of socialism
by encouraging irrational superstition."

"They only want to save you," Hong said. "They only want your soul."

"Let them save somebody else," the cadre snapped, annoyed at not finding a kindred barbarian-hater. "Let them save you."

Palm trees rose up as the plane descended. A billboard at the end of the runway proclaimed HAINAN, PROFITABLE HAVEN FOR INVESTORS, inviting foreign money to develop rubber, rosewood and ebony, offshore oil, sugar. And hotels, of course. A thousand years ago the Emperor exiled his troublesome courtiers here. Any day now the tropical beaches would sprout resorts.

No soldiers waited in the terminal, no rifles.

The leprosarium lay twenty miles to the west, on the island's coast. Public Security at the airport supplied Hong with a car and two young officers of the Li minority, one of whom could take stenography. They drove the coast road through vibrant sugarcane fields, quartz quarries, coffee plantations, and faraway smokestacks pouring a stench of burning rubber, while the South China Sea roared and foamed against the beach. From their basket of provisions the two Li officers offered Hong lichees and pomegranates, but soon lapsed into anxious silence. Considering their destination, Hong understood why. Only one disease was cited in the Family Law of the People's Republic: infection with leprosy was grounds for prohibiting marriage.

The director of the leprosarium met them at the gates. He was a broad-nosed Miao, a man of the hills, wearing a faded blue turban and a belted saffron-colored vest, and had the smooth skin of his Vietnamese ancestors, brown as loam. With a crooked smile he dispensed white plastic face masks and gloves. "Just keep the masks on," he said cheerfully, "and wear the gloves. Almost no one here is contagious, and anyway, only five percent of those exposed ever get leprosy."

The two Li officers were not reassured. They eyed each other, then slipped on the gloves and tied their masks tight. So did Hong.

The visitors' log showed not a single guest for Lieutenant Shun Tsung, not in the past year, not in the past ten years, which was as far back as the records went, and the director, for the life of him, had no recollection of any guests who might have avoided signing their names. "Then again, I'm not always here, I might have been in town," the director said. "Why not talk to the lieutenant yourself? He's quite a hero. Get him to tell you about his enlistment after the Marco Polo Bridge incident, he can go on about it for days, how he was with the Eighth Route Army for the evacuation of Nanjing, how he fought the Japanese hand-to-hand at Wuhan—had his own brigade, he says, if you can believe it. He actually tried to convince us he worked undercover, blowing up bridges and things. He likes to make up stories."

"Yes, old men do," Hong said, feeling no need to explain that Lieutenant Shun had undoubtedly blown up a great many bridges, and probably a lot of Japanese soldiers with them.

Through his office window the director pointed Hong toward a contorted figure reclining on a folding canvas cot under a laurel. "He remembers the war, but for anything else his brain's gone soft," the director cautioned. "And he's fairly blind."

Hong walked toward the laurel tree, expecting the worst, but for this his imagination was insufficient, and when he got close the sight nearly stopped his heart. The old lieutenant had no face, only a mass of congealed, yellowed lesions dotted by swollen eyes and a sunken nose deteriorated into two bulbous holes. He had no hair. He had no hands or feet, only clawed fingers and warped toes. There were only the outlines of what had once been a mouth.

Hong took a canvas chair opposite the lieutenant and announced himself as an investigator from Beijing, here on a special assignment, the particular nature of which he could not reveal. Lieutenant Shun Tsung nodded, and Hong began with the matter of the visitors' log. Was it true that no one had paid a visit to the lieutenant in ten years? Did he not have brothers, sisters, wife, children?

"I have no wife," the lieutenant said in a voice so gentle that Hong felt an overwhelming rush of pity. "I have no children."

"Brothers, then? Sisters?"

"No, they were killed during the war. I have only my friends here."

"How long have you been here?"

"A long time, as long as I can remember."

"And how many years is that?"

"Many, many years," Shun Tsung said.

"Last summer," Hong said, "did you have other visitors from Beijing?"

Shun Tsung lifted a clawed arm and touched the top of his disfigured head. "From Beijing, yes."

"Two visitors," Hong said, "a high cadre and a foreigner. A British foreigner."

The lieutenant could not recall.

"But you remember the cadre?" Hong said. "A woman?"

"No...maybe, there might have been a woman, I don't remember."

Hong nearly grabbed the old soldier, but the cruelty was beyond him. And despite the director's reassurance, the plastic gloves gave Hong less faith than he would have liked.

He turned to the two Public Security officers who had accompanied him from the airport. "Take notes now, please," he said. He unzipped his briefcase, making as much noise as possible, removed the folder containing his travel papers, and turned back to the lieutenant. "I have with me your record, your official Army record. Perhaps we can go over it together to verify the facts."

At the mention of an official record, the tiny dots that were once the lieutenant's eyes seemed to take on light, and he stirred faintly on the cot, lifting his head higher on the backrest.

In a formal voice, Hong began with the lieutenant's enlistment following the Marco Polo Bridge Incident in 1937, and his service in the Eighth Route Army.

"Let's see," Hong said, flipping the pages, "what division?" From his dim recollection of history, he took a guess: "The 112th..."

"No, the 115th," the lieutenant said.

"Yes, I'm sorry, I misread it."

Hong continued, pretending to skim the pages in front of

him, remarking on the lieutenant's presence at the evacuation of Nanjing, his eventual rise to command his own brigade against the Japanese at Wuhan.

"And so are we correct to this point?" Hong asked.

"Yes, everything is correct," the lieutenant said.

"Good. Now let's look at your service behind enemy lines starting in..." Hong flipped the sheets of paper back and forth.

"In 1939," the lieutenant volunteered.

"Yes, in 1939." Here Hong fired his best shot. If it went astray, this particular war might be over. "You were working under direct supervision from Yanan, under orders from Comrade Wei Ye. Is that correct?"

The lieutenant hesitated.

"Lieutenant Shung Tsung, the stenographer is waiting for your answer."

"Yes, you are correct," the lieutenant said. "My superior officer was Comrade Wei Ye."

Here, in a moment of elation, Hong paused. "Excuse me a second," he said, then rustled his papers loudly. "Now, let me ask you again. A year ago, did you have other visitors from Beijing?"

"Yes, yes, you were right."

"A foreigner," Hong said. "A British foreigner."

"Yes, a British foreigner."

"And he came with...it says here he came with the Director of Investigations of the Public Security Ministry. That would be Wei Ye, wouldn't it?"

"I...I can't recall," the lieutenant said.

"Really? It wasn't so long ago, just last year, wasn't it? Last August, to be exact."

"My memory isn't so good..."

"But I have the record right here," Hong said. "You received a visit from a British foreigner and Comrade Wei Ye in August of last year."

"No, I can't remember."

Hong brushed flies from his face. The lieutenant flinched, twisting his clawed hands over his head as if to ward off a blow.

"If I can propose an idea to you," Hong said, "perhaps your memory will return."

"Perhaps," the lieutenant said.

"We're talking about events that occurred when you served behind enemy lines. You were a good soldier, you had a good record."

"It was said that I performed well, yes."

"And it was a hard war, you were fighting two enemies, the Japanese and the Guomindang. You in particular had a harsh assignment . . . relying on the local people, some of whom might have been sympathetic to the Guomindang. Maybe some were in the pay of the Japanese. So you had to be careful."

The lieutenant braced his arms against his hips to shift his body, but it was a labor of pain. After a moment he had adjusted himself on the cot and appeared more comfortable. "We were very careful," he allowed.

"Naturally you were, your life was at stake every day. I imagine that you had many lines of communication to your superior officers. Maybe they sent very secret orders now and then."

"We received many secret orders," the lieutenant said.

"Let's suppose, just to help your memory, that you carried out secret orders for a high officer, possibly even your most superior officer, Wei Ye. And let us also suppose that since that time you've never discussed those orders with anyone. There were spies then, there might be spies now."

"We worried about traitors," the lieutenant admitted.

"Of course you did, you were prudent. And when these secret orders arrived—or maybe they were delivered personally—you didn't question them. If they required you to deal with foreigners, you were given a reasonable explanation. If you were required to dispose of a traitor, you might have doubted the evidence against him, but you were a soldier, you followed your orders because that's what a soldier does." Hong leaned closer, and the lieutenant's deep-socketed eyes seemed to follow every movement, responding to shadows and light. "For example, did you ever shoot a traitor yourself?"

"I . . . I seem to remember I did. Yes, I shot many traitors."

"On direct orders from your superior officer."

"Such orders came from many people at Yanan."

"But by 1941, for example, they came mostly from Comrade Wei Ye."

"Yes, mostly from her," the lieutenant agreed.

"And do you recall one case, an underground organizer for the Party, a man who had been loyal and trusted, but who was said to be a Japanese collaborator? Near Baoding, it would have been, in early 1941. In February, to be exact."

The mention of Baoding brought the second noticeable sign that Hong might be better informed than the lieutenant had expected. He raised his disfigured head even higher on the backrest and said, "Baoding, a Japanese collaborator shot, I might recall that."

"Lieutenant Shun Tsung, I'm sure you've been warned, you've been told about enemies of the people, bad elements. But we are not bad elements. Here is an order"—Hong fumbled for his travel papers and held them in front of the lieutenant's face—"that you should now speak to me about your service in 1940 and 1941."

Shun Tsung peered at the travel orders from the scarred sockets of his swollen blind eyes, but said nothing.

Hong moved closer. "I will explain to you," he said. "You are at the center of a conspiracy of which you know nothing. But now it is imperative that you give testimony." He folded the travel papers into his pocket and waited, but still the lieutenant said nothing. "The man you shot as a Japanese collaborator was innocent," Hong continued more forcefully. "He was a loyal Party member, and an error was made. Now we must correct the error, we must rehabilitate this man's reputation. You are the only witness, and without your testimony the injustice cannot be undone."

The lieutenant lowered his disfigured head. "I am not going to live much longer," he said simply. "They threatened to take me from here, from my friends. They threatened me with prison."

"But you won't be sent to prison," Hong said, "I assure you."

There was another long silence, until the lieutenant lifted his head and sighed. "Caffey," he said at last, "the Englishman from the war."

Hong pointed a finger at the Li officer. "Get this down. Every word of it."

Gulls swooped over the treetops, an ocean breeze rustled the leaves, and finally the story came out.

They had arrived, the Englishman and Wei Ye, last August—in late afternoon and unannounced, the lieutenant elaborated in his soldierly way. From the time the lieutenant had taken his troops behind enemy lines, all his orders had come directly from Wei Ye, an honor he spoke of with pride. "I was her most important officer in the area around Beijing. All orders from Yanan were sent to me. I relayed them to my men, to three separate regiments. We made raids on the Japanese. We were there to disrupt, to blow up their trains, sabotage their food lines. We had spies, informants, peasants who alerted us to enemy troops."

"And you, as Wei Ye's most important officer, did you have special functions?"

"I carried out numerous special missions. She once told me that she trusted no one else more, that I was her best officer."

"About the Japanese collaborator in Baoding," Hong said.

The lieutenant remembered the man well, a Party organizer from near Choukoutien.

"Name?" Hong asked in his military voice.

"Liang Bairong," the lieutenant supplied—Liang Yushang's father, Cheng Hai-lin's husband. The old lieutenant's brain was not as soft as the director thought.

"And what was he allegedly guilty of?"

"We had organized three teams of peasants around Choukoutien, given them guns, bombs, to sabotage shipments on the roads, and to cause damage on the railway from Tianjin to Beijing. It was the most effective way to strike at the Japanese. Two of the three teams were captured. They were tortured, and then shot. All of them. Someone had given their location to the Japanese."

"And why would anyone suspect Liang Bairong? Why was he held responsible?"

"One of the men in my command had asked him to investigate, but Comrade Wei Ye discovered that Liang Bairong himself was responsible, that he had informed the local Japanese colonel. He was investigating his own crime."

It was so simple, Hong thought. If Liang Bairong were allowed to investigate, he might discover the truth. More likely, by the time he was shot he had already discovered it, and had to be disposed of before he told anyone.

"And so you were ordered to kill him," Hong said.

"Yes, we went to Choukoutien in the middle of the night, found him in his bed. We had been told to shoot his wife as well, but there was no sign of her. We assumed she escaped into the countryside."

No, she had already gone to Beijing, to work for the foreigners there. "But if you shot him in Choukoutien," Hong asked, "why does the record say Baoding?"

"That was how I reported it," the lieutenant said.

"And the reason for that?" Hong prodded.

"For our own protection. Communications weren't secure, you see, and even in messages to Yanan we often disguised our location. If the Japanese searched for us near Baoding, they wouldn't find us. It was standard procedure. Even we had spies among us."

Yes, you did, Hong thought. Your superior officer, for one. "And did you question that this man was a traitor?"

"Why should we? It was true that his reputation was good, the people relied on him, but when an order came from Yanan we had little choice. Comrade Wei Ye said he was a double agent, betraying our troops. There had been raids against us, the enemy tracked us too well. We had already suspected someone of reporting our locations."

Someone had, but the traitor had not been Liang Bairong.

"But when Wei Ye and the Englishman came last year, it wasn't about the shooting at Baoding."

No, the lieutenant said, the Englishman had been involved in a separate mission, several months later. "It's a long time ago, the months all seem the same." The lieutenant's superiors at Yanan feared that the treasured fossils uncovered at Choukoutien would fall into the hands of the Japanese, or that the foreign scientists might steal them. Foreigners had no loyalty to China, the lieutenant explained. So an offer would be made to buy the fossils from them, to pay the greedy foreign devils. The Communists had friends, friends with money who loved China and who hated to see her plundered. "The Englishman, he was a friend of China, he could help spirit the treasure out of the country, to Hong Kong, until the war was over."

"Wei Ye told you that Caffey was a friend of China."

Not directly, the lieutenant said, but in a message brought by courier. The message directed him to approach an American in Beijing, a scientist named Ostrander, with an offer to pay, in British money, for him to steal the fossils and help the Englishman deliver them to Hong Kong.

"How much money?" Hong asked.

"I did as I was ordered, I was loyal."

"Of course you were, we know that," Hong said. "How much money?"

"Fifty thousand British pounds."

"And what did Ostrander say?"

"It was strange," the lieutenant said. "Ostrander had expected me. He had already heard of the offer, you see, and the Englishman. He even knew the Englishman's name."

Naturally, Hong thought. Caffey and Wei Ye had already approached Ostrander in Guangzhou to plan the bargain.

"Perhaps you were a little suspicious," Hong said, "about Ostrander expecting you."

"He led me to understand that he had been waiting for an acceptable offer."

Ostrander must have refused an earlier proposition— made by Caffey and Wei Ye in Guangzhou—and demanded more money. By the time Caffey and Wei Ye decided to meet his price, it was too late, Ostrander had returned to Beijing. All those references in Cheng Hai-lin's diary—how Ostrander was working to save the scientists' research. But with Ostrander in Japanese-occupied territory, Wei Ye had needed an intermediary, and who else would she choose but her own most trusted officer? Hong wondered now if Caffey had solicited Dr. Guo Ke with a bribe as well. Had Dr. Guo suspected Theodore Ostrander of secretly arranging to steal the fossils? To those questions, there would never be answers.

"So Ostrander agreed to sell the fossils," Hong said, "to help carry them out of China."

"Yes, when he was paid."

Peter Ostrander's father had been a thief, a scoundrel. "And did you pay him?"

"I received half the money, a packet of British bills. It was difficult to move then, Japanese troops were everywhere, but I delivered the package to Beijing. Please, the sun." It was beating down on him, and Hong moved to block the heat with his body. "I was almost caught by the Japanese."

But why now, forty years later, had Wei Ye visited him here? What had she wanted now?

"The fossils were never delivered."

"By Ostrander, you mean. You paid him, but he didn't bring the fossils."

"Yes, we met him, me and the Englishman, but Ostrander demanded the rest of his money. The Englishman wanted to see the fossils first—"

"Where?" Hong interrupted. "Where did you meet?"

"Near Beijing, I don't remember. It was arranged by the Englishman. But Ostrander hadn't brought them, and the Englishman pulled a gun. I was surprised, I didn't know he was armed. He said he knew where the fossils were, that we didn't need Ostrander anymore. And so he shot him. Through the head."

"What made Caffey so certain he could find the fossils?"

"My men had trailed the American scientist on two trips out of the city. Caffey was convinced that the American had left them somewhere along his route."

Caffey had been so greedy that he thought he could keep the money and find the fossils. He killed Peter Ostrander's father—a fight among thieves. "Still, it was more than forty years ago," Hong said. "What could you do about it now?"

"I was useless, but Comrade Wei Ye thought I had followed Ostrander, that I had seen his hiding place."

"But she could have asked you forty years ago," Hong suggested, "when you returned to Yanan."

The lieutenant's warped mouth skewed upward into a curve resembling a smile. "But that's just it, I never returned," he said. "I was captured two weeks later and spent the rest of the war in a Japanese camp. In Yanan, you see, they thought I was dead. All these years, she thought I was dead."

* * *

It was one o'clock in the morning when the flight from Guangzhou descended toward Beijing. The plane had been held on the runway because of the rains, and had taken off four hours late. Hong had remained awake, praying that the flight wouldn't be canceled, and that the true reasons for his absence had not yet been discovered. When the plane finally rose from the runway he gave in to his body's needs and slept the entire way to Beijing, almost three hours.

The stewardess woke him as they approached the airport. Hong heard the wheel bays open and the landing wheels lower with a crunch. Did the other passengers on the plane, he wondered, notice the look on the face of a condemned man? He observed his fellow cadres zipping and unzipping their overnight bags and briefcases, pulling out their raincoats, rubbing their fingers in the dark hollows under their eyes. They had a condemned look themselves.

With the lieutenant's confession, witnessed by the two officers, Hong had fit together the last links in the chain. As he suspected, it had not been the Japanese who killed Liang Yu-shang's father. Wei Ye had ordered him shot—and his wife, Cheng Hai-lin, had kept evidence of the betrayal. *An old woman...letters...diaries*, Cui Chun had said. Caffey, in his phone call to England, had spoken of a shipment, which could only mean the fossils, but Wei Ye wanted something else—the old woman's evidence. *If the Marines cannot do the job, Professor Ostrander will try himself. I pray that he succeeds, for my sake. Who knows if I will survive the war?* Hong saw now what the old woman had meant. She had given her evidence to Theodore Ostrander to hide. Another item he might have sold—the old woman's sacred evidence along with the fossils.

As for Peter Ostrander, he was everyone's pawn. Only he could find the evidence that would destroy Wei Ye. Hong wondered how Deng Bo had begun his pursuit. Had the old woman's daughter found Deng, or had he found her—an actress singing for the military? Seek revenge for your father, Deng would have said, whore yourself with Ostrander, and I promise you freedom. He had not, however, managed to protect her mother. Soon the last witnesses would be dead.

But not quite all of them, Hong said to himself, I'm still alive.

It had rained in Beijing, too, while he was gone. Pools on the pavement outside the airport glistened, white mirrors on the cloak of the night. Hong boldly strode past the Bureau's cars and took a taxi stationed opposite the doors. Waiting while the driver found the keys, he watched a Boeing 747, its wing lights flashing, land at the international terminal: the flight from Tokyo, which in the next hour would turn around and fly back, across the Yellow Sea and the Korean Strait, and then over the Pacific to the United States. Hong wondered idly how he would feel if he were on it, with Yamei at his side.

Bulldozers blocked the entrance to his apartment building. He settled for the eastern end of Sanlihe Road, collected his taxi receipt. The rain had washed the sky, and the sliver of moon courted by a million stars winked from its sparkling black blanket. By their light Hong sluggishly made his way past the Widow Ou's window. His eyelids were deadweights, but he wanted his files to make his appeal.

Inside the door on the first floor he took a reasonable precaution: he removed the lieutenant's confession from his briefcase, folded it in half, then again and again, until it was a small square. With his pen he chipped a loose strip of mortar from between two bricks above the door and jammed the paper in, then forced pieces of mortar back into the hole.

On the fifth floor, rounding the corner toward his apartment, he stopped. His own alertness mystified him. A day with almost no sleep, exhaustion...maybe it was a will to live that had sharpened his senses. He listened. There was a faint rustle at the end of the corridor. Had there been someone hiding at the bottom of the steps, too? Hong put his ear against the concrete and heard a shuffling. One from behind, one in front. Would they risk shooting him here?

He rubbed the stiffening muscles in his neck, straightened his shoulders, confidently marched forward. At the

alcove just short of his door he spun around, tossed his suitcase at the figure in the shadows, threw a fist at the two
eyes. His knuckles met flesh. He ducked and waited for the
crash of a falling pistol.

Peter Ostrander stumbled into the moonlight, caressing
his bleeding face.

Hong nearly laughed. He dug for his handkerchief and
pressed it on Ostrander. "How did you get here?" he whispered.

"I . . . I've been waiting all night for you." He dabbed the
handkerchief to his lip, touched his nose and winced in
pain. "I think my nose might be broken."

"I'm sorry," Hong said. "That's what happens when you
hide in corners and wait for people in the dark. How did
you find out where I live? Did anyone see you?"

"Dr. Yan told me. I waited until they all went to sleep."

"You're a fool, my friend Peter. You could be arrested if
they found you here." He unlocked the door to his apartment. "Hurry, come inside before someone hears us."

Ostrander hesitated.

"All right, stay where you are," Hong said, starting in. "I
don't have time to waste."

Ostrander clamped a hand on his shoulder. "You put
Liang Yu-shang in jail. I want you to release her."

"It was a mistake," Hong said, "but I can't do anything
about it."

"Yes, you can. You're in Public Security, Dr. Yan said
you're very powerful."

"Dr. Yan is a fool, too." He yanked his shoulder from
Ostrander's grip. "Go to your government, file a protest,
ask your embassy to get your beloved released."

"I did," Ostrander said, dabbing again at his lip. "They
told me I was only going to cause trouble for myself."

"And you will," Hong said. "Have you ever been in a Chinese jail? It will make yours look like Heaven."

"Why did you arrest Yu-shang? What has she done?"

"She worked for them," Hong said, "she made love to you
so you'd find the fossils for them. Why do you think they
invited you? Forget Yu-shang, she's a whore, forget you
ever came to China, go home while you still can."

"But my father, the painting and the letter . . ."

"Your father's dead, shot by your friend Caffey."

"That's absurd, it's ridiculous...you're lying."

Was it also ridiculous that his father had schemed to steal a great treasure? Hong wondered what Peter would think of that information.

No doors along the corridor had opened, no curious light sleepers peeking at whoever might be causing a ruckus. "You should leave, before the street militia arrives."

"Dr. Yan won't tell them I'm here," Ostrander said.

"They're not coming for you. They're coming for me."

Hong stepped over the threshold and started to elbow the door closed. Ostrander wedged his foot over the doorsill and tore at Hong's arm, pulling him against the wall and scraping his forehead and hands on the concrete. But Hong was younger, and stronger, and easily pitched Ostrander off, sending him sprawling, thumping onto the hallway floor.

"Go home," Hong said, "get out of China. There's nothing for you here."

He gathered his files quickly, planned the speech he would make to the Minister. But his strength ebbed, he succumbed to weariness and rested in his chair for what seemed only a moment. He dozed, he woke, he dozed again. When he was finally able to drag himself from the chair he found he had lost almost an hour.

The moon had slipped into the night, the gray horizon bled into black. In the courtyard he strapped the files to the rack on his bicycle and pedaled toward Fuchengmen, taking the straightest route. If an arrest order had already been issued, they would never expect to find him here, alone on his bicycle. They would expect him to run.

The compound on Tsungenwai was a sleeping fortress. No lights shone from the houses, no cars waited in the courtyard. Hong slowly rode past the gate once, out to Chang'an, then circled back past Dongdan Park, where Red Flags all in a row were parked diagonally to the curb. The streetlamps reflected sparkles from the polished black cars and from puddles on the wet street. Hong looked in all directions for Public Security cars, for a jeep with a waiting driver, for thugs who might be hidden in the willows.

But he saw no one. On the pavement below the edge of the park he paused and peered toward Tsungenwai. If they were waiting for him, they were well hidden. He pedaled up the alley behind the compound, turned the corner, and coasted to the steel-gated entrance. At the very instant he touched his brakes, a soldier stepped from the guardhouse.

"You can't stop here," the guard said.

Hong realized that the soldier would be wary at his disheveled appearance—his wrinkled clothes, the scrapes on his hands and face from his fight with Ostrander. He presented his identification folder so that it caught the light from the streetlamp. "I want to see the Minister of Public Security," he said. "It's very urgent."

The soldier glanced at Hong's identification, then at his clothes and face. "The Minister is away. Now, you must move on."

"This is very important," Hong said. "I'll speak to the Deputy Minister."

The soldier reluctantly accepted the identification folder and retreated to the guardhouse, closing the door behind him. Hong watched as he made a note in his duty register, picked up his phone, and dialed a four-digit number—an internal extension. He spoke to someone very briefly, then returned, holding out Hong's card. "I can write down your request, but that's all. We have strict orders not to disturb anyone."

Hong fought off his panic, took a breath. "You must summon the Deputy Minister! It's urgent! I have to speak to the Deputy Minister now!"

"Assistant Deputy Director Lu Hong, you must leave. Your request has been recorded."

With that, the soldier slipped back into the guardhouse and closed the door.

Unable to think clearly, Hong climbed onto his bike, pedaled out to Chang'an and turned toward Fuchengmen. What now? Should he go to the front gate of Zhongnannai, attempt an appeal directly to the Premier? If Deputy Ministers left orders not to be roused from sleep, would the Premier's guards respond differently?

He rode west the whole way to Fuchengmen, thought of

going to the compound of the highest leaders, but instead turned north and headed for home. He would make his appeal in prison, he told himself, he would expose Wei Ye at his trial. But this was a desperate hope, a delusion. There would be no trial.

Passing the trolley stop at Baiwanzhang, he saw someone waving from a bicycle; it was Boda, pedaling frantically toward him. The sculptor's untamed hair stood straight up in the wind.

Boda braked to a stop, his chest heaving for air, his damp shirt sticking to his sides. "I was on my way...to your place...," he said breathlessly. "They came half an hour ago...I couldn't leave sooner. You've been accused, there's a list of charges."

"Slow down," Hong said, rolling his bike to the sidewalk. "What were the charges?"

Boda caught his breath and wiped the sweat from his forehead. "Smuggling, conspiring with foreigners. They say everybody's drawing a clear border, separating themselves from you...your brother, Chan, your cousin Hu, and..." Boda stared at his feet.

"Finish with it. Who else?"

"They said Yamei and her parents, but I don't believe it. She wouldn't."

Was it too late to present a case against Wei Ye? She had already jerryrigged one against him. "I hope you drew the border around yourself, too," Hong said.

"Of course not."

"You should have," Hong said. "It'll be bad for you and Min." He turned, took the files from his bicycle rack. "I want you to hold these, and when Ma Sufei returns from Guangzhou—"

The tautness in Boda's face stopped him.

"She's not—"

Boda nodded. "We heard there had been an accident at the hotel."

"Take these, keep them for me," Hong said, and then, as Boda extended his hand, yanked the files back. "No, it's not worth it. You'll have troubles enough."

Boda snatched the packet of papers. "Good deeds always

bring trouble. Has it ever been different? What are you going to do now?"

A few workers heading for the morning shift were lining up at the trolley stop, and a long dim plume of orange rose into the sky. Hong touched Boda's hand. "If I run, I'm guilty," he said, moving away, "and if I stay I'm guilty. If I live I'm guilty, and if I die I'm guilty. I guess I'll have to figure out something else."

"Which is what?" Boda called.

Something between running and staying, Hong thought as he turned and waved what he knew might be a last good-bye. Something between life and death.

At the gymnasium, morning practice had just begun. Her teams gleamed in the water, swimming relays. Look at them, they were long skinny fish with black stripes around the middle, they were glorious socialist fish. Hong thought about his son. What would become of Bai, with a traitor for a father?

Yamei, on the diving board, leaned over with a stopwatch, cheering and exhorting her relay teams. Pull, pull, harder, another lap, just one more. Hong stood behind the glass window in the coaches' office that faced onto the pool. Somewhere above him other swimmers were exercising. The ceiling shook and the ventilation fan let out a whine.

Two girls climbed out of the pool and Yamei lay down next to them on a mat. Leg up, out—see, it's done this way, this is the more economical stroke. Hong saw the curve of her arm, the line of her cheek. He had found her, she had found him, she would give birth to a little swimmer and they would raise a socialist hero of their own. Now he was going to lose her.

When she stood to blow her whistle and call a break, she saw him. Her eyes searched wildly all around the pool. Did she expect to see soldiers? Was she surprised only because it was morning and he ought to be at work? Or because he ought to be in jail?

Her mouth open in horror, her tears already starting to flow, she ran toward him on the black mat alongside the tiered bleachers, though she seemed so far away that she could run forever and never reach him. But reach him she did, sprinting into the office and closing the door. She pulled him behind it, took him in her arms. "I thought they'd arrested you," she said through her tears.

"Not yet," Hong said. "Soon enough, though."

She began apologizing for her parents. The procurate had arrived in the middle of the night, her father was frightened, her mother reported Hong's jokes about Chairman Mao, they agreed that Hong might be a criminal.

"And you," Hong said, "what did you tell them?"

She whimpered, hugging him tighter.

"It's all right," Hong said. "You didn't have any choice."

"I told them I knew nothing, I said you had always been loyal and devoted to the Party, but what could I do? I had to agree you might have caused trouble. They would have arrested me, Hong, they would have taken me to prison and I...I couldn't..." She fought for breath. "You're not a smuggler, it's not true!"

No, it wasn't true, Hong said.

"How can this happen, we're so happy, you work so hard..."

She broke down, weeping and choking back sobs, and he stroked her round shoulders where the straps of her suit had become twisted. He had never known her to cry like this.

"Listen to me," he said, taking her face in his hands. "Listen," he repeated when she continued sobbing. "If they ask you to testify against me, then do it. You musn't try to defend me."

"You have to go away," she replied with sudden firmness. Her crying ceased and she grew efficient. She rubbed her hands together and paced. "You can go to the west—yes, of course, that's the best way, the whole way to Tibet, they'll never find you, and then when we've cleared your name you can come home, you'll hide and—"

"They'll find me," Hong said. "I can't run."

Her cheeks filled with air. "They *won't* find you," she burst out. "You can cross the border if you have to, into the hills, or maybe go south, that would be better, to Hong Kong..."

"Stop." She was doomed herself, and still worrying about

him. He took hold of her shoulders. "I can't run far enough, they'll find me eventually. And I can't cross into Hong Kong on my own papers. Even if I could, they might find me and bring me back. I only wanted to . . . to say good-bye. I don't think you'll get to see me in prison."

Or anywhere else, he thought.

She broke free of his hands and pivoted away to a locked filing cabinet in the corner. Fumbling with the key, she released the top drawer. "I have our travel documents," she said triumphantly. "For the team's trip to Hong Kong."

She produced a stack of external passports. The dark brown booklets were opened and flattened, held together by a thick rubber band. She slipped the rubber band off and fanned them in front of his face. "Look, exit visas! They're stamped!"

"Yamei, it won't work . . ."

"No!" she shrieked. Her voice echoed from the tiles. "No," she repeated, more quietly, "you can hide there, someone will take you in, you can't quit, I won't see you go to jail."

"Yamei . . ."

She shushed him and riffled through the passports, then turned and held one up—gleefully, like a child with a pretty new toy. The whole idea was absolutely crazy. "He looks just like you."

Hong smiled at her naivete. It was the passport of an assistant coach whose face might have been Hong's five years ago.

"But I'd need an internal identification to match," he said, trying to dissuade her from this insanity. "Put them away."

She dipped into the same drawer, extracting another bundle—plastic red folders, the team's internal papers. "We sent these for the visas and I haven't distributed them yet. We're all carrying temporary cards."

Hong considered the two documents. The photo on the internal passport resembled his own. With the barest luck, if the border police were sloppy, if he had the opportunity to try . . . the documents might sneak past a quick glance.

"If they catch me with these," he said, "you'd go to prison, too."

"You're wasting time," she said frantically. "Please, please take them. Please hurry..." She embraced him, she kissed him, she cried again. "Please, go..."

He was about to suggest that if he managed to escape maybe someday she would join him, but it seemed the wrong kind of farewell.

Down the long tiled corridor to the gymnasium steps, he considered escape. Three years ago he had chased a band of robbers halfway across the country, day and night without pause. He lost them, months went by, they were sighted, and he pursued them again. They were captured in the end and met their fate in front of a firing squad. The odds of getting to Guangzhou and on a train to Hong Kong were infinitesimally small, even on false papers. Yamei had been right only about fleeing west; he might have a chance of disappearing in Tibet, if only for a little while.

None of the alternatives was appealing: fifteen or twenty years in prison, a bullet in the back of his neck, or running west and scavenging food until he starved or froze to death. Maybe there was yet a chance of heading south.

He was staring at two guns when he stepped outside, and they were in the hands of two thugs he had seen around the Bureau for years.

Wei Ye stood next to them, behind the open door of a new Shanghai sedan.

"I thought you'd come here," she said as he walked toward her. "So you found the lieutenant. You weren't expected to go that far."

"But you were the one who told me that if a man says one thing, I understand three."

"Four, five...you understand too much. You've created a problem for me down there, stationing a guard at the leprosarium. Please get into the car."

"How much did Sun Sheng understand?" Hong asked, his rage rising in his throat. "How far did he go?"

"Not far enough," she said. "He was your hero, wasn't he?"

"He was a great and wise man," Hong said.

"But error is always in a hurry. He wanted to be Minister of Public Security. He was no different from any of us." She paused and smiled at him. "Except you, that is. You carry the burden of goodness."

Sun Sheng might have wanted to be Minister, but he was different from Wei Ye. Attribute to others your own base motives, Hong thought. Defame him all you want. What do we expect from a hog but a grunt?

"A year ago," Hong said, "what led you to the lieutenant?"

She smiled. "That was the Englishman's idea. When I told him that Ostrander had been invited to China, he cleverly suggested that we go back and check everything. Poor Mr. Caffey . . . clever, but not clever enough."

Another car had pulled up, and four officers climbed out. They went up the steps into the gymnasium.

"Why are they here?"

"To take your fellow conspirator's confession," Wei Ye replied smoothly. "We must pursue all the evidence. Now again, please get in the car or we'll be forced to put you in, which will only make everyone uncomfortable."

What point was there in arresting Yamei now? What more could she tell them? Only that she had given him travel documents, and with a sickening feeling in his stomach Hong knew she would submit to torture before she revealed anything.

He slid into the back seat and Wei Ye joined him. The two officers got in front, one behind the wheel and the other with a gun trained on Hong's head. A little melodramatic, Hong thought. "You can put that away. I'm not jumping from a moving car."

Wei Ye nodded, the gun was instantly tucked into a shoulder holster, and the officer switched his focus to his protectress.

"Where is the picture?" Wei Ye asked. "Of Caffey and Deng Bo."

"Why? What use is it now?"

"But it's the evidence," she said righteously. "To hold an Englishman and a high cadre in jail we need evidence."

"Caffey is in jail?"

"Obviously. I had him arrested at the airport. He was conspiring with Comrade Deng Bo."

So Caffey, the accomplished middleman, had been caught

in the middle. Even Deng had been suspicious of him, Hong realized. That moment in Beidaihe, when Deng mentioned Public Security's interest in Ostrander: Deng had wanted Hong to investigate Caffey, had wanted him to help keep Caffey in line. Caffey had played on both sides and Deng had known, but Wei Ye had triumphed over both of them. The photograph of Caffey was in his office, Hong told her, in the same drawer she had already opened once.

The car was turning on West Dianmen, so they weren't going to the Bureau, or to Qin Cheng Prison Number One, or to 44 Banbuqiao. Where was she taking him?

"You didn't let me arrest Caffey," he said, "and then you did it yourself. Why?"

"Because if I'd given you a chance to question him, especially with that brute assistant of yours, you would have understood too much. And I needed you to continue with Ostrander. As it happened, Comrade Deng accompanied Caffey to the airport, which I suspected when you informed me that he'd changed his flight. Comrade Deng, as you're aware by now, has been plotting against me ever since he had Ostrander admitted to the country. Finding him with Caffey, I had no choice but to arrest them myself."

Hong had not really expected her to answer, but as she talked he heard a sense of release in her voice, and a strange pride. She had lived an entire life of deception, and now, finally, she had someone in whom to confide. Needing an audience for her brilliant treachery, she seemed almost to be boasting of her success.

"So the tiger wins," he said. "Even in Yanan your comrades wondered about you."

"My comrades were weak."

"I suppose Caffey and Deng will die in jail. Of an infectious disease, maybe. When do I join them, or will I succumb to a heart attack?"

"You're not going to prison," said Wei Ye. "You're going to find the fossils."

Now he knew why Wei Ye had sent the officers into the gymnasium for Yamei: to ensure his silence. "It's not just the fossils," he said. "You want the diary that's hidden with them."

"Congratulations!" she exclaimed scornfully. "A man says one thing, you understand six."

"Ostrander doesn't know where the fossils are. If he did, I would have found them already."

"His father left the painting for a reason," Wei Ye said confidently. "The information is in Ostrander's head. As his friend, you can get it out."

"He no longer thinks of me as a friend," Hong said.

"You'll find a way," she assured him.

Until now he had done everything wrong. Here was a chance to do something right. "If you released Liang Yu-shang..."

"She's been charged," Wei Ye said. "Releasing her is impossible."

"Ostrander wants her. To have his cooperation, it's the only way. And without him, you have nothing."

She looked down and studied her hand, turning it over and over. "You may approach him with the idea," she said finally.

"And if I refuse?"

"Why would you? At the very least you'd spend the rest of your life in a reeducation camp. Twenty years of shoveling coal where it's always winter, that's not an appetizing prospect, is it? And your friend Cao Yamei? Fortune might befriend her with an invitation to help colonize Qinghai Province. It's a little dull, though. All she'd see out there are camels. And she's soft, she's lived in the city too long, I don't think she could survive it. When someone steals food in Qinghai they tie his thumbs together with wire. I hear if the wire stays on too long they have to amputate."

Hong knew that he would never see the high walls and barbed wire of a labor camp. He would die long before any charges were filed; in becoming the witness whom Wei Ye so desperately needed, he had sentenced himself to death. But if to him death now seemed almost preferable, who could tell what horrors might befall Yamei? "If I agree to help with Ostrander," Hong asked, "what will happen to my friends?"

"It's as easy to rehabilitate them as it is to punish them for knowing you. We'll say it was an error, have your girlfriend promoted, have your sculptor assigned to a post at the Art Institute."

There was no prayer for any of them. Yamei would be demoted forever, perhaps even be sentenced to prison, her father would lose his bonuses, Boda's apartment would be raided for subversive artwork and literature, Lin would be removed from his lucrative factory directorship. Even Kuang would be considered dangerous now, and Bai would be branded forever with the mark of his criminal father. Only Chan, perhaps, could take care of himself.

"And what about the charges against me?"

"They'll be removed. You'll awaken from this bad dream and you'll be free."

Free to be shot, Hong thought, while attempting to escape. "There's one aspect I still can't see clearly," he said. "Why did you assign me to Ostrander in the first place? Was it only because of Sun Sheng?"

Wei Ye laughed. "That would have been no problem, none at all. A list of dead cadres, doctors who would never say a word against me . . . maybe in a few years you'd build a case. Besides, once I'm on the Central Committee nobody will be able to touch me. No, it wasn't your silly suspicion about Sun Sheng, it was your mother. The minute she wrote that story for *People's Daily*, I had to worry. Heaven only knows what she told the editors. Not the truth, naturally. But sooner or later, I realized, the two of you might succeed in bringing me down."

"Why not dispose of her, too?" Hong asked.

Wei Ye took the problem under consideration. "It would be hard. It's not so easy to kill someone, you know, even with the best doctors. Your mother lives in that compound surrounded by peasants, she never leaves the house. And she has those damn caretakers from the Army, they see who comes and goes. If she were shot, if she had an accident, too many people would ask questions. Sometimes I think she moved out there for protection. But if I could put you in a position where I could build a case against you, it would shut her up long enough for me to take care of Ostrander."

The car stopped at the corner of Wangfujing and Chaoyangmen. Wei Ye reached across Hong's chest and opened the door. "Let's walk," she said. "You have an appointment."

She led him toward the medical college, with the car cruising along behind them. To the crowds on the street they were objects of envy, contented high cadres on a morning stroll, and people parted like the wake of a ship to let them pass. It must be painful, Hong thought, so ungratifying, to live one's truest life always in the dark, to scheme so cleverly and have no one recognize your greatness, no one to salute your genius. Even as his loathing grew, even as his repulsion at the magnitude of her murderousness turned him cold with terror, Hong discovered in himself a perverse admiration. Was she so unlike the others who had preceded her? Or was she separated from them only by the boldness of her deceit?

"There's one other mystery," Hong said. "Maybe you could clear it up for me."

"It would be a pleasure."

"You were one of the Chairman's favorites. Why sell information to the Japanese or the Guomindang? Why try to make money from the fossils? Whatever happened, you would have lived well."

"Only if we'd won," Wei Ye said, lighting a cigarette. "What if we lost?"

"That's too easy. Nobody becomes a spy only for money."

"It wasn't only money, it was a guarantee. Whoever won, I would be in power. And I think maybe that I was never a dedicated Communist."

"You'd like to think that," Hong said. "But I don't. It was really that you hated your comrades for how they'd treated you. They thought you were stupid, they looked down on you, on your lack of education. It wasn't their cause you wanted to hurt, it was them."

Wei Ye came to a halt in front of the hospital complex. Workmen were carting new beds, desks, room dividers. She turned to him with fury in her face. "Think what you like," she said. "Your friend Ostrander is waiting."

25.

MEMORY

Ostrander denied everything. He denied that he was a pawn, he denied that Liang Yu-shang was a whore, he denied that Hong was innocent. Throughout his denials he swore and threatened. The man who had loved China and her wonderful people had grown a hatred to match the childish anger in his heart. Everything had become simple: China was a hellhole, a fascist state that existed only to thwart his love.

"We're not fascist, we're Marxist-Leninist," Hong insisted, and then added, trying for a joke, "although these days we're not even too confident about that."

His jokes no longer amused his friend. "You disgust me," Ostrander said. He rubbed the bandage on his nose.

They were in Dr. Yan's office, guarded by one of Wei Ye's thugs in the corridor. The sun coming through the windows planted bars of light on Ostrander's face, as though to make him the prisoner he was. But we have no tribunal, Hong thought, we have no judges to free or condemn us.

"I called you a fool," he said to Ostrander. "Accept my apology. I was one, too."

"You lie pretty well, don't you?" Ostrander sneered. "But I forgot, you're trained for that."

Ostrander's insults were annoying. Here we are arguing, Hong thought, with both of us soon to die. "You have two choices," he said. "If you trust me, we can retrieve the fossils and exchange them for Liang Yu-shang. That's the bargain I made. And if you don't trust me, I'll be dead and she'll rot in prison for the rest of her life, which may be short."

"And if I decide not to trust you," Ostrander asked, "what do you plan to do with me?"

"This is only a humble cadre's speculation, you understand—and one who is thinking with his head at the end of a gun barrel—but either they'll send you home on the next flight or you'll be arrested as a spy and they'll beat the information out of you. If you would accept my knowledgeable guess, I would pick the latter."

"This is incredible," Ostrander bellowed, "you can't treat people like this. My government will lodge a protest, the ambassador—"

"Won't get his phone calls answered. You think of your embassy as some kind of magic. You think because you're a foreigner you'll be protected, the way you're protected inside your housing compound. But your ambassador won't even hear about you until it's too late. Believe me, please, Peter. You have to trust me."

Ostrander sulked, and Hong sat opposite Dr. Yan's desk. He began to comprehend, for the first time in his life, what it meant to have faith in embassies and ambassadors, in laws and governments. It must be an extraordinary condition, he thought for a moment, until it struck him that precisely the opposite was true. It was not extraordinary at all; to Ostrander, it was as unremarkable as buying a box of his ballpoint pens, a camera, his leatherbound notebooks. It was the most ordinary thing in the world.

"Do you remember what you told me about secret desires?" Hong asked. "It turns out that you were right. I know more about freedom now. I know how valuable it is."

"Is that so? Then maybe you ought to realize—"

A fracas erupted in the hall, Dr. Yan quarreling with the guard.

Hong opened the door. "Let him in," he said sharply.

Dr. Yan, brushing his shoulders and straightening the flaps of his white jacket, stormed past a startled nurse, tugging his weak leg behind him and venomously slapping the door shut with his cane.

"So you've been denounced," he said brusquely to Hong. "A smuggler? A counterrevolutionary? You amaze me. I would never have marked you for such courage."

"My recent reputation is undeserved," Hong said.

Dr. Yan circled around to his desk. To Ostrander, in a more muted tone, he said, "And sadly you're part of the conspiracy, too. I will be sorry to lose you."

"I'm not part of a conspiracy," Ostrander protested.

"In our reality, no, but in theirs, yes. I have already explained to you the multiple realities we live with in China, and I am not referring to those of psychotics and schizophrenics. They say you're a conspirator, and therefore you are." He turned to Hong. "They want his memories, is that it?"

"That's it," Hong agreed.

"Ah, my laggard mind," said Dr. Yan, distractedly running a hand through his thick white hair. "It was all available to the eye of any sharp-witted idiot, if only I had bothered to look. Will they live?"

"I hope so," Hong said.

"Just a minute here," Ostrander cut in angrily, "will *who* live?"

"You and your woman," said Dr. Yan. "Comrade Lu Hong is responsible for your fate."

"Are you telling me I should trust him?"

"Do you want the woman to leave with you?" Dr. Yan asked, and hurried on, not disposed to wait for an answer. "Then yes, you should trust him."

On the table, Ostrander lay with his eyes closed. Dr. Yan worked the needles into his head, his neck, and the small muscled area at the top of his spine. When the needles were in place, Dr. Yan boosted the power from the generator.

"Can you see the scene in the painting?" he asked.

"No, I see a train," Ostrander said, "I'm in a sleeper, folded down inside the car. My mother and father are opposite me. We're going to visit...it's a friend of his, someone who does the same kind of work."

"The scene in the painting," Hong said.

"I'm getting there," Ostrander said. "I think about the house in the painting and it starts on the train."

Hong suggested that Dr. Yan retreat into the anteroom. "You don't want to hear this," he said.

Dr. Yan picked up his cane and backed awkwardly toward the door, like a supplicant leaving incense at the Buddha. "I'll be right here, call me if I can help."

"Why do you want him to go?" Ostrander asked.

"This is between us," Hong said. "We're safer this way. Continue."

Ostrander closed his eyes. For a moment he was silent. "It's like a dream, I have a little puppet with me, a marionette, the kind with strings attached to the hands and feet..."

"Yes, I know," Hong said.

"The puppet! I must be eight because I got it for my birthday."

So it was after January 1941. "But where are you going?"

"The train's very nice," Ostrander went on, "the conductors all make a fuss over the puppet." He moved his hand to the generator and adjusted the current. "We've come to a place to catch a boat. We get off the train and they load our suitcases onto a wagon, big suitcases and trunks..."

"Two trunks," Hong said.

Ostrander paused. "Yes, two big footlockers. We take a car and ride through all these hills, we're riding down. It has a big steam engine, this boat, and it's at the bottom of a hill. There's a city behind us, we've come from the train station. I'm wearing a little backpack, the straps are cutting into my shoulders and my mother takes it off. There's a bridge just down the river, and behind us houses on stilts above the harbor, and there's the incline, it's a car running on tracks down to the harbor, that's how we came down to the boat..."

There was only one such incline on the Yangtze River. "Chongqing," Hong said.

"That's right, that's where we are, where the train took us. We're getting on the boat, everybody's staring at us because we're foreigners. We're not going very far, my mother tells me, just down the river, and pretty soon we're pulling into the shore, a small dock. A friend of my father's is coming down to meet us, he calls out my name, and I run up to him, it's Uncle . . . Uncle Bill. He's from the university. He's doing here the same thing my father does, they're excavating something. They're talking about a temple . . . it's on the other side of the town . . . they're telling my mother about a poet, it's the poet's temple, she's going to take me there."

"A temple," Hong repeated, thinking aloud. "A place you could reach in one morning. Zhongxian County, maybe." What archaeological sites were nearby? He had read about them. "Of course, it's the Tang Dynasty poet's memorial . . . what's his name? Bai Juyi."

"So they were excavating a temple," Ostrander said, sitting up.

"No, an older site near there, it was closed down two months later." He turned the generator off. "Qian Jinggou," he said, "east of Fengdu, on the Yangtze."

Dr. Yan made his farewells and wished Ostrander a safe journey. Like two brothers on a train platform, one going to war and the other staying behind, they expressed their improbable hopes for meeting again. After a suitable interlude, Hong pulled Ostrander aside and in his most authoritarian cadences issued a catalogue of instructions to be followed exactly, without deviation. Prepare the smallest suitcase possible, he said, no excess weight, we'll be moving quickly. Leave everything else—research materials, cameras, tape recorders, clothing—in your room. Inform no one at either your embassy or the foreigners' compound of your destination.

"When am I supposed to accomplish all this?" Ostrander asked.

"Immediately," Hong said. "We're leaving today."

In the meantime, though there was as yet no earthly reason for telling Ostrander, Hong occupied his attention with other arrangements. He recited equally strenuous instructions to himself, for he had plans of his own to set in motion—plans that with luck would come to fruition a good deal earlier than those being orchestrated by Wei Ye.

The thugs took him to the Bureau, where with the door open they stood guard outside his office and waited while he collected his internal passport.

Chan leapt from his chair when Hong entered. "You're a disgrace to your country and the Party," he said loudly, for the benefit of the guards and the tapped telephone. He crossed the room, scribbled a note, and slid it onto Hong's desk.

Where are you going?

"I'm innocent," Hong said.

Stand in front of me, he wrote on Chan's pad.

"Innocent?" Chan said angrily. "Would you be charged with such crimes if you were innocent? I suspected you all along. Don't continue trying to make a conspirator out of me." Blocking the guards' view, Chan continued to condemn Hong and ventured angry recommendations for the quality and length of his imprisonment. Hong finished writing, and Chan, gesturing to a folder of case reports on the top of the radio cabinet, turned to the door.

"I can't bear to be in the same room with you," he said finally, stalking out past the guards. "Wherever you're sent for punishment," he called from the hall, "it will be too good for the likes of you."

Hong left his message in the case report file, and under the watchful eyes of the thugs continued on to his apartment. He packed his green cloth suitcase and, while the thugs turned their backs and helped themselves to cold beer at his invitation, he tucked the pieces of his disassembled revolver and a small innocuous box of ammunition inside a clean shirt. He was in a reverie, he was invisible, he could walk through walls. On his way to the car the old women hanging clothes to dry in the courtyard stared at him as if he were a ghost.

At three that afternoon he and Ostrander were driven to Capital Airport, escorted by Army officers in motorcycle sidecars. The monsoons had blown in with full force, releasing sheets of rain dense as a plastic curtain. The sky turned black. Hong fidgeted with the handle of his suitcase, worrying about whether the rain would let up long enough for the plane to take off, while Ostrander wrapped himself in sullen silence. To him the schedule was irrelevant; for Hong it was timed as closely as the firing pin of an automatic artillery cannon. Neither spoke a word until they had passed through the old embassy district, crossed the Wenyu River bridge, and entered the long maple-lined stretch of the restricted airport road. The trees beat back and forth in the wind, as if even they, too, were readied for the battle ahead.

"Where's Yu-shang?" Ostrander asked.

"She'll be there."

"I'm not going anywhere without her."

"Neither am I," Hong said.

Madness reigned at the domestic departure hall. It was as hot as a public bath and far more steamy. Nanjing, Kunming, Hohhot, Shanghai, Xian, Shenyang—long lines snaked from every counter. Every passenger was burdened by duffel bags, lunch sacks, cardboard boxes of clothes for the rural relatives. Clerks handed out luggage checks, debated the validity of tickets: this reservation is not correct, that flight has been canceled.

At the counter for Chongqing, Yu-shang waited, surrounded by Public Security officers—out of uniform, but Hong recognized them. Despite her guards she had the air of a stranded passenger, a child accidentally abandoned to a world of uncaring strangers. Ostrander ran up and nearly kissed her, but with her arms she held him away. Already everyone in the line was staring. The guards parted and Hong eased in behind her.

"You're scum," she said softly, "you killed my mother," and then to Ostrander: "This is a trap. He's not a guide."

Ostrander held up his palms. "Everything's been arranged," he said. "Don't worry. They're going to let us leave together."

"Whatever he promised you," she said, "whatever you're going to do for them, we'll be shot anyway."

Hong felt sorry for her, but her blind arrogance infuriated him. He had a slim enough chance to save her life, and a far slimmer one of saving his own, if only she would let him. "Deng Bo is in jail," he said. "Do you understand? Without me, there's no hope."

"Pig," she said.

"Enough," Hong said evenly. "Why don't you tell him why you seduced him?"

For a moment his language left even Liang Yu-shang in shock. To talk of sex privately required a rare immodesty; in public it was simply crude.

"You're not only scum," she said, "you're vulgar and without manners."

"Tell him," Hong pressed her.

Her face tightened and she said nothing.

"Go on, tell him," Hong said more harshly. "Tell him how Deng Bo recruited you. Explain how you were transferred to Beijing."

Still she was silent.

"She used you," Hong said to Ostrander. "They told her to sleep with you and she did. They told her to get information, and they offered her freedom. They offered her... what did you talk about? Palm trees."

Ostrander looked from Hong to Liang Yu-shang, and in his eyes he begged not for the truth, but for the satisfactory lie. No matter what a man pretends, he needs to be desired as much as a woman.

Liang Yu-shang bowed her head. "Yes, at the beginning," she said uneasily, "yes, it was true. I wasn't supposed to fall in love with you. But I did." She looked up. "Don't do anything for him. He won't let us go."

They were at the counter. Behind the battered luggage scales were two harried clerks, both women, one a plump homely creature with a white pen in the pocket of her blue jacket. What if she hadn't been here? What if she'd been suddenly assigned to another post? Hong passed her the envelope with the tickets. She stared at it, at him, and then excused herself.

"What's the trouble?" Ostrander asked.

"There's no trouble, be quiet."

The woman reappeared and scribbled three boarding passes. When she handed the envelope back, it was much thicker. Hong looked inside and made his silent hallelujahs. Bless Chan, bless the secret brotherhood of cadres everywhere for whom the back door meant more than personal gain. Most of all, bless those who would stick their necks out and not fear the gun. They had come through for him.

He bent down and tied diamond-shaped luggage tags on Ostrander's bag, on his own, on Liang Yu-shang's.

"It's a trap," she said.

"We're going," Hong said. "Now."

On the plane Hong surveyed the other passengers. Which ones, he wondered, had been sent to tail them? There was a pair of twin doorposts—a bushy-browed ox in the rear on the aisle and a heavyset tree stump in the front, both traveling alone and reading newspapers. Hong had missed them in the boarding lounge. Under their jackets were bulges at their waists, which neither had tried to hide. They were rough players, Hong thought, not given to the niceties of deputy ministers or investigators.

The plane was a Trident, which Hong had been counting on; the Ilyushins had no restrooms. He took his bag and walked to the back of the plane, giving the ox a long healthy stare as he passed. Inside, with the door locked, he sat on the toilet seat and assembled his revolver. He worked fast—cylinder in, breech tight, bullets loaded—and wiped the excess oil from the barrel with a paper towel. He was gone no more than three minutes.

When he returned Yu-shang was talking quietly with Ostrander. "They killed my father, my mother wanted justice. She waited almost fifty years and then they killed her, too. And now they'll kill us. We're nothing to them, we're not even human."

Hong leaned across the aisle, touched her bare arm. "Do you think no one here understands English?"

"He's filth," she said to Ostrander, jerking her arm away. With her fingertips she touched the faint bruises on her face, symbols of her certainty.

"I'm sorry you were hit," Hong said, "but conserve your anger. You'll need the energy."

The great Sichuan vegetable basket, rich and green, glistened below, fields terraced across red mountains that stretched on forever, the edge of a vast trough from which an entire country fed. From above, Chongqing seemed a single gray roof that sloped down, wing-shaped, to the confluence of the two rivers—the Jialing and the mighty Yangtze. Over the Jialing hung the suspended wire of the cable-car tramway that carried workers across the river from the northern suburbs, on the other was the Yangtze bridge over Shanhuba Island, and from the middle of the peninsula a slender bent finger jutted out, its ridges the steep hills of the central city. The rainbow lights on the domed Renmin Guesthouse and on the pavilion atop Loquat Hill, nighttime haunt of lovers, were already glowing as the plane banked and dipped. In the dusk the city resembled nothing so much as a giant floating palace. Did it appear that way to Ostrander? What did he see in the mighty Yangtze, water railroad of a hundred million peasants? Was the river to him also a ribbon of majesty?

The plane dropped through a cloud of gray coal-polluted air that seemed to penetrate the cracks of its skin, then skidded onto the runway. Hong took his small suitcase from under the seat, stood, and caught a long glance from the heavy-browed ox. Sizing me up for the noose, he thought.

The airport, which had once been a military field, lay in a valley beneath the western hills, near Bishan, and consisted of nothing more than a low ramshackle passenger hall and an ice-stick stand. The humidity was so dank and thick that Beijing was in winter by comparison. Old men sat in the terminal, drinking tea and beer and watching the planes take off and land. Hong felt a momentary nostalgia for the peacefulness of his youth—cricket fights with Boda, old men on street corners playing chess, trips to the countryside to work in the garden. But his memories only made him realize how selective nostalgia was; no starving peasants marred the picture, no victims of anti-rightist movements, no friends who suffered when their parents were denounced. How incredible, he thought, that his mind drifted this way. The mind only tolerated fear for so long, and then retreated to the daily routine of life. You could not be frightened all the time.

It was astonishing: he had run out of fear, and what had replaced it was a weird tranquility. He had stopped worrying about his own death.

Looking for a car with Public Security plates, he led Ostrander and Liang Yu-shang around the terminal, watching
all the while as the ox and the tree stump strolled right past
them to a beat-up Warsaw sedan. They got into the back
seat and waited. This is my true punishment, Hong
thought, this is worse than death. To be in the charge, even
temporarily, of these two lumbering snakes.

"Jesus, it's hot," Ostrander said, wiping his sleeve across
his face.

Directly ahead of the Warsaw, straddling the road, was a
green Datsun. The door opened and the driver waved to
Hong. The engine was already running.

"Our car," Hong said, pointing the way.

They got in and the Datsun turned out of the airport
onto Gelou Road. The Warsaw followed tight behind.

The steamer boats of the Yangtze's passenger line, *The
East Is Red,* stopped running at dusk, and Wei Ye had arranged for rooms at a small hotel near the dock. Hong slept
five hours, more than enough, and after waking he lay on
his bed, dressed and ready to go. The single room was
shabby, the walls decayed by moisture. By the faint light of
his bedside lamp Hong counted the holes in one of the ceiling's soundproofing tiles. The lamp, with its fringed, water-
stained shade in the French style and a base decorated with
small cut globes of red and green glass, was an object of
tawdry luxury that had not been seen in a State store for at
least a decade. The mattress was lumpy, the air conditioner
churned out a steady flow of warm air, the blond chairs and
the old large-character scrollwork on the walls sagged as if
overcome by the heat. It was a middle-level room for a
middle-level cadre; the system adhered to its hierarchy even
with a prisoner.

Hong reached for his gun and the envelope of tickets
under his pillow. He examined the two passports, internal
and external, belonging to the assistant swimming coach.
Hidden in the folder behind his own papers, they had been
missed when Wei Ye's thugs searched him before he left for
the airport. Yamei could always say he had stolen them
from her, but she would suffer nonetheless. He prayed only
that they would let her live. Forget your fine young stu-

dents, Hong thought, forget a trip to the Olympics. He wondered how the role of overseas Chinese would fit him, if by some miracle he should assume it, and whether one day he would be allowed to come back, if only to sweep the graves of his ancestors.

The ox and the tree stump were waking up in the next room, taking their showers, bantering noisily. In the distance Hong heard the *putt-putt* of motorcycles, the city coming alive. He slipped the gun into his waistband, left his shirt hanging loose, and stepped into the open-air passageway. The heat gave off an acrid whiff of coal and smelting iron. Across the bowl of earth in which the hotel lay were the hills of Chongqing—gray-shingled rooftops descending to the harbor, houses on stilts hugging together for protection, narrow alleys where employees from the motorcycle factory lived. Above them white-banded apartment towers rose. Crows cawed in the sky. Hong walked down the passageway and put his ear to Ostrander's door. There was no sound. He turned the knob, went in, and saw that the bed had not been slept in. So it always was for the condemned: a final night of love.

The door to Liang Yu-shang's room opened, and Ostrander came into the passageway.

"Good morning," he said, flustered and embarrassed.

"Yes, good morning," Hong replied.

"Are we going soon?"

"As soon as you're ready. Why didn't you try to escape during the night?"

"She told me it was hopeless, a foreigner could never travel unnoticed."

"She's getting smarter," said Hong. "Why didn't she try?"

"She wants to stay with me."

"True love," Hong said, missing Yamei. "Precious as jade. Did she tell you about the diaries?"

"What diaries?"

"If anybody's going to set her free, we need the diaries. I promise you, if we find them, both of you will be free."

Ostrander turned away and gazed out at the city. "Why do you keep insisting that we trust you?"

The cawing crows returned, circling overhead like dust motes on the wind. Hong looked up at the black birds and said, "Maybe because I'm one of you now."

The pollution was settling, and Hong felt it on his skin, in his eyes and throat. Ostrander came closer, glanced quickly up and down the passageway, and whispered, "Yu-shang thinks there are two men following us."

"That's observant of her," Hong said. "But they won't be following us for long."

"Do they work for you?"

"For me?" Hong threw his head back and laughed, longer and louder than he had laughed in years, a great whoop that rolled out into the hills and came back to him as an echo. "No one works for me anymore," he said.

26.

ON
THE
YANGTZE

The morning stayed hazy, the heat built to a sweltering bubble that made sweat run like tears. From the hotel they rode to an old stone terrace overlooking the harbor embankment and shadowed by great budding elms. There seemed to be an order from somewhere that Hong not show up personally at the terminal. At the terrace's windowed stone gazebo a clerk telephoned the harbormaster, who in short order strolled in from Shaanxi Street bearing three tickets for *The East Is Red*, boat number 11. One was written in Ostrander's name, one in Hong's, and one for a Macao compatriot, a Miss Ling. No records would show Liang Yu-shang ever having arrived in or departed from Chongqing, which was a hopeful sign: if she was untraceable, then maybe Wei Ye planned to let her vanish. On the other hand, Yu-shang could vanish just as conveniently into a labor camp as onto a plane from Shanghai. Hong lit a cigarette and studied Ostrander, whose face was taut and drained of color from lack of sleep. The muscles in the corners of his eyes were twitching.

Following the harbormaster, they circled back from the terrace and through the free markets lining a steep concrete stairway on a cliff above Qiansimen Road. Under corrugated tin roofs, open booths were selling persimmons and sandals and white fungus and ginger root, and from below rose a clatter of pickaxes on rock, workers breaking up the macadam for repaving. At the bottom of the market they boarded the incline cable car for the ride down to Chaotianmen Dock.

"They're behind us," Ostrander whispered. "Two of them."

Hong looked over his shoulder at the ox and the tree stump. "Yes, I know, don't worry about it."

The first steamer of the day left from wharf 4 on the eastern tip of the peninsula. The steamer's loudspeakers, accompanied by an orchestra of foghorns, played taped martial music from the previous October's Liberation Day parade. The clock atop the harbor terminal chimed five and the tape changed to a clanging version of the national anthem sung by a military chorus, "Stand up, stand up, all you who refuse to be slaves..."

For some reason, the music failed to stir Hong's heart.

Liang Yu-shang, wearing makeup in her role of wealthy Macao tourist, led the way across the sand to the steamer. So dainty, Hong thought, an Emperor's concubine, she could be walking on silk. At the edge of the ramp Ostrander's stretched nerves snapped and he lost control. He tugged violently at Hong's sleeve and pointed toward the ox and the tree stump, who stood at the bottom of the incline by the cable car. "They can follow us anywhere. What makes you sure they'll let us out?"

"Once we're on the boat, Wei Ye can't search for us. She'd have to explain why we were here in the first place."

"Why?" Ostrander asked urgently. "Who would care?"

"She *needs* us," Hong said. "Don't you see? Until she gets what she's looking for, we're as dangerous to her as she is to us."

"Do you believe that?"

"Maybe I do," Hong said, "maybe I don't."

"The passport you have for Yu-shang, the plane tickets, what good are they? Who says they'll even allow us on the plane at Shanghai?"

"The plane leaves Shanghai on Thursday night," Hong said. "But we're not going to Shanghai." He lifted his shirt to reveal the butt of his revolver. "And if she tries to have us followed downriver, I'll have to threaten to shoot you, then me."

Ostrander half-smiled. "Would you?"

"The boat's leaving," Hong said, also smiling, and nudged him forward.

At Fuling, two stops to the east, they disembarked *The East Is Red* and in the harbor Hong found a barge just preparing to depart for Wuhan. The tired crew had already loaded enormous clay jars of hot pickled mustard and barrels of tung oil onto the greasy deck, and had settled into a poker game. The captain was a tough former Navy colonel with the square, squashed face of a bulldog—fat lips, nose like a spigot. To a glimpse of Hong's identification card and two ten-yuan notes, he responded, "I'm always happy to help an officer of Public Security." The money slipped into his waist pouch as though it had wings. Hong wondered: what if we get there and find nothing? What if I have nothing to barter?

Liang Yu-shang wrapped her hair in a plum-colored scarf and leaned on the railing as the poker game ended and the barge maneuvered around the junks in Fuling harbor. The crew gaped at her, this haughty powdered beauty who might have stepped whole from the pages of a cinema magazine to grace their lives. But their attention escaped her notice, or so her pose pretended.

Hong scanned the shoreline for more surveillance teams. He trusted his instincts, he could smell a man's shadow, but he was nervous and his instincts might be having an off day. He had seen no one on *The East Is Red* with even the remotest air of Public Security, not a single sweating figure with Beijing written on his clothes or his face, but it was possible that Wei Ye had recruited help in Chongqing.

The shoreline, however, seemed clear, satisfying Hong that his faith in Wei Ye's overweening confidence had not been misplaced. With Yamei in prison, Wei Ye was convinced Hong would never try to escape, especially while burdened with Ostrander and Liang Yu-shang. Still, there had been a rough moment when he demanded that they not be trailed downriver. If there were guards, Hong argued, Ostrander would balk. He would refuse to cooperate if he felt any threat to himself or Yu-shang. Wei Ye had accepted Hong's conditions because she felt there was no way she could lose. Ostrander would hardly risk Yu-shang's life by letting Hong take her for an appeal to a procurate or Public Security branch in a city along the river—not with Deng Bo in jail, not with the case Wei Ye had already built against all of them. And what, in any case, were the odds of three people—one of them a foreigner—leaving the country undetected?

Hong strolled across the barge and sat near the perforated casing over the engine block. Spreading his legs and resting his chin in his palm, he peered down through the open door of the cargo hold, where he caught sight of three sets of handlebars. They were no doubt attached to three stolen motorcycles. Contraband goods, contraband passengers: the captain was getting rich. Not a bad job, Hong thought. Good pay, lots of travel, and a private little black market. He looked up as Ostrander left Yu-shang by the railing and crossed the deck.

Ostrander took out his pipe, filled it. Hong put a cigarette between his lips, flicked his lighter, and cupped the flame in his hand. "It's illegal to smoke on the deck of a barge," he said. "But let's be daring."

"I can't figure you out," Ostrander said, sitting down.

"That makes two of us. Beautiful day for a boat ride, isn't it?"

"What I mean is, I understand what happened to me, but I still don't understand how this happened to you."

"To tell you the truth," Hong said, "neither do I." He took off his glasses to wipe away the river's spray with the tail of his shirt. "Wei Ye wanted me to be your friend," he went on. "If you trusted me, if you liked me, you might reveal what you knew. And she counted on my liking you."

Painfully, Hong saw how well Wei Ye had used him. The sum of his evasions, everything he had left out of his reports, his stubborn denial of Ostrander's guilt—all this was evidence for the charges against him. It was not merely that Wei Ye had wanted to ensure his mother's silence, but rather that she had sensed in him a fundamental weakness, his infatuation with absurd notions of right and wrong. She had known his dreams would draw him in, that he and Ostrander were two halves of a single secret, that in the end he would protect Ostrander from her, and so be unable to protect himself. What had she said? *You carry the burden of goodness.* Was that really her idea of a burden? He should have asked what her burdens were.

"How did they get you to arrest Yu-shang?" Ostrander asked. "Why are you in as much trouble as she is?"

"It's really very simple," Hong said. "A man died, he was killed, I cared about him. That's all."

"A friend of yours," Ostrander said.

"A friend, yes... more than a friend."

Ostrander fell silent, respecting the memory of someone he had never met, but after a moment he asked, "Who is this Wei Ye?"

"A very good question, as it happens. She's many people. She's a powerful cadre with revolutionary credentials, and she's a thief. She's a defender of the peace, and she's a murderer and a traitor."

"That's a fairly big contradiction in the great Communist state. I thought everybody served the people."

"But there are many contradictions," Hong replied amicably, "internal contradictions, external contradictions. Without them the great Communist state wouldn't function."

"You helped it function," Ostrander said.

"That's correct," Hong said. "I'm the biggest contradiction of all."

The barge reached the city of Zhongzhou, Zhongxian County, an hour later. Lush bamboo groves swelled on the marshy banks. In the land of the hungry, no fertile ground went uncultivated. Hong walked into the barge's steering shed and opened his wallet in front of the captain, who was sitting and working over his cargo manifest.

"How long from here to Yichang?" he asked.

"Depends on the currents through the gorges," the captain answered, eyeing the thick wad of bills. "Six hours, maybe seven. Longer if there's a storm. The sky looks bad."

Through the tiny window above the rudder controls Hong put his hand to the breeze. The air was heavy with unshed rain.

"I'd like you to wait for us, if you can. We might be several hours."

"Well, I don't know..."

Hong laid two ten-yuan notes in his hand.

"Maybe I could give you two hours," the captain said.

Hong took out another twenty yuan. "There's fifty more if you're here when we come back, and another hundred when we get to Yichang."

The money swiftly vanished into the captain's pocket. "Take your time," he said with a yawn, stretching his legs and leaning back to rest his head on his palms.

Hong joined Ostrander and Liang Yu-shang on the small pier.

"What were you doing in there?" Ostrander asked.

"Discussing economic reforms," Hong said.

"What?"

"I was teaching him a lesson in the power of incentives."

Objects of curiosity, they climbed the wooden steps. Strangers were rare enough, foreign strangers a cause for ogling. In the center of town was a soy processing plant, and the fumes from its round latticed windows soaked the misty air with the rich smell of fermented bean curd. Hong was treated as a most important dignitary. You're from Beijing? Good. Listen to our complaints. The plant foreman welcomed him into the reception hall with glasses of tea. On the walls hung productivity charts and framed portraits of Chairman Mao, Stalin, Marx, and Lenin. Here in the heart of the country Chairman Mao was still a god and the Russians his loyal theorists. After hearing tales of interference from Beijing and strong socialist praise for the plant's excellent workers, Hong commandeered a truck, half a dozen shovels, and three men. He assumed the fossils would be buried.

The site at Qian Jinggou, east of the county seat, had been abandoned by scientists in the early 1960s, when the last of

its Bronze Age axes and hoes were excavated. The out-
buildings erected for the archaeologists had then been
stripped bare by peasants during the Cultural Revolution
—a modest sacrifice of the valuable lumber—leaving
three cement foundations that sat on the ground like
ancient funeral pyres. Only one structure survived: a
sturdy rectangular box with high narrow windows and a
front porch of dark red brick in the British legation style.
The building had been converted into a primary school,
and the ground closest to the river paved over with as-
phalt surrounded by chain-link fencing with basketball
hoops at either end.

"That's the cabin in the painting," Hong said. "Where do
we dig?"

Ostrander scanned the scene, shaking his head. "This is
where we were," he said, bewildered, "but I didn't see them
bury anything."

"Think," Hong instructed. "He wanted you to know."

Liang Yu-shang stepped between them. "Don't," she said.

Ostrander laid his hands on her shoulders. "It's our only
chance."

She followed him as he walked around the school. The
children, having heard the truck's backfiring exhaust, were
peeking from the open windows. Hong flashed his identification at the teacher and she sent them back to their low
tables to cut paper birds. Paper birds, Hong thought: for
children and depressives.

Ostrander rounded the corner and crossed the brick
porch. Gesturing first with his left hand, then his right, he
paced from one end of the playground to the other, conjur-
ing aloud a vision of the past. We sat here, he said, and then
over there, near an open pit. There were mounds of dirt,
my father showed me fishnet hooks excavated from the pit.
We slept in a building near the river, it had shutters, and I
played here, digging with a toy shovel. My father showed
me how to dig, how to be a scientist, we dug a big hole, the
next day it was filled in . . .

Ostrander was next to the porch at the edge of the black-
top.

Hong pointed to the three workers and took a shovel
himself. "We'll dig here," he said.

• • •

The day was eternal, but time was short. They opened a hole three meters deep and four meters square, and there was nothing. But at least the ground was soft; it had rained here, too. When Hong allowed himself a respite from shoveling, he stared at his watch, as though under the power of his will the hands would slow down. It was eight o'clock, then nine. Add six or seven hours, Hong thought, eight if the current proved too strong, more if a storm should blow in from nowhere. Twice he sent one of the workmen from the soy factory to see if the barge still waited by the small rickety pier. It still waited, the crew had drifted ashore, the captain napped in his steering shed.

Ostrander stared into the hole. "It's the wrong place," he announced.

Hong ordered the workmen to keep digging. The father had played with his son, made a hole in the ground. He had not traveled to the Guomindang capital in wartime to visit friends.

They were using buckets now to haul up the muck. Another meter down, two, three. Hong climbed to ground level and brushed the damp soil from his arms and face. Mud had caked on stains of sweat; he was a zebra, striped brown on his chest, under his arms. The barrel of his revolver had rubbed his groin raw.

The front door of the school opened, the children burst onto the porch, and the boys, adventurous, excitedly converged on the hole.

"What are you digging for?" one of them asked.

"The treasure of an ancient princess," Hong said, wiping the back of his hand across his forehead.

The teacher called the boys to the playground, where they played basketball while the girls held a contest, using chopsticks to move marbles from one dish to another. Ostrander and Liang Yu-shang sat on the porch, murmuring like doves. Let them coo, Hong thought. Let them do whatever lovers do when they're afraid they'll never see each other again. Was there a special pleasure, reserved for lovers only, in dreaming of what might never be?

"You said Caffey killed my father."

Hong looked up. He had not even heard Ostrander approach. "Yes," he said.

"Why?"

It was a question Hong had dreaded, had known Ostrander would ask ever since his night of foolish heroism in the dark corridor outside Hong's apartment. Did the truth serve any purpose? Did Ostrander want the truth? Your father betrayed, too; he betrayed his own comrades and he betrayed my country.

Ostrander gazed down at him. Protect me, his face said. Deceive me.

Hong had no idea of the answer he would give until it was already on his lips. "Caffey offered your father money for the fossils. He tried to convince your father to sell them. But your father was an honest man and refused, and Caffey shot him."

It was shaky, and not quite convincing. Of that Hong had no doubt. And for one brief instant there was a flicker of knowledge in Ostrander's eyes, a lucid, unwavering stare that seemed to demand both the truth and absolution. But Ostrander no more desired to hear the truth than Hong wished to deliver it, and the moment passed.

Hong consulted his watch again, blew dust from its crystal. In another country, he thought, he could exchange the precious Rolex for new clothes.

"Why do you keep checking the time?" Ostrander asked.

"Because we're running out of it," Hong said. "We have a train to catch."

Yu-shang was walking toward them, squinting into the sun, when they heard the sound of metal hitting metal. From inside the hole came the crack of the striking shovel.

Hong called down to the workmen: "What have you found?"

Out of the dirt a trunk emerged, green metal banded by black and rusted in jagged streaks. The men hoisted it over their heads and, digging their feet like mountain climbers into the walls of the hole, heaved it onto the ground.

"It's light," one of them yelled. "There's something rattling inside."

A rusted lock dangled from the front, but the bolt was

intact. Hong kicked away encrusted clods of root, grabbed a shovel and slammed at the lock. The trunk skidded across the dirt into the chain-link fence. Hong chased it, swatted again. The lock held firm, but the fixture tore away.

The crash against the fence had shaken a layer of dust from the top, revealing a red painted *V*, and had drawn the interest of the children, who scampered to the edge of the playground. Ostrander knelt, brushing the rest of the dirt away and revealing the letter *A*, upside down. Forcing the edge of a shovel under the lid, he pried it open.

There were a few loose rocks and pebbles, but otherwise the trunk was empty. For a long moment none of them spoke.

"Where's the treasure, where's the princess's treasure?" one of the little boys cried.

Hong crouched next to Ostrander, ran his hands along the inside of the trunk. A fine white powder clung to his damp fingertips, filled the skinfolds of his palm.

"After all this," he said, defeated, looking at his ghostly hands. "Nothing. He must have come back for the fossils, or emptied the trunks before he got here, or someone else—"

Behind them another footlocker was being hoisted from the hole. Of course, there were supposed to be two. Hong felt his heart galloping in his chest. Let the diaries be inside, he prayed, then asked himself which god would listen. He had never believed in any of them, not even Chairman Mao.

"This one's heavier," one of the diggers yelled.

The painted red letter on the top showed more clearly this time—a *B*—but the lock and its fixture were less rusted and stronger. Hong waved the children aside, turned the trunk on its back, and brought his shovel down with all his weight behind it. Not a dent. Again and again he smashed at the lock, but three blows failed to snap the bolt.

"I need a tire iron," he said.

Had he spoken aloud? Was he talking to the wind? The three plant workers, like masked opera performers, stared at him blankly.

"I said go get a tire iron from the truck, a crowbar."

One of them, who had been the driver, bestirred himself

to amble to the cab. Yes, well I should have gotten it myself, Hong thought. The driver returned at the same slow trot carrying a toolbox. Hong found a screwdriver and slipped the shaft between the lock housing and the bolt. He propped the shaft straight, anchored it and wedged it tight. Lifting the shovel, he had a vision of Red Guards setting fires and smashing the doors of the Union Hospital with axes and the stocks of their rifles, and he brought the flat end of the shovel blade down with a crash. The screwdriver handle shattered, but the job was done: the lock housing sheared from its rivets.

Ostrander was there first, throwing the lid open.

The weight was a pile of redwood planking. No fossils. The redwood had once been the boxes used to pack them. Where were they? Who had come to retrieve them? Watching for nails—this was no time to puncture his hand—Hong lifted the planks one by one and tossed them over the side until he had emptied the trunk.

Or rather, almost emptied. At the bottom in the middle lay an old varnished leather box, long and shallow for holding checkers or maybe an instrument of some kind, a flute.

The top was painted in strokes of gold leaf over a thin coat of crimson, a hand-tooled scene of the Emperor's court. Ostrander reached down for it, but in an explosion of relief and jubilation Hong pushed him away, lifted the box like an offering, and set it on the ground. Its brass clasp sprung open as though obstinately rejecting more than forty years of the earth's moisture.

Inside lay a leatherbound book.

Hong turned the cover to the first parchment page: a diary, a dead man's diary, the evidence of an underground Party organizer whose reports that his dead comrades might be the victims of a traitor had reached only the traitor herself. Hong turned to the next page, and the next, until he heard as if it were a shout the author's frantic voice, his suspicions that coincidence could no longer account for the increasing bad luck of his comrades. Your evidence has been found, Hong thought, the evidence so many people died looking for. He closed the diary, set it back inside the box.

"You have no right," Liang Yu-shang said, standing over him.

Hong picked up the leather box and walked past her toward the truck. He recalled what the little bandit Bun had said, the beggar: a dead man can't hurt anyone. But he can, Hong thought. A dead man can.

27.

LOOKING

FOR

LIFE

The rains began before Yichang, east of Hubei. The sky darkened, the river steamed, and a typhoon rolled over the Yangtze, a swirling column of gray clouds. In seconds a pelting downpour washed the deck clean, as if swept suddenly by a long brush from Heaven. Hong, standing in the prow, felt the barge slow and veer toward the shore. The typhoon was an omen, he thought, like the earthquake that had foretold the death of Chairman Mao. On the southern cliffs above Badong, waterfalls roared down the silvery limestone, and trackers pulling a three-sailed junk upstream were thrown to the ground.

Clinging to the railing hand-over-hand, and cursing himself for falling prey to superstition, Hong started toward the steering shed, his legs sliding against the huge clay jars. Ostrander, draped in a poncho of canvas sheeting, met him halfway. The barge's foghorn hooted into the storm.

"We're stopping," Ostrander bellowed excitedly. "We're not going to make it."

"Get back down into the hold," Hong ordered. "We're not stopping."

Battered by the rain and using the corked tops of the jars to steady himself, Hong crossed the deck. The captain was calling to his crew, who struggled against the wind and the stubborn rusted winch that lowered the anchor ropes.

Hong followed the captain into the steering shed.

"We don't have time to stop," he yelled over the beating of the rain on the shed's tarred roof. "You have to keep going."

"In this?" the captain exclaimed. "Are you crazy?"

"We have to be in Yichang by seven, no later."

"I can't move until this passes. We'll run aground, or we'll tip and lose my cargo."

"We'll have to risk that," Hong said.

"Not with *my* barge," the captain shouted adamantly.

The barge bucked and dipped, throwing Hong against the bulkhead. The anchors had dropped. Hong righted himself and asked, "How soon do you think the storm will pass?"

"An hour, not much more," the captain said. He cut his engines.

"We don't have an hour," Hong said.

"You don't, but I do. My cargo is more important than you are."

"I'm paying you," Hong said evenly.

"You're not paying me to die."

"This is a matter of highest importance to the security of the State."

"If money isn't enough for my life," the captain said, "the security of the State means even less."

Ostrander had reached the open doorway of the shed. Gripping the jamb, he looked from Hong to the captain, the worry creased on his face.

Hong felt for his revolver. Until now he had carried the black object as a talisman, never imagining he would use it. The grip gave off heat, warm from his body, and he wondered if had the nerve to fire the gun, or the steadiness to aim. It came up in his hand like a root unexpectedly loosened from the earth, a surprise. Here, what's this? A gun, and it was inches from the captain's head aimed at his jaw.

The captain's face showed no change of expression. He was a man who had seen guns before. "You *are* crazy," he said with amazement, but not fear. "Hijacking is a capital crime. Are you really in Public Security? Where I come from, officers are—"

"Instruct your crew to bring in the anchors." Hong fought the trembling in his voice, and in his hand. He pressed the gun barrel against the captain's neck, and it puckered the skin. Hong supposed that finding a bullet a few inches from your brain would break even the strongest spirit.

"You don't dare shoot me," the captain said, but less confident than he had seemed a moment ago. "Can you steer a barge?"

"I can learn," Hong said, hearing the catch in his throat.

"What crimes are you charged with?" the captain asked.

"Crimes?" Hong asked. "I told you, I'm involved in a confidential matter of the highest importance to the State."

"Only a guilty man uses a gun."

"Not in this case."

"Maybe you're innocent," the captain said, "but we're not lifting anchor."

Hong slid the gun to the left and before he felt the grease from the trigger on his finger he fired. Glass cracked behind the captain's head and the tiny windowpane was gone. An old framed schedule of maritime regulations fell from its nail. Hong looked down at the gun, stunned by his own violence.

The bullet was in the river, but the barrel had been close enough to leave a line of black powder and a small blotchy burn at the top of the captain's spine. The captain's hand flew to his neck; he grunted and his breath heaved.

"I'm sorry," Hong said, "but we're going to Yichang."

The captain picked up a rag and pressed it to his neck. "You could have killed me," he said.

"But I didn't. Let's get under way."

Squeezing past Ostrander, with Hong behind him, the captain called to the crew to winch the anchors in, then eased behind the wheel.

Hong waved the gun at Ostrander. "Go back down."

Ostrander studied him in wonder. "I've been wrong

about you, haven't I? You do want to save us."

"I want to save me," Hong said harshly. "Go back to the hold."

"No, you care about us, me and Yu-shang. You care about what's right."

The captain twisted a lever, hit a button; the engine growled and the barge started forward, downriver. A wave washed over the railings, thrashing the cargo and nearly toppling Ostrander into the Yangtze. "Get below deck before you're blown overboard," Hong shouted.

He watched until Ostrander had disappeared through the door of the cargo hold, and with the gun still in his hand turned into the shed. The captain was fighting the wheel and the rudder controls; the engine whined. Keeping the gun in the captain's view, Hong braced himself in the corner. He looked at the revolver and thought of what he had been taught about criminals, the bad thinking of men who broke the law, who robbed and murdered and hijacked boats and could only be rehabilitated in struggle sessions and at hard labor. But no one had ever taught him how he might become a criminal himself.

"It's getting worse ahead," the captain said.

In more ways than one, Hong thought.

The rains abated by the time they reached Yichang harbor. They had come down the long stretch of alluvial plain from the Nanjin Pass and through the locks of the Gezhouba Dam into the setting sun, having lost only a single bundle of tow ropes to the storm. At the pier Hong offered the captain the hundred yuan he had been promised, and fifty more for the ropes.

The captain took the money and said, "The minute you leave, I'm alerting Public Security."

"Really? And what will you tell them? That you brought us through the storm at the point of a gun? Who will they believe, a captain who has no doubt taken bribes before, or an esteemed officer of Public Security?"

"I have a broken window, a burn—"

"And no bullet hole," Hong said. "Let's suppose I call Public Security. Let's suppose that they need an example for an anti-bribery campaign. Good officer that I am, I feel compelled to do my patriotic duty, and so I suggest that they examine your cargo hold for three stolen motorcycles. Oh, you could unload them, but they can be traced, and I'm sure you've come close to being caught before. Economic crimes are punished severely these days."

"Get off my barge," said the captain.

"Have a safe journey to Wuhan," Hong said.

The taxi brought them to the train station at ten to seven. A few beggars with straw baskets and bedrolls squatted on the steps, smoking. These people did not exist. They were a mirage. How long have you been here, Hong wondered, and where are you going? Hoping for an urban permit? Or merely a meal? A new pair of shoes?

There were only four tracks; three were empty and the bell for the overnight train to Guangzhou was already sounding—a steady pulsing ring. The train made local stops until Changsha, then turned express. Hong stood under the arch leading from the ticket hall to the platforms. A claque of tired Public Security guards sat in a corner, none of them paying the least bit of attention to the crowd. Men said good-bye to women, women to men, girls to boys, boys to girls. Lovers everywhere to remind him of what he was leaving behind.

From the upstairs platform two stairways led down to the tracks—one for soft seat, one for hard. Hong pulled out the envelope given to him by the check-in clerk at the airport in Beijing.

"You take soft sleeper," he said to Ostrander, handing him a ticket.

"I'm staying with Yu-shang," Ostrander said.

"It's too conspicuous. Three of us together will attract attention. A foreigner alone is no problem. And if anyone's looking for us, they're looking for three. Do you want to get to Hong Kong?"

Liang Yu-shang snickered. "It doesn't matter, Peter. We're not going anywhere. Where did he buy those tickets? They were supplied to him. We'll be shot trying to escape."

"Is she right, Hong? Would you give her up to save yourself?"

Hong seethed. Have patience for a moment, he thought,

save yourself trouble for a thousand years. "A friend of mine risked his neck for these tickets," he said. "As did his friends, and their friends. Be grateful to all of them, as I am. And now move, we can't miss this train."

Liang Yu-shang set her bag down. Her lips quivered and for the first time her haughty facade completely crumbled. She started to cry. "Good-bye," she said, reaching out to Ostrander. "Think of me, if you can. Remember that I loved you."

"She'll be on the train," Hong said through clenched teeth, pushing Ostrander toward the stairs. "Hurry."

Ostrander started toward the stairway, then stopped. They waved, and he continued on.

Liang Yu-shang reached for her bag and turned into the station. "Who's waiting for us?" she asked. "The Army? More of your murderers?"

Hong grasped her arm and forcibly steered her to the steps. At first disbelieving, she held her ground and stared. He yanked her again and she followed him down. Through the windows of the hard-seat cars he saw peasants unwrapping food and pouring tea. Relatives waved, passed in last pieces of luggage. Which of them would be glad to report an errant cadre to the nearest train security officer? Perhaps that couple over there, a factory foreman and his wife with their patriotic son in Army uniform. Could you reason with them, explain that to make the law work you had to break it?

The hard-berth aisles teemed with middle-level cadres going to Tongren, Hengyang, Guilin, and the conductor moved efficiently along the row of compartments, clipping tickets. She was a stout old workhorse with close-cropped hair, and she gave Yu-shang a particularly nasty glare. Too much makeup, a decadent bourgeois habit. Yu-shang's rouge was stained with tears, it had run down her cheek.

When the conductor left, Hong went into the compartment, poured tea from the thermos on the drop-leaf table beneath the window, sipped, and peered up and down the track. No soldiers, no white-coated Public Security officers.

"Why are you doing this?" Liang Yu-shang asked.

"Ah, suddenly I'm not a pig," Hong said, his eyes still on

the platform. The last bell sounded, the train pulled out, jerked, accelerated.

"You could give them my father's diary," she said, "you could turn me over to them now."

Hong took the bench across from her. "Didn't Deng Bo promise you freedom? You deserve at least that."

"Why? Why do I deserve that?"

"You've had a difficult life," Hong said.

"You don't know me or how I've lived. You don't know a thing about my life."

"Maybe I'll be on the train out of Guangzhou myself," Hong said. "Maybe I'm leaving with you."

"I don't believe that."

"You don't believe anything. I wouldn't either, if I were you."

He found that her bitterness actually soothed him; it was a predictable friend, steady, consistent. He looked out the window. The train crossed a highway and ran parallel to a road lined with silk factories. Buses emptied armies of women going to work. Trucks unloaded mountains of cocoons.

"You have a family," Yu-shang said, trying to convince herself, "you have a place in the world, membership in the Party, a high position."

"Do you remember the birds you told me about? The ones that had no place to land and died in the air. What if I told you I was a bird who wanted to land?"

"You're not," she said. "You've never suffered, you've always had the best, you and your revolutionary parents."

"Where did you learn your contempt?" Hong asked. "Did you attend special schools in the United States that taught you to hate your country? You tell me I don't know anything about you or how you've lived. But you think you know me." He stood up. "I'm starved. Would you like some noodles? The food on this train is very good."

He walked out and left her in the compartment.

In the middle of the night the train's bell woke him. He had been dreaming of a hot summer train ride to Shenyang with his father, to the countryside where Yamei stood before a firing squad in the rain. A corporal cocked a rifle, handed it to Hong, told him to fire. "You've killed her anyway," the corporal said.

Hong sat up, rubbed his eyes, and looked across at Liang Yu-shang, then reached over and raised the window shade. The train was on the outskirts of Hengyang, changing tracks for the leg to Guangzhou. In the distance were limestone mountains, and near the interchange, dimly lit but breaking through the darkness, was a giant red billboard: "RELIEVE POISON" BRAND COUGH DROPS. From the end of the car came a babble of raised voices. Investigators from Beijing? Hong squirmed on his wooden bunk and reached for his gun. The conversation grew louder and passed near the compartment.

"The mechanics earn more, the cooks earn more, we should earn more," said an irate female voice.

A political discussion on the product of one's labors. Loudly, of course, and in the middle of the night.

Hong pulled down the shade and slid back into sleep.

Yu-shang's bunk was folded closed. Hong woke quickly, sitting up too fast and bumping his head, then slipped onto the floor. He opened the compartment door, blinked at the sun, glanced in both directions. Could she have left the train? No, there had been only one stop during the night, and he was certain that she still hoped, dreamed of escape, lived in her mind somewhere on the other side of the border.

She had gone to Ostrander's compartment, which was stupid.

Hong changed his shirt, raised the shades on the door and window, and poured himself a cup of lukewarm tea. The attendant would be barging in with a breakfast call soon. Outside the compartment a young Army officer stopped and leaned on the windows. He had an unformed face, like one of Boda's rare chunks of polished stone—not a wrinkle, not a line of age or even a prickle of beard. He turned from the wind to light a cigarette and his profile threw Hong back into time—it was Lieutenant Wang, his neighbor of twenty years ago. Hong was cowering behind the door of his parents' apartment and could see Lieutenant

Wang's head bouncing on the concrete as he was dragged down the flight of steps, leaving a trail of blood. What could a boy make of such events? His own brother leading a pack of Red Guards, revered scholars sent to shovel sewage, Army officers purged. His father's decline had started even then, even before they sent him to the countryside during the Cultural Revolution. Hong wondered what his parents saw when they looked back. Only another moment in history, his mother had once told him. Time was not an inexorable Marxist march to the future, she said; time was a spiral, it moved forward, backward, wound around on itself and went on.

The young soldier made room for Liang Yu-shang to pass. She opened the door, came in and sat down.

"You'll get us caught," Hong said.

"At least he could see me and know I'm here."

"And maybe not see you at the end."

"In the midst of death," she said, "I look for life." It was an old saying about taking chances: when threatened with the worst, risk everything. "The train is running late," she went on. "We lost time during the night."

Hong looked at his watch, consulted the train schedule. They had been due to arrive in Guangzhou in two hours, at five past nine, which would have allowed more than an hour to cross the city to East Station. Until last year the Guangzhou-Kowloon express had departed from the main station, but was moved for better security. "Have we passed Qujiang yet?"

"The last sign was Shaoguan."

The train would be almost an hour behind schedule. So much for socialist efficiency, Hong thought. The trains were the country's pride and glory.

The hard-berth conductor opened the door without knocking. "Breakfast," she said.

"We're not hungry," Hong said.

"You must eat breakfast. You've paid for it."

"We'll be right along then," Hong said.

The fear he had lost for two days returned, but mutated into terror. He was becoming like her, dreaming of the border. The express to Kowloon departed at 10:30, and was never delayed. If they missed it, there would be no hope of hiding until tomorrow morning. When they failed to appear at Shanghai, Wei Ye would put out an alert. Hong closed his eyes; he saw before him a prison camp, walls with wire atop the crenellations, his thumbs wired together as he sipped a bowl of gruel.

"Let's eat," he said, opening his eyes. "We deserve a last meal."

Banyan trees whizzed by. The river and rice paddies blurred. The train picked up speed at Sanshui, careened through a strip of cement factories, shipbuilding yards, textile mills. Hong assumed the engineer had a reason to make up for lost time. Possibly it was pride. The railway people were a different breed.

The train screeched into Guangzhou's main station fifty minutes late. Hong and Liang Yu-shang were at the end of the car when the conductor opened the door and kicked the stairs down. It occurred to Hong that he had never in his life stepped from a train without being met by someone— his mother or father, Shen Kuang or Yamei, at the very least by an official car. On the platform he searched for evidence of a welcoming party. No one even met his glance. Good, perhaps he was invisible. With a grip on Yu-shang's arm he started for the soft-berth cars; she tried to break loose, but he easily held her back. It was hard to run in high heels. "A broken leg now would finish us," he whispered.

Ostrander was standing at the base of the first stairwell.

"You leave separately," Hong told him. "You hand in your ticket stub at the first counter. You go straight through the front door and you avoid the beggars. You cross the street and wait near the taxi queue. Is that clear?"

Ostrander nodded and started up the steps. This was too easy, Hong thought. Even the normal contingent of Public Security officers was missing. He watched Ostrander pass the stub collector without incident, then sailed through himself behind Yu-shang. They had barely thirty minutes to reach East Station.

And then? And then whatever came next, he thought.

"We'll ride to Hongyun Street," he said when they reached Ostrander across the street, "and then we'll walk down to East Station. Don't move too fast, don't attract attention."

They were at the front of the taxi line, the dispatcher opened the door, and they got in—Ostrander first, then Liang Yu-shang. Hong wanted one of them in the middle, someone he could hold on to in case they should be struck by the ridiculous notion of making it on their own.

"Long-distance bus terminal," Hong told the driver. "Hongyun Street."

"The terminal on South Huanshi is a lot closer," the driver said.

"Thank you, but we're meeting friends."

The taxi driver took North Huanshi Road along the edge of the city, past the telegraph office and around a traffic circle bordering the bright green of Yuxieu Park. The morning traffic was thick, jeeps and farm trucks and a million more cars than Beijing. To the right was the broadcasting tower of Guangzhou Television, to the left the tracks of the railway to Hong Kong. Through the cloth of his suitcase Hong felt the hard leather box containing the diary. He touched his shirt pocket, where the assistant swimming coach's passport and internal papers stuck to the sweat dripping on his chest. What if the guards looked too closely? What if they asked him for further identification? Ostrander would easily get through, and Yu-shang's Hong Kong passport was genuine, even if the name on it was not. But his own? He felt in his pants pocket for the Kowloon tickets that Chan had booked at some unimaginable cost. The tickets gave him hope. The guard would compare the name on the swimming coach's passport with the name on the ticket, and that might be enough.

How could he leave Yamei? Heat rose to his cheeks, he swallowed again and again but nothing worked, the dryness in his throat expanded, the lump was a tumor. He fought the tears back. Don't think about Yamei. Think about the bullet, think about prison camps. Think about the Chinese in Hong Kong, in the United States, all over the world. You'll come home someday, they'll clear your name and you'll come home.

Who would he become in another country, who would he love? Who would love him?

The taxi turned on Zhongshan Road. A code name, Hong thought. Even Dr. Sun Yat-sen had needed code names; he had called himself Zhongshan in messages during the war. So today I am a swimming coach. He looked at his watch—twenty minutes before the Kowloon express departed. They passed the old willow-shaded Confucian temple that had become the Peasant Movement Institute and the red ten-tiered gates of the Memorial Garden to the Martyrs of the 1927 Uprising. The traffic thinned, they sped down Dongchuan, banked into Hongyun Road, downhill toward the river.

Hong paid the fare, then took off his glasses; the swimming coach didn't wear them. Ostrander opened his door and Liang Yu-shang slid over to follow him, but Hong caught her arm and pulled her out on his side. He held tight to her as they walked down the street and across to East Station.

"Shouldn't we hurry?" Ostrander asked.

"Better to be in the last crowd boarding," Hong said. "They won't be looking at papers so carefully."

The renovations had just begun. Inside the station were sawhorses and gutted walls, plumbing pipes protruding from plaster like unlit sticks of dynamite, girders jutting out where holes had been cut for electric cables. Rivers flowed between hills of sodden plasterboard and broken concrete. Above the desolation, rows of ceiling fans whipped a muggy soup.

Ostrander whispered, "I'm scared, Hong."

"So am I," Hong said.

The first control point was ahead of them, just beyond the two lines of passengers at the end of a temporary plywood passageway. Three nuns clattered by, towing suitcases on wheels; from behind, in Hong's blurry vision, their white headdresses looked like winged helmets. Service counters on their right issued luggage checks and customs stamps. Posters on their left forbade the carrying of firearms or explosives on the train. A phalanx of Japanese businessmen in identical black ties and gray suits rushed past the nuns, bunching together as they crossed passport control—a roped-off desk and a makeshift booth.

At the desk Yu-shang, the tourist from Macao, regally waved her false papers at the guard, who checked her name, handed her a customs declaration form, and waved her on. A good thing they didn't ask to see her luggage receipts, Hong thought. A tourist carries luggage, but there were limits to Chan's resources, and preparing dummy suitcases for the checkroom went beyond them. Hong and Ostrander fell in step ahead of a group of British businessmen, then edged into the other line and stopped at the booth.

Ostrander went through with no difficulty. Hong handed the guard his two booklets, one brown and one red. The guard looked at the photo of the swimming coach, checked his list, and pushed the customs form forward. Looking into the guard's young face, Hong wondered how they would punish him. Not too severely, he hoped. Thinking about the guard kept Hong's mind where he wanted it: here, nowhere else, in the present. Not in the past or the future. *Take the jellyfish, for example. A primitive nervous system. It has no past, no future. The ultimate freedom, you might say.*

"That's all," the guard said.

"Yes, thank you."

Hong emerged into the high main hall, put on his glasses, and headed for the seating area, a large square of benches enclosed by sawhorses. His feet felt sluggish, dragged under in swamp. Only one more gate to the other side, he thought. He would chase criminals there, maybe. No, he was finished with criminals. Let someone else chase them. He saw that Yu-shang's eyes were following Ostrander, and he was about to signal her to move away when he noticed the slight gray figure standing near the edge of the second passport gate.

It was Deng Bo, with two other men. Army, probably. When two tigers fight, Hong remembered, one is sure to get wounded.

No wonder they had made it this far. Wei Ye had been brought down, and Deng Bo had triumphed. The Central Department of Investigation had lived up to its reputation

—with Chan's help, probably. But the moment had no
glory, not even justice, and as Hong's mind went back to his
peculiar admiration for Wei Ye, he realized that he pitied
her too. She had betrayed her country and her friends, but
hadn't they all betrayed her in their turn, and themselves as
well? Murder, treachery, the never-ending fight for power
—had they not all lived by the same despicable rules, inspired fear in each other as they had in their enemies?
Revolution is not a dinner party. From the barrel of a gun
comes power. And in a single moment Hong thought of Dr.
Yan's friends, dead by suicide, of Boda's parents who had
died anonymous, meaningless deaths, of his own father
driven mad, and of his mother living in the gray half-light
of her dead dreams. He thought of countless others, the
revolutionary heroes who had perished at the hands of
their former comrades. If Wei Ye had been caught in her
own trap, it was not by a hunter anyone could respect.

Hong stopped, lowered his hand. Deng smiled at him and
nodded, made a small bowing gesture. One of the soldiers
took a step forward toward the sawhorses, but Deng motioned for him to stop.

Was there no reward for the journey? Did it end for them
here, Hong wondered, as prisoners of the whoremaster for
whom they were all no better than cards in a game?

Hong turned, took Ostrander's hand, and led him to
Liang Yu-shang.

"Go straight through," he said quietly, "don't stop. Don't
look back."

Deng started toward them. Yu-shang, watching him, was
raising her hands to her mouth in shock.

"What's wrong?" Ostrander asked.

With an arm to Ostrander's back, Hong gave him a hard
shove. "Take her, go through now."

They moved away, Ostrander staring over his shoulder.
Hong pivoted to face Deng, who seemed to be approaching
on air, floating above the concrete floor.

"You're off the tiger's back at last," he said.

"And you untied the bell," Hong said.

"Not without some assistance," Deng said. "I've been
building my case for a long time now, and not alone." He
looked down at Hong's suitcase. "You have something for

me, I think. I'll need it as evidence for her trial."

Everyone needed evidence—false pictures, real diaries, what was the difference? The bell for the Kowloon express started to ring. Hong felt his left hand involuntarily tighten on the handle of his suitcase. "I'll leave it on the train," he said uselessly.

"That won't be sufficient," Deng said.

"Then I'll mail it to you."

Deng's smile broadened as he glanced toward the two men standing ten meters away. "Comrade Xu, over there, he's a very good shot, an excellent marksman. And no one would blame him. A Public Security officer attempting to escape with important State documents, for that they'd give him a medal."

Hong's right hand moved imperceptibly toward the bulge at his waist.

"Lu Hong, do you seriously think you could shoot me, or take me hostage, before Corporal Xu fired a bullet into your head? Why would you want to do that?"

Hong unzipped the suitcase and took out the leather box that contained the dead man's diary, the evidence of Wei Ye's treachery.

"Now you're thinking clearly," Deng said. He took the box, opened the lid and looked in, then closed it. "So. From your friend Boda we have your files and the lieutenant's confession that you secured in Haikou. Soon we will have the testimony of the old woman's husband from Choukoutien, and now we have the diary of the man Wei Ye ordered shot. She will be convicted and she will face the firing squad."

"And me?" Hong asked.

"Did you think I was going to arrest you? You're not important in this case. As a swimming instructor, Lu Hong, you can leave, board the train, I don't care. Or as a witness for the State, you can stay. Otherwise you're irrelevant to me. Do as you please."

Deng stared a moment, then walked away, the two soldiers trailing behind him toward the passport control gate.

What a blessing it was to be irrelevant. Supremely and ultimately useless, that was what he had always feared most, and wanted most. Who troubles the useless?

Hong watched the two soldiers disappear into the temporary passageway, and he wondered how Deng had known about the swimming instructor's papers.

The bell for the train rang insistently, like an alarm that had been set off in the middle of the night and that no one cared to stop. The crowd behind the barricades had risen in unison and melted into a wedge, crushing each other to reach the train. All but Liang Yu-shang and Ostrander, who stood apart, not moving toward the doors. Shadows fluttered across the wall behind them, over their faces. Hong raised his eyes, lifted his head, almost expecting to see... what? A flock of birds? The shadows were cast by the revolving ceiling fans.

The departure area had emptied. Hong took a step toward the sawhorses, toward the last passport gate, then stopped.

Ostrander called out, "Come with us, Hong."

The distance between them already seemed to be visibly receding into a long narrow tunnel, stretching out longer and longer by the moment. Hong could see the green railroad cars through the far windows. Come with you? To where?

The passport officer had left his cage to latch the gate.

Hong felt her behind him before he turned to see her. Someone was lurking near the customs booth. He saw her hand first, her slender arm, her dark smooth hair as she peeked, one eye, around the edge of the counter... Yamei. Had she expected him to leave? Had she always sensed that a part of him, too, lived on the other side of the border?

The last bell sounded, stopped. The hall was quiet but for the whoosh of the fans. Ostrander and Liang Yu-shang stood in the far doorway, half inside the hall. Ostrander raised his arm, either in beckoning or good-bye, but Hong started in the opposite direction before he could tell. As he walked toward the doors, he thought that maybe a Red Flag would be waiting, how nice it would be to ride in one. When he passed the counter Yamei came alongside him, took his hand, said nothing. Let me be useless, he thought, let me be innocent like you and have your faith. Was she still so innocent? So full of faith? Never mind, she would find her faith again, and maybe he would find it, too. He brushed a tear from her cheek, smoothed her hair back, and she leaned against him, resting her head on his shoulder. Hand in hand they walked through the open doors, where a Red Flag sedan was indeed sitting at the curb, but they passed it by. The sky was clear, the sun rising red. They turned toward the Pearl River, down toward the quay, where gulls were swooping, swooping, soaring and diving, landing in the harbor.